KU-605-390

REVIEWS FOR *THE WEIGHT OF NUMBERS*

'A Scheherazade of a novel, executed with scope, daring, and humour. *The Weight of Numbers* is unerringly well written, and engrossing to the last page.' **Lionel Shriver, author of *We Need to Talk About Kevin***

'Captivating... a shimmering tapestry, a truly networked work of fiction... In the corner of the literary landscape in which a few of us sit, hunting for ways to work ever exciting and dynamic thinking from the sciences into the contemporary novel, *The Weight of Numbers* is extremely good news. It's a dynamic, innovative, and compelling book that brings into focus some of the most interesting trends in contemporary fiction, and Simon Ings deserves more than a sniff of at least one prize for his efforts.' ***Daily Telegraph***

'And so it goes on, this rolling story, with its dazzling, admirable narrative nerve, travelling through space and time, across continents and generations... In Ings's world we all become different people, less than the sum of our parts... A novel of explosions, of historical chain reactions... A new heart of darkness... It is unlikely there will be a finer written fiction this year.' ***Guardian***

'The scale of Ings's ambition is proportionally matched by the precision of his prose. Every sentence, image and line of dialogue is balanced and true. It isn't its clever design or technical achievement that makes it compelling so much as its beating human heart.' ***Independent on Sunday***

'Ings weaves an ingenious, shimmering web of contiguity and chance... A feat of meticulous plotting... Ings's project is not dissimilar from David Mitchell's *Cloud Atlas*, with which it has been compared.' ***New Statesman***

'An ambitious, exciting novel... Ings's prose can ascend into theoretical, visionary territory, but is rooted in the mess of human experience. A sudden sexual encounter in a bombed-out London library, an anorexic slicing a muffin in a Florida restaurant, a horror show of violence in Mozambique – these are unforgettable scenes, evoked with a lean, immediate physicality. The thrill of its unfolding connections pulls you inexorably to the end, and – if you're like me – straight back to the beginning, to pick up your pencil and try the sums all over again.'
The Times

'Ings displays great technical mastery in the construction of this novel... His ability to recreate history is keenly expressed... This novel triumphs, thanks to Ings's discipline and quite fierce powers of imagination.'
Sunday Business Post

'A virtuoso display of imaginative plotting.' *Financial Times*

'This stunning, gutsy novel takes a single incident and traces back its causes through the life stories of those involved. Dozens of deftly drawn characters, an acute understanding of geopolitics, an epic historical sweep and a serious talent for storytelling make this one of the most exciting – and relevant – books of the last year. Booker material, for sure.' *Arena*

'Like Don DeLillo's *Underworld*, Simon Ings's remarkable new work delivers nothing less than a secret key, a counterhistory, of the last sixty years. Ings's fiction is vivid and swift, a thing of scenes and people, smugglers and astronauts, spies and revolutionaries. But beyond the topical excitements lies something even grander – a vision of our culture as a death ship. *The Weight of Numbers* is amazing.' **Mark Costello, author of *Big If***

Dead Water

SIMON INGS

CORVUS

Published in hardback, eBook, and export and airside trade paperback in Great Britain in 2011 by Corvus, an imprint of Atlantic Books Ltd.

This is a work of fiction. All characters, organizations, and events portrayed in this novel are either products of the author's imagination or are used fictitiously.

1 3 5 7 9 10 8 6 4 2

A CIP catalogue record for this book is available from the British Library.

Hardback ISBN: 978-1-84887-888-4
Trade Paperback ISBN: 978-1-84887-889-1
Ebook ISBN: 978-1-84887-891-4

Printed in Great Britain by the MPG Books Group

Corvus
An imprint of Atlantic Books Ltd
Ormond House
26-27 Boswell Street
London WC1N 3JZ

www.corvus-books.co.uk

For Steve, who said
'Everyone is in the intelligence business now'

and for Leo, born into this:
story time.

CONTENTS

Part One

∞

Part Two

Part Three

Part Four

'The truth is, everything in this universe has its regular waves and tides. Electricity, sound, the wind, and I believe every part of organic nature will be brought some day within this law. But my philosophy teaches me, and I firmly believe it, that the laws which govern animated beings will be ultimately found to be at bottom the same with those which rule inanimate nature, and, as I entertain a profound conviction of the littleness of our kind, and of the curious enormity of creation, I am quite ready to receive with pleasure any basis for a systematic conception of it all.'

Henry Adams to his brother Charles, October 1863

Part One

ONE

Friday, 25 May 1928: half past ten in the morning

Returning from its successful transit over the North Pole, at a point about seventy-five miles north of Spitsbergen, the airship *Italia* falls out of the sky. The gondola strikes the pack and cracks, scattering crew and equipment over the ice.

Incredibly, all but a couple of the spilled men climb to their feet, uninjured, and go running across the ice after their ship. It's hopeless: the envelope, trailing the remains of the gondola's roof, ropes, and canvas shreds and spars, begins to rise. A massive tear has opened in the airship's outer skin, exposing twisted fabric guts. Faces lean out of the hole. Half the crew were sleeping in the envelope, in a crude bunk space next to the keel. Now the storm is bearing them away.

Arduino's up there. The chief engineer. He knows he's finished: marooned aboard an ungovernable balloon, plaything of a polar gale. He hurls supplies through the ragged gap where the companionway should be. Cargo rains down on to the ice: fuel, food, gear, whatever he can lay his hands on. Spanners. Pemmican. Oatmeal biscuits. Tobacco. Voltol oil. Arduino devotes his last moments to the welfare of those left on the ice.

The bag is carried up into the fog and disappears.

On the ice, the leader of the expedition, General Umberto Nobile, lies prone, his legs and right arm broken, drifting in and out of consciousness. The motor chief has a broken leg and a mechanic is dying amid the wreckage of the rear motor gondola. Lothar Eling, the ship's Swedish meteorologist, lies bruised and winded under a wooden box he embraced a split second before the impact. Some minutes pass before he realizes what he has done. He lets out a shout.

The *Italia*'s field radio is intact.

A day later, the radio is operating. The aerial's made of scraps of steel tubing, braced with scavenged lengths of control wire. There's even a flag of sorts fluttering at its tip: scraps of cloth that add up to a crude Italian Tricolore.

Biagi, the radio operator, is not happy. The *Italia*'s support ship, the *Città di Milano*, lies at anchor in King's Bay and the ship's crew are making the most of its radio: a popular novelty. The first message Biagi picked up read '*infine il mio pollo caro ha fatto il suo uovo*'. Some sailor's chick has laid her egg at last. The ship spends so much time transmitting sweet nothings to the girls back home, it's impossible to get a message through. More infuriating still, the ship keeps sending out these meaningless reassurances: 'Trust in us. Trust in us.' 'They keep telling us we're near fucking Spitsbergen.'

Eling grunts acknowledgement; he's not really listening. He writes in his notebook: an ugly thing, red leather. He is calculating how long their supplies will last.

Prunes.
Curry powder.
Jelly crystals.
Bags of coal.
Tripe.

Assuming three hundred grams of solid nourishment per man, their supplies will last less than a month. They may be able to supplement their diet. There are clear channels where they can fish. There's also the chance that the airship came down within a few miles, along with the rest of their gear. Depending on how far and how fast it came down, there may even be other survivors. Every hour or so someone stumbles across another find.

A seal pick.
A small plankton net.
A barrel of kerosene crystals.
A Newman and Guardia quarter-plate hand-held camera.

(Eling itemizes everything.)

Spratt's dog biscuits.
Seal oil.
A box of Brock's flares.
Pants.

Now and again, he turns back the pages of his notebook, to read what's written at its start:

To Uncle Lothar
Wishing you a Merry Christmas
Vibeke

Sometimes, when he thinks no one is looking, Eling traces the words with gloved fingers. He closes his eyes. He remembers.

Five months earlier: Christmas Eve, 1927

'Merry Christmas, Uncle Lothar!'

Professor Jakob Dunfjeld's fifteen-year-old daughter, Vibeke, hands Lothar Eling a brown-paper package. Eling tugs the string and slips off the paper. The girl has got him a hideous red leather something. He turns it over and over. It is a pouch, cleverly stitched. Waterproof. Inside the pouch is a notebook covered in the same leather.

'I'm sorry about the colour. It's all they had.'

'It's perfect.'

'For your expedition.'

'Yes.' Eling tries to swallow. 'It is just what I need.'

The next day, Christmas Day, while the professor attacks his ever-mounting pile of correspondence, Eling accompanies Vibeke to the funicular that runs up the side of Mount Fløyen, biggest of the seven mountains ringing the city of Bergen on Norway's south-west coast. Together they explore the peak, the parapet, the cafe and the heavy telescopes, trained on the city below. Ten years have passed since the great fire and the city still carries the scars.

'You have a look,' says Vibeke, stepping away from the telescope.

Eling puts his eye to the heavy barrel. It's trained on the harbour, seed of the disaster that has shaped his career. In July 1916 three men were stocktaking in a wharfside warehouse and one of their candles brushed against a bundle of tarred oakum, setting it alight. Neighbouring bundles caught light immediately. The men threw the bundles into the sea, where they floated, burning, and the wind drove sparks of flaming hemp back on to the jetty, setting it alight, and a gale sprang up, driving fragments of burning wood deep among the crowded alleys of the town.

The fire bankrupted the city and left Professor Jakob Dunfjeld in sole charge of its brand-new Meterological Institute. Lothar Eling is a Swede: a young physics graduate fresh from the meteorological laboratory in Trappes. He has spent the last couple of winters helping the professor turn his modest town house into the hub of an empire of the winds.

Together the professor and his protégé have clad the eaves of the attic with pine, and little by little the grandly named West Norway Weather Bureau's scent of ink and industry has come to replace the old, sour smell of damp and gull droppings. Two rows of desks face each other along the length of the attic. New dormer windows add light for a staff of twelve to work by, and additional edges and corners on which to crack their heads. The headroom is so meagre, some promising students have been turned down for being too tall. It is Dunfjeld's bitter joke that, having lifted meteorology out of the mire of folklore, he is having to staff his bureau with elves.

Meanwhile, in his few free moments, Eling entertains Vibeke, Jakob Dunfjeld's daughter. At fifteen, she is hardly a child. Still, Eling feels sorry for the girl. It's a lonely life she leads, with her mother dead and her father engaged so fiercely upon his work.

Christmases are especially hard. The professor has let slip, in unguarded moments, how much he dreads the Christmas season. Christmas reminds him of all the ways in which he must be both father and mother to his child. He fears – he *knows* – that the tree will never be colourful enough, the salted lamb ribs never browned to the right sweetness, the carols never hearty, the dances never boisterous enough. How can a family of two expect to form a ring around the tree? So Eling takes it upon himself to prance about the Dunfjeld household like a helpful but cheeky imp – the *fjosnisse*, or barn-elf, of the fairy tales – a bottomless source of sweets and riddles, practical jokes . . .

Eling looks up from the telescope. 'Vibeke?'

The girl has wandered away.

Eling catches up with her a minute later, not far along the path, behind a rocky spur.

'Vibeke.'

But Vibeke is as still as a statue, her attention riveted by something out of Jakob's line of sight.

'Vibeke –'

'Shh!' She waves him to silence.

The spell is broken. Her impatient gesture has disturbed the bird she has found. It rises like an angel in the air, terrible and huge and beautiful: a white eagle, breasting the wind that comes off the sea, funnelling between the spurs of Mount Fløyen: an inverted cascade, solid and unseen. The eagle does not move a muscle but simply rises on that escalator of air, cruciform, magnificent: 'Oh, Lothar,' Vibeke gasps. 'Oh, Uncle Lothar –

Look!'

∞

Monday, 28 May 1928: eleven in the morning

Three days have passed since the crash of the *Italia*. The fog has lifted a little and with equipment scavenged from the crash site – a Britannia pattern sextant, Bessel's refraction tables, a chronometer, a mercury artificial horizon – the survivors have established their position.

Now, against the white, hummocked horizon, a dot has risen. A pencil fleck. A rock. The men gather outside Nobile's tent, staring south, trying to decide whether this apparition is a good thing or not. They've been up for hours, those who can still stand, unnerved by last night's tremors and explosions. (Their floe has begun to fracture.) Their mittens, those who have them, drip red on to the snow as they stand and stare. They've been using dye from shattered altitude bombs to paint the walls of their tent, to make it more visible from the air. They look like hunters, caught cutting up a kill.

Inside the tent, crouched near the opening, Eling examines one of their two surviving charts. The rock is Foyn. The island of Foyn. Ninety-four miles from King Charles Land. North of Hope. He says: 'We can walk off the ice.'

Bonfanti, one of the engineers, turns and hunkers down beside him.

'Assume eight miles a day,' Eling says. 'Nearer land the ice will be more smooth, so reckon on twelve miles.'

Bonfanti shakes his head. Quietly: 'The general will never agree to splitting the party.'

But Nobile is halfway to delirium with pain. Listening to Eling's plan, he is halfway persuaded. In the gloom of the tent, its blue-tinted walls made muddy by the dye they've slathered over it, he strokes his little terrier, Titina, behind her ears and asks Biagi's opinion.

The radio operator is crouched in his corner, disconsolate, nursing the unit's dying batteries. He's still to get a message through. It is clear enough by now that the support ship's captain, Romagna, would sooner let them all perish on the ice, and no one else has managed to pick up Biagi's transmissions. No one knows where they are. The airwaves are full of rescue plans and not one mission is heading in the right direction. The floe is carrying them towards the barren wilderness of Franz Josef Land . . .

'Look,' says Eling, pressing his advantage, and Nobile, his eyes swimming with pain, leans up on an elbow to peer at Eling's calculations. Rates of progress. Currents. Forecasts. Supplies. Two pounds of butter. Three pounds of malted milk. Half a box of Liebig's meat extract. A lump of Provolone cheese . . .

∞

Wednesday, 14 September 1927: eight months before the *Italia* comes to grief on Arctic ice

Sprawled under the funnel, out of the wind, his ears ringing with the rattle of the engine (as the Svolvaer–Narvik ferry labours in vain to tear a passage through Arctic waters) Lothar Eling writes his last letter of the season to Vibeke Dunfjeld:

> Nobile intends that his new ship (the *Italia*, naturally) should be able to anchor at the pole, allowing us to explore the surface. It is a risky business, as a sudden change in the force or direction of the wind could see us cast adrift on the ice while the *Italia* scurries for safety. For every man on the ice, supplies and equipment sufficient for several weeks' survival must be lowered – an arduous carry-on.
>
> You ask whether Amundsen's absence this time around concerns me. My answer is, with all respect to the old man, no. The people I have spoken to did not see him so much as lift a sextant or take a bearing aboard last year's flight on the Norge: he left all that to Riiser-Larsen. General Nobile himself I set no great store by as an explorer, but he is a peculiar and contradictory figure and I cannot help liking him. He is the future – much as it hurts my national pride to admit it. He would design away all the hardship and heroism of our voyage if he could, and if this delivers a blow to my idea of myself as an outdoorsman, the sting is much salved by the thought that, alone of all the machines of the earth, only his

> extraordinary ship can possibly bring us home alive from such an overweening enterprise.

Eling is returning to Bergen now. Soon he'll be on the mainland, and aboard the evening train. He'll be chasing his own letter home. He pauses to study the rock needles as they emerge from the sea, sharp as the hatchings of a mapping pen: island peaks of Landegode and Moskenes. The Blue Mountains are the colour, this evening, of the vivid purple saxifrage that splashes the rocks beneath the vast, canted bulk of Stetind.

All summer long, eager, puppyish and hopelessly unfit, he has been spluttering through the Arctic waters in woollen swimwear, trying to position Professor Dunfjeld's heavy, hydrological apparatus in the complex, treacherous currents of Norway's Lofoten archipelago. Nose held shut with a wooden peg, arms wrapped around whatever weight comes to hand – a stone, a link of chain, a brick – he has been jumping feet-first through the banded cold into a world of corals, sponges and scuttling things.

> In Norwegian waters the difference between water layers is so marked, as regards their temperature, salinity, and density, that it is a simple matter to determine their boundaries, as well as their respective movements.

Each evening, wrapped in blankets before the hearth, and plied with egg-nog by their host, the region's *nessekøng*, Eric Moyse, Eling has taken it in turns with the professor to write to Vibeke. She has visited these Arctic islands before, and misses them. This year, school studies have stranded her in Bergen. Thinking of her, looked after by a nurse she has long since outgrown, Eling has tried to amuse her.

> Everything here boils down to fish except the fish which boil down to glue. Roast cod, poached cod, cod in batter, milk, beer, batter, breadcrumbs, salt cod, minced cod, cod pie, cod's head, morning, noon and night, oh for a loaded gun.

More successful are the caricatures: Professor Dunfjeld sunbathing naked on the deck of Eric Moyse's yacht, swaddled and made decent in the wrapper of his own prodigious beard. Their host Eric Moyse (over the caption 'His mind turneth more slowly and more coldly than the gyre') wresting coins with menaces from the fishermen who rent his *rorbu* cabins. Eling himself, tangled up in climbing gear, suspended by one foot like the Hanged Man in Vibeke's tarot deck.

Now Eling and the professor are returning to the mainland. The professor's in his cabin; Eling's stayed on deck, despite the cold. He smokes, sprawled under the ferry's funnel, hidden as far as possible from the wind. Vibrations from the engine room have put the muscles of his back into spasm, so when the engine's labour turns, with a change of gear, from a felt thing to a heard thing, his relief is immediate. It feels as though constricting chains have snapped from around his chest. His backbone, no longer a conducting rod for the engine's vibrations, ripples and flexes: free at last. He writes some more:

> Are there bears at the pole? A wizard? A Christmas elf? They tell me that last year, the *Norge* dropped its little flags – Italian, Norwegian – in an unutterably dull place. A flat waste of jumbled ice. Seriously, the discovery that there is no lost continent at the North Pole is bad news for your father and me. If everything we thought might flow from such a land mass flows instead from a dynamic system, then our whole model of the weather in these latitudes must acquire a whole other level of complexity.
>
> This is too disappointing. They are hiding something. I believe in a lost continent peopled by malign and frigid elves *and so should you.*

Lothar Eling stretches. His summer in the Lofotens with Professor Jakob Dunfjeld, studying winds and currents, has rooted him strongly in his body. As each day has passed, and his fitness has improved, he has felt ever more the explorer, the sailor, the mountain man. That the balance can never be struck in him, that intellect and exertion must collide and roil around each other constantly, suggests, at least in his own case, a psychical application for Professor Dunfjeld's work about the weather.

> THE DUNFJELD CIRCULATION THEOREM
> If it is unbounded – wrapped, say, round a globe, where every forward impulse is also a return – then perturbations will disrupt even an ideal, frictionless fluid.

This is why the weather will not die. This is why the waters will not stop in their courses. Why the winds will not cease to blow. Why the heart will not cease to desire!

Stiff now, freezing cold, hidden from the wind under the ferry's funnel, Eling finds that his spine is once again stuck in its channel, as the hull of the ferry is stuck fast in the water, held there not by bone and glue and linkage but by the peculiar boundary conditions that pertain between iron and water, flesh and ice, and fluids of variable density. Eling and Eling's spine and the icy deck and the ferry's hull and the waters of Svolvaer: all are bonded together like the layers of a fancy French pastry by forces that Eling (explorer, hydrographer) understands only now, after years of study, and too late.

Tuesday, 12 June 1928

Eighteen days have passed since the *Italia* foundered, spilling half its crew on to the polar icecap. Lothar Eling and Giovanni Bonfanti, the *Italia*'s chief engineer, have decided to try and walk off the ice. The airship crashed on pack ice north of the island of Foyn. If they can make it on foot to Foyn, they can wait there in reasonable safety for the first rescuers to arrive, then return to camp with help.

So they will walk towards Foyn, as they have walked towards Foyn before, as they have walked towards Foyn every day since they left the crash site. Having made their decision, Eling and Bonfanti have no choice but to persevere. But they are like ants on a gramophone turntable. Yes, the ice drifts south, towards the island, the only fixed point in that corner of the Arctic map. Yes, it brings them closer and closer to dry land and the possibility of rescue. But even as the island looms out of the mist, the current swerves and carries the pack east, away from Foyn, and bears its struggling human burden into uncharted territory. They cannot find a way off their spinning hell because the ground moves under them. Worse, the ground moves relative to itself. It is a shattered gramophone whose pieces shift against each other, eddying and waltzing, so that even relative movement is impossible to plot.

For twelve days they have walked towards Foyn. Each time, with the target barely a day away, their energy failed them. Then followed days of whiteout. Navigating blind, stumbling into cracks and puddles, they entered a surreal war zone where the ice, cracking as it warmed, fired pistols at them. When good visibility returned, Foyn lay at an intermediate distance that mocked their whole enterprise.

After that Eling begins to lose track. What he sees and what he thinks are becoming increasingly hard to separate. His imagination, freed by degrees from its obligation to the dying body, wanders at will over the mist's grey screen. If there is a mist. And if there is a mist, how much the worse, for spring mists in the Arctic rot the ice so that puddles of freezing water form on the surface, and at night thin crusts form over the puddles, and breezes scatter a little snow over the crusts, and every day Bonfanti and Eling fall for the trick: they step into the puddles, sometimes up to their knees in the gelid water, and there is nothing they can do – they are being carried further into the warm and rotten unknown.

Thursday, 3 May 1928: Three weeks before the *Italia* destroys itself

Eling takes out his red notebook and writes: 'Off to North Pole. Thought you might like this brick.' He tears the page out of the book and tucks it into his sheepskin flying jacket. His thick reindeer-skin boots, stuffed with grass, get in his way as he climbs up into the envelope of the *Italia*. Bags like great bellows rise either side of him, filling the space forward and aft: bloated columns to support a soft grey ceiling. The columns come in two mismatched parts: under the gas bags are air bags which are filled from an opening in the bow. When the hydrogen in the gas bags contracts, the air bags swell. The airship breathes. Breathing, it keeps its shape.

A narrow keelson runs the length of the envelope. Either side of the keelson lie the expedition's supplies. Food, clothing, tents, sleds, balloons, glass altitude bombs: shapes indistinct under sheets of blood-brown tarpaulin. Eling thinks of a ribcage: brown muscles packed between slim metal bones. There is gear here to anchor the airship in an emergency. Chains and wicked hooks, ropes – even bricks, though he can't imagine what purpose they might serve. He steals one. It is yellow, and porous as a sponge. He ties his message round the brick with a piece of twine.

A catspaw swipes the *Italia*'s bow and the whole ship surges and billows. Eling watches the wave travelling towards him through the fabric of the ship. He's used to the *Italia*'s eccentricities. He relaxes, feet apart, loose-hipped, hands on the wire handrails strung either side of the keelson. The flexible keelson gives a mild kick, softened further by the felt soles of his Russian-made boots.

A gangway crosses the keelson and out through openings to port and starboard, providing access to the motor nacelles. In the draught of the port-side opening, one of General Nobile's engineers, Giovanni Bonfanti, is brushing rubber cement over the bottom of an airbag.

Out in the open air at last, poised on the narrow gangplank connecting the envelope to the nacelle, Eling looks down. The suburbs of Stockholm turn and turn. He unbuttons his coat and takes out the brick. Far below him, his mother waves. She is standing in her garden, both arms upraised, reaching for him. Clutching a brick to his chest, Eling falls forward. The wire handrail catches him across the stomach and flips him over. He falls. Bonfanti's cry of surprise is the last thing Eling hears before he hits the water.

He hits the water.

He hits the water.

He hits the water.

He plunges through boundary layers between waters of different thicknesses. The colder the water becomes, the thicker it gets. At freezing point, water releases energy and expands catastrophically and Eling rises, cased in ice.

∞

Saturday, 16 June 1928

They have not moved in three days. The chocolate is all gone. They have nothing to eat. The only ice that is remotely potable forms in yellow icicles and they sucked their last one to nothing over a day ago.

Sprawled in the lee of a hummock of broken ice, Eling moves his arms and plates of ice fall from his flying jacket. The tips of his big felt boots poke out of the spindrift. The lack of sensation in his legs is total. He tries moving his feet and he sees the tips of the boots move back and forth, left and right. Dare he believe his eyes?

In the flat glare of the ice field, the edges of Bonfanti's bundled form are impossible to map. Only where snow has failed to adhere to the material is there anything to see at all: an irregular scattering of brown patches, each distinct, sharp-edged, the shards of a gramophone record scattered over a marble surface. With so little to see, just a pattern of brown patches against an even white, vision can proceed only by analogy. Now the bundle is like a wave. The brown squares are patches of turbid water, peaking through a web-work of foam.

Air hits the wave, is driven up over it, curls under itself as it rises, curls back, rubbing itself against itself – and knots itself in place.

Eling stares at the bundle.

The wind knots itself in place.

After so many years of study, and too late, the insight comes. He needs his notebook. He needs to write this down. He tucks his right mitten under his arm, meaning to pull his hand free so that he might unbutton his coat and get at his notebook. But the mitten is tied securely with a cord. It takes him a second to understand this – long enough to realize his folly. He must not take his mittens off.

Concentrate.

He will have to remember this. He will have to keep this in mind, for as long as his mind holds.

His eyelashes have frozen shut. He nudges his goggles aside to rub his eyes. They tear up in an instant against the beat of sun on snow. Refracted by his tears, the sunlight curls into a coloured rope. It moves around him on the ice: a snake. He catches his breath, the illusion is so beautiful, essing towards him through colour fields that change as his tears cool, leaving their salt to crust around his eyes.

And then, without warning, the snake strikes at his eyes, all fangs and scales, shards of colour, glass fragments, glass dust, and he shakes and squirms, squealing, frantic to be free of his hallucination. His eyes are burning in the light. Where are his snow goggles? In a panic, he wrestles off his mittens and feels for his goggles. They are hanging over his right ear. His fingers are frozen and without feeling, and he uses his hands like blocks to knock the goggles back over his face. He tries to put his mittens back on but he cannot think straight enough or move freely enough to manage it. He crawls on his hands and knees over the ice. 'Bonfanti, listen! The gale is passed!'

His fingers are swollen white tubes. Weeping, Eling uses his teeth to pull the mittens over his clubbed hands. He staggers to his feet. The wind has dropped, the sky has cleared. What time is it?

All around him, ice lies piled: there is no level ground. Edging out from behind a nearby hummock, topped by an unlikely crown of ice spires: something black. A rock.

It is Foyn. Again: the island of Foyn. Their destination. Their goal.

Lothar Eling explains to Giovanni Bonfanti that the hull of the ferry is trapped in standing waves on the boundary between water layers of different density. The ferryman can spin his propellers as fast as he likes, his vessel will make no headway.

The logs of every voyage of Arctic discovery, from the *Dobbs* to the *Fram*, contain reports, sometimes several in a day, of how their steering suddenly gave way. A hull can come unstuck from these waters as surely as the wings of a plane, caught in an eddy, can lose their grip on the air. When waters of different densities and temperatures pour into each other they do not mix. Instead, they settle into layers. Run a propeller through these layers and you will make no headway, however fiercely you drive the engine. You're just cavitating: chopping up waves into froth.

'The locals have a name for it,' he says.

Who says?

He says.

'Yes?'

'Yes,' he says. 'Dead water.'

Eling has forgotten that Bonfanti is dead.

Bonfanti's huddled form casts a shadow over the hideous red leather something in which Eling writes, the pencil jammed between crooked black fingers.

The notebook falls out of his grip. He bends down, but his fingers are swollen, he cannot pick it up, and as he bends over, staring at it, it – *flexes*. It squirms uselessly. The ice provides no purchase, it cannot get away. A hideous red leather something. Eling thinks of the flexible keelson of the *Italia*: equipment, shapeless under blood-brown tarpaulin, squeezed between sleek metal bones, like the compact muscles of the back.

Eling sits frozen to the ground, marvelling at the compact musculature of Bonfanti's back, laid open before him upon the ice as though upon the marble slab of a mortuary.

Bonfanti's spine, torn away at last, a hideous red something, spasms and contracts to form a shallow spiral. Eling blinks, dazzled, unbelieving. The meat snake sparkles. Glass shards rise between knuckles of bare bone: new scales, new skin. It esses. Back. Forth. Back. Forth. It is waving to him. Signalling to him. It is trying to tell him something. Eling copies the spiral in his notebook. Beneath it he writes:

'Towards a Unified Theory of Ocean Circulation.'

He puts the book away in his jacket, topples forward, and hits the water again and again and again. He descends. On the sea floor there are sponges. He picks one. He will give it to Vibeke, Professor Dunfjeld's daughter, as a present. He jackknifes, gazes up at the silver undersides of the waves, and strokes powerfully for the surface – but he does not rise.

In his sudden terror he exhales. The bubbles go straight down. These are forces Lothar Eling understands only now, after years of study, and too late. Why the weather will not die. Why the waters will not stop in their courses. Why the winds will not cease to blow. Why the heart will not cease to desire.

He glimpses open arms, outstretched arms, the arms of his mother perhaps, waving to him from her garden in Stockholm, reaching for him, drawing him in. The blow from those arms is so powerful, so fast, he does not see it coming. It all but decapitates him. In the few seconds left to him he is vaguely aware of a lump in his throat. How the lump pulses. How it squirms and explores.

But the bear has gorged on Bonfanti already and it leaves most of Eling to other bears, to arctic foxes, and gulls.

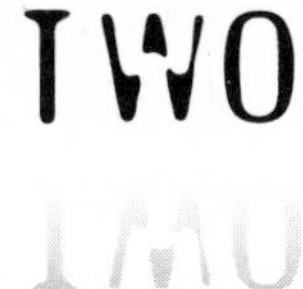

TWO

The Musandam peninsula extends into the Strait of Hormuz, guarding the entrance to the Persian Gulf. It's a rocky fretwork, an outlandish calligraphy. There is no level ground. In the folds of its cursive script pale green squares stand for gardens, their soil gathered laboriously from miles around and contained by dry-stone walls. Alfalfa one year. The next year, nothing. Musandam is the homeland of the Shihuh, the *ichthyophagoi* of Ptolemy, who speak Kumzari, a language all their own, and spring from some nameless corner of Central Asia; who are said to bark like dogs after a meal and who, having nowhere else to put them, once buried their dead under their floorboards.

Musandam's coastline is so scooped, so ragged, only a thread of broken rocks attaches the place to the mainland. West of this thread is a deep scoop of all-but-landlocked water called Elphinstone Inlet. In the middle of the inlet, Telegraph Island, so called because from 1864 to 1869 it was the terminus for the Persian Gulf telegraph cable. Signals were received here from Europe and retransmitted along another cable under the Arabian Sea and beyond, across the Indian Ocean, all the way to Calcutta.

George Curzon, Viceroy of India and later British Foreign Secretary, was convinced the station was vital to British security. He made sure that Britain flew a flag here. The Admiralty grumbled: flags must be defended, and how was the Navy to defend this godforsaken mote, surrounded by treacherous down-currents, whirlpools, rips?

The Admiralty won the argument and the flag got taken down.

A century later to the day, David Brooks, a British Desert Intelligence Officer seconded to the Armed Forces of the Sultan of Oman, hobbles on his stick through the hamlet of Khomsa. In common with every village on the peninsula, Khomsa is accessible only by sea. He sailed in past boats, each high prow painted with an eye. The men are all out fishing, so he's walking through streets populated entirely by women and children. Not that there are streets – just a series of interconnecting backyards.

The children follow him, the women ignore him. Some are bare-faced; others wear a stylized version of the rigid masks he's seen used in the Empty Quarter – objects monstrous to Western eyes but which act like chimneys in the heat, cooling the wearer's face. The masks here are purely decorative, their panels reduced to a meshwork of rods: exotic spectacle frames.

David moves gingerly, careful with his walking stick. The bone's mended, more or less, and he needs to put on muscle now to bind his shattered leg together. It's a precarious business.

David's seen action, quelling the rebellion in Dhofar in the south of the country. He's driven Gurkhas into battle and dragged one away under fire, his jaw shot off and dying. He's led raiding parties up 'beaches' that, when they got there, black-faced and saddled with artillery, turned out to be cliff-faces. His unit, outflanked, once defended a stone house against Yemeni-backed mortar fire armed with nothing but small arms, command of the local dialect, and guile. He's come through all this, commended, congratulated, only to crash his Land Rover into a gully, avoiding a camel. The damage to his leg was severe enough; he was flown back to England, to the RAF hospital at Wroughton, and it was while he was having his leg pinned together that he first caught wind of the British-backed plot to bring the Sultan's son to power.

He should not be playing here, he should not be risking himself on loose scree, dust and tumbled rocks, but with every foot he gains above the hamlet the freer his breathing becomes. He is still a young man after all. The time of adventures is not over.

In a cleft in the rock towering over the town, David casts around for a place to rest. There really is *no* level ground in Musandam: even finding a rock to sit on is a challenge. David leans his backside against a canted boulder. His eyes adjust to the dimness. He takes off his sunglasses. There's a sack lying near the entrance to this shallow cave. Even a sack is a point of interest around here. Whose sack? Is it one of his?

Since his return to Oman, and while he recuperates, David's been assigned to what could well be Britain's smallest military base: hardly more there than a couple of chairs under a *sumr* tree. Day after day he sits under the shade of the tree, doling out supplies of water, rice and coffee to the Shihuh tribesmen. The bay here is shallow, so supplies are brought in by landing craft and dumped on the sands, and if he's called away for any reason the Shihuh forget all about the supplies. Whole consignments have been ignored, left to float away on the tide.

What's in this sack that's worth anyone caring about?

David levers himself to his feet and shuffles over. It's not a sack. It's a scrap of some unfamiliar material. It's impregnated with a greyish powder. He turns it over with his stick and the cloth shatters. He cannot kneel: he hunkers down. He rubs a tatter of the cloth between his fingers. The dust is slick on his fingers. Not rock dust. He tastes it. Metal. He picks up the cloth and the sun-rotted parts fall away, leaving a lacework bound together with a bituminous black paint.

A metallized skin. He thinks of biplanes. Mail-carriers from the heroic age of aviation. Saint-Exupéry at the mercy of unmapped thermals. John William Alcock, imprisoned on the shores of Moudros in Turkey, assembling a plane from the parts of other crashed aircraft. Europe's empires were held together with seaplanes and the coasts here are dotted with old refuelling stations.

Long as he's been stationed here, there's a limit to the level of interest David can bring to a scrap of cloth. He tests his knee. The soreness there is trivial: he's good for another half-hour's tottering before he minces back to town.

Round the corner, through a defile thick with goat droppings, the ground falls away and opposite, on a hill-face so broken, so rotten, it looks more like the workings of a quarry, an expanse of silver cloth flutters.

Metal dust catches the light. Staring without sunglasses, David's eyes tear up. Black letters flex and bend and ess, fragmenting even as he reads:

ITALIA

∞

A year goes by, it is Thursday, 23 July 1970. A sea fog is sweeping across the town of Salalah, in the region of Dhofar, facing the Arabian Sea.

There is a royal palace at Salalah called Al Hisn. Each summer, come the monsoon, fog smothers the beach, then the palace, then the avenue, palm tree by palm tree, then the double-gated tower. Reaching inland, it swallows the nearby RAF aerodrome with its toffee-coloured leather armchairs, pale pine panelling, and inevitable David Shepherd print. Soon it has smothered the whole city.

The afternoon is hot, humid and foggy, with bursts of heavy rain. Sheikh Braik bin Hamid Al Ghafri, son of the Wali of Dhofar, arrives at the tower with his usual retinue and seeks an urgent audience with his sovereign. Braik is a regular and esteemed royal visitor, and Sultan Said bin Taimur's personal servants, the Khadeem, descendants of African slaves, have no qualms about opening the gate. Plumes of frankincense rise from incense burners in every winding corridor as Braik and his men dog-leg their way through Al Hisn's maze, towards the Sultan's private chambers.

The plot has had a comparatively easy ride through Whitehall. In office barely a month and with his focus set firmly on Europe, the new prime minister, Edward Heath, signed off on the plan after only the most cursory glance. The plan makes sense. The Americans' honeymoon with the House of Saud has let the Wahhabi genie out of the bottle, undoing over a century of British containment. Replacing the obscurantist Sultan of Muscat and Oman with Qaboos, his Sandhurst-educated son, will rebalance power in the region, maintain British oil interests after the meltdown of Suez, and do something to contain the threat of Soviet insurgency through Yemen. It may even lead to the building of a few hospitals and schools if Qaboos has his way.

So Sheikh Braik has come to request that Sultan Said bin Taimur abdicate. At once. Braik does not anticipate trouble. Qaboos is, after all, Said's own son, and already named as his successor.

Said, alas, has no desire to step down.

Braik, nevertheless, will not take no for an answer.

And it is at this point that Said feels obliged to give Braik a definitive royal response. Braik has no time to defend himself and in any event he would never dream of drawing a weapon against his sovereign. Said's like an uncle to him!

Some uncle. The slug to his stomach comes as a complete surprise and Braik wanders around for a while, looking bemused, clearing his throat, before falling flat on his face.

There are no metalled roads in Oman and most towns are accessed by sea or by Skyvan, a British military transport rigged to carry paratroops. David Brooks, his knee a screaming bolus of pain, clambers stiffly in through the cargo door of the plane, followed by a dozen goats. There are canvas seats strung down either side of the fuselage and crates of fish stacked in the central aisle. A whiskery old shepherd offers him a handful of cotton wool, none too clean, for his ears. The noise in the unpressurized cabin is terrible. It's cold, too: even on a short-haul flight a Skyvan climbs to seven thousand feet.

Around 4.00 p.m. they enter the fog bank rolling in over the city of Salalah. David arrives at the palace early in the evening in the company of Lieutenant Colonel Edward Turnhill of the Sultan's Desert Regiment. Braik's men are manning the entrance tower and open the gate.

For an hour and a half the British-backed conspirators have been chasing the Sultan through the labyrinthine corridors of his palace. In this region rulers and their nobles carry guns, but they don't all know how to use them. Two men lie dead: one royal bodyguard and one of

Braik's men. Braik is still alive, his condition stable. Said, meanwhile, has contrived to put a bullet through his own foot.

Pinned down at last, Said says that he is ready to capitulate – but only to a British officer. He wants to look the men who've betrayed him in the eye. David lays his Browning aside, straightens his tie, and grips the pommel of his stick. He wishes to God he hadn't gone clambering over the rocks like an idiot yesterday. He can barely think, he hurts so much. He marches as evenly as he can down the stone-flagged corridor, careful not to slip in the bloody smears the Sultan has left behind. He clears his throat, hobbles one step at a time up a flight of spiral stairs up to the open door, and salutes.

The room is lit by two windows, one opposite the other. Above one window there is a second, semicircular, window made of plaster wrought into the form of the word 'Muhammad'. Gaps in the ornate Arabic calligraphy are filled with coloured glass.

'What a cunt.'

The room is full of parrots. Some share tall cages – gilded cages – that sit either side of a samovar so huge and so complex it looks as though it could serve as the controls for a steam locomotive. In the middle of the room is a generous four-poster bed in carved wood. The Sultan sits at the foot of the bed, his injured foot extended. He holds his gun by the barrel, ready to present it to the man come to depose him.

'What a *cunt*.'

The Sultan does not stir. His face is an empty bag. Above him feathers rustle. There's a line of parrots above the bedpost. Favoured birds. Familiars. Uncaged. Presumably the sounds mean something different in Arabic. 'Pretty Polly.' 'Who's a clever boy, then?'

David bows. 'Your majesty.' There is a form of words for this. A protocol, if you can believe this, for throwing an old man out of his realm. David's been practising, he's got the form down pat, but he's not ready for the Sultan's stare. The face is lifeless but the eyes burn with an intensity David finds increasingly frightening. He employs a schoolboy trick, focusing on the tip of the man's ear – black and dry as a scrap of *boerewors* – as he recites. An Edwardian pupil tackling *Casabianca* was not more proper, or more nervous.

The Sultan makes to stand. David hobbles forward, but the Sultan waves him angrily away. He'll surrender on his own terms. He'll exit the world's stage under his own power, thank you. If necessary, he'll hop.

In fact, they can both hop. Christ, thinks David, teeth gritted against laughter, what a pair they make.

At the door, the Sultan presents him with his gun, an old service Browning, and David tries again, offering the old man his arm. The Sultan's birds, outraged, take flight around the room. In a mirror hung in the hall, David glimpses them: a rope of many colours snaking, shiny as glass, above the bed. 'What a cunt,' they cry. '*What* a cunt.' 'What a *cunt*.'

David sees Said and Braik on to the same plane, a Bristol Britannia headed for Bahrain, where doctors are waiting. He flies on to the UK the same night and is there waiting on the apron when Sultan Said lands at Brize Norton. A cold, rattly car ride bears them to the RAF hospital at Wroughton in Wiltshire. Once discharged, Said and his favourite parrot take a suite in London's Dorchester Hotel. David Brooks quits the army and acts as the Sultan's Home Office liaison until Said's death, on 19 October 1972. It's during this period that he meets and befriends Havard, adopted son of the eccentric shipping magnate Eric Moyse.

Towards the end of 1972, David returns to Oman, where, working as a civilian consultant, he runs the public affairs office of Moyse Line. He meets Ann, an Australian geologist, and they move to Melbourne, Ann's home town, in time for the birth of their daughter.

Though he quit Oman, David likes to say that he's remained one of Moyse Line's crack team of 'political officers'. The company clearly finds him useful for something. Since the separation he has been spending ever larger fractions of his life crossing continents at thirty thousand feet.

THREE

India's epic, continent-spanning Grand Trunk Road is the vessel to which the village of Chhaphandi clings: a tapeworm sucking feebly from a greedy gut. The point is: the GTR splits at Kanpur and sends two highways sprawling westwards over the fields and paddies of Uttar Pradesh towards a distant reunion in New Delhi. The northern road has no separate name. The southern one is called the Sher Shah Suri Marg.

It is 1976, and raining.

In Chhaphandi's market place children garlanded with flowers run from puddle to puddle, stamping and laughing. Old men sit grinning at nothing, displaying their dental decay. In the fields the first pale green rice shoots tremble in the downpour.

On the third day, under skies so low, so heavy, it's as if you could reach up and stir the clouds with your fingers, it begins to dawn on the region that this is not a normal rain.

Cattle take shelter under the trees. Lovers retire to their rooms. The rain beats down all day and all night, and all the next day, and the next, heavier and heavier, filling ditches, bursting pipes, drowning the villagers' crops under four inches of slurry and smearing the village of Chhaphandi with a weak solution of human and animal shit.

The rain stops. Chhaphandi holds its breath. Here and there the bank of a paddy collapses silently into the surrounding mud. A patch of the highway loses a couple of feet from its northern bank. A landslide buries two boys inside a latrine. The rivers swell but do not break their banks. It takes four days for the waters to drain away.

Under the eyes of jealous rain gods, the farmers of Chhaphandi walk their ruined fields. They stick their fingers surreptitiously into the sodden soil, testing its crumb. Some raindrops fall. By the afternoon the shower stops. In the evening it rains again, but not much, and the following day it stays dry, and some say that the skies are lighter, though they aren't. On the sixth day the village comes alive again. Tata trucks laden with oxen draw up in the market place. Tempos rattle their way to this farm or that, labourers clinging to their sides. Under a sky the colour of lead the villagers begin to plough.

Rishi hasn't even got his fly properly fastened before his mother is thrusting a basket into his hands. She leads him out into the pre-dawn gloaming, across sodden fields, to where his brothers are already at work. He is eight years old.

Over the years, the Ansaris have dug a network of ponds and canals to water their land. The rainwater in these ponds is still high and it wouldn't take much for them to overflow again, inundating the fields. The water makes pale discs in the half-light: counters in some monstrous game of *pachisi*. Rishi becomes aware that he is surrounded, as in a dream, by virtually his entire family. His father Keshav. His two elder brothers, Aadi and Ram. Cousins, aunts, uncles. Still more distant relations – ones who live far off, in the next village or the next – grown men and women whose names Rishi barely knows. Together they work their way across the paddy, bent-backed, plucking and planting to a rhythm sustained by nothing but a common urgency – no chant, no clap, no song. They tread the flood's yellow leavings deeper underfoot, into mud made oily by hurriedly scattered ox shit.

Hours later, and with much of the work finished, Rishi's mother sends him back to the house to fetch the lunchtime chapattis. He returns, wobbling precariously along the narrow, mud-slimed embankments that parcel the paddies into regular squares, the grid forcing him into comic turns and switchbacks, like the gobbling yellow Pac-Man sprite he once saw in a fairground booth in Firozabad. It's raining again, and the women, already soaked from the day's labour, shelter under folds of sari. The men, in shirts plastered to their skin and trousers that look as if made of mud, chew their soggy bread, listless as cows. Seizing the chance of escape, Rishi slides away behind a line of trees.

The margosa trees mark the line of a stream fed by waters running off the Sher Shah Suri Marg. Old Samey Yadav's Komatsu has straightened and narrowed the watercourse, making a sluice through which his own and the Ansaris' paddies can drain. In so doing, Old Samey's excavations have turned a gently meandering brook into a foul-smelling drain. Rishi knows better than to approach the edge of the culvert. Even from here, by the trees, he can see an edge of silver where the rushing waters lick the bank, far higher than usual.

He follows the watercourse upstream, towards the Sher Shah Suri Marg. There's a stand of margosas beneath the embankment. Their serrated leaves, curved like the blades of ornamental knives, shiver in the downpour. Rishi looks up through the foliage at the road. Despite the rain there's no let-up in the traffic at all. If anything it's heavier, as farms and businesses haul plant and stores out of the path of the spreading flood. Horns bellow continually.

In the rain and the obscuring tremble of leaves, the traffic blends into one: a silver ribbon extending from horizon to horizon, a rope of silver that forever flows back on itself, like a propeller that, on reaching a certain speed, appears to slow and rotate the other way. Rishi rubs his eyes, but the illusion will not be shaken off. Tata trucks decked out like shrines add bright colours to the silver skin: glassy scales of blue and red and green. The great snake howls – and suddenly the trees are toppling around him, what was far is near, and Rishi's eyes, too late, begin to process what has happened here: a truck has fallen, tipping a container down the embankment and through the trees towards him, over and over, booming and bellowing, like one of those elongated dice from the Howzat! cricket game.

It rocks to rest a few feet away from where little Rishi is standing, frozen with horror, under a rain of leaves. There's a word painted along the box. He tries to read.

Ǝ S ⅄ O M

He tilts his head. He reaches up and runs his hand over the letters, back and forth, as though this might release their meaning.

The container doors swing open.

Though it's gloomy outside, a false dusk, Rishi's day-adapted eyes cannot make out the back of the container. The box might go on forever. He waits for his eyes to adjust. The darkness persists. He steps inside, over the aluminium lintel. His footfalls make no sound as he edges into the dark. Behind him the door swings in the wind, dimming and brightening the interior walls, and yet the back wall remains invisible. It becomes a dare for him, that welling dark. He takes another step, another – and stops dead. There is something in here with him. He hears a susurration so faint it could be anything: a sound, a scent, a movement of lightless surfaces against a lightless ground.

There's commotion outside. Rishi turns gratefully back to the light.

Travellers on the Sher Shah Suri Marg have pulled over to investigate the accident. They're slipping down the embankment, gathering around a margosa tree where the driver, thrown out of his cab, hangs from the topmost branches, dying.

The truck lies some way off on its back: a crumpled catastrophe, a ball of silver paper, screwed up and thrown away. An old, exhaust-filmed shoe dangles from its tailgate; the beam's been snapped like a spent match into a careless V. So much for the trucker's charm.

Washed up on the shores of Chhaphandi, the container's pillaged as swiftly and efficiently as any sea-wreck cast against a cliff. Ancient feuds are forgotten, bad blood made good as the onlookers form a human chain to empty it. Old Samey turns up at the wheel of his Komatsu to haul the container away. He can use it for storage. Aadi and Ram come running up the track to see what's going on, but the haul's a disappointment.

Wastepaper. Crushed glass. Plastic bags. Men wander off, muttering, back to their Tatas, their Tempos, their Standard Gazelles. Small white plastic barrels. They're heat-sealed and the labelling on them makes no sense.

Barrels, small white plastic / US$000 TEU / 24.

Aadi pulls a machete from his belt, turns a barrel on its side – they're easy to handle, no bigger than large paint cans – and chops through its neck.

The barrels contain a caustic granular yellow paste. Aadi pokes at the stuff with the tip of his knife. He cleans his knife off on the grass. The stuff is slightly reactive: soapy bubbles form where the edges of it react with the raindrops clinging to the grass. And there's a smell, both caustic and rotten: mould growing on meal. Old Samey's conclusion: it's paint-stripper. Disappointed, he kicks the barrel into the stream. A few villagers, standing around, pick up canisters for themselves. Could come in useful.

At least the shipping container is in good nick. Aadi and Ram help Old Samey secure it to the bucket of his Komatsu and, yard by painful yard, he drags it out of sight of the road.

Halfway down the track, Rishi's mum comes running up, wailing and rending her kameez. The Ansaris' house has foundered in the flood! It is splitting, ruined, done! The roof beam has snapped! 'Keshav! Keshav, what shall we do?'

That night, while Aadi and Ram and the other young men of the family fight to wrest the family's belongings from the worsening flood, Rishi, his mum and dad, and his sister bed down in a barn belonging to their neighbour Old Samey. Safia curls against Rishi in the straw, gently snoring, while Mum mutters angrily in the dark to her husband, who wants only to sleep. What are we doing in a barn? Is there no room in the house? Of course there's room. Who the hell does old Samey Yadav think he is, herding us into a barn like so many cattle? Go and speak to him, Keshav. Cause a merry stink, Keshav. Go on: show your son what you are made of. Show me.

A bad smell, both mealy and caustic, brings Rishi back to wakefulness. He opens his eyes. Light slides under the barn door. It ropes toward him, tangling across the dusty concrete floor. Red stars on a field of blue. Shreds of yellow light ribbon between softly glowing fields where the colours intermingle to make a white as soft and wet as peach flesh. Rishi's breath catches in his throat. It's beautiful. Uncanny. A dream that's slipped into the waking world.

Aadi and Ram do not return that night, and in the morning they are nowhere to be found. Rishi follows his dad to the ruins of their home. It is not there. In its place, a muddy river flows. Something has happened to the land. It has buckled under the weight of the flood and the receding waters have dug new channels, shortcutting the river's old weave.

Chhaphandi's every field is mud. The flood has daubed every hedgerow with mud so thick the fields appear walled. There's no green leaf anywhere. Buffaloes starve in their pens. Cows keel over in the roads. For two weeks the villagers of Chhaphandi wait to see which of their dead the disaster will leave behind for them to bury.

The drowned bodies of Rishi's elder brothers are found wrapped around each other, tangled in the roots of a dead tree. Their funeral is postponed because there's not enough dry timber for a pyre. Garlands have to be taxied over from Firozabad.

Rishi's father, Keshav Ansari, walks around the funeral pyre, a flaming paper in his hand, lighting Aadi and Ram into the otherworld. The pyre's been smeared with that yellow paint-stripper stuff to help it burn. In the overcast the flames spreading over the pyre are pale and yellow and harmless-looking, and the garlands smothering the corpse seem to be shrivelling and blackening by themselves.

FOUR

At 2.00 p.m. on Sunday, 20 August 1995, the Kalindi Express to New Delhi hits a cow a mile and a half outside Firozabad, in the Indian state of Uttar Pradesh.

The cow makes no sound as it is swallowed. The rush of gas from its mouth, its anus, its ears, and from the corners of its eyes is consumed by the hiss of the train's state-of-the-art braking system. The cow spasms as it vanishes under the locomotive: a steak jiggled into a blender. The cow's hooves snap cleanly off, scissored between wheel and rail. Its chest, compressed, bursts open like a peach, revealing wormy innards that whip up to a froth, drowning the cow's only, involuntary, moo.

The neatness of this butchery, its symmetry, impresses even this hardened driver and his engineer. Climbing down from their locomotive, they inspect the damage. 'Is that a part of the cow, or a part of the train?' Immune to revulsion, they are gripped by a childlike curiosity.

The cow's assumption seems to have done very little damage to the locomotive and the driver and his engineer marvel at the ease with which the animal has given itself up to the machine's appetite, almost as though it had been standing there pre-boned, cut up into living chuck and loins, ready for the instant of collision.

They shunt the train back a few yards, steeling themselves for the shovel-work to come. Perhaps they can throw a few coins to the locals and save themselves the labour. People are running over now: fieldworkers and ditch-sleepers thrown out of their dreams by the squeal of brakes, and even businessmen in suits and ties, driving home, the worse for wear from drinking dens and roadhouses. They have abandoned their cars by the side of the Sher Shah Suri Marg to join the gathering crowd.

The locomotive moves off smoothly enough. Gingerly, the driver tries the brakes. The train rattles and lurches to a ragged halt. The driver looks at the engineer, and the engineer looks at the driver. There is damage after all: their brakes are shot.

The cacophony that erupts from the spectators – the trade in opinions, speculations, criticisms and even gobbets of philosophy – is more constructive than it might seem to an outsider. Living and working beside the low-level atrocity that is the Sher Shah Suri Marg, these people are used to accidents. They react promptly and well to emergencies. In barely a minute, and with their bare hands, men have scoured the rails, bringing to the driver and his engineer anything that might belong to the innards of the train. Others have worked their way underneath, into the stinking, tripey rain dripping from axle and driveshaft. Still others, frustrated by the ambiguity of reports coming from the scene, work instead from theoretical principles. How should a train's brakes work, and what might make them fail? 'In my car . . .' they begin. 'When I was a boy . . .'

In the cab, the driver and his engineer argue disconsolately over the meaning of the lights chasing each other across their dashboards. Cascading electrical failures have left the train's systems impossible to unpick. Dare they drive on with bad brakes? This would be extremely dangerous, but they are stalled on one of the busiest stretches of line in the Lucknow region. It cannot be long before another train is due.

And here it comes. The Purushottam Express: 1,300 sleeping passengers bound for New Delhi on a train twice as heavy as any on the Kalindi service and twice as fast.

In the rearmost carriage of the Kalindi Express twin six-year-olds, the Nankars' boys, sit neat and proper, one on each side of their overseer, the kiln-owner Vinod Yadav. On the way to the station, crouched in the back of the truck, Vinod cowed them with soft, deadly mutterings and sharp, professional jabs of his heavy fingers under their sternums and into their groins. These unfamiliar tactics, meant to wound more than to control, have convinced the boys that they are in the presence of something hungry and unpredictable. They would no more ignore him than you would turn your back on a snarling dog.

Why has the train stopped? Abhik Nankar leans forward, wanting to see out. Vinod cuffs him back in his seat. Abhik studies the scene reflected in the eyeglasses of the man opposite. Sparking in each glass, right to left: headlamps. The train has come to a halt near a road – but which one?

Abhik's brother Kaneer has his eyes closed. Another move. Another compound. Another foreman. Another gang of big boys they must learn to avoid. It's happening again. Kaneer was not cut out for this life. He wants his mum, Samjhoria. He wants their little brick house in the Chhaphandi works and his dad, Manjit, always complaining about his back. He wants to sleep on familiar foam, smell familiar sewage, he wants to feel the old clay setting under his nails. This is not the first time the twins have been carted off without their parents, in this truck or that, only to be reunited with them half a day later, hungry and frightened, in the shadow of this kiln, that barn. It happens – but never before like this. They have never been put aboard a train before. He wants his mum. He must not cry. He wants his dad.

News of the train's collision with a cow spreads through the train in a human shock wave. Suddenly everyone is standing. Here and there people are opening doors. They jump out of the carriage, into the dark, and (Abhik leans forward to see) they vanish! Even their heads disappear! Abhik has never been on a train before: who would have thought they were riding so high off the ground? Vinod pulls him roughly back in his seat, where there is nothing to see. Abhik has seen enough. The embankment, the sweep of headlights: they have halted beside the Sher Shah Suri Marg! They have only to time this well and they can make a break for it. With the road to guide them they can find their way home! He must get a message to his brother, but how? Vinod is sitting between them. There is a metal panel beneath their bench. Abhik kicks his heels against it: bang bang, rattle rattle. He waits, half-expecting Vinod to cuff him again, the way he cuffs their mum. But Vinod, stuck in his seat with the boys, is distracted: he is straining to hear the gossip. An accident? A collision?

Again, then: bang bang, rattle rattle. Kaneer does not respond. Abhik scowls in frustration. Is his brother asleep?

Unable any longer to ignore the drama engulfing the train, Vinod stands. The boys turn and blink at each other. Vinod steps towards the carriage door and Abhik slips behind him, aiming for the door opposite. Once they are outside the boys will have the train between them and their jailer. They are small enough to scamper at will under the carriage, so they can cat-mouse this lumbering bully all night if they want, before losing themselves in the dark. They will be free! Abhik does not doubt he can communicate all this in an eye-blink and as he rushes for the door he glances at Kaneer, beckoning him with his eyes.

Kaneer follows all right.

With the full force of the Purushottam Express at his back, propelled from nought to sixty miles an hour by a wall of superheated vapour, Kaneer the human bullet traverses the shuffle-space between him and his brother faster than human nerves can carry the news into Abhik's uncomplaining brain.

Knees first, a rider in mid-air, Kaneer catches Abhik's torso between his legs. Coupled at the groin, the boys' heads whiplash against each other, into each other. They are, by fractions of a second, the first victims of the second-worst rail crash in Indian history.

The boy's skulls do more than shatter on impact: they explode. Their brains are liquid haggises whose meningeal skins are lacerated to chaff by shards of frontal and maxillary. The ballistic paths of a thousand bone fragments agitate the spewing and unbounded broth: a formula in which what was Kaneer can no longer be distinguished from what was Abhik.

Once, each boy's brain was a forest, magical and sparkling. Each brain cell was a tree, with a taproot for incoming news and branches spread to pass its 'I am' to its neighbours. Now both forests fall through the same chipper and out the end comes something new: a turbulent spew, self-blending, a seething soup of single cells. The force of the blast has sent each brain cell spinning. Each cell is a brush, rapidly whirling, a Tesla device, a friction-maker, a halo of spinning bristles. The cells revolve and touch each other, and as they contact, they spark. Something new is being made here. The boys' minds, sea-changed, spin and whirl into a second life.

As one they bloom; as one they see. They see Vinod hurled the length of the carriage. He tumbles like a doomed parachutist. His left hand strikes a wire luggage rack. With his full weight behind it, here's force enough to spit his fingers into the air – onetwothree! – as though he's plunged his hand into a mincer. The bulk of him, ballistically driven, passes over the rack. His arm, firmly snagged, buckles in a hundred places before it comes away, waving and spitting like a different order of life, an anemone browning in the hot vapour of collision.

The carriage, punched into the air, turns end over end and for a split second it seems as though Vinod is stationary: the tumbling car's centre and pivot. Then the carriage collides in mid-air with the car in front of it and everything buckles. The illusion is broken. Vinod is sucked into a bench-seat as it folds and the halves of its frame scissor his flailing stump. Heat washes through the carriage, cauterizing the wound. The carriage splits in two and Vinod's half plunges end-on through the roof of car number eight, instantly killing half a dozen. Slowly the carriage topples over, crushing almost everyone else in the car. Cloud-borne, the Nankar twins marvel to see how Vinod, encased in the seat, survives the impact.

(Vinod, enveloped by the sandwiched seat, smells seared meat. The disaster is barely seconds old: too new for his mind to register. As far as Vinod is aware, the train is still becalmed outside Firozabad, the Nankar twins are seated on their bench, and he is standing before the open door, looking out at the night, the embankment, the road. It seems to him that a great, scratchy tongue has curled out of the dark and wound him into a hot, close, savoury space: the mouth of a cat.)

The twins' bodies are chopped wreckage by now: smoke-curls and fragments of char, roiling in a spinning metal maze. Theirs is a bodily annihilation so abrupt, so comprehensive, it leaves the boys agape at their own extinction. But who needs flesh? Not Kaneer, not Abhik. They are literally disembodied: interpenetrating clouds of pink steam. A nova seen double through a gravitational lens. They bob and tremble on the edge of a shock wave that even now hurls them out of the open mouth of the sundered carriage and into the night.

Vaporous, expanding constantly, the twins flow through new conductors, race each other down whipping wires, dance thillanas through a businessman's mobile phone, play demolition derby round the looped infinity of a pair of spectacle frames, and trace the rills and saddles of a foil sandwich wrapper. Distributed and dispersed, they comprehend the disaster around them in all its fullness, while the maimed and the dying have barely had time to notice anything amiss.

A woman without legs flies by, clutching beaded bags. It is Pali, Rishi Ansari's wife, off to New Delhi to promote her district's bangles and kangans, chandelier ornaments and cut-glass figurines. Of course, Kaneer and Abhik do not know who she is. They are not yet gods. They see only a determined businesswoman, her mouth scrunched with disappointment, her hands tight around the handles of bags which are themselves samples. See the finish! Feel the quality of the stitching! But the blast has ripped through her wares as comprehensively as it has ripped through her thighs, and her treasures spray out behind her through smoking rents: rivers of glass.

The Nankar twins watch the rivers twine and sparkle half-seen against the stars. They stare and, staring, lose themselves in toils of reflected light, refracting and recombining as the hot and close-packed shards smash into each other, rendering themselves down to powder. Pali's bangles, her district's labour, the bitter fruit of whip-backed hours, the pride of eyes gone yellow from the scarring of a hundred thousand glass flecks – it is a rainbow, or it would be, were there light enough to see.

The boys hang in the air, holographed in glass: their new home. The rainbow flexes. The rainbow lives. The rainbow wriggles through the air like a snake. It runs like a blindfold across Pali's eyes as she tumbles, scraping her corneas to a fine translucence: she does not see the tangle of steaming metal that waits for her as she begins her descent. The rainbow flexes, dashes, roils. Riding the heat of the collision, it surfs away from the railway, the Kalindi and Purushottam Expresses.

Tacking back and forth, it finds at last a stable cushion of warm air along which to flow. Like a varicose vein, the Sher Shah Suri Marg runs over the land, raised on earth embankments. Warmth rises, even at this late hour, from its metalled top.

Meanwhile, at the Yadav Brickworks outside Chhaphandi, not ten miles away, the Lohardaga girls have gathered, nervous and disoriented, on the edge of the compound. They know nothing of the railway accident: they are being kept awake by a more proximate calamity. The geometry of their home has been disturbed. Where is the Nankar family's hut? Where are the Nankars? What are these lights in the sky? Above their heads, half-glimpsed in the roiling flash of oil-drum fires, the rainbow skips, agitated, around the perimeter of the work camp. The Nankar twins are looking for their home. They are looking for their mum and dad. Something terrible has happened. What? Fine grains of glass cascade from the sky. The girls, cursing the smoke and embers, wipe their eyes as unseen supernatural forces read the secrets from their frightened hearts.

Beyond the kilns and out towards the river, a fickle tributary of the sacred Yamuna, the criss-crossing tracks and paths of the brickworks give way at last to channelled mud and weeds, cowpats, discarded fence posts and broken kerb stones, screes of woodchip and pebbledash. Among the trash left from the factory's construction there is a pit, newly dug and newly filled, and overlooking the pit, a saffron-yellow Komatsu. Its engine is warm. The pit is warmer: wisps of labile smoke rise from a crumble of burning tyres.

Even gods would have a hard time sifting evidence from the smeared and crumbled leavings buried here, crushed beneath so much rubble, scoop upon scoop of river gravel and bails of rusted barbed wire. But Kaneer and Abhik smell their kin well enough. They flex as one above the pit in an agony of loss. Mummy! Daddy! The Nankar boys are home.

The rainbow flexes in the air, swelling, stretching, deforming. It haloes the ground, a screaming mouth. Its needle teeth glisten in the dark. It's only a child. It's only two children, hugging each other against the dark. They're lonely. They're lost. They're dead. What comfort for them now?

They loop back to the only home they know: mud walls and corrugated-iron roofs and dogs. The compound is asleep. Their hut is a disordered, kerosene-drenched heap of mud, straw and ash: very few clues remain here to remind them of their life. The bowl of a frying pan; the handle's burnt away. Scorched and shrivelled scraps of green polyester: it was their mum's only good kameez. Potatoes. Now, this is a puzzle. Potatoes? They haven't seen a potato for days. Round here, and under Vinod Yadav's vindictive rule, potatoes have been a weekly luxury for the Nankar family. What are all these potatoes doing here? Handsome, fresh, blemishless baked potatoes, their insides soft and creamy, their skins crispy under a smothering of fat – what fat? White fat. Lard. Mummy . . .

The twofold djinn spins together a scenario of unspeakable, sickening horror, then jackknifes away from the ruined hut, repulsed by its own powerful imagination.

Marking the southern boundary of the compound, half-hidden behind piled pallets and rolls of rusty, half-unravelled chain-link, there's an old forty-foot shipping container, 'MOYSE' still just about readable on its flank. It's the only secure structure on the site, the only corner of that busy desolation where they are guaranteed some peace. They need space to breathe. To come to terms. They need to understand what they are. The boys unravel and fan in under the lip of the padlocked door.

Among old buckets, tools, drums of fuel oil and kerosene, bottles of paint-stripper, turpentine and white spirit, the boys curl around themselves, each the other's nest, and whisper stories in the dark. And for a while, they are comforted. These tales, at least, are familiar. 'The Qazi of Jaunpur'. 'Wangu and the Lion'. Folklore from a land since pocked with breeze blocks and landfill. But it's a limited repertoire and very soon exhausted.

They try spinning new tales out of old, but story-time's a luxury almost unheard of in their little lives; they're only young and bricks are all they really know.

It goes like this: Wangu is the oldest man in the village and he cannot bear to see anyone happy.

No, like this: Wangu finds good, loamy clay soil from the side of a hill.

How about this? Wangu just wants more money, more land, more sheep. He knows to avoid old stream beds and flood plains and digs a hole in the ground four feet long by three feet wide by three feet deep. When day dawns he has wandered far, far away from the valley of the stone lion and he fills the hole with water.

No, no.

Like this, then: When day dawns he swings his legs over the rail and plucks the brick from his mother's grasp. It is an ordinary yellow house brick, poorly made, porous as a sponge. He folds it in his arms and falls into the water.

Something has happened. Something important. But the transition from the old, familiar shipping container to some other, quite alien, story-space is so abrupt and so seamless it takes the boys a moment to realize the enormity of it. For a little while they read their old surroundings on to the new: Pink jellyfish: paper dishcloths. Darting crabs: rats. Rocks wrapped in gold weed: sacks of cement. Then, looking up, they see that the roof of the container is turned to sea and the silver undersides of waves plash their glassy sides with bluing light.

The boys rise cased in ice, infused with wonder. What is this place?

This landscape's so strange it might have leaked from someone else's dream. Land made of ice. Ahead of them a dark fang punctures the grey horizon. Foyn. They walk and walk. They stumble into puddles, shield their eyes, suck buttons torn from their coats to keep their thirst at bay. They wear felt boots. They carry axes, pistols. Now here's a story worth the telling, a boy's adventure tale, if only they can.

The blow is so fast the boys don't even see it coming. Howling, swiped out of story-time, they flex into the air, fleeing white bears, smashed ice, and the red ruins of strange men.

Buoyant, briefly becalmed, the boys take stock. Somehow, they've fallen through the skein of things. How it happened is a question that can wait. Now all that matters is, how on earth are they going to get home?

They spin and spin, but there's no traction here, no headway, they are adrift. Is this it, then? Is this the end? They're only children. Little. They're aghast. How can stories end in such a way? Where's the moral? Where's the justice? Brought up on old tales, and precious few of them, they're unprepared for this. The way lives churn and churn, going nowhere, just frothing time into what might have been.

At the eleventh hour, a rescue. A wrecked and flapping bladder happens by, a plaything of the air. A complex fabric bag, sheened with aluminium paint. Now, this is new. Pure Jules Verne. Shit-kickers they may be, but they're boys, and know of Nemo. Once, stumbling on some distant village fair, they snuck in under the tent wall to watch. James Mason in white polo-neck, Kirk Douglas in red stripy T. Ever afterwards, for as long as they were flesh, they carried the marks of their transgression. A scar above Kaneer's right eye. Abhik's cauliflower ear. A movie's not for *bhangi* kids.

Well, look at them now! Squealing with joy, the boys wriggle round the stricken airship's balloonettes and grid themselves along its flexible metal skeleton. There are men here, survivors of the first crash, but marooned now. Lost men. Dead men. One, despairing, leaps, embracing chilly dark and death.

Furiously, the boys work to keep the airship afloat. Snatches of the film return to their powerful and twofold mind and they use it to plug the airship's holes. Kirk Douglas crouches by a gap in the wall, looking out into the Arctic night, hunting in vain for some last-minute, third-act solution. James Mason lies across a mat of muscle-red tarpaulin, greeting the tragic failure of his ship with dignity and cigarette. Mutters: 'Should have stuck to submarines.' Mason's a reassuring name for these kids: kids whose clay- and mica-blotched skins once glittered greenly in the dusk like week-old fish. Mason's swarthy, flattened looks make him every inch a Nemo, too. Prince Dakkar, son of the Rajah of Bundelkund, who plundered sunken galleons for gold and preyed on British ships to fuck the hated Empire up . . .

The boys will spin this story out for as long as they can, they're learning fast, they're getting good at this, but narrative logic demands that what goes up must come down. The shattered airship will crash again – and finally, this time. The ship must crash . . .

But the winds do not stop in their courses and the oceans do not cease to turn, and the bag, a ruined, wheezing lung, flies higher, higher, hits a slipstream, bends, deforms, stretches and shreds, its luggage spilled, its Nemo hurled without complaint to earth, roll-up sparking in his clay-white fist. World-wrapping winds whip shreds of fabric bag round and round the earth and drop them, years later, on a barren hill.

ITALIA

The boys slither over dry, smashed rock, dizzy with adventure. They have no idea where they are, or when, but they are beginning to grasp that geography matters less to them than it matters to the living. They make their own journeys with the stories they tell. They fashion – somehow, they don't yet know how – their own escapes. They survived a barren and virtually unpeopled Arctic: they'll make a story of this place too. Stories are their breath. Their food. Their blood. And they're getting stronger.

On the hill opposite, perched in a shadowy defile, a wounded officer of the Sultan's Desert Regiment blinks, sun-dazzled, as letters spill and blur across the shattered wastes, into the defile and up, unseen, towards his heart and brain.

The boys bed in, tense, waiting for the crash, the screaming plummet, the blow from the monstrous white bear. (For all they know, it's their presence brought such ill-luck on their former host.) But nothing bad happens: just a stumbling descent on one good leg to the town and the shore and the motorboat. David Brooks rides in the prow, watching a pod of dolphins. He wonders why he feels so nauseous, who never had a day's seasickness in his life. The boys, winding boisterously around his guts, fight for the view afforded by his eyes.

The aeroplane ride to the southern city of Salalah is exhilarating, though the Skyvan's interior is cramped and smelly and not nearly as comfortable as the airship. Riding in the Land Rover with David Brooks and Edward Turnhill brings them back to territory with which they are almost familiar: dust, rock, broken concrete, jerry-rigged phone and power lines. It's when they get to the palace that things begin to fall apart. This David man's no hero, it turns out. He's come to steal a kingdom. No hero hides behind a gun, a uniform. No. The boys will none of him. They'd sooner tease the old man's parrots.

When they look up from their play, David has gone. Turnhill and the Sultan have gone. The palace is deserted.

The palace doors are open. One by one the Sultan's birds flump their way towards the great outdoors. Funnelled to an unlikely height by the strange, reverse vertigo of once-captive birds, the parrots spiral over their palatial home, up and up, until they hit a cold layer, whipping counter to the sea fog's flow. Airs of different temperatures and densities do not mix. They rub against each other and waves form along the join. An inverse wave, like a great tongue, scoops the birds up into the cold layer and the wind flings them, bright as rockets fired from Nemo's ship, out over the ocean.

Around noon the next day a lump of something, a rough parallelepiped, yellow as a cheap housebrick, drops out of the Indian Ocean's blue empyrean and lands on the roof of a forty-foot-long shipping container. The container is one of eight lashed to the hatch covers of a small Chinese-built cargo ship called *Malacca Queen*. Bricked in ice, deep-frozen, Sultan Said's second-favourite parrot (a rare Senegal) shatters against the roof of the container and the container, 'MOYSE' stencilled on its side, rings like a bell. It's empty – or may as well be, for what its contents are worth:

Wastepaper / US$100 TEU / 01 TEU.

Crouched in the dark between this container and the next –

MSKU7176658: Vehicles, cars, buses, trucks, lorries, motorcycles, bicycles, used.

– fifteen-year-old Egaz Nageen ducks. *Gunfire*? RIB pilot, machete boy and look-out, Nageen is so far out of his comfort zone here he's imagining all kinds of shit. His idea of piracy is sneaking aboard some Sydney tourist's yacht while they're busy getting pissed portside. He's never clambered aboard so big a ship, never mind in mid-ocean.

Something colourful and frilled convulses at his feet and Nageen falls back, fumbling with his knock-off AK. At last he has the thing pointed in the snake's approximate direction – but now that he looks closer, what he took for the hood of a monstrous serpent turns out to be nothing of the sort. He nudges it with a horny toe. What the fuck? Just a few bloody feathers stuck together with a skin of grey glue. Must have been a bird flew into the ship's exhausts. He nudges the dead fragment under the container with his foot, shuddering. Where are they? What's taking them so long? What was that sound? He imagines all kinds of grief. A crew wielding knives from the galley. Fire hoses. Flare pistols. He lays down his AK a second and wipes his eyes with the edge of his T. He's had enough of this shit. If he gets out of this alive he's catching a bus, well away from Tarutao and the boys and all the stunted hand-to-mouth with which his youth's been filled so far. He's not stupid, and he's not broke. There has to be something better he could be doing with his life.

Meanwhile the boys slither under the container, round to the doors, and in. Wrapped around each other for warmth, for safety, and for the sharing of strange tales, they explore the container. Their awakening senses tell them that they will not come this way again or see this box again. Still, they are excited. They are overjoyed, for every such container affords a feast for story-eating creatures.

Boxes and boxes and boxes. Millions of boxes. *Tens* of millions of boxes – and every one a dedicated explorer of the earth! Follow the boxes and you follow the stories of every grain and fruit and paste and spice. Every nail and screw and handle. Every ointment, adhesive, moisturizer, syrup. Every rebar. Every book. The drug-run done, the ship's released, rebadged, re-crewed. MSKU 7176658 is unloaded in Istanbul and transferred to a Suezmax behemoth bound for Nagasaki. From there, stuffed with electronic components, it heads back north to Tilbury and on to a ship bound for Newfoundland. Fifty further voyages are enough to bring Abhik and Kaneer to Mumbai. From here it's an easy business to ride a box back home.

Stretches of the GTR are as busy as the Strait of Malacca, just as dangerous and just as pirate-infested. At 2.00 a.m. the truck they're riding in splits its tyres, jackknifes, and rocks to a halt in a cloud of dust. Youths rush out of the shadows and up to the cab, wielding iron reinforcing rods. But the boys are long gone, bellied by the warm air rising from the Sher Shah Suri Marg. They know what they are now. They have the measure of their power. Howling, they hurl their way home, their colours startling drivers bound for shifts in the emergency wards of Agra, Mathura and Bharatpur.

The sun rockets into the sky to meet them near Firozabad, city of burns, city of scars, and lights the cooling metal mash that was their train and still contains, in smears and scraps and soaps, their lost remains.

They're story-eaters now. They're djinn. They'll pull a story from this mess. They'll find a way to make a meaning from their lives, their deaths, their lives-in-death. They'll find a way to make this right: their dad's death, their mum's death, their stunted, hopeless birthright and all the petty cruelties of their world. They'll find the sense in this.

They settle over the wreckage and weep their glass into each undefended eye. No child, no bird, no dog is safe: all must give up what they know. Glimpses, rumours, histories: the brothers drink them in.

Names, faces, places.

Smells, sights, memories.

Banyan trees. Hindu swastikas. Bad typography.

Cooking fires in a parking lot.

A foul smell. Christmas dinners. Pink Australians. Yadav.

The twofold genie lurches. *Yadav*? Blue flame erupts across the sky as the boys scurry and slither through the wreckage, among the living and the dying, the human and the animal, hunting down this errant thought. (Mortal men, hiding as they must from too much reality, assume that this fierce blue blaze that does not burn is simply sunlight, catching against the bright metal of the Purushottam's carriages. The birds aren't fooled: they wheel and caw.)

The blue fire winds itself up again and slides through many colours into the invisible as it curls towards a young woman, her face as bright, iconic and ambisexual as the emblem on a stamp. Hers is a smile to stagger the heart. Hers is a heart that yearns for love. They wrap her round, their instant auntie, loving her for her smile and her heart. They lick a forked and twofold tongue into her ear, all glass, to tease out what she knows.

Mmm. (They sip and cogitate.) *A cheeky little number, this:*

Engine grease / US$38 barrel / 27 barrels
Revolvers (assorted) / US$ N/A piece / 37
Ammunition (assorted) / US$ N/A / 128 x 10rds box

And an aftertaste of silencer.

And here, with uniformed retinue, he comes: a big policeman in civilian clothes.

Yadav.

It's no Yadav the boys have ever met. There's story here, for sure. The boys will stick around for this. They slide in, bed down, twine around the bright young woman's silky guts (none too gently – the old mistake) and the little tea she's drunk today drools off her chin as Roopa Vish, Bombay child, father's daughter and police spy, heaves . . .

Part Two

FIVE

Sion: a suburb of Bombay.

It is 1993, two years before the Purushottam Express collides with the stalled Kalindi service just outside Firozabad, causing the second-worst rail crash in Indian history.

Hardik Singh and his boys have arrived early at the community centre. Police Probationer Roopa Vish finds them loitering in the portico. Muscular poster-boys for the hardline saffronist Rashtriya Swayamsevak Sangh, right now they're stuffing their faces with egg sandwiches. Why so many of them? She feels their eyes on her as she unlocks the door. Their smiles are speculative, halfway insolent. Her dear dead father warned her about boys like these. Boys who shelter under a religious banner. Boys who think they're God's gift.

'The meeting's not until six.'

They watch her. They await her next important pronouncement. Oh God, is she blushing? The youngest is barely a teenager. The oldest is no older than her. He offers her his hand. Unthinking, she shakes it. 'Hardik.' His features are delicate and expressive. Not handsome. She cannot hold his gaze.

The venue is a former Scout hut. (This is Roopa's job, six months into her service with the Bombay police: community events.) Stacking chairs. Dusty windows. Peeling paint. They build fast round here and they build cheap. When they need concrete they dredge sand from the nearby creeks. When it rains the concrete acquires streaks and stains and it cracks and crumbles and, yes, collapses, as though these blocks were ancient, weathering to failure over centuries.

Hardik and his boys want to reassure the locals about their organization. They will explain to the law-abiding and aspirational communities of Sion that their children have joined a benign outward-bound movement. Any cheaply produced pamphlets they may have found under their darlings' beds – banyan trees, Hindu swastikas, bad typography – are nothing to do with the RSS.

The boys wrap up their sandwiches as they enter the hall. One of them disappears through a door into the little galley kitchen at the rear of the room. He comes out with a rubbish sack. The boys throw their half-eaten sandwiches in the sack. The sack disappears into the kitchen and the boys set out the chairs. The first residents arrive to find tea already hot in the urn, the room already arranged.

They're not grateful. These are the old, the halt, the lame. The ones who come just for the free cups of tea. Had the boys repainted the hall saffron-yellow and thrown rice at their feet, it wouldn't have made any difference to them. No one of any significance turns up until the room is already half-full and by then it is no longer obvious that the boys had anything to do with the setting up. Outnumbered, the RSS boys gather at the back of the hall. They haven't a clue how to work a room.

Hardik meets Roopa's gaze. His friends whisper in his ear. She watches him, his face, his small mouth, and for some reason she recalls the moment they touched: the warm, dry grip of his hand in her hand. The memory is shockingly vivid. She tries to get rid of it, wiping her hand against her nasty nylon slacks – the dismal uniform of the police probationer. The meeting is called to order. Hardik watches as people take their seats. As though he were waking out of a dream, he approaches the lectern.

He is not used to this. He's on the defensive before he's even begun. His voice is pitched too high, hectoring people. He tells his audience he's a *pracharak*: a full-time RSS volunteer. He tells them enough about his life, and with enough humour, to establish his rough-diamond credentials, but the tone of his voice tells a different story entirely. It is the voice of someone frantic for respect.

Seated at the back of the hall, Roopa loses the sense of what Hardik is saying. His words are being drowned out by the rattle of the air-conditioning unit. It's not even keeping the room cool. Roopa squirms in her hard chair. Her slacks are sticking to her legs, it's disgusting. She gets up and goes to the back of the hall. Now that she is nearer the air-conditioning unit, Hardik's speech is completely inaudible. This is good. There is something sad and small and vulnerable about Hardik. She does not want it to touch her.

Plenty of Sion's residents have turned out to hear the RSS put their case. But there are no teenagers here. This meeting is about them, so why aren't they here to fight their corner? Have their parents told them not to come? And if they retain that much authority over their children, why are they so worked up about the RSS? A few yoga exercises? Advertisements for a wrestling tournament?

Then the meeting is over and, again, here they are, Hardik and the boys, ostracized in their corner while their audience mills around the tea urn. The boys are learning that they are not so controversial, after all.

The next time Roopa sees Hardik he is in an American magazine, covered in blood. His picture accompanies an article describing the worst terrorist atrocities yet perpetrated in post-Partition India: the bombs let off across Bombay on 12 March 1993 by Dawood Ibrahim's D-Company.

Roopa has been taking witness statements. Every day, she visits a different hospital. Two hundred and fifty people killed, seven hundred injured. Roopa thought that the more she heard the clearer her picture of events would become. (She is her father's daughter, youngest child of Kabir Vish, who caught the Stoneman, who beachcombed the streets of Matunga for meaning – pure police.) But each statement she takes is virtually identical to the last. There was a loud bang. I fell over. I saw blood. Impossible to get frustrated with these people. Impossible to despise the recall abilities of a man without arms or a mother mourning a child. They remember well enough. The problem is what they remember. It will not fall into words. Logic will not parse it. It is story-proof.

Yesterday she was weaving past cooking fires in the parking lot, shouldering through knots of weeping, jabbering relatives in the corridors. Today's rota has her at Pushpanjali Hospital, talking to the private sector. A better class of paraplegic. A more educated burns victim. While she waits for the ward sister to admit her, she picks up a magazine. It is not one you often see. Not *Cine Blitz*, not *Sportsworld*. It has been dropped here by a recent visitor. A British colour supplement. She reads:

> Young, frustrated, politically engaged, Hardik Singh has amassed a file of misdemeanours following trouble at rallies of one sort or another. Now his saffron-dyed politics have achieved legitimacy. He is a hero, and his cause is one the city's liberal intelligentsia can no longer belittle.
>
> Within minutes of the explosions, the RSS were pulling people out of the rubble and tearing the injured free of mangled vehicle wreckage. Long before the ambulances got there, the RSS's trained first-aiders were hammering hearts to life again and kissing breath into deflated lungs. RSS boys gathered maimed and bleeding children in their arms and ran relays, bearing them to hospitals at a speed the city's rescue crews could not match. Fire trucks arrived to find that local RSS boys had put out their fires with nothing more than blankets and dirt. It was what RSS shakhas all over the city had been training for, planning for (cynics said, hoping for). It is their finest hour, and Hardik Singh, covered in filth and soot and other people's blood, and obviously annoyed by my questions, knows it.

In the photograph Hardik is standing in front of a wrecked car. He has been saving the injured. He is smeared with other people's blood. The photographer has captured him shouting orders. His delicate face is distorted by a fierce intensity.

Riots begin in earnest a few weeks later. Whole streets burn. Entire families roast. Hardik is arrested. He still thinks he's a hero. Roopa watches him in the holding cell. Milling there with a dozen others, already he has the poise and dignity of a political prisoner.

Roopa speaks to the desk sergeant, then goes and waits outside the station for Hardik to come out. There are Tempos and mopeds pulled up outside the front gate. There are boys: RSS and Shiv Sena. When Hardik comes out, a free man, he ignores their cheers. He hunts the crowd. He spots her. He walks towards her.

Roopa snaps to attention: her father's daughter. She is as tall as he is. He stands before her for the longest time, looking at her. She wishes he would say something. She wishes he would take her hand, at least.

And he does.

Bombay's Anti-Corruption Bureau ('Raise your voice and it shall be heard!') operates out of an industrial estate in Worli, next door to Raj Electricals. The ACB has a twofold remit: to weed out government corruption, and to tackle the city's long-established mafias. Organized crime in Bombay is divided along religious lines. The Muslim syndicates receive clandestine backing from Pakistan's intelligence community and pose a serious terrorist threat to the Indian state. The saffronist mafias have connections to domestic far-right groups and hide beneath a banner of Hindu patriotism.

Of the saffronist families currently operating in Bombay, the Yadavs are the most notorious. The ACB has files on the Yadav family going back to Partition. Whole careers have been expended poring over the family's business affairs, its influence in the port, its political connections. 'The deepest fissure in Bombay's black economy is the traditional rivalry between the Indian Ocean commercial–criminal nexus and the land-based nexus stretching from Bombay to Delhi to Kashmir. The Yash syndicate has begun to square this circle for itself, through a programme of intimidation, assassination and a series of strategic alliances across religious boundaries.'

To put it in plain English, the Yadavs are everywhere. Roopa Vish finds this out for herself shortly after passing her police probation. Roopa has been working at the ACB for six months, matching names and addresses across commercial and contractual paperwork, when she comes across a small import–export concern called EastSpan Imports. Uncovering connections between the company and other Yadav family interests, Roopa tips off the Bombay Port Trust. The most she expects, and the most her bosses expect of her, is that the Trust might intercept some low-pressure cold extraction gear: plant associated with the Yadav family's sandalwood scam.

What they get are twenty-seven barrels of engine grease which, when emptied over the quay, disgorge thirty-seven revolvers, 1,280 rounds of ammunition and a silencer.

It's been common knowledge for years that the Yadavs of Bombay have been importing Tanzanian sandalwood and using it to adulterate genuine sandalwood oil. The family's rural branches, meanwhile, have been smuggling protected sandalwood from Kerala and distilling it in mobile factories all over Uttar Pradesh. It's a profitable trade and a relatively bloodless one. What the hell do the Yadavs need all this hardware for?

Roopa Vish, meanwhile, has uncovered something even more peculiar. One of the Yadav family's country cousins has moved to Bombay and joined the police.

With a family this big, you expect a few recidivists to find themselves legitimate careers. It's only when they start doing exceptionally well that alarm bells ring. Sub-Inspector Yash Yadav has been doing very well indeed. Bank frauds, financial frauds, foreign exchange violations: Yash Yadav's case files record success after success. Now strings have been pulled to draw him up the police ranks and into the elite Central Bureau of Investigation. Roopa Vish wonders whether, underneath his uniform, this country cousin, this yokel, might not be working for the Bombay branch of the family. She picks up the phone.

Roopa has a new boss: Kala Subadrah, formerly the Deputy Inspector General of the Central Industrial Security Force, providing security cover to nearly three hundred sensitive industrial locations all over India. Kala's just had twins, though you'd never know it to look at her. She has one of those labour-proof bodies: easy to picture her on the front cover of a maternity magazine, working out with small hand-weights. Only the bags under her eyes give her away. If she's getting four hours of sleep a night, she's lucky. For all that, Kala finds time to meet Roopa out of office hours, and this is a very good sign. Kala is new to her job and has a lot to prove. Roopa's discovery may be the answer to Kala's prayers.

The restaurant is pink with Australian tourists. You can smell the sunblock from here. And there's a foul odour coming from the restaurant. Christmas dinners.

'Well,' Kala says, over tea and sweets: straight down to business. 'This is a bloody mess, isn't it?'

Roopa chews her halwa.

'A decorated officer. Gallantry. Meritorious Service. And here you are dragging his name through the mud on no better grounds than that he has a notorious surname. What on earth do you think you're doing, Assistant Sub-Inspector?'

Roopa stares at her plate.

'Roopa.'

It takes a moment for Roopa to twig: Kala is smiling.

'Roopa Vish.' She pours them more tea. 'Are you related?'

'My father,' Roopa says, her voice barely audible over the raucous chatter of the Australians.

'Kabir Vish. Caught the Stoneman. Ugly bugger, as I remember. Terrible teeth. Your mum must be a beauty.'

'Ma'am?'

Kala laughs. 'Relax, Roopa. I know quality when it's under my nose. Your father, may he rest in peace, taught me everything I know.'

Installed in her own office, with her own assistant and even a phone of her own, Roopa works long hours on Yash Yadav. She could recite you the highlights of his police career without recourse to the file. Armed encounters with Islamist mafiosi. Police shoot-outs and legal kills. Roopa studies statements, photographs, autopsy reports, official denials. The legal kill: it is, she thinks, with a thrill of mischief, one hell of a way to get rid of your family's business rivals.

In bed at night, alone, she thinks of Yash Yadav: a big man, taking aim. Naked, self-aroused, she dreams the just blow and its aftermath. Shock and recoil. She pushes a finger inside herself as she comes. Afterwards, trembling, disgusted, she wonders how it is that she finds any of this erotic.

She clambers out of bed. She moves around it, as you would shy away from a bad memory. What time is it?

After midnight.

After one.

Where is her husband? Where is Hardik? Of course she knows the truth about Hardik by now. Any wife would. Once, in desperation, she tried to get him to watch her masturbate. What a farce that was.

Roopa and Hardik have been married barely a year. In the beginning, they were gossip-worthy: the daughter of a decorated police martyr come to rub the rough edges off a gutter patriot! A fairytale of the city's New Right. But it's a dizzying time for the RSS and Hardik's volunteer work has been keeping him out late. Roopa has been staying up for him, keeping his meals hot. It is not easy, in her line of work, to be always putting Hardik first.

Hardik is riding the wagon of saffronist resurgence: a force that will soon transform Bombay down to its very name. He wants her to know that she is not part of this. He wants her lack of understanding established: a fact as secure and protective as a wall. He has been dabbling at the edges of political violence for years. Now he wants her to think he has been drawn into some sinister activity. How can a bourgeois girl like Roopa hope to understand the plight of the slums? It is Hardik's very big alibi for betrayals that have nothing to do with politics.

Under the bed, in a suitcase filmed with dust, Roopa's old probationer's uniform lies neatly pressed and folded. She shakes it out. She finds a shirt of Hardik's which, at a distance, will pass for a service garment. She dresses the part.

She is her father's daughter: Kabir Vish, who never let the spoor of the Stoneman go, though many said he was just a fairytale the *bhangis* told to keep their brats in check. For a woman of such pedigree, tracking down her husband is a very small matter. Last night she followed him to Kamala Nehru. Tonight – she knows his habits by now – she will find him in Shivaji Park.

Roopa's old uniform prickles and sticks. Still, it is necessary. It gives her a reason for being here, a woman alone at night in Bombay's biggest public space. The wildlife will leave her alone. At the same time, any upright citizen – any fellow officer, God forbid – will feel that he can call on her. Officer, I've lost my dog! My child! My service weapon! My mind! If she's caught impersonating an officer, there will be hell to pay.

It's out of her hands. She follows her husband. She slides off the broad avenue after him, off raked gravel and on to mown dirt. She follows him into the dark, around cricket pitches, past the Scout hut and the temple of Ganesh, into ornamental shrubberies where abandoned cricket balls dome like fungi out of a salad of leaf-mould and tissues. She follows him past the tinkling of bells and the susurration of silks. The men who congregate here wear their make-up so thick its river-bottom smell overpowers any amount of cheap perfume. Roopa knows what goes on here. The *hijras* of Shivaji were her father's eyes and ears. Each time a superintendent got it into his head to clean up the parks, Kabir Vish tipped off his fancy-dressed friends. It's how he caught the Stoneman.

What is Hardik doing here? What investigations does he pursue? Tonight, watching him, his antics and caresses, Roopa knows that she has always known.

Roopa retires to her mother's house in Thane and for a few weeks she tries to knit herself into the old solid, suburban life.

Her mother is sympathetic. Her daughter's disgrace is, in some half-acknowledged way, an opportunity for her. A chance to exert some authority. She schools her daughter in the art of managing shame. For Roopa, it is like being buried. With no work for her to do, and no husband to look after, she is bored out of her mind. But staying with Hardik is impossible.

'You can stay here as long as you like, dear.' Long enough for the city to change its name, and every street and every street corner. When Roopa finally returns to work she feels as though she is visiting the city after an absence of years. She arrives at the ACB to find that her phone is gone, her office is gone, her clerical help has been reassigned. Kala Subadrah calls her into her office. 'I'm sorry, Roopa,' she says, 'it's out of my hands.'

'Then why –'

Kala throws up her hands in exasperation. 'Yash Yadav has resigned from the Central Bureau of Investigation.'

'*What*?'

Kala hands her the file.

Yash Yadav has secured a transfer to Uttar Pradesh. A paper promotion, and a whopping cut in salary. Why has Yash Yadav abandoned his CBI career just to run anti-terror in *Firozabad*, of all places? Why rise so effortlessly through the ranks in Bombay only to return to the provinces?

Roopa knows. Long before she was copying out chalkboard diagrams in the classrooms of Marol – 'Assets disproportionate to known sources of income amassed by a Public Servant', 'Public Servant obtaining valuable thing without consideration from person concerned in proceeding or business transacted by such Public Servant' – Daddy explained to her, without all this verbal hoopla, how saffronist mafias tick. Yash Yadav's appointment as Firozabad's anti-terror tsar leaves him plenty of time to take up the reins of the family's regional business interests. The construction work. The haulage concern. 'Ma'am, Mumbai has been an apprenticeship for him! The family doesn't need him in Mumbai any longer. They need him in Firozabad. They're putting him to work!'

Police Superintendent Kala Subadrah sighs. 'Write it all down if you must, but I can't promise you anything.'

Roopa writes it down all right. Every nuance of the case she's so far amassed against Yash Yadav. Stated baldly, and without the circumspection of a legal document, her argument against Yadav is a thing of pure spite.

Roopa assumes this is an exercise of sorts. A way of keeping her occupied while she adjusts to her disappointment.

On the contrary, her investigation into Yash's too-perfect record and too-healthy bank balance have won her more friends than she knows. Kala takes Roopa's 'exercise' to meetings at the highest level and when eventually a decision is made to send someone out to the sticks to keep an eye on Yash Yadav, they call on Roopa Vish.

'In Firozabad you will be tackling women's issues,' Kala tells her. 'Errant husbands. Domestic violence.'

'Yes.'

'The hours will be long.'

'Yes.'

'Plus, they don't have much experience of women officers.'

'No.'

'If it goes badly for you we can't help you. The ACB has no jurisdiction outside Maharashtra.'

'I understand.'

'This is not an official posting. It will not appear on our records.'

Roopa can barely contain her excitement.

It is a new beginning for her. From her mother's house, and with her mother by her, squeezing her hand, she phones Hardik and tells him what she has decided to do. She asks him to come with her. She wants them to try again. Hardik is her husband, after all.

'What the hell is there for us in Firozabad?' he complains. 'We should have talked about this!'

Nonetheless, he follows her.

Firozabad: city of ovens and cutting wheels, city of fires and flapping skin. This is the place where people breathe more glass than air. 'You imagine this is a flourish, heh? Go there! Feel your lungs bleed!'

Firozabad: city of asthma. City of tuberculosis. City of burns and scars. Virtually every glass ornament, bangle, kangan and kara is pulled from Firozabad's furnaces on asbestos trays. Boys carry skewers tipped with molten glass across the factory floor. The heat of the skewers calluses their palms, turning them green. The boys gather bangles from baking trays and stack them on trolleys, and men pull the trolleys out of the factory gates and down the hill, along roads crusted with broken glass, to the warrens of Devnagar.

Devnagar. Washing on a thousand lines: cheap saris from China, white shirts and baggy grey salwars. Firewood. Dogs on chains. Children playing cricket with bats and stumps torn from packing crates. Sparks and sudden outages. Bags of cement, stacks of bricks. Cementation rods spilled everywhere. It is never quiet. Spinning wheels and screaming babies. Arguments over water, about who is tapping whose electricity. Insults hurled from house to house. Generators that will not start. Cars that will, but only on a hill. Squeal of pulleys. Snap of clothes pegs. Scrape of metal wool against the bottoms of ten thousand pans. Water poured from bowl to bowl, water poured into the gutter, water poured from a high window. Snap of washing in the wind. Slam of ten thousand doors.

In Devnagar, girls sit cross-legged before single flames, soldering bangles. Specks of flying glass make tiny scars that turn their eye-whites bright yellow. The City of Glass is a city of child labour, and if indeed the times are changing – if indeed there is such a thing as progress, as the government claims – it is expressed here in time-honoured fashion: the authorities send junior officers, probationers, do-gooders, and, at a pinch, women like Roopa Vish, to check that everyone's papers are in order.

Knock, knock.

Who's there?

Police.

Scrabble, scrabble.

Come in, do! Yes, madam, these are all my children. Twelve of them, madam? If you say so, madam. I must confess I had lost count. Why so many? Well, madam, I am also bringing up my sister's children. Because she is dead, madam. Yes, madam, I am pleased to say I have that certificate kept safe about my person. Here it is. Read it. Feel it. Judge it. Admire it. Yes, my children go to school, madam, and here are their papers. Read them. Feel how the boss of gelatinous ink on each letterhead forms a poignant contrast to the cheapness of the type beneath. No, madam, of course not. I know the law! Not one of these darlings is younger than twelve, I would not dream of such a thing. Besides, read what is printed there. Feel and judge. But I understand your mistake, madam, for indeed the little darlings are small, they are scrawny, they do not thrive. And you can see why, madam. After all, I have so many. Allow me to present you with this token of my esteem, madam. Thank you, madam, until next year, then, goodbye.

Roopa pockets every bribe. Not so naive, she knows better than to raise her head above the parapet. She's new here. She must work to fit in. She knows full well that, the moment her back is turned, the women in that house will turn their home back into a factory for the finishing, soldering and decoration of bangles. With flicks of their lathis, the businesswomen of Devnagar will go on imparting life's dirty lesson to children who will never see the inside of a school.

For Roopa and Hardik, since they moved to Firozabad, 'home' is a box in a half-finished housing estate on Swami Dayanand Road, opposite Gandhi Park. They arrived to exposed sewage lines, live electrical cables and mud. Hardik has work that occupies his days and most evenings as well. Roopa suspects he has male lovers, but she no longer beats herself up over it. She has her mission. She is an agent working semi-legally on an investigation of national importance.

Of course, Hardik (rustling the local paper – yet another exposé of taxi touts cluttering the Taj Mahal) knows nothing of her secret life.

Roopa showers in tepid water, sloughing off the day. She dries, dresses, puts on her make-up. Milk to cleanse her skin; moisturizer, foundation, eyeliner, mascara, lipstick. She cleans her teeth with bicarb to make her smile shine.

Hardik, nettled that she no longer stays in to cook for him, once asked her which of her many men she was meeting. 'Just my pimp,' she told him. 'Which man are you meeting?' Hardik slapped her. This was a mistake. Roopa is her father's daughter. Hardik lost a tooth. He told his *shakha* that Muslim youths had ambushed him in the street.

Roopa Vish does not meet men. She calls round on mousy, forty-year-old Nidra, one of the secretaries from the station. Together they take a taxi to the Apsara Cinema Hall in nearby Agra. Sometimes Nidra's husband Arun accompanies them: a man so kind and handsome and happy and funny and charming and attentive, sometimes Roopa could just give up and fall weeping into his lap.

The central police station of the city of Firozabad is a small building into which the authorities have crammed several miles of corridor. The corridors have many doors, all of them locked. They have windows of frosted glass and behind the glass, indistinct, fractured forms shuffle past. There is no daylight in this building. Along the ceiling, slung through loops of torn plastic carrier bag, run lengths of cheap concertina ducting: paper over wire. Once they fed air to portable air conditioners. Now they're disconnected and bulge and slump their way over the heads of the crowds in the corridors like discarded skins.

'Name.'

'Samjhoria Nankar.'

'Address.'

'The brickworks in Chhaphandi.'

'Do you have an occupation?'

'I work there.'

'Are you married?'

'Yes.'

'Give me his name.'

'Manjit Nankar.'

'Spell it for me.'

Silence.

'Can you spell?'

'M-a-n-j-i-t N-a-n-k-a-r.'

'His occupation?'

Silence.

'What does your husband do?'

'He works at the brickworks in Chhaphandi.'

'He is a labourer?'

'Yes.'

'Do you have children?'

'Yes. Two boys.'

'What are their names? How old are they?'

'Abhik and Kaneer.'

'How old are they?'

'They're twins.'

'How old?'

Samjhoria shrugs.

Nettled now: 'What's your date of birth? Have you even the faintest idea?'

'July the seventeenth, 1955.'

'Better. What's your place of birth?'

Silence.

'Where were you born?'

'Lohardaga.'

The form is complex and poorly carboned. It is three pages long. When it is done, Roopa puts down her pencil. 'I am Assistant Sub-Inspector Roopa Vish. You are –' She consults her form in two places. 'Samjhoria Nankar.'

'Yes,'

'Sit down.'

Samjhoria sits.

'You're complaining.'

Silence.

'You are making a complaint.'

'Yes.'

'What are you complaining about?'

'My back –'

'Your back?'

'My employer.'

'Your employer.'

'He beats me.'

'Your employer beats you.'

'Yes.'

'Your employer beats you across your back?'

Silence.

'Is that what you are saying?'

'Yes.'

Sighing, Roopa rises to her feet and studies the wall behind her. The entire wall is pigeonholed. There are forms in every pigeonhole except for the one that's meant to hold diagrams explaining which form goes in which pigeon hole.

Roopa makes her best guess, pulls a form out of a pigeonhole and scans it. 'Where did you say you worked?'

'The brickworks in Chhaphandi.'

God. That benighted dump.

'What's its name?'

'The Chhaphandi Brickworks.'

It figures. 'There's only one brickworks in Chhaphandi?'

'I don't know.'

'So who's your employer?'

Silence.

'Who employs you? Who do you work for?'

'The brickworks.'

'Who beats you?'

'My boss.'

'Who's your boss?'

'Vinod Yadav.'

'Yadav?'

'Vinod Yadav.'

'*Yadav*.'

'Yes.'

'Yadav, in Chhaphandi.'

'Yes.'

Roopa places the form on the table in front of Samjhoria Nankar. She takes a pen from the drawer of her desk. It doesn't work. She takes out another.

Little by little, Samjhoria Nankar grinds out her story, a depressingly familiar tale of withheld wages, bullying and near-starvation. Dalit matters. Sensitive issues of a female nature. Roopa's been wading through this weak shit since she arrived here. She doesn't mind. She needs to get her feet under the table before she forges a friendship with the district's new anti-terror chief. Samjhoria's complaint gives her a first small 'in' to the Yadav family's local interests.

'Wait here.'

She leaves the room and heads for the toilets. She will come back by the kitchen and fetch tea for them both. She will devote time to this. She will tease out every detail. Every scrap of dirt on this Vinod character and his brick kilns.

She washes her hands and throws water in her face. She grins into the mirror, checking her teeth. Her dear dead dad used to say that her smile was her best feature. She is her father's daughter, after all. Kabir Vish, who apprehended the Stoneman and died in a hail of bullets, during a shoot-out with Yadav syndicate men, on the streets of Matunga in 1983.

She knows how to follow a trail.

Roopa contacts Vinod Yadav at the Chhaphandi brickworks and arranges for him to attend Firozabad police station for an official interview – but on the morning of the interview, Roopa is awoken at 4:45 a.m. by a phone call from the station. She dresses quickly and takes the car into town. At the station she is issued with a helmet and a billy club and told to report to field headquarters in the south-west quadrant of the city. There has been a train crash: one of the worst in her country's history. More than half the townsfolk have turned out to gawp. She's being assigned to crowd control.

It takes her the best part of an hour to work her way around gridlocked cars and clustered, story-telling streets, to the armoured truck that's meant to keep crises like this in bounds. It's marooned beside the railway line some quarter of a mile from the scene of the wreck. From the top of its rickety aluminium steps Roopa sees what she can see, which isn't much. A shoal of heads. She's a Bombay girl and used to crowds, God knows, but this is crazy. The crowd is pliant enough, lumberingly curious as a herd of cattle, but densely packed, corralled by the walls of the cutting. Its collective breathing rocks the police truck from side to side.

A screw of brown smoke marks the wreck site. It rises through the sheltered air of the cutting, then a breeze shears it away, smearing it across the northern embankment. There are vehicles parked there: plainclothes four-by-fours with detachable lights spinning blue.

'Who are they?' Roopa asks nobody in particular.

It's Yash Yadav, the region's counter-terror tsar. 'Now off you go.'

Go where? Roopa has no radio, there's no real chain of command, and it's all she can do to elbow through to where the Purushottam and Kalindi have collided – or, to speak more accurately, to where they have achieved a ghastly fusion. Coaches have burst like bags, sending bodies into the branches of trees. There are clothes everywhere, ripped to rags, and ribbons of flesh, intestine, hair.

Around the carriages the police have established a cordon and the crowds are climbing the walls of the embankment, away from the tracks. It's hardly less crowded now they've gone. Milling around her, stepping round corkscrewed metal spars and crinkled sheets of granulated glass, round shattered pallets and pools of lubricant and here and there, for God alone knows what reason, bars of hot pink hand soap, there are uniforms that Roopa doesn't even recognize. Police probationers, army cadets, nurses, paramedics, railways workers, masked and booted paramilitaries from every academy within fifty miles. No one seems to know what to do with Roopa, and Roopa is so preoccupied that no one thinks to call her to their heel.

Slipping in bloody turds and ponds of oil, Roopa rounds a sleeping carriage of the Purushottam. Hydrostatic shock blew out its glass. Bodies slump shapeless, bladderized, across its steel sides. Roopa imagines the moment of impact: the shock-front waving passengers like bloody flags through the carriage's tiny window frames.

A sudden gust clears the smoke from the sky for a second and sunlight hits the train carriage. Light erupts from its polished walls and Roopa winces in the glare. Through her half-closed eyes the light from the carriage is a sheet of blue fire that, even now, is winding itself into a rope of many colours. She staggers under its imaginary weight. In the moment it takes for her to clear her head of the hallucination, the snake curls around her shoulders and stabs disconsolately at the train carriages, as though in dwindling hope of finding survivors.

She shrugs it off, and a fleck of something drops in her eye. She's trying to remove it with a corner of her shirt cuff when a big man in civilian mufti, leading a retinue of suits and mobile phones, approaches from the other end of the carriage. From pictures, file entries and newspapers, Roopa recognizes Yash Yadav. He's bigger than she imagined, and fitter: a workhorse of a man. Veteran of a dozen kills. Scion of the house that murdered her father.

Next to her, something moves. Someone.

Yash imagines she's been crying. 'Are you all right?' He lays his hand on her shoulder. Beside them, a young man, propelled through a window, scalped, his head a beating polyp, rolls his head from side to side. Impossible to say where the face is. His skull's a white nubbin, peering through red tissue like an eye.

The tea she's drunk today drools off her chin as Roopa heaves.

'Come on,' Yash says, bearing her up. 'This is no place for a woman.'

Yash half-leads, half-carries Roopa away from the carriages to where a concrete stair leads up the northern embankment. Roopa is afraid to look at him. All the time she's spent planning how best to approach him – and now this! She feels as though a door she's been battering has suddenly come open against her shoulder.

Footfalls on gravel. She opens her eyes and sees her feet and his. His steps subtly guiding hers. A pair of shoes, city-made, half-hidden beneath

European-style suit trousers. The trousers are meticulously pressed. His shoes are clean. There's not a speck of dust, not a smear of dirt. Impossible. He must be held above the ground on wires. On wings.

The shoes vanish. Footfalls pass around her. She feels his hands. He helps her to his car. He helps her bend so that she can climb inside.

He closes her door and walks round to the driver's side. She tries to turn her head. She's too weary to move: shock is closing her down. Her eyes will not focus. She smells him. A good smell. Shampoo and spice. Yash Yadav. Veteran of a dozen encounters. Pirates and mafiosi.

He says: 'I'll drive you home.' But he doesn't.

Yash Yadav lives in a freshly painted apartment block on Vyapar Marg. 'Let's get you cleaned up.' Roopa hobbles after him, past the watchman's cubbyhole (empty), through the gate (Yash has a magnetic key) and into the elevator.

Yash's apartment isn't what she expected. The whole place is decked out like a teenager's bedroom. The walls are hidden behind movie posters. Yash shows her the bathroom and hands her a towel. 'Where do you live?'

She gives him her address.

'I'll go fetch your husband.'

She goes to the bathroom. Yash has a bathtub. A rarity round here. A luxury. There's a robe hanging from the door. She undresses and draws the robe around herself. While she waits for the tub to fill, she wanders back into the living room and up to the window. She watches as Yash Yadav lets himself out through the security gate, crosses the road, and points his key at his car, unlocking it: a new Opel Corsa. She leans against the glass. She wants Yash to pause. She wants him to turn. She wants him to see her there, against the glass, naked under his robe. She watches him drive away. He is everything she thought he'd be. More. Big and dangerous. Magnificent.

They dine in restaurants in Agra, far from Firozabad's rumour mill. They drink in Mughal Bar and Downtown Club, Le Bar and Downing Street. He meets her in a side street behind the town hall. He pays for them. He chooses their food. He orders their drinks. At the end of the evening he pays her cab fare home. He buys her gifts: jewellery and shoes and scarves. She hides them from her husband. She keeps them in her locker at work. She takes them out only for him. She dresses only for him. She scents and shaves herself only for him. She dreams of him.

She remembers the flak she took, leaving Bombay. The cheap humour flying around as she packed up her desk at the ACB: beanpole-slim Roopa following wobble-hipped Yash Yadav into the outback. Even her superintendent, even Kala Subadrah, could not resist a gag as she returned Roopa's salute: 'I hope he's worth it.'

Yash has not slimmed down. He's hardened up: an engine, big and square, trembling with controlled violence. She fucks him and fucks him. She is sore from him. It is what her hard, athlete's body was built for, has longed for, screamed out for.

He's serious, direct, utterly two-dimensional: a blank on to which she might project any desire. A hero of sorts; impervious, at any rate, to the ironies and doubts that hedge round ordinary men. He is a motive force and as earnest as a child. He lifts himself out of her and kneels over her and fills her mouth. He buries his tongue inside her. He slaps her, and she bends for him. He squeezes her breasts as though there were milk there. He'd eat her if he could. The bite marks show sometimes, but Hardik does not notice. Hardik never gets close enough to see – and if he could bring himself to do so, and he saw, would he even care?

This cannot last. This heat. This turbulence. But then, it does not have to. Roopa's not forgotten why she's here.

She's drunk on Yash, yes, but it's her betrayal of him that drives her to heat, quite as much as his passion. Bedding Yash Yadav, she finds quite easily the things she needs to incriminate him and smoothe her path in glory back to Kala and the ACB. 'Raise your voice and it shall be heard!' She'll raise her voice, all right. She'll make front page, if this goes well.

Yash rolls off to the bathroom; she reads the messages stored in his phone. She writes down his recently dialled numbers. Sometimes Yash leaves her in his flat when he goes out to work: the region's anti-terror tsar. In a bedroom lined with movie posters – curry westerns, war films, historical epics – she reads his diaries. She trawls the trash under his desk. She undeletes the files binned on his laptop. She tabulates, cross-references. She'd eat him if she could. Instead she'll tear him down.

There's a solicitor, Mohinder Gidh, works for Yash Yadav. He spends his nights in a room lit entirely from lights whirling underneath a raised plastic dance floor, throwing single, low-denomination notes on to the floor, more or less at random, as he tries to decide which heavily made-up girl to fall in love with tonight. Later he will hurl money by the handful at his chosen muse. Whole weeks' wages. He is lucky that the club, a recent and controversial import from Mumbai, is a Yadav enterprise.

By day, Gidh sails close to the wind, orchestrating a land-grab backed by some possibly forged paperwork. A car-repair business has been acquired by the Yadav family on terms so unfavourable intimidation must have been a factor in the sale.

And it goes on: a steady stream of petty and not so petty extortion, fraud and theft. She'll have her lover locked away long before his fire is out: her pet. She'll get her man.

The severity of the Firozabad rail disaster keeps the station busy for many weeks. Only when the missing have been officially presumed dead can Roopa Vish pick up the loose threads of her ongoing enquiries. Top of her list is Samjhoria Nankar's complaint into mistreatment and non-payment of wages at the Chhaphandi brickworks: Vinod Yadav's fiefdom and the Yadav family's weakest link. She calls Vinod on the phone to discuss Samjhoria Nankar's accusations.

'Samjhoria and her family absconded months ago.'

'Nonetheless,' she says, hoping to haze him into an interview.

It works: they set a date and time. 'Whereabouts are you?'

The way Vinod describes it over the phone you'd think the Chhaphandi brickworks was a well-run, bureaucratic operation. You only have to see the compound from the road to know the truth. You only have to smell the children hunkered down in the dirt, chipping away with hammers at chunks of coal, their faces black with coal dust.

A girl, perhaps eight or nine years old, her face smeared with dirt and sweat, walks right in front of Roopa's car, oblivious. She is balancing four heavy bricks on her head. At the edge of the nearest kiln she lifts her burden up to her father, who's standing on top of an enormous heap of dun-coloured bricks. Then a boy runs under Roopa's wheels, so close that she stalls, braking to save his silly life.

It's all for nothing, anyway. Vinod's blown her out. He's left his Komatsu driver, Rishi Ansari, to answer her questions. He's waiting for her by an old shipping container – 'MOYSE' dimly visible on its flank – which marks the southern boundary of the compound. 'He's had to go back to hospital to have his stump seen to,' Rishi tells her. A persistent infection, apparently. There are many persistent infections round here. Stillbirths. Mysterious goitres. Birth defects. All the kids round here have these funny little bibbly-bobbly heads. Mind you, Chhaphandi's always had a reputation for inbreeding. What else is there to do?

Rishi is here to set her right about Vinod Yadav, his medical problems, his important schedule, the need to confirm all appointments on the day. 'He can't be at everybody's beck and call, you know.' As though she'd come round here to try and sell him something. He turns his back on her a moment, swinging the door shut on the old shipping container.

As the door swings, Roopa feels suddenly ill, as though something is roping itself around her chest. She staggers, tugged by some impossible, invisible muscle, away from the shipping container. Another tug.

Another. Is she going to be sick?

There is a stale, mealy smell on the air. She puts her hand to her nose, instantly revolted.

Rishi hasn't noticed anything. He secures the doors with a padlock, chuntering on, and the smell fades, the tugging ceases. 'The Nankars? Vanished. God knows where they went. I mean, this Lohardaga scum. Excuse me, but you know how it is.' Rishi Ansari: a forgettable man with a forgettable face. 'A complaint?' He sucks his teeth. 'No, don't know nothing about that.'

The thing around her chest lets go. It slides away. Roopa feels its dry rasp as it relinquishes her and she has this nonsensical impression that she has been rescued from some terrible, unseen danger.

She drives out of the compound, still on edge, sucking up air in shallow, panting breaths. She is afraid the smell will come back. She is afraid it will surprise her again, in the car, on a bend in the road. It was one of those fundamentally wrong odours that lodges in the memory, ready to trigger a fierce, unpredictable reflex. But the air in the car stays clean, cut only with the tang of the vehicle's own hot oil.

The following morning, Roopa lies in Yash Yadav's bed, testing the air. His room is full of smells, smells she has never noticed before. None of them are *that* smell, but the tugging sensation is still there. It has moved off her chest. Now it's squeezing her stomach, stirring the acids there. She sits up, breathing the fit away.

The morning after, waking in her husband's bed, she pulls herself from the bed and runs, dry-heaving, to the toilet.

A couple of weeks later and Roopa is standing in Yash Yadav's bathroom, holding a plastic wand to the light.

Within seconds – faster and more surely than any Polaroid – two blue lines appear across the white of the window. Roopa feels the walls and floor of the bathroom slide away as the bars set a new vertical for her: a new, tilted reality. How many periods has her silly, sprinter's body missed? They're so irregular she finds it hard to count them.

She wraps the test in a fistful of toilet paper, opens her handbag and tucks the expensive white wand inside, losing it in a mulch of tissues, tickets and receipts.

Yash will be here in the couple of hours. She dresses in the bedroom. The walls are smothered in movie posters. Action classics. *Line of Control. Sholay*. A teenager might have collected them, she thought, the first time Yash brought her here, months ago. His hands, his bulk, the taste of his penis, the feel of him splashing her breasts, dear God, months ago! How far along is she?

She sweeps a hand across her midriff. She can't feel a thing. What an infuriating machine her body is! What's the use of a body that will not take you into its confidence? She imagines the changes a baby will wreak on it. How the stomach wall splits like a peach, how the ribcage bells out.

She forces herself to breathe. Could the test be wrong? What if it's too late to terminate? What if it will not die? What if she only succeeds in, well, *damaging* it?

She searches in her handbag for her mobile. Her husband Hardik has a meeting tonight, a *shakha*, so there is no need for her to hurry home (if you can call that love-abandoned shell a home: a breeze-block box tossed about on a sea of mud). She will get Yash to take her out tonight, somewhere they will not be recognized. There is a hotel in Agra with a good restaurant, far beyond her means but well within his. She will get him drunk on his own generosity (it is important for her to play to his vanity) and she will tell him about the baby.

She dials and is put through to Yash's voicemail. She risks a call to his office, but he is not there. She opens the door of the apartment and breathes in the communal smell of rose carpet shampoo and cigarettes. She wants to leave but she has nowhere to go. She aches in Yash Yadav's absence. Yash has become a physical need. Strange how these things happen. Yash, veteran of a dozen legal kills – and yet the violence attaching to him, which so excited her at first, does nothing for her now. The attraction she feels for him, now that she knows him, is simpler and oh, so much more corrupt. Yash's home, his tastes, his childish comforts. His film posters. His DVD collection. His simple, strenuous appetites in bed. She fucks the boy, not the man. If it wasn't Yash, it would have been someone equally adolescent. Why should she always be drawn to boys? Hardik and Yash: both are vulnerable men. What's in this to trigger her desire?

She puts her phone away. Yash will greet her news with horror. The scandal of her pregnancy is enough to ruin his standing as Firozabad's counter-terror tsar. The affair – the madness of it, and the pleasure – is done.

Away from the Anti-Corruption Bureau and its levelling realities she has been dreaming up a heroic role for herself. A female detective, alone against the system! A city cop hacking her way through rural corruption! What, in the end, has she uncovered? Some argument at the Chhaphandi brickworks between Yash's cousin Vinod and a Dalit labourer. This was how she planned to build a case against Yash Yadav – all the while managing to get herself nicely groped! And now this!

She steps back inside the apartment and slams the door. She knows Yash better than she has ever known her husband. She knows the way his family works. She would make a good gangster's wife. She imagines a future with Yash Yadav. She must speak to him, tonight, before her conscience and the ghost of her poor dead father weaken her resolve. She takes her phone out of her bag again.

This time her call gets through, but the conversation does not go well.

Another month, and now Roopa's key no longer opens the door of the house she shares with her husband on Swami Dayanand Road. She hammers on the door.

'All right! I'm coming!'

In the moment before Hardik scrapes open the door, Roopa notices that the frame is damaged. The wood has been gouged here and there by something with clean edges: a crowbar. She recognizes the pattern. She has seen it before, during her probation in Bombay. The door opens.

Caught between relief and disappointment, Hardik's words come out stripped of affect. A machine might be speaking. 'I thought you were the police.'

Hardik will not tell her what went on in the interrogation room, but she can guess. Yash wants Hardik to acknowledge the baby as his. For as long as Hardik resists, Yash's counter-terrorist teams will be raiding their home, 'searching for seditious literature'. This time they have outdone themselves. The level of damage suggests relish more than thoroughness. Skirting boards have been jemmied away from the walls. Most of the antique furniture from her mother's home in Thane has been smashed.

Hardik scuffs through the remains. A sock, a mobile-phone charger, a disposable razor, a cup. Roopa picks her way after him, her arms wrapped around her belly, as though she might shield the child from his sight. The kitchen is mostly put away. The door to one of the cupboards is missing. 'Do you want to sit down? There's still a chair.'

Roopa sits.

'Do you want a cup of tea?' Hardik fills the kettle from a plastic bottle. 'They've cut off the water.' His face is grey. There are no obvious bruises. Yash Yadav's crew are too well trained for that. Hardik is spent and demoralized but not visibly damaged. He puts the kettle on the stove and lights the gas with a cigarette lighter. It putters: the cylinder is running empty.

Roopa slips her hands around the hot thing lying inside her. This other self. This slip of human possibility. All day she has been working at words, conjuring them into phrases that might tie her and her husband back into each others' lives. She stands. She takes her hands away from her belly. She wants him to see this. She wants him to confront this.

Hardik does not want to touch her. Then again, when has he ever wanted to touch her? Will he not even look at her? 'It's yours.' She returns her husband's incredulous look steadily, without flinching, without shame. She knows what he is thinking: How can she hold her head so high? 'Do you understand? If you want it, the child is yours.'

If she and Hardik and Yash Yadav can only buy into the same lie, then everything will come right. Better than right, because she and her husband will have gained a child. If the baby is Hardik's, if they make it Hardik's by saying so, then they can begin again. 'In Bombay!' The child will grow, and it will be happy, and their life will go on being the life they know: a predictable life among people who know them and define them. 'In Bombay. Hardik. Husband! In Bombay!'

'Mumbai.'

'Yes,' she says, wrong-footed by this leaden correction. 'In *Mumbai*.'

'Roopa. I need to give you some money.'

'What?'

'A little money. I need to give you money.'

'I don't want money.'

'I am going to give you money so you can stay here for a while.'

She stares at him.

'The rent. If you're staying here you will need to cover the rent.'

'Where are you going?'

He shrugs. 'Mumbai.'

'But –'

'I have plans already, Roopa. It's a chance for the party. It's a chance for me.'

The rechristened city is a haven for right-wingers. The D-Company's bombs have woken the saffron tiger: this is what they are singing, in *shakhas* and public rallies up and down the Sher Shah Suri Marg. Hardik has already reinvented himself. He is going to Mumbai without her.

At 6.30 p.m. a car pulls up outside the house and sounds its horn. Roopa goes to the window. She cannot see the driver. Is he young? Is he pretty? Is he kind? There is no reason for her to suppose that this is Hardik's lover. He could as easily be just a driver. She will never know and there is no point asking Hardik. She knows what he would say. 'You wouldn't understand.'

Hardik comes to say goodbye. The sun is low in the sky. The room is full of saffron-yellow light.

'Yash wants to get rid of us,' she says. 'He wants to drive us out of town. This –' She sees her mother's furniture again, what's left of it, strewn about the hall, and swallows, fighting tears.

'Roopa, that's nothing to me.'

She cannot tell whether he is being kind or cruel.

Outside, the driver hits his horn again. Hardik takes her hand. He wants, in these final moments, to be gentle. 'You have your family. You have Thane. Go home.'

When he is gone, Roopa tidies the house. Her weeping has numbed her. The piece of her that is capable of powerful feeling is missing suddenly: perhaps Hardik took it away with him. She will rescue what she can of her mother's furniture. Her kid brother Ijay can drive it back to Thane. A heavy bureau that used to stand in her father's study. An ornate sandalwood box, big as a table, that a distant auntie brought home from Malawi. All but one of the wicker-bottom chairs has been staved in. As a child she used to drape sheets over these chairs, making a cave for herself. Her father crawled around it on his hands and knees, roaring like a lion.

She tires. She will finish this another day. For now, she will pick up a handful of personal things to take back to Arun and Nidra's house. A book or two and some make-up. The make-up she wants has been trodden into the linoleum, and she can't find her books anywhere. Were they taken in the raid?

Roopa remembers her report. A hollowness opens inside her. *Her report*. Her half-finished investigations into the Yadav family. She goes into the bedroom, gets down on her hands and knees and reaches under her bed. The blue suitcase isn't there. She finds it by the window. Its locks have been forced open. It is empty. She casts around for stray papers but this is pure avoidance. Yash Yadav's men have confiscated her report.

She imagines it landing on Yash's desk. Yash reading it: a dossier compiled by his pregnant ex-lover. Notes on his business dealings. Unsubstantiated accusations of impropriety, extortion and fraud. She imagines Yash, with the resources of a state-wide counter-terrorist apparatus at his fingertips, finding out who she is, where she comes from, who she works for.

It is getting dark now. She fumbles her phone out of her bag. She calls the Anti-Corruption Bureau's head office in Worli. She thumbs through half-familiar options, pausing a second to jiggle the bedroom light switch. The electricity is off.

Kala's extension: 'Superintendent's office.' It is not Kala's voice, nor anyone's she knows. 'Kala Subadrah? I'm sorry, she no longer works in this department.'

Panic streams through Roopa's softened and expanded body: it flutters in her throat, delivers a ghost-kick to her diaphragm, commands her to pee – the body as slapstick. She says, 'I have information relevant to the Yadav case file, Maharashtra Port Authority One through Three, Y-A-D-A-V.'

The line goes dead a moment, then clatters back to life: 'I will transfer you.' The dialling tone is replaced almost immediately with an out-of-office message. Roopa listens with growing incredulity: she's been put through to the archive.

If Kala is gone and the case on Yadav is abandoned, then how is she to return to Worli and the ACB? How is she going to get home? She thumbs the red button to kill the call, then scrolls through the names on her phone. She will find an old colleague to talk to. Someone to tell her that this is all a mistake.

Headlights sweep the darkening room. An expensive Hyundai saloon draws up behind another, virtually identical car, parked opposite the house. Now the car in front starts its engine. Its sidelights come on. It pulls away, leaving the newcomer in its place. Roopa moves away from the window. She imagines Yash Yadav, her report in his hands. She knows how he thinks. She heads for the door. A shadow appears behind the glass.

She hesitates. 'Hardik?'

The pane shatters. A gloved hand reaches round for the catch.

She runs into the bedroom.

The door bangs open.

There are footsteps in the hall. And here they are. Hoods, cricket bats, trowels and wrenches. Their smell fills the room: ash, wet clay and burning tyres. A country smell. A brick-kiln smell. They rush into the room and fall upon her.

For the briefest instant there is only breathing and the tussle of prone bodies in the darkness and it seems as though there might be passion here. But this is something else and Roopa finds the strength at last to scream. Two men pick her up by the arms and throw her against the wall, getting the air out of her. They haul her back on to the bed and fall upon her, lying across her, pinning her down. One of them rubs himself against her.

Things are slowing down. Violence is giving way to performance. A man comes in with a thick green rubbish bag. He empties it on the floor. It is full of glass. Coloured glass. Broken glass. The shattered wastes of

Firozabad and Devnagar. They pick Roopa up and pull off her clothes and sit her on the glass and while they hold her there, down in the red puddle she is making, a man kneels down in front of her, brandishing a pair of pliers. His breath is nauseating: rotten and sweet and laden with alcohol. Working from one side of her scream to the other, he crushes her teeth.

SIX

Friday, 15 June 1928

In the middle of the Barents Sea, halfway between the mainland and Spitsbergen, Bear Island forms an irregular arrowhead pointing due south towards Tromsø. There is coal here. For years, people have talked about mining it. A few spindly iron crosses along the northern coast mark the resting places of nineteenth-century Russian bureaucrats, marooned here by their own ambition or disfavour at home. Imagine them building their houses, writing diaries and prospectuses, staring at the calendar: only three months to go until the next boat! Coffee, letters, good news!

The costs of extracting coal at such a latitude, and at a location so remote – fog-bound in summer, ice-bound in winter, and lacking even a harbour – bested them. All of them, sooner or later, turned away from the sea; were drawn to face south, across flat, treeless, yellow-orange lowlands, across six hundred shallow lakes, to confront the peaks of Fugle, Hamberg, Alfred. Black whaleback mountains on sheer black pedestals. East of the group, standing 536 metres above sea level, is the highest peak on Bear Island. It is called Misery.

Their huts stand deserted now and the wind has torn the shingles from their roofs. The locomotive, hoppers and carriages of the mining operation are orange with rust. A narrow-gauge railway runs along low cliffs above the only anchorage. The wooden ties are bleached white, dry and cracked. At the end of the line the cliffs have crumbled and the tracks spill into the sea.

Eric Moyse, twenty-eight years old, whaling and fishing magnate, landowner, mayor, lollops over stones overgrown with scurvy grass, slippery with yellow moss, past splashes of purple saxifrage, to the meteorological station at Herwighamna. He has a vested interest in the weather, and in the newfangled meteorology, and twice a year, spring and autumn, his ships convey supplies and personnel to this most isolated of Norway's weather stations. The huts, repainted every year at his expense, are the only green things on the island. The adjoining radio station is Eric's own work.

Maintaining the weather station gives Eric some welcome distraction from the news dribbling out of Vadsø and King's Bay. The airship *Italia* has crashed on pack ice near the Pole. The few survivors are all but unreachable. One of them, Lothar Eling, is Eric's protégé. His climbing pupil. His friend.

It is getting late: nearly 4 a.m. The skies are clearing, but the glass tells a different story and the weathervane points obstinately south. Even as he stands recording his observations – barometric pressure, temperature, humidity – the breeze tickles him through his beard.

CLOUD COVER BROKE 4.15 A.M.
CONTRARY WINDS DOWN TO 15 MPH.

The rest of Eric's weather report, morsed in tonic train at 1,400 metres, is mostly raw number, but the amateur weatherman in him cannot resist adding an editorial.

STRONG HEAD WIND EXPECTED FROM NORTH.

He knows full well that Tromsø's tough-minded analysts, pupils of Professor Jakob Dunfjeld, will ignore him.

Visibility is deteriorating fast. Eric wobbles over rubble covered in moss, between tufts of grass. The weather breaks, and the rain turns the rocks to glass under his boots.

*

An hour later, in the shelter and relative warmth of the weather station, Eric Moyse listens to Stavanger.

> BETWEEN BEAR ISLAND AND SPITSBERGEN EASTWARDS DEPRESSION, PRESSURE FALLING IN FRONT OF CENTRE. OVER OCEAN BETWEEN SPITSBERGEN AND JAN MEYEN N TO NW BEAUFORT 5.

He tries again to catch radio signals sent by the survivors of Nobile's ill-fated expedition. A farmer in Archangel picked up the camp's SOS two weeks ago. So far, Eric has been unable to pick up their transmissions. Eric has come to the end of his time on Bear Island. He is waiting for a boat to carry him back to the mainland and his responsibilities as *nessekøng* (loosely, squire) of Svolvaer, capital of Norway's Lofoten archipelago. Early in the evening it appears: the *Cormorant*, a fishing vessel from his own fleet. Of the four men on board, two are new to him: a Bergen-trained meteorologist and a radio engineer, come to take over the running of the weather station. Accompanying them are two men Eric recognizes. A rowboat, absurdly small, serves as the *Cormorant*'s cutter, and the couple have their backs to him as they pull the boat to shore, but there is no mistaking Tor Dalebø's red hair, or Peder Halstad's rounded shoulders.

Bear Island's weather station is meant for two and built small, making it easier to heat. The five men hunker down in the living area, squeezed in as best they can. The weathermen crouch on the unmade bottom bunk, as nervous and proper as new boys entering a school dormitory.

Eric serves coffee. Already they are talking about the *Italia*.

'Amundsen's rescue crew is off at last.' Dalebø says.

'That took him a while.'

The young men look uncomfortable. Roald Amundsen is practically a saint. You cannot talk of a saint this way, as though he were just one more exhausted explorer, drumming up a little publicity for himself.

The truth is Amundsen is old and broke. Whether he saves the explorers or not, a first-hand account of the *Italia* affair, with lantern slides, should be good for a season or two on the after-dinner circuit. After that, God knows what will happen to the poor bugger. You see them often enough: veterans of the *Vega* and the *Fram* haunting quarterly meetings of the Geographical Society, ancient mariners sprung from Coleridge, stuffing their pockets with canapés when they think no one is looking.

After coffee, Eric shows the newcomers around the station.

The Stevenson screen stands a minute's walk away from the radio hut, over boulders worn clean of gravel and dirt by twice-daily visits. The screen is sheltered from the constant sun of Arctic summer by a sailcloth canopy which requires constant mending and attention. It stands two metres high, so that there is room underneath to swing an L-shaped aluminium ice detector. A spare detector, wrapped in sailcloth, lies under a prominent rock, next to a spare snow vase.

Eric warns the newcomers always to wear their winter jackets fully fastened when they open the screen, or the thermometers inside will respond to their body heat. Paint is peeling from the screen's louvres already, though it was brushed up less than a year ago. A short distance away, on a plinth fashioned from a ship's mast, a Robinson anemometer is furiously spinning. It has small cups and its arms turn more slowly than on most models: three and a quarter times slower than the wind. The snow gauge is in a dip to the west. 'See?'

The newcomers' eyes slip back and forth, hunting for purchase on the bare horizon, the yellow, puddle-pocked flatlands. They expected more.

Eric takes them into the radio hut. Now they are really up against each other: there is barely room to close the door. Here is the spare generator: a 3hp Douglas. The short-wave receiver has a range of between ten and a hundred metres. Mind the reaction-coil under the table. Eric shows them the logbooks and leaves them to make a hash of their first readings and to discover, by painful experience, how to sit at the radio table without drawing off a spark from an oscillating circuit.

In twenty minutes he will come and rescue them. Another set of readings in the morning will iron out any kinks and by then they should have mastered everything they need to know about the station. And when the chronometer strikes noon and Eric and his friends, chugging south aboard the *Cormorant*, vanish at last into the perpetual summer fog, then the newcomers will confront their most serious difficulty: not their reports, which are regular and simple to prepare, but the gaps of time that stretch, plastic and hallucinatory, between them.

The next boat is not due until the end of summer.

In the living quarters, Dalebø has made more coffee. Halstad, relieved of the obligation to behave properly around the two greenhorns, is revelling in the latest gossip. 'They say Il Duce wants the general dead. Nobile's a thorn in his backside, apparently. A decorated war hero who refuses to join the fascists.' He pulls out a handkerchief and blows his nose. 'This farce is certainly one way to go about a murder.'

Dalebø grunts: 'Be thankful. As long as Romagna's men are cooped up on their ship with their dicks in their hands, that's a hundred-odd fewer clowns we'll be expected to go fish out of the water.' The Arctic is awash with undirected, piecemeal rescue crews. 'If it carries on this way there's going to be bodies littering the beaches from Murmansk to Dikson.'

Halstad agrees: 'There are more rescuers pulling other rescuers out of trouble than there are teams heading for the Red Tent. So,' he turns to his companion, 'Captain Dalebø, sir: are you going to tell him about our brilliant plan or am I?'

Halstad loves drawing attention to Dalebø: it is so easy to throw the old sod out of his stride. Dalebø stares into his coffee cup. 'Well,' he says, put on the spot. 'Well. It's like this.'

Then Halstad, who cannot contain his excitement a moment longer: 'Hey ho! Listen to this! We're off to get ourselves killed!'

At 4.10 a.m. on 18 June, a crew hired among the miners at King's Bay brings the *Cormorant* into Beverly Sound, overladen with equipment, impossibly cramped, rowdy with dogs.

Eric Moyse, Peder Halstad and Tor Dalebø disembark and spend the evening loading their sleds. With the dogs in harness they set off, shortly after 1.00 a.m. on 19 June. The sky is clear. The sun, low in the west, casts their shadows before them across the snow.

The survivors of the *Italia* disaster have split into two. Engineer Giovanni Bonfanti and meteorologist Lothar Eling are trying to walk off the ice. They are heading for the island of Foyn. Dalebø's plan is to rendezvous with Bonfanti and Eling on Foyn. Dalebø, Peder and Eric will walk from Cape North as far as Cape Platen. From there they'll take their chances on the frozen, crevasse-riddled waters of Dove Bay. Nearby, barely half a day's trek away, lies another beach, the starting point for an even more daunting sea crossing: a journey on churning pack ice all the way north to barren Foyn and their hoped-for rendezvous.

The landscape changes subtly as they advance. The accretion of ice on a succession of low peaks, the angle and extent of bare scree, the texture of the snow: all these things, to the sensitive eye, reveal the nature and strength of that other, invisible territory of winds and weather which sculpts, with a slow and cruel hand, the solid world, and will outlast it.

Fourteen hours in, their difficulties begin. Eric is making tea when he notices Peder Halstad, goggles off, eyes screwed shut, pinching the bridge of his nose with an ungloved hand. 'What's up?'

Halstad shakes his head. He fumbles the goggles back over his face and adjusts his mittens.

Dalebø takes his cup from Eric and gives a little shake of his head: let it go. 'One more run and the dogs'll need feeding. Then we may as well call it a day.'

It is early afternoon. Dalebø wants them resting within the hour, and on the move again by midnight. Nights under such a sky, at such a season, can be murky, but the fractional drop in night-time temperature improves the snow under their runners.

Dalebø, so composed, so taciturn, becomes a different man once you get him inside a tent: a windmill of ineffectual fuss. He has surrounded himself with junk: a compass, a penknife, chocolate bars, spare bootlaces, a whistle, silk socks, pencils. He is taking things out of his pockets and putting them into other pockets, seemingly at random. Eric taps a finger to the corner of his eye. Dalebø understands. 'Let's get a good sleep,' he says.

Halstad keeps his goggles on. He turns on his side, away from his companions. He is doing everything right. If his eyes are troubling him, then rest is the only cure. There's no point fussing over him.

An hour before they are due to rise Halstad sits up, struggling with the toggle of his sleeping bag. He gets a hand free and pulls off his goggles and presses his hands over his face.

'Peder?'

'*Fuck*.'

Dalebø sits up, arms still pinned inside his bag, stiff and symmetrical as a corpse rising from an open coffin. Eric hides a smile.

'It's not fucking funny.'

Sharp pains are shooting through Peder's eyeballs. The snow-glare has burnt his corneas.

For another half-day, from Cape Wrede to Cape Platen, Peder Halstad struggles to keep up, over slushy snow that has refrozen, forming treacherous crusts. His vision has begun to darken. He can go no further.

It is about eight in the morning: the snow already has an edge of rot about it and the sleds' runners are bogging down.

'Go on,' Halstad insists.

'That's all very well.' Dalebø is angry with himself for bringing Halstad this far. 'We're hardly going to leave you out here alone on the ice, silly sod.'

'Why not?' Halstad, slumped against his sled, looks up at them with eyes made huge and black and blind by snow goggles. He still has to shade his eyes from the sun. 'I know what I'm doing. In a day or two my eyes will be better and I'll walk out.'

His plan is to return to Cape North and wait for a boat. There are enough of them involved in the rescue effort: he is sure to be picked up. It is a good plan – assuming he sticks to it.

Eric hunkers down beside him. 'You can't follow us.'

Halstad laughs.

'You mustn't try to catch up with us.'

'Do you take me for a complete fool? Well, I won't follow you.'

'Good.'

'Bloody sod, you, in fact.'

Eric grins: 'That's the spirit.'

Even so, he does not entirely trust Halstad's promise. Halstad is a gifted outdoorsman but he has come late to the discipline. He lacks a northerner's caution.

A couple of hours later, Peder Halstad is settled comfortably in his bivouac, surrounded by two weeks' supplies. They have rearranged the sleds, overloading the larger ones so as to leave Halstad with a burden he can pull by hand. 'Even when you're better, keep wearing your goggles when you sleep,' Dalebø warns him when they are ready to leave. He gives Halstad the rifle. 'Try not to blow your foot off.'

Halstad makes a facetious salute.

Eric and Dalebø pitch camp on Cape Platen and rise again at 9 p.m. to begin their crossing of Dove Bay.

Wave action and the swirling currents of the bay have shattered the ice field. The danger is not so much open water – there is very little of that – but the amount of time it takes them to negotiate mazes of piled ice. The weather is slowly deteriorating: by mid-morning there are snow flurries. They are halfway across the bay when a violent front moves over them, bringing squalls that reduce visibility to a few feet. Unable to progress, Eric and Dalebø secure the dogs and hunker down in the shelter of jagged blocks of ice.

For two days they lie trapped, listening as the storm wears the dogs down to a frenzy. By the time the storm has passed one dog has been mauled to death, another has had her leg broken, and a third is down with a fever. The pistol is to hand but Dalebø seems dissatisfied: he checks and rechecks the breach. Saying nothing, Eric takes the gun from him. Like most lifelong hunters, Dalebø has grown sentimental with age.

Eric leads the casualties away and shoots them cleanly in the head.

On the morning of 29 June, Eric Moyse and Tor Dalebø complete their crossing of Dove Bay. After their enforced bivouac on the pack ice they have no need of their planned half-day's rest. Instead, they press on, over the headland, steadying the overburdened sled as the dogs struggle through snow that leaves their coats suspiciously wet.

Having seen to their dogs and erected their tent, the two men climb a rocky promontory of Cape Bruun. There they sit and smoke, contemplating the nightmare to which their efforts have brought them. The pack is shattered like a window pane. You could be slipping and staggering from one platform to another for hours and never venture more than a stone's throw from your starting point.

The next day Dalebø and Eric repack their gear and erect a snow cairn over the items they intend to abandon. It is not likely they will be back this way and any further retreat on foot is not even an option since, following the storm, the ice on Dove Bay will be dangerously rotten. Once on the pack and headed for Foyn, they are committed. Boats and planes involved in the rescue attempt will be using Foyn for their navigation and will spot them there.

The rest of the day they spend making a desultory survey of the coast. Great blocks of ice have been cast up like ships upon the lichenous rocks. The blocks, in their scale and disarray, are an absolute barrier. Only where rip tides keep the surface ice thin and fragile is there any hope of reaching the ice pack.

'We will have to chance our luck where we began,' says Dalebø, even more morose than usual. In the golden overcast that serves here for night, the men strike camp, harness the dogs, and head for a precariously thin ice platform, jammed by the tide between lines of rocks. They detach the dogs and wrestle the sled, foot by foot, on to and across the cambered ice. On its seaward side the waves are wedging another small berg under the lip of the platform. The drop from one block to the other is, even at the peak of a swell, a good three feet. When the waves withdraw the block slides away another foot or two and grinds the shingle beneath it: a dull sound.

To negotiate a drop of that sort they should first unload the sled, but there is no time: the pull of the water is scraping the platform past them even as they stand debating their next move. Eric waits for Dalebø to say something. Finally Dalebø turns and shoots Eric an exasperated look.

'What?'

Dalebø mutters something and then, without warning, jumps.

He lands without difficulty, knees bent, feet apart, on the further block, which is just now grounded on the shelving beach. The waters advance, lifting the block off the gravel and Dalebø turns, arms outstretched for balance as the berg tips, accommodating his weight. He rises into Eric's view – shoulders, chest, hips – as the block rises. At the top of the cycle he leans forward and takes hold of the sled. Whether he means to pull the sled, or simply to steady himself, is unclear – but suddenly the rip causes Dalebø's berg to swing and Dalebø, still clinging to the sled, brings it bearing down on top of him. He steps aside, slips, and falls on his backside. The sled lands beside him. Dalebø cries out and sits up, reaching for his foot.

Eric, furious, shouts an obscenity. Dalebø gets to his feet, limping. A swell lifts Eric's block off the shingle. A couple of dull collisions shake the platform, and Eric jumps.

His timing is bad: the berg is rising to meet him and he lands heavily, out of balance. He keeps his footing, but then the dogs make up their minds to follow him. They knock him back against the sled. There is a deep, resonant crack and the ice rocks beneath him. Dalebø shouts a warning, and the platform shears.

One dog tumbles into the water, then another. Eric crawls to the edge of the ice. He reaches into the water, fishing for fur, a bit of leash, something to grab on to.

'For Christ's sake!'

Eric glances up. Dalebø is standing on the other side of the crack with their sled and all their supplies. The gap widens. Eric gets to his feet. Dalebø steadies himself with his axe, pressing hard upon the shaft while he extends his other hand. With a puff of splinters, the ice under Dalebø's axe explodes and Dalebø staggers. All his weight comes down on his injured foot and he gapes in silent agony.

Dalebø's berg moves toward deeper water and begins to tilt. The sled slides towards the water and Dalebø after it, slithering head-first down the ice as the berg rolls. Dalebø's left hand paddles frantically for the axe leashed to his wrist. He gets hold of the leash. The axe slithers towards him, past him, and into the water. Dalebø follows.

Seawater slops over Eric's knees and he falls, his gloved fingers digging for purchase on the ice. The platform steadies. The surviving dogs dance round each other in futile circles. The ones in the water are silent, beyond panic. They pull each other down into the freezing water. Eric uses his axe to fish a leash out of the water. He yanks a struggling dog towards him. The dog bites his sleeve, hangs on, and drags him in.

He flounders. He kicks something. He thinks at first it is a dog. Then he finds his footing. He stands. The water laps at his chest.

There is a rock under the water. A large, flat rock. He is standing on a rock and the water comes up to his chest. A big wave comes in and he loses his footing. The wave goes out and here he is again, on the rock. He turns around. He is about ten metres away from the beach. He laughs. 'Tor!'

He looks about him. There is open water all around. The bergs and ice plates they had meant to ride have vanished, drawn away as swiftly as flats in a theatre. The dogs are paddling to shore.

'Tor!'

The sled is bobbing in the water, half-submerged. Eric wades out to it. He has to move quickly, before his shock falls off him and he begins to freeze. His skin is already burning with the cold. He spots the end of a rope. He grabs it and pulls. The lashing around the sled unravels. A sleeping bag bobs to the surface of the water. The sled, losing buoyancy, sinks deeper into the waves. Eric paddles frantically over to the sled. He takes hold of it and the combined weight of sled and man submerges both. He slaps his way back to the surface and struggles there, the water suddenly deep, bottomless. 'Tor, damn you!'

He tows the sled to shore. By the time his feet touch shingle, he feels as though he is walking on knives. He strips and hobbles up and down the beach, forcing the blood around his body, tottering on legs that are as toneless as columns of tinned meat. He unloads the sled, hurling equipment carelessly up the beach. Ham-fisted, he twists and punches his way into dry clothes. Once the sled is light enough to manoeuvre he heaves it a couple of feet up the beach and anchors it with stones.

He huddles with the dogs on the shingle and, screwing up his eyes, hunts for his companion. There is a break in the cloud cover. Sunlight hits the water. The sea erupts in blue fire. The fire winds itself into a snake. The snake curls around him and strikes randomly at the beach, as though it too is hunting for Tor Dalebø, desperately, among the empty spaces that are even now invading the peripheries of Eric's vision. Eric shuts his eyes against the hallucination, the glare, the blind-spot dark that's swallowing his sight. His snow goggles. That's all this is.

His snow goggles.

He has lost his snow goggles.

Eric's best hope is to head for Foyn, holding out there long enough for the pack to disintegrate, permitting a rescue by boat or seaplane.

He fashions a blindfold from a pair of silk long-johns, makes a tiny tear to see through, and goes on with his preparations. A first-aid kit. Matches. A compass. Water. Pemmican: several weeks' supply. Chocolate. Dalebø's handgun: a Colt M1911. Plenty of ammunition. His packing is limited only by what the dogs can pull. He is at this moment – and setting aside the crucial loss of his goggles – the best-equipped man on the cap.

After a short nap Eric Moyse scouts a suitable crossing place. He expects to find Tor's body washed up on the beach. There is no sign of him.

Eric leashes his dogs to the sled and, with barely a nudge of the runners, negotiates three easy cracks in the ice. In twenty minutes he is on the pack. The irony implicit in this easy passage is choking: he forces it down.

He rides all night, a lone figure hurtling as fast as he can from the scene of disaster, yet dragging every detail of it with him, the images stored indelibly behind his eyes. For hours he follows a wide canal which runs due north, and so straight you could land seaplanes in it. Eventually a line of jumbled ice on the horizon forces him to steer away. He beds down around noon the next day and wraps more rags around his eyes.

The dogs wake him. He has staked them out in a protective triangle, the way Dalebø once taught him, and he listens a moment, assessing the direction of their cries. He reaches for the pistol.

The sky is clear. The sun is bright, high in the sky. His blindfolds have fallen off in the night. His whole body sings with the cold. He climbs a rising shelf of ice and looks down at the dogs. Stiff and alert, they are watching three polar bears. It is a family group, moving west, some fifty or sixty yards away. The dogs' clamour has made the bears curious, but they do not seem aggressive. Eric raises his gun and takes aim. The bears amble out of range. Eric lowers the gun, returns to his tent, and breaks camp.

The air is still, the sky acquires an even overcast, and the going is good on adequate ice with a healthy covering of snow. Thirty hours after his encounter with the bears, Eric reaches the shores of Foyn. There are no birds here, no plants, no soil. Eagerly he seeks out dry lichen to make a fire, but the stuff stubbornly refuses to burn. Demoralized, Eric chews down some chocolate, sleeps for a couple of hours in a cleft in the rock, then scouts for a place to establish a more permanent camp.

As he struggles in snow shoes over icy rocks, the dogs bound away from him, snarling and yapping. They gather round an outlying rock. Eric approaches. The snow around the rock is darkly splashed. He runs forward, yelling and waving his axe. The dogs retire, whining.

The rock is a man. For a split second, Eric has the crazy idea that it must be Tor Dalebø. It has been badly mauled. The face has been chewed off, the remains so black and swollen they suggest something vegetable – a mess of tubers.

Eric tries to read the remains the bears have left behind. This looks more like a monkey than a man. The arms of his blue flight jacket are overstuffed. Shirts and jerseys: too many layers, packed too close together to hold warmth. The bears must have had a hell of a time tearing through all that cloth. They have had to practically rip him in two to get at the meat.

Eric tries to turn the body but it is stuck to the ice by its own blood. He takes off his snow shoes. He works his way round the body, kicking it, jamming the toe of his boot in to break the bond between the ice and the man's clothing. When the body is free, he rolls it over – and there are the dead man's snow goggles, unbroken, waiting for him in a nest of blood spots. He tugs them off the ice and pulls them over his head. He fumbles the lenses over his eyes. The relief is instant, as though cool water is pouring down the insides of his skull.

This has to be one of the *Italia*'s crew. The short, inadequate jacket, the amateurish layering beneath: this is a man who had no business being on the ice. At least they found him some decent felt boots. Is it Eling or Bonfanti? He tugs at the shreds of the man's jacket, searching for pockets. The dogs, gaining confidence, approach. They sniff the ice. One paws at the ground and begins to truffle. It tugs something red out of the snow. Eric gets to his feet. The dog scampers up the slope, defending its prize. Eric goes after it. At last he manages to extract the thing from the dog's jaws.

It is a red leather pouch. He wipes the dog's drool away with a gloved hand. Inside the pouch is a notebook, bound in the same leather. He opens it.

To Uncle Lothar
Wishing you a Merry Christmas
Vibeke

He turns the pages, trying to make sense of it. Clumsy scribbles criss-cross each other every which way in a palimpsest. There are matrices and chequerboards, graphs and diagrams, ruler-straight and upward-pointing arrows crossed with strange, sinusoidal lines. There's stranger imagery, too: shamanic eyes and scales and fangs.

Behind him, the dogs edge forward, circling the shambles in the snow.

SEVEN

In the S.N. Medical College in Agra surgeons gather round Roopa's bed. Their arguments disturb her morphine sleep. Students lean in to peer inside her mouth, and worse, to prod. Police constables hover outside her curtain to catch a glimpse of the damage.

She cannot talk. Her mouth is broken. Her lips. Her tongue. She wakes on a wet pillow. Pink stains, drying, have made maps on the cotton. Her mouth is a mess of stitches and swellings. The stumps of her teeth are white with ulcers. She drinks cold soup through a straw. When she speaks, or tries to speak, saliva runs over the ruin of her bottom lip and gathers under her chin. She mops up the stringy droplets with the edge of her sheet. Pink.

Yash Yadav comes to see her, pressing a handful of pamphlets to his chest. 'Nice company your husband keeps.'

Roopa cannot speak, cannot grimace, cannot communicate. She makes a sound.

'There's no need to defend him, Roopa.' Yash lays his hand on hers. 'Hardik confessed.'

She says nothing.

'Very much the wounded husband. Never mind that we picked him up in a motel off the GTR with another man. That's honour for you. Very keen on honour, these fascist fags.' He sits on her bed and leafs through the pamphlets. 'They tell me the baby is all right.'

She will give him nothing. Not a tear. Not a sigh. Nothing.

'If anything had happened to the baby – well, Hardik would have been looking at some serious charges.'

One by one he drops the pamphlets on the bed where she cannot help but see them. Amateurish typography. Banyan trees. Hindu swastikas. 'We picked up the men who raped you. You should be pleased. Vermin like that off the streets. Incidentally, we stumbled over these in your apartment.'

She doesn't need to open the pamphlets to know what's inside. She's familiar with the crazy edges of Hardik's sort of politics.

'Stumbled,' she mouths. Saliva burns through a tear in her bottom lip.

Yash leans over, handkerchief extended to wipe the spittle from her chin.

She turns her head.

'We have to make a decision. About your husband. Teaching his wife a lesson is one thing. Something like that gets so easily out of control. You can see how it happens. But his politics. I'm worried, Roopa.' He strokes her hair. 'Anyway,' he says, tiring of the game, 'it's not up to me any more. Next week I leave the force. Well, why make the scandal any worse? There are family interests in Chhaphandi that I can be looking after. It's a fresh start, you might say.'

Roopa understands that this is the outcome Yash expected. It is what he wanted. She understands that she has failed. Her heart hammers in her chest.

That evening she writes a letter. 'Yash Yadav is in no way derailed.' She writes to the new Police Superintendent at the Maharashtra ACB. 'I will accept any posting, however menial.'

Two anti-terror officers in plain clothes come to talk to her about her husband's political activities. They will not tell her where they are holding him.

Ijay, Roopa's youngest brother, comes all the way from Mumbai to see Roopa home. He is stiff, reticent, appalled. 'You know,' he says, 'we will look after you. Whatever has happened. Whatever it is you've done. The family is behind you one hundred and ten per cent.' This is a phrase he has picked up at work.

In Thane, Roopa gets better, after a fashion. Her nerves heal. Her shattered sleep sticks itself back together. Her face changes character as it heals. The smile is gone. What emerges in its place is not ugly or deformed. The most you can say about her now is that she looks unremarkable. She has the face of another woman completely now. Her own father wouldn't recognize her. The assault has made her plain.

It fills her with a terrible glee, that she has somehow escaped herself. Sometimes she thinks about getting rid of her body, not because of its pain or its shame, but simply to realize her freedom completely. Anytime I want, she thinks, I can walk this thing under a truck. Then her baby kicks. It spasms. It shakes in dumb horror, and she is overwhelmed by an intense, nauseating remorse.

She learns to look upon herself as a machine. A machine acquires dignity by operating smoothly over a long period of service. You cannot humiliate a machine. Here is this baby, baking inside her, bubbling, rising. By the third trimester her future is clear. It is up to her to reinvent herself.

The priests call. Ceremonies follow in their proper sequence. The baby is born early in August 1996. It is a boy. When he is six days old he is laid on a blanket and his palms and the soles of his feet are painted with a red paste. The family gathers around the blanket and prays. This is the point at which the child is supposed to acquire a soul. On the eleventh day he is named. Roopa calls him Nitesh. He is happy and placid and he looks exactly like Yash Yadav.

A couple of months later, Roopa Vish boards a coach heading inland, along the Sher Shah Suri Marg, back to Firozabad. Little Nitesh lies across her lap, hands spooling as though already set to some industry.

The coach's on-board video offers instant Technicolor relief for eyes bruised by too many miles of the same thing, too many frilled and tattooed Tata trucks rattling past, too many mayfly villages, but Roopa pays no more attention to the screen than she does to the view through her window. The lovers' on-screen agonies, their ecstatic musical interludes, their battleaxe of a mother-in-law: it's all one to her. Underneath the folds of her child's blanket, Roopa's knuckles are white. She is her father's daughter and she is going to get her man.

A *bhangi* can go anywhere. A *bhangi* is invisible. A *bhangi* cleans the toilets and carries the shit away in a bucket on her head: who the hell ever looks, or wants to look, at a *bhangi*?

A *bhangi* is never short of work, because everybody shits. A *bhangi* gets to know everybody's shit, eventually. Chhaphandi's elementary school is full of shit. Odd-smelling, mealy, faintly caustic, faintly rotten shit. The school governors obeyed the state-wide ban on dry toilets and installed a modern flush-operated system and within days they were wading through – well . . .

A *bhangi* is invisible. A *bhangi* doesn't count. A *bhangi* can scoop shit out of a toilet in one cubicle while boys are picking on a child in the next. A *bhangi* hears everything. Every hateful, shitty thing. Your mother sucks your uncle's prick.

A *bhangi* learns.

Roopa has dental plates to replace her missing teeth. They are temporary things, grey, like shark's teeth. She does not wear them. She has money: she does not spend it. She has a plan: she does not share it. She rents a room in a block owned by Ekram Badbhagi, Chhaphandi's postmaster. Badbhagi divorced his wife after her fifth miscarriage and he's all over little Nitesh, the son he never had.

For all its surface clutter, posters and cheap glass ornaments, this place is typical of the buildings erected by Yadav Construction and Homes Ltd. You can find their rabbit hutches thrown up in villages all along the Sher Shah Suri Marg: single-occupancy accommodation for transients moving, with painful slowness, from one menial job to the next, one village to the next, towards the mega-cities of Delhi and Mumbai. The walls of the room do not quite join. There are no shutters and no rails for curtains.

The monsoon is coming. Yesterday, banks of filthy, sand-laden moisture from the Arabian Sea roiled through the sky and broke over the village. Roopa's walls dribbled and steamed.

Roopa wakes in darkness, Nitesh sprawled in the crook of her arm, the room's air sweetened by the smell of a soiled nappy. After the elementary school and Chhaphandi's kids – their weird little heads and their weird rabbit-droppings, small and hard as bullets – cleaning up after Nitesh is an active pleasure.

There is enough light in the yard below to clean her son by, because a couple of wall-mounted arc lamps light up the back of the roadhouse where lorry drivers plying the Sher Shah Suri Marg come for their medicine. This trade's an open secret. The Grand Trunk Road is one and a half thousand miles long and something has to get them through the night. The trade is swift, smooth, discreet. The drivers are not furtive, not delinquent, not ashamed. They are professionals, with legitimate needs: athletes of the long-haul.

Off to the side there are string mattresses stretched across posts in the earth. Only one hammock is occupied tonight. Some derelict.

Nitesh sleeps late into the morning. Once she has fed him, Roopa carries him across the yard and lays him in one of the string cots while she goes to buy breakfast. Her walking so brazenly into that space – a woman, and barely touchable at that – is calculated to turn heads and ruin conversation. The regulars here know she rents a room off Badbhagi, so there is nothing they can say about it. She asks for chai, and gets it. She leaves her coin on the counter. The proprietor leaves it on the counter until she has gone. He doesn't want to encourage her.

Coming out, she sees the derelict from the night before lying sprawled across his cot, playing peek-a-boo with Nitesh. Trying to: Nitesh is too small to respond.

The tramp sits up. He's in a bad way. He has only one arm. 'Good morning.'

She knows who this is now. She says to him: 'We had an appointment.'

'What?'

She shakes her head. 'More than a year ago now.'

'What?'

Roopa picks Nitesh up and carries him back to the accommodation block. She can be patient. A *bhangi* learns. A kiln-worker whipped. A family vanished. *Your mother sucks your uncle's prick*. Decline and fall. Roopa sits by her window and looks out at Vinod Yadav sprawled there, derelict, upon his string bunk. She drinks her chai. She smiles a ghastly, toothless smile.

A *bhangi* handles all kinds of shit. From thin stews to gritty lumps, shit is the *bhangi*'s proper field, her métier. The schemes, the threats, the feuds. The hot nastiness that prevails over everything and everyone. In this idiot- and stillborn-stricken village the bereaved sneer at the barren and the barren laugh at the burdened, and the nights are a-mutter with the rehearsal of nested blames and intractable vendettas. Moany old Vinod, maimed in that rail crash last year and turning day by day into his dad until at last, they say, his mind gave out completely. And what about his cousin Yash, who couldn't keep it in his pants? Some squire, some Lord Muck he turned out to be!

Roopa is her father's daughter: Kabir Vish, who took tales from a city's vagrants and rough sleepers, *hijras* and prostitutes, and wove them into a net to catch the Stoneman. There's nothing here in this sleepy backwater can frighten a woman who, as a child, listened wide-eyed to her father's tales of the maniac who dropped paving slabs on to the heads of rough sleepers in the midnight gutters of King's Circle.

Tonight, as the monsoon approaches and the parched sky sings with tension, Roopa puts her baby to bed and comes to the window and counts the mattresses stretched out beneath the margosa tree. A handful of drivers are asleep there, weary from the road. One is awake: Vinod Yadav. He looks up at her. Just another deadbeat. One of hundreds of small-time dealers lubricating the Sher Shah Suri Marg.

Vinod Yadav: the toothless old men of Chhaphandi are mystified by his precipitate decline. He had enough to live for, you would think. A pretty wife. Two kids, and so what if their heads are a funny shape? Shubi and Ravi aren't the worst-afflicted kids around here, not by a long stretch. He had his father's house. He had the brickworks to run. Vinod, you would think, was set up for life – and yet he has contrived to piss the whole lot of it away. Vinod's drunken no-shows have matured into wholesale vanishing acts, sometimes days, sometimes weeks in duration. What's got into him? People talk about the rail crash as though that might be a trauma sufficient to explain his decline, but there has to be more to it than that.

She leans out the window. She beckons Vinod off his hammock. She beckons him in. A *bhangi* learns all kinds of shit. Today, unseen, she discovered why the sons Vinod has abandoned – Ravi, Shubi – come home from school with bruises on their knobbly little heads and bad reports: *Your mother sucks your uncle's prick*.

She opens her door. Vinod staggers in. He's very drunk. His smell is so pungent she is afraid it will wake the baby. More than rum, this smell. Fires. Truck exhaust. Rancid cooking oil. Vinod holds out his remaining hand. He tries to touch her. She pushes him away. He reaches for her again. She's been stoking him for weeks now. Glad-eyeing him from her window. Sashaying past his little bed. She's asked for this. She backs away towards the bed. He reaches under his shirt, fanning his stink through the room, and pulls out a gun. An old Browning Hi-Power.

She sits back on the pallet.

'Take off your clothes.' He watches her, one hand waving the gun.

'Vinod, for God's sake, put it down. Look. I'm giving it to you. This is what you want. Is this what you want?' She raises her feet onto the edge of the bed and parts her knees. 'Is it? Vinod?' You cannot humiliate a machine.

Vinod hesitates, then bends down and lays the Browning on the bed.

'Go and wash yourself first. It's all right.'

He swallows. He sits beside her on the bed. 'It's not loaded.' And when she does not reply: 'How do you know my name?'

'Vinod? Everybody knows you, Vinod. You're famous. You're Yash Yadav's cousin.'

Vinod's in no state to unpick riddles, but Roopa is going to make it simple for him. 'Tomorrow,' she says, 'I'm going to show you something.'

The next morning a green Honda rolls into view around the corner of the roadhouse and stops in the shade of a lone neem tree. The monsoon is hours away. There are no clouds, but the sky is thickening, the heat is building, everything is buzzing. The whole countryside is stretching and bubbling. Vinod shambles over and leans on the door sill, breathing the fumes of the old car.

'You can drive.'

Roopa smiles.

'You have a car.'

She has grown teeth. Terrible, sharp, grey teeth. 'Get in.' Her baby is in a basket on the back seat. It sleeps soundly, lulled by the rhythms of the engine as they curl their way onto the Sher Shah Suri Marg.

Vinod stares at the sky. There is something wrong with it. There are no clouds, but its whole fabric has haemorrhaged from blue to mauve. Sand from Arabia: that's what this is. Vinod sits up. The horizon is shimmering, the whole landscape is bubbling and bursting: the monsoon is coming to put out this fire. Out of his side window he can see birds flocking, preparing to outrun the poison cloud.

In the corner of his eye, something yellow catches the sun. He turns his head just in time to see a car, a saffron-yellow Maruti Zen, spun half-off the road. The driver's by the side of the road, waving at them to stop, but why would they?

It's his brother-in-law. Vinod turns in his seat, but the sun against the dusty rear window does not allow him a view. Rishi. It was Rishi. He's sure of it. The kid he played with as a child. His workman at the kilns. The man who helped burn –

Rishi, at the wheel of a Maruti! Who'd have thought it? But this is the point. Vinod understands now. They have none of them grown up. Their childhood games have never ended. They have simply acquired a darker, more adult coloration. Now Yash is top of the heap and Rishi is on the rise, while he is falling, falling – and this was always on the cards. Even when they were little, you could have seen this coming: the turn of fortune's wheel.

The Yadav family's garage is easy enough to find because of the giant peeling sign by the roadside advertising Apollo tyres. The house itself stands at the end of a dirt track lined with deodar trees and choked with elephant grass.

'But this is Yash's place.'

She says, 'We'll walk from here.' She picks up Nitesh and leads Vinod through brushy shade and down the hill, towards the house.

Vinod knows this place, and its history. It is the garage whose mechanics' mistakes killed his father. The place belongs to the family now. Which is to say: his cousin, Yash. 'Here, Vinod. Hunker down.'

It's harder to do than you would think, one-handed. Vinod slumps and sprawls. They crouch for many minutes in weeds and shadows. What if the baby wakes?

'You see?'

Yash Yadav's car, the Opel Corsa, is parked under the corrugated-iron roof of the lean-to. Two young boys come running out of the house. Two funny little heads wobble about on long, weak necks. Two miniature motor scooters zip back and forth across the dirt yard.

'Are they yours? Vinod? Are those your boys?'

Vinod watches his sons playing in the yard.

'Shubi and Ravi.'

Vinod swallows.

'Where do you suppose their mother is?'

Poor Vinod.

'Their mother's inside. Safia. Can you guess who she's with?'

Your mother sucks your uncle's prick.

'In there.'

'Yes.'

With Yash Yadav.

Roopa drives them back to Chhaphandi. The monsoon is coming. The earth is baking. Things are rising. It no longer matters if Badbhagi calls by for the rent and a game of peek-a-boo with Nitesh and finds a man in her room. It doesn't matter what rumours go round – a lone *bhangi* mother at the wheel of an old but serviceable green Honda. She does not need her cover any more. She is peeling off her skin of other people's shit. She is becoming something else. The plainest butterfly.

In her room the air fizzes and the walls drip. Roopa peels off her torn and filthy sari. Underneath she is clean. She is sweet. 'Vinod. There's no need for you to be afraid.'

He sits in front of her and bows his head. She kisses the top of his head. 'Poor man,' she croons. 'You loved her so.' He reaches up. He cups her breasts. 'The police, they're not interested in you. They're not interested in Samjhoria Nankar. Some *bhangi* family gets into a row, then scarpers, who's to know? Yash Yadav, though. Yash is another matter. He matters. He counts.'

She understands the politics of this, better than the precinct shit-kickers do. If she can get Vinod to implicate Yash Yadav in violent activity – violent activity involving a scheduled caste employee – it will bring the case to life again. She will bypass Firozabad and go straight to Lucknow, the state capital. Look, sirs! Slavery, alive and well in the City of Glass! With such a story, hell, she can go straight to the office of the Director General!

'Vinod,' she whispers, cradling his head. Vinod falls back, his arm over his face. She climbs on top of him. Her belly, baby-softened, brushes his. Again. Again. 'Tell me. What happened to Samjhoria? What happened to the Nankars? Was Yash involved? Tell me what he did.'

Vinod sobs out his anger at his wife's betrayal.

'Tell me: where did they go? Samjhoria? Manjit? Little Abhik? Little Kaneer? What did Yash do to them? '

Little by little, Vinod sobs out his fear of Roopa's grey smile.

'Tell me.'

At last, the seam comes open, releasing not one tale but dozens. How the Yadavs acquired their garage business with menaces. Their land-grabs.

Their trucks. The pick-me-up trade, and what little Vinod understands about the adulterated sandalwood scam. The brickworks. The Nankars. 'It wasn't me,' he says. At last: the killings. *Killings!* 'It wasn't my idea . . .'

So this is what has beaten him: the sight of Yash Yadav taking control. Yash managing the situation at the brickworks, with a clinical cruelty learned in a dozen police encounters on the streets of Mumbai, and honed by Professor Doctor Rao's Advance Commando Combat System. One enemy. One chance. One strike. One kill. Poor Samjhoria. Whatever did Yash do to her?

Vinod says he doesn't know. 'It wasn't my idea. I didn't do anything. I wasn't there. I took the boys away. Yash wanted –' He bites his tongue. (No matter: it is loosening, she needn't press him harder now.) 'But I snuck the boys away.'

'Where did you take them?'

I was going to lose them in New Delhi.'

'What happened?'

A stupid question. She knows what happened. The second-worst rail crash in Indian history happened. Even Vinod, in his agitation, won't give that question the dignity of a reply. He simply lifts his stump and sobs and, sobbing, weeps away a year of pent-up horror, regret, self-disgust. 'They never found the boys.' Splashes it out. 'Poor boys.' Splashes it into her. Is – or seems to be – done.

They lie beside each other, panting and sobbing; panting and grinning a terrible, shark-grey grin. The sky changes colour, turning from blue to grey to charcoal. The darker it gets, the more Roopa's grey teeth shine. The first clouds arrive. They are made of birds. Grass withers, leaving a thin dust that gathers itself up into twisters no taller than a man. Even the dust is impatient for rain. And it comes: black as coal and wrinkled like a brain. Stand out in this, you'll catch your death. This is the first cloud. The pollution cloud. Worms, released from their baked-earth tombs, wriggle in a mass across the roadhouse parking lot, steaming in the acid washout.

*

Roopa wakes. The baby, little Nitesh, is crying. Roopa peels herself off the pallet and shivers. The whole rooms glimmers like a cave. The walls are running wet. Absently she runs a hand beneath her breasts. She gathers Nitesh into her arms to feed.

At last, heavy-headed, she registers the change: Vinod is gone.

Her heart skips a beat. Where is he? She is so close to victory. Vinod's the man who can bring Yash Yadav down. She has only to keep him near.

She hears the gush of a tap. A footfall. He's in the bathroom, that's all. He doesn't sleep so well. His stump is hurting him.

The bathroom door opens, but the footsteps go straight by her door and down the hall. It isn't Vinod.

So where is he? She goes to the window, her baby at her breast. The branches of the neem tree turn and toss under poison rain. The courtyard is a lake. It is empty. There are no sleepers, and no cars –

No cars.

Her green Honda is gone.

EIGHT

Wednesday, 2 April 1930

On beaches up and down Austvågøy, chief island of Norway's Lofoten archipelago, sides of cod hang drying on wooden frames. Leathery and mummified, the fillets chock against each other in the wind.

Eric Moyse slumps in an old rocking chair before the kitchen stove. A mug of coffee cools, forgotten, on the floor beside him. Nine months have passed since the Russian icebreaker *Krassin* rescued him, snowblind and raving, from the shores of Foyn. Deep in the lassitude that has overtaken him since then, he listens to the clock-clocking of dried fish and turns the pages of Lothar Eling's red notebook. Its gnomic sketches and its even more gnomic sentences.

> Between air and water *and* between waters of different density: the formation of WAVES.

If the notebook belongs to anyone now, it belongs to the old professor, Jakob Dunfjeld. He alone might be able to make sense of it.

> You don't expect a propeller to function half out of the water. And this comes to the same thing. *Cavitation*: generating empty space within a solid body.

The sun is high enough to warm him now. Eric will go visiting. It is expected of him. He squeezes the notebook into the pocket of his coat. He steps outside and his eyes fill with thin, insipid light. It will be good, after nearly a year, to see the professor again, even if their talk must come round, sooner or later, to the *Italia*. Absently, he presses his hand against his coat, feeling the notebook there. His missing toes tingle.

To the east of Svolvaer, at the head of a small inlet, the Oslo government leases a cottage for the use of visiting officials: men from departments to do with meteorology and fisheries. At high tide the sea comes up almost to the house. The water is brilliantly clear. Where Eric's shadow falls across it, reflections are banished, revealing jellyfish-like pink balloons, starfish, darting crabs, pebbles woven with golden weed.

Footfalls in the shingle serve, better than any bell, to alert the house to a visitor's arrival. As Eric approaches, Jakob Dunfjeld opens the door. Eric follows him into the warmth of the kitchen. There is the stove and a kettle steaming. The room is unlit and there are lamps on the table waiting to be filled. Beyond the window a field rises steeply to a line of trees. The grass looks buttered in the sun's declining light. Nets lie in the sun. The fields here are too steep for horse and wagon and the farmers use nets to gather in their hay.

He wishes he did not have to go through it all again. That daring mission for which he is known. His failure and spurious fame. There is a malign satisfaction to be got from telling people about Dalebø's death and disappearance in four feet of water. 'He may as well have slipped in the bath.' Afraid of his own motives, Eric more often maintains an aggressive silence.

A patch of deeper darkness detaches itself from the wall by the window. A young woman, bright, confident. She extends her hand and the professor says: 'You've met my daughter, of course.'

'I remember you,' says Vibeke. 'Are you actually wearing the same jumper?' The sleek symmetry of the young woman's face is so striking Eric finds it impossible, afterwards, to remember anything else about her. 'Your housekeeper kept hugging me and weeping. She smelled of liquorice. Not sweets. I think it was booze.'

This comes as a complete surprise to Eric: how a few years will carry a child into adulthood. Yes, he has met the professor's daughter before, on a previous visit: a polite, contained little girl.

'Daddy says you're going to take us sailing. He got me all excited but now he says I have to go diving for him. I have to pay for my pleasures by helping him set up his apparatus. If the octopuses eat me I am counting on you to have him arraigned.'

How old is she – sixteen? She seems already to have leapt into the surety of her twenties.

'Do you really wring out whales to get the oil? You know, like dishcloths? I find it hard to know when Daddy's teasing me.'

A bread board. Dishes and a tureen. A plate of berries gathered from the hill behind the house. Eric watches Vibeke move about the room. There is a confidence to her movements. 'Do start, please.' Her face has matured in an unexpected way. The flesh around her eyes has retained its childish fullness: a hint of Lappish ancestry. A drop of Arctic wildness under the skin.

Eric takes Lothar Eling's notebook from his pocket and lays it on the table. Vibeke recognizes it. She feels her way into her chair. The professor comes over with the coffee pot and sees the book lying on the table between his daughter and his guest. He looks from one to the other of them, nonplussed. Vibeke reaches across the table and picks up the notebook. She pulls it free of its waterproof pouch. Eric studies her hands. Long, delicate fingers, the nails short, the tips a little flattened. Strong at the joints. A climber's hands. Eric recalls what Professor Dunfjeld has told him: how Vibeke has taken to climbing the ring of mountains surrounding their home city of Bergen.

'Thank you,' she says. She does not look at him. She says to her father: 'This is Lothar's. This is the book I gave him.'

Eric finds his voice: 'It found its way into my bag after I was rescued from Foyn. I didn't know who to give it to. That's not true. I could have found someone. His mother is still alive. The Geographical Society. Something made me hang on to it.' He has never felt more in the wrong, though he can't imagine why.

*

It appears an easy business, reaching the ice. Hopping boulders, bounding across stretches of shingle and gravel, surely Eric Moyse and his new mountaineering pupil will reach the foot of the route with ease?

Eric knows better. He explains to Vibeke Dunfjeld the miseries of that obvious route. The broken and slimy terrain. 'There's no real floor. Just a litter of smashed stone.' In summer the ferns grow taller than a man. You forget your feet and in seconds something underfoot comes along to ruin your whole year. A birch root. A hole.

He points out the better path: a green and greasy granite wall. It's a drear prospect from a distance but at close quarters it gives up a line of obvious handholds and axe placements.

Vibeke folds her arms, contemplating it. Contour the slab and climb down to the ice. The descent is steep and exhilarating, over broken slabs and down a chimney in the rock, flared just enough to give the pulse a kick.

Eric, already on the ice, leans on his axe and watches as Vibeke Dunfjeld slips into position, her body falling as neatly into the chimney as a keystone drops into an arch.

He lets Vibeke lead the ascent of the glacier. She is faster than he is, a natural with the axe, carving steps with easy, effective strokes. For Eric, the loss of three toes has made walking a precarious business and he is more than happy to follow. For an hour and a half they toil up the snow bank in the shelter of damp, high walls. It is exhilarating at last to reach the saddle, to sit on a rock and look across open water to the chain of mainland peaks: blue fangs set in a green gum of sea ice.

'Daddy told me last night, it takes a thousand years for water to pass from the Pacific to the Atlantic.'

'Really?'

'I thought you'd like that.'

'Good grief.'

They are sitting in full sun, confident of the weather, though there are clouds out to sea – shreds left behind by last night's rain. Beneath the clouds the waves are a deep red that is almost black. Flecks of mica, close to the horizon, are reflections off the cabin windows of fishing boats.

'Daddy says we may not be coming to the Lofotens any more.'

'Oh?'

'He says the work is finished. Now that Eling – well.'

'Oh.'

'He says Lothar Eling used dead water to solve the weather. You know, the way a propeller churns up waters of different densities so it can't go anywhere. Airs of different densities, waters of different temperatures, they do the same thing. It's all fluid, you see. It all obeys the same laws. There isn't this big boundary between the ocean and air. At least, there *is*, but it's only special because it's the fluid boundary that's obvious to us. The visible one. The one we can touch. But there are hundreds of invisible boundaries too, up in the sky, running through the ocean, all cluttered up with each other. Waves under the ocean and waves halfway to outer space. One gigantic fluid-dynamical problem. And it never stops. Never. When the sun explodes and boils the oceans into gas, the gas will still be turning over itself, over and over.'

Something else from Eling's notebook comes to Eric's spinning mind: '*Why the heart will not cease to desire.*'

'When we get home to Oslo, Daddy's going to write a paper about it.'

They sit in silence.

'What will you do in Oslo?'

Vibeke shrugs. 'Maintain the diary of a great man or two. They will let me attend classes. Some of them will.'

Her father has plans for her. Some carefully chosen study. She can become a teacher. The professor can have no idea how deadly his schemes are. To him, Vibeke's love of the outdoors must appear no more than a tomboy's eccentricity, amusing in its way, even admirable, but not very serious when set against the real and pressing business of her future.

'Miss Dunfjeld.'

She will not look at him.

'Vibeke.'

Vibeke rests a hand on his shoulder.

Steadily, as the days have passed, maturing into weeks, so Eric has come to hope for this – and it has come. His heart leaps. His face contorts with sudden yearning. Her head is turned away. Her face is hidden behind her wildly curling hair. Is she crying? Crying, to be going away forever? Crying, to be leaving him? He leans towards her. He raises a hand to touch her hair. He thinks that he might kiss her. So beautiful. So young. He leans in and sees, not twenty feet away, on a snow-covered boulder, a white-feathered eagle.

A male. It sits and preens, its great primaries spread against the sky like hands, then it leans into the wind and is carried off over their heads. Vibeke, letting go of Eric's shoulder, turns to him, her face aglow with an innocent, ornithological delight.

Eric dissembles well and fast. He has dug snow holes for himself before now, out-waiting Arctic blizzards. He is a master of self-burial. There comes from him not a single outward sign, not a blink, not a breath, *not a fucking hint*, of what has just happened to him.

In the evening, exhausted and chilled through, the pair accept tall glasses of egg-nog and join Professor Dunfjeld by the fire. Vibeke is full of questions tonight, as though making up for all the visits she will not make now, and all the Lofoten summers she will miss. She asks Eric about his explorations, his seafaring, his role as the islands' *nessekøng*.

For all her courtesy – pantaloon gestures that inadvertently parody her father – she is mining him. Vibeke brings to her interviews the same speculative eye she brings to bear on the birds pecking crumbs at her window sill, and the animals sheltering in the hedgerows. What drives her ceaseless questioning? Eric has the strange and morose suspicion that she is going to repeat every word he utters to agents of a foreign power.

Eric's paranoia has some foundation. Earlier this year, representatives of a new national conglomerate came calling: men who have links to Norway's Hitler-worshipping Nasjonal Sammling, whose own ventures are capitalized in Germany and who owe their commercial loyalty, ultimately, to IG Farben. No one seriously doubts that another war is coming. Since whale oil is used in the manufacture of plastic explosives, Eric has in effect been selling the Germans precursor ingredients for tomorrow's bombs.

Of more immediate concern is the decline in the archipelago's economy. The Lofoten fishing fleet mechanized itself only to expose itself to recession. No one can get spare parts for their faltering engines. A good third of the fleet is laid up. It pains Eric to sit by and watch so many boats rotting at anchor.

This summer, in the pages of the Geographical Society's bulletin, some student published a fulsomely ungrammatical essay about maritime life in the Lofotens. (Eric imagines a cow-licked disciple of Hans Gude, Grieg's *Sixty-Six Lyric Pieces* under one arm and *Peer Gynt* under the other.)

> In midsummer, small whales come to the VestFjord area. From end of summer to late autumn, shoals of herring, and then the arrival of cod.

Less a work of scholarship, more an upwelling of national sentiment. The pictures were pretty enough, though more suited to Washington's *National Geographic* ('the world in your living room') than Oslo's sober *Geografisk Tidsskrift*. A woman strings together a fishing net from wool on a wooden spool. Peat cutters. Mown grass is hauled from the steep fields in nets. A crow's nest is tied to the mast of a fishing boat, a harpoon gun bolted to its bow. These are common enough scenes, familiar from Eric's boyhood and not too rare among the archipelago's poorer communities. Taken together, they speak of an aspect of island life that is slowly but steadily disappearing.

Why record nothing of the business proper? The factory ships made of old tankers? The boilers and the great round tanks that squat to the side of every quay?

> Returning home from the hunt, a successful gunner is treated to a hero's welcome – and well deserves it!

'I would have done it better,' Vibeke agrees, handing the journal to her father.

For some reason, Vibeke's dismissal of the article inclines Eric to its defence. 'How would you have done it differently?'

'I would have interviewed you, for a start.'

'Oh?'

'Or not interviewed you at all. Perhaps I would leave the people out altogether and write about the foxes.'

'They interest you, do they?'

'Everywhere else, foxes chase after chickens and people chase after foxes. This is the only place I know where foxes and people rub along.'

This is true. The thickets are so well stocked with willow grouse that the island's foxes have never developed a taste for domestic fowl. Here, before the fireside, Vibeke has never looked more wild or more unapproachable. Tanned, bright-eyed, her hair tied back in a rough ponytail. A Lapp virgin. An ice princess. She does not look at him. She knows that he is watching her.

'Stay.'

Vibeke looks up from the fire.

'At least for the summer. Stay longer if you want. See these islands in winter. In different seasons. Stay for a year. Make something of all this. Don't go copying out the scrawls of great men. What you're doing. The climbing. Your observations. It could be something.' He has run out of words. He has still not declared himself. How can he possibly declare himself with her father slumped there between them, complacent, by the fire? Does she know how he feels? How can she?

Jakob Dunfjeld stretches and yawns. He sets his glass down on the rug. 'It could be something.' Is the professor agreeing with him, or making fun of him?

In any event, Vibeke stays.

∞

Years go by.

In Kastrup, on the Danish coast, Eric sits waiting for his flight to be called: the Orange Horror to Poole. When he lands it's a quick, if uncomfortable, train ride to London and his next meeting.

One of the ironies of Eric's change of life – from local fishing magnate to international shipping entrepreneur – has been the growing frequency and duration of such trips. For years now he has been languishing, week after week, month after month, in one hotel after another, in this capital city or that, alone, unmarried, his feelings for Vibeke still undeclared – and to think that all this while his secret love has been tramping, dark and supple, among the hills of his island kingdom!

From Svolvaer, Vibeke writes him letters full of observations of animals and birds. He's reading one now:

> The older greylags have enjoyed the run of the house for over a year, and have learnt to treat the dogs as their social inferiors. The dogs, in their turn, barely tolerate the ducks.
>
> Pippi holds himself aloof, as always. Without a companion, he grows ever more neurotic. He is terrorized by the sight of the end of his own tail, poking up from under the shreds of newspaper lining the bottom of his cage. When I take him out he hides behind the curtains and does not make a sound. If I leave the room for a moment, I return to find him perched on the pelmet, screaming with loneliness.

When Pippi first made his appearance in her letters, Vibeke omitted, in a welter of other domestic and zoological detail, to say what kind of animal he was. In his reply Eric forgot to ask. Now it is impossible for him to admit to his own ignorance. He imagines an unhappy, indeterminate creature with bright red fur, somewhere between squirrel, cat and monkey.

A policeman leans in through the door and calls the waiting businessmen to attention: the flight is refuelled and ready for boarding.

As he crosses the apron, clouds peel away from the sun: light turns the orange hull to a slab of flame so that Eric, disoriented, must grope half-blind for the handrail. Tin steps wobble underfoot.

Eric's contact, sitting by the window near the front of the aircraft, arrived with the plane. Though the man's eye is keen and his handshake is firm, his torso is sunken, twisted, as though the hours spent in his seat have caused an essential mechanism to unwind.

The pair sit in a silence that you could not really call companionable until the DC3 takes off and the racket of the propellers is sure to mask their conversation. 'Nice day,' the man says, with a certain sourness.

Eric, whose humour is simple and direct, never knows what to do with sarcasm. 'Yes,' he says, in a neutral tone, falling back on his usual reticence: the fisherman's friend.

The DC3 is circling Kastrup as it gains cruising height. Winter sun flushes their side of the plane, filling the cabin with a light that is, in all senses of the word, neutral. Neutral by the common accord of hostile parties; neutral, too, in its lack of heat, its absence of association, the way it accentuates edges while robbing surfaces of their texture, so that it feels for a moment as if they are sitting in some photographic developing agent, their surroundings only half-realized.

The young Frenchman speaks. His accent reveals a German education, which is only to be expected given his area of expertise: 'The by-product represents little in terms of bulk. Less than a hundred kilos.'

Eric is not interested in reassurances, least of all reassurances that assume his ignorance concerning deuterium oxide. As if bulk were the issue!

Deuterium, a regular hydrogen atom with a newfangled neutron at its heart, bonds with oxygen to make a kind of water, and if you filled a bucket with it, and filled another from the tap, you might just be able to guess which bucket was heavier. In every cup of ordinary water there's a little heavy water. To get at it you have to electrolyse the ordinary water away – an expensive business, but not if you need to split oxygen and hydrogen for some other profitable process – say, the production of fertilizer. Which is what the plant at Vemork is – or was, before the new physics arrived: a fertilizer factory. The Frenchman's talk of 'by-product' is accurate in its coy way.

'I would feel a lot more comfortable if you would allow me to float a little oil over the contents of each barrel. Carting drums of water across the North Sea would attract anyone's attention.' It pleases Eric to play the fool sometimes with these scientific types, as Svolvaer's practised whaling crews once played the fool with him.

'Maintaining the purity of the by-product is our first priority.' The Frenchman sounds as though he is reciting from a book. Eric admires the man's control.

How much do the French assume he understands? The role of heavy water as a neutron modulator is most definitely *not* a piece of information the French expect Eric to possess, and it is almost worth dropping it into conversation just to see what colour the Frenchman's face will turn in this acidic orange light.

Of course, Eric will not do any such thing. Because he is Eric. Because the stakes are too high. Most of all, because the experiment would fail. This light would fail to conduct the fiercest passion; would shine alike on lovemaking and murder, so that you would not be able to tell one from the other; would dull the passions themselves in time. Why did they have to paint over the windows anyway?

The Frenchman wants to dictate the route. He wants Eric's sea captain to ply the coast as far as Tromsø, then sail west to Skye. The naivety of the plan is predictable: it assumes the sea is as neutral and featureless as the charts that represent it. Eric replies: 'Your route at least doubles the risk to your cargo from the weather and increases the journey time fourfold.' This last is a lie, but Eric has grown used to the business of bluff. You don't get to relocate your fleet in foreign harbours – at a discount, at that – without acquiring some of the flashier tricks of the persuasion game.

Quite what this man thinks German agents will make of an unfamiliar cargo vessel heading so far north, into the haunts of Lappish reindeer-herders and fishermen, is another point against the plan, but not one worth airing since the plan is void anyway. Eric's captains have his complete confidence and they choose their own routes. 'Your people will be welcome on board, as before,' Eric offers, and the man's abrupt and immediate acquiescence leads him to wonder whether this whole argument was not a red herring, a test of his urgency in acquiring the shipment – too much keenness being deemed suspicious.

Their business done, the Frenchman loses interest in him and reaches under the seat in front for his briefcase. He has been far too long in his seat; his balance is shot. He has to lean with his free hand on the seat in front to keep himself from slipping sideways. He balances the case across his legs. Eric stares for a second, then looks quickly away. The material of the man's trouser leg has folded up under the weight of the case, flattening to a shape that cannot be natural. The man has lost a leg. Maybe he has lost two legs. A child casualty of the last war? Anyway, he is wearing at least one artificial leg.

Eric wonders how he could have failed to notice this till now. Were the man's trousers structured to assume a natural fullness when not crushed by the weight of some object? What kind of arrangement would that involve? Some form of inflation, perhaps. Balloonettes. He wonders how far these mechanisms extend.

Can the operating company simply not pay someone sometime to scrape the windows of this aircraft clear of orange paint? A small square would be enough. A chink scraped clean with a razor blade, just enough so that the world might catch its breath. Without that chink of earth-blue light it is impossible to associate this interior with the idea of forward motion. The propellers rattle and churn but they don't seem to be going anywhere.

Is the man's torso real? His arms are real, because Eric can see the man's hands, leafing through his papers – but is this inference justified? Might real hands be attached to unreal arms? His head is real. Is his chest real? Or are the real parts connected to an artificial centre, like gondolas hung from an airship? How much does he weigh? If the pilot decreases the plane's altitude, and the cabin's pressure rises, will the Frenchman levitate?

Caught up in these thoughts, if you can call them thoughts, tangled in absurd speculations, Eric doesn't even notice they are descending until the Horror's wheels hit the tarmac at Poole.

With a stifled little cry, Eric clambers out of his seat, even while the plane is taxiing to a standstill. He isn't the only one. Week by week, as the news worsens and the European war spreads west, this fragile flight is becoming a test of nerves. Eric allows the crush of eager passengers to carry him away towards the front of the plane. He glances back at the Frenchman, who gives him the curtest of nods. He has not tried to leave his seat. Naturally, he is waiting until everyone else has left the plane. It will take him some time to arrange his artificial leg, to get his balance, to move, crabwise, through the plane, and this is why he has not yet moved. Though it comes to Eric that he never saw the man move from his seat, so it is possible – not likely, but possible – that the man has somehow been made part of the plane.

Vibeke tells Eric in her letter that her camera is broken: Pippi knocked it off a shelf and it is beyond repair. She is saving up for another.

Once in London, Eric buys Vibeke a camera. Heavy. Specialized. A Tropen Adoro: its teak body was conceived to withstand the humidity of the East Indies, 'so I think you will find that it will prove more than equal to the mists and drizzle of Voksenkollen'.

In his room in the Dorchester Hotel he stares at his letter, the complacency of it, the hint of self-congratulation: this is the warmest his correspondence ever gets.

He unscrews his pen and stares through the sparse, pale green of new foliage, over Park Lane to Hyde Park and the crackled grey hide of the Serpentine, drained to deprive German bombers of a landmark. His insides churning like an overworked Kvaerner blubber digester, he writes:

> Invasion of the south seems inevitable, but you will be safe enough on the Lofotens, I think. And you will always have a home here in London should you need it. It may be prudent to arrange your

> passage while these dealings can be conducted openly. Take what money you need from the house and speak to Frodhi, a trustworthy man and a good seaman – and no friend of the Hun.

He could weep with frustration. No matter how close he comes to her in thought, his words serve only to carry him further and further away. He will have to find some other way to express his clotted feelings. He walks into town and visits Liberty's department store to buy Vibeke a gift. After an hour's wandering, he drifts into the orbit of the perfumery. There's pre-war stock here, on sale at an eye-watering mark-up. He settles on the most expensive brand he can find. *Étude*. The salesgirl, unable to believe her luck, insists on delivering her pitch anyway. In common with the world's finest perfumes, she explains, *Étude* contains 'ambergris'!

Listening to her, Eric wonders idly, mischievously, what the girl would say if he were to tell her what he knows of this rare and magical stuff. That sperm whales subsist largely on a diet of Antarctic octopus. That the octopus wrap themselves around the heads of their attackers, and the whales dive, head-butting their prey to death against the ocean floor.

'. . . with a top-note of patchouli . . .'

The octopus can only cling; it has no other defence. Its arms are not muscular. Its suckers, though, are blade-edged and tear fiercely at its foe. The octopuses are big; their tentacles reach as far as a whale's rectum.

'. . . Jean-François Houbigant . . .'

That a whale coming away from battle with a sore arse will manufacture a foul-smelling grease to cleanse and soothe its wounds. And men who work for Eric Moyse, killing the whale, will look for this grease. Retching, they will scrape it out of the whale's arsehole. And they will put it in jars and sell it to dealers in Oslo, who will sell it to parfumiers in Paris and Amsterdam and New York.

'. . . presented in a flacon by Cristalleries Baccarat . . .'

'I said, I'll take it.'

Back in his room at the Dorch, Eric inspects the gift. He turns the thing over and over in his hands, aware of a growing dissatisfaction. The bottle, as chunky and irregular as a salt crystal, rests on a silver-plated base. The more he thinks about it, the more he tries to imagine it, the more impossible it seems that Vibeke will show the slightest interest in it. He may as well have bought her a ball gown, or a lapdog, or a season ticket to the opera. His mistake appears doubly inept when he thinks of the trouble he has gone to in encouraging the girl, in his long absence, to adopt a life of loneliness and high purpose.

Her notes. Her observations. Her science and fieldwork. Studies to rival anything by Austria's Konrad Lorenz or the Netherlands' Niko Tinbergen. Nights spent sleeping rough in barns and ditches. An endorsement from the Geographical Society. By encouraging her love of the Arctic seaboard he has successfully sequestered her from outside influence. He has made her a myth. A sprite. He has made her untouchable.

Sunday, 29 September 1941

London's Dorchester Hotel is made out of concrete, its wall cavities filled with seaweed to deaden the sound of traffic on Park Lane. It is a new kind of building, built to insulate its clientele from a new kind of world. It is, simply, the most sumptuous air-raid shelter in London.

Tonight the Luftwaffe are dropping wave after wave of high explosive over Whitehall, but nothing short of multiple direct hits could breach the hotel's reinforced concrete shell. The restaurant – it has been moved to the Gold Room to avoid the danger of flying glass – is sumptuously decorated, a mass of gilded stucco, and the bombardment is shaking it free, piece by piece: an absurd, decadent rain. The diners shelter under their tables, entertaining each other as best they can: titles, MPs, American spies, minor royalty. Mrs Greville of Polesden Lacy. Ministers, ambassadors, industrialists. It-girls of every hue and stripe. Emerald, Lady Cunard has come prepared. Self-contained, unflappable, seated among folds of tablecloth like Scheherazade in Shahryar's tent, she reads to her party from a volume of Paul Verlaine. Eric's French is rusty enough to shield him from the poet's more baroque indecencies.

Dans un palais, soie et or, dans Ecbatane,
De beaux démons, des satans adolescents,
Au son d'une musique mahométane,
Font litière aux Sept Péchés de leurs cinq sens.

Good grief.

The Ministry of Shipping has written to Eric requesting that he hand over his merchant fleet to the British authorities under a demise charter. They're uncomfortable to be entrusting sensitive military and industrial surpluses to a fleet owned by a foreign national.

Ronald Cross turned up in person today: a young, smiling, insufferably self-confident Old Etonian, chopping logic as though the pair of them were at a school debate. 'Mr Moyse, British registered companies control your ships!'

'They have majority voting rights. They don't have the right to interfere in management.'

'But –'

'Given what you have been asking me to manage,' Eric says, fed up with this, 'I would have thought the English expression "over a barrel" would serve quite nicely here.'

'I must say –'

'For example, the ships you're talking about are actually owned by *Panamanian* companies.'

'But –'

'For example, the major shareholders in the British companies you speak of are *Norwegians*.'

Too hot. Too strong.

'Look –' Laying down the law to a minister of His Majesty's government. No wonder they won't give him his permit to travel to America. 'Look, I'm not against you having the ships. Sign a bloody time charter like everybody else.'

When he is not getting into arguments with the British government,

Eric spends his hours looking for Vibeke Dunfjeld. There is no word from her and no report of her from fishermen crossing from the Lofotens. She has surely reached London by now! Dowdy men in frayed suits show no special discretion as they follow Eric out of the hotel and on to trams bound east for Deptford and Bermondsey and Rotherhithe. They haunt his passage from wharf to wharf, church to church, mission to mission. He has half a mind to confront them – 'If you're being paid to shadow me, you may as well help me' – but he won't. Vibeke Dunfjeld is his affair.

Pamela Harriman slides in beside him under the dining table. He feels her warmth, her static charge of sex. How old is she? Not as young as the role she plays: the flighty, precocious schoolgirl of many a middle-aged MP's fantasy. She lays a cool hand on his. 'My dear,' she whispers. She knows his story. His dramatic escape from Norway. His troubles with the authorities. His hunt for his fiancée. Under cover of intrigue and sympathy, she flirts with him. 'Any news of Miss Dunfjeld?'

Everybody knows she's Churchill's spy, his eyes and ears in the bedrooms of this staff officer, that politician. It is impossible to resent her and only an invert could resist her, although a cool eye might register, in the conscientious way she feminizes every gesture, that sex has become an act she performs more than a quality she embodies. 'No news? Oh, my poor dear.' She squeezes his hand. The hot response of his loins to this simple gesture is so abrupt, so mechanical, he feels no more real than a puppet. He wonders at this appetite he has acquired for the women of the Dorchester. Pamela Harriman. Nancy Cunard. Women who know what it is to be feminine, who understand its power and wield it well. They have been taught about it, trained up to it, as to a birthright.

He thinks about Vibeke. This girl he took under his wing. This girl he shaped so strangely. He has always assumed that what he did with her was motivated by care, even love. The cameras. The maps. Papers in the *Geografisk Tidsskrift*. Lying in the arms of the women of the Dorchester, he can no longer be so sure of his motives. What, after all, did Vibeke become in the end? (He has begun, unconsciously, to think of her in the past tense.) A vagabond. A woman closer to her animals and birds than to the people of the islands. An Arctic nymph – or an Arctic witch. A scarfed girl shod in heavy boots. Not feminine at all.

This is what keeps him awake, troubled and oh-so-fascinatingly mysterious between the sheets. The thought that all his care and encouragement of Vibeke Dunfjeld might after all have been directed against her sex, against her power, against her womanhood. That he took a girl he was afraid of loving and year by year made her unlovable.

A bomb lands near the building. Light wheels, sunlight under water, as the chandeliers swing. Another explosion whomps the dining room. A plate topples off the edge and lands on the floor by Eric's hand. Instinctively he catches it as it bounces. It pulses for a second between his fingers as though it were made of rubber. The harmonics die away, damped in his thick-fingered grip, leaving him holding a dish greasy with turbot and cheese.

There is applause.

Eric thinks of his smart, chilly bedroom on the roof, thinner-walled, and several degrees colder, than the apartments below. He says: 'I wonder if my room will survive.'

Pamela's little voice is hot in his ear: 'I shouldn't worry about that tonight, dear.'

Wharfingers with hooks for hands beetle four-limbed among the boxes, barrels and bails of Tooley Street. Case-hooks of hardened steel, split-handled, piratical and huge, tug and trawl the city's goods about its rumbling yards. Hands of leather, gristle, chipped bone and scar tissue wield hooks aloft, careless and savage, as shifts retire and shifts awake: ceaseless waves of burdened men. Gutters run with weak beer, vomit, essences, sump oil, spit. From Tooley Street, Eric Moyse makes desultory sorties into the terraces: a nervous stranger with a thick accent, apologetic and uncomfortable. Resting wharfingers and cracked old men, oblivious so far to the injunctions posted up on public buildings – 'Keep mum she's not so dumb!', 'Talk less, you never know!' – whisper behind his back and cast around, uneasy, for the nearest policeman.

They should recognize Eric by now. He comes here three times a week at least to explore and explain, traipsing back and forth from London Bridge to Rotherhithe, Shad Thames to the Old Kent Road: anywhere there's a knot of refugee Norse blood. It is a solitary and dispiriting business to be hunting one woman in a city of exiles and refugees, firewatchers, fantasists, Blimpish ex-cavalrymen, calculators, damp-handed cadets. Hopeless, anyway, to be looking for Vibeke as though she were some child mislaid in a market! She might be anywhere. Processing refugees in Fife. Translating decrypts in some nameless Nissen hut in the home counties.

So, steadily, inexorably, Eric's original quest falls away and his visits to this 'little Norway' acquire their own justification. He learns his way around the streets of Bermondsey and Rotherhithe by smell. Lavender from Yardley's. Fruit from Hartley's. Baking from Peek Frean's. Over all, the stench of tanneries. Walking by wharfs and factories, breathing the spicy miasma of lime and decay spilling from James Garner and Sons and Barrow, Hepburn and Gale, Eric finds himself ever more at ease in this place. Something draws him here. Some as yet unformed idea. A magnetism. A hope.

On Tower Bridge Road, at the mouths of alleys and in the porticoes of defunct shops, local children, saving up for Saturday's tuppenny rush at the cinema, build grottoes out of fruit boxes lined with shredded grass. They arrange daisies and dandelions in small vases filched from their mothers' mantelpieces. They prop holy pictures, even cigarette cards, behind a stub of candle. They sit by their shrines like sadhus. It is a form of begging: they kick the grottoes to pieces and scamper off if a policeman happens by.

In the shadow of a railway viaduct a different kind of grotto is tended by two boys – twins, by the look of them, wilder than the rest and darker-skinned. They have no pictures, no candles. They create no mood. The boys are obviously idiots. They have grasped that their crate is a kind of box and that boxes are for putting things in, but that's as far as their arrested understanding takes them. One fills their crate with shoeboxes and the other fills the shoeboxes with matchboxes. They have no jar, and were you to drop a copper or two on the pavement beside them – Eric has done this, many times – they will either ignore it or, less often, one will pick it up and slip it into a matchbox, one coin per matchbox, as though preparing the apparatus for a complex three-dimensional game.

Eric, fascinated, hunkers down to watch. The boys stack and fill their boxes methodically. Boxes in boxes in boxes. Eric stares. Something is taking shape inside him: a bright new idea that will propel him beyond the confines of this silly war and into the future.

The sirens sound.

The street is already emptied out. (The locals have their own, private early warning system: old men sit in their backyards, watching air-raid signals shuttling up the railway lines from Kent.) Eric stands. The nearest shelter's obvious enough: the viaduct's only a few yards off. 'Come on!'

The twins, oblivious, persevere with their little boxes, their shrine to who knows what private divinity.

Evening has gathered, yellowing the sky, stripping the blue from every shadow. The first detonations shiver the air: the guns in Southwark Park have opened up. Shadows shimmy across the road. A warden springs out at him, waving his arms. The blast is so close Eric doesn't even hear it and the warden vanishes in a cloud so white it must be flour.

Eric turns back towards the boys and their grotto. The children have vanished. A wriggle of shadow cees and esses around their shrine: their perfect cube, their intricate, perfectly squared-off stack of boxes. The shadow vanishes. The air stinks of vinegar. Eric walks through clouds of pearly white. There are bells. White figures move amidst the clouds. Some are on fire. He finds himself on Tower Bridge. In the river, just a few hundred yards away, a boat is burning fiercely. He retreats.

In Tooley Street, London's larder fries in coconut oil, palm oil, fat. Walls of yellow heat corral him into reservoirs of smoking grain and bails of burning twigs. Drums and barrels burst and jump, cartoon-like, at his approach. Canvas sheets flame and spin like Hollywood dancers. All the variety of the material world sings to him.

Another blast, very close, hurls him to his knees. He cannot breathe.

The mess and chaos of the port, its complexity and industry, evaporate before the flames and, with a terrible abruptness, the whole landscape flips, like one of those trick geometrical figures, into something mean and disordered: a rubbish tip on fire.

The air rushes in from behind, urging Eric towards the flames' bright centre. He knows he must run. He cannot move. He is fixed to the spot by a strange and burdensome thought. The fire will sweep all this away. These heaps and stacks and barrows of jumbled stuff. It will clean the slate for a more ordered world. A cleaner trade. Contained. No stench of sweat, no broken limbs, no sores, no sprains. No ham-boned supermen rolling drunk of a Friday night on wages that their children never see.

The future, when it comes, will come in boxes. From port to port, big, square-built ships will carry ever bigger quantities of the future about the earth. Great cranes will lift the future from open holds and deposit it on trucks and railway locomotives, and they will bear the future inland, to every town, every settlement. Ships that today are shackled, constipated, squeezing out their goods for weeks on end on the backs of men made beasts, will then evacuate themselves in a matter of hours! Eric pictures them: great tanker hulls converted to dry storage . . .

For a moment, the white core of the fire is obscured by smoke as thick and black as ink dropped in water. An autumnal smell – burning stubble-fields – sweeps thickly over him, as though the season itself were come to carry him out of time. Eric finds his feet and staggers, propelled towards the future. Boxes. Boxes and boxes and boxes in boxes, boxes everywhere and every box the same. He falls to his knees, buckling under the weight of his vision, and crawls through the litter of the old world: swatches of banana hemp and drifts of ash and the stubs of hand-rolled cigarettes and burlap threads and, here and there, surreal and precious, the greenish heads of discarded pub-lunch prawns. He has to stand. He lies with his back against the rippling tar of the road while heat rolls over him like blankets. He has to sleep. The vision is bigger than he is. It overcomes him.

Presently, out of the rain of ash, the red drizzle of molten shrapnel, something else impends. A tower. A statue. An angel. 'Moyse?'

Something human. Vast. Red.

'Eric!'

Stalin. Satan. A red death.

'Eric, come on! Come *on* . . .' A bearded balloon swims drunkenly toward him. Two eyes veer and vanish. Eric feels himself gripped under the arms. A ring around his chest. He's lifted. He staggers as an invisible muscle rasps round him, round and round, drawing him clear of the sucking blaze. His heels drag against hot cobblestones. He feels under him, around him, a muscular labour, as though a motor were trying to drive his hull of flesh out of its doldrum channel and into clear water, and it comes to him, by some faint signature of breath and muscular rhythm, that this figure is a man, a man he knows. If only he could –

'Eric! Heaven's sake, move!'

Eric struggles and frees himself. He kneels and wraps frail arms around his old friend's legs. 'Oh . . .' He looks up through his tears, blinks salt and ash away and there, haloed by the bright sulphurous light of the future, is Peder Halstad.

Part Three

NINE

Sion: a suburb of Mumbai.

Centuries ago the Jesuits built a chapel here and named it after Mount Zion in Jerusalem. The chapel has vanished, and even the British fort on its hill, which once marked the boundary between Bombay and Salsette Island, is vandalized and done, its few remaining timbers scored and scorched. Close your eyes. The drone of the Eastern Express Highway competes with the rustle of used prophylactics. Open them. Woods. Parrots. Broken paths and exposed plumbing.

To the east, in the shadow of the K. J. Somaiya Institute of Engineering and Information Technology, a slum line sheathes the railway line to Chunabhatti. To the west, suburbs nibble like a grey leprosy at the skirts of Maharashtra Nature Park.

The dead boys, Abhik and Kaneer, becalmed, take the chapel for their own and lick their wounds with a forked tongue. They are accomplished djinn by now. They shape the narratives through which they flow. Still, their parents' murder remains an open wound: a mystery they cannot yet explain.

Lovely Auntie Roopa has rented a cramped apartment for herself and her son overlooking the rain trees and casual cricketers of Shivaji Park. The plumbing here is bad: she has to wait until 2.00 a.m. to have a shit. Day after day, while Nitesh is hauled, at some expense, from one bin to another – nursery, breakfast club, supper club, homework club, school – Roopa sits slumped in front of the television. The TV is the family that no longer speaks to her. The TV is the circle of friends she no longer has.

Now and again she dabs at her ruined mouth with a balled-up tissue. Her spit comes away pink as fragments of tooth circulate in her gums.

Her dentures lie forgotten in the bottom of a drawer. She watches movies. Bollywood noirs. Frustrated at her inaction, her defeat, Abhik and Kaneer break her television. It's an old cathode-ray tube model, and it takes no more than a tail-flick to damage the set.

And if this was the kind of movie Roopa spends her days watching, there would be an important beat here. The dead boys would rip off the back of the set and there, tucked into the housing, taped there, would be a brand-new Glock wrapped in an oilcloth and about one hundred thousand rupees in small denomination bills. The discovery would signal a new act.

This is not a movie. The boys achieve precisely nothing. The first thing Roopa does when she discovers the TV isn't working is to phone the rental company. By lunchtime there they are again, Auntie Roopa, baby Nitesh, dead Abhik, dead Kaneer, eating *vada pav* sandwiches in front of an LG flat-screen, watching a rerun of *The Stoneman Murders*. Vikram Gokhale plays Roopa's dad.

The green Honda is gone. Vinod is gone. Yash Yadav himself is gone: disappeared, scot-free. As for mum and dad, no one living even brings them to mind any more. The Nankars may as well have never lived. What more can Roopa do? There's only so much that djinn can ask of one small, broken woman.

Feeling sorry for themselves, Abhik and Kaneer take themselves off again to the ruins of the Chapel of Zion and curl up in the litter there. Bags of glue. Old needles. Shitty tissues. Shattered rum bottles. Glass flecks sting the eyes and disturb the sleep of every glue-sniffing vagrant who passes out in this place.

'I told her to make the chapattis and then, when she was leaning over the bowl, kneading the dough, I took the pan from the wall and I lifted it over my head and I brought it down on her head and it rang like a bell.'

The boys flex, steeped in horror and pity, and the failure of the world.

'I expected her to fall over. That was the idea. To fall over empty, eyes shut. She didn't fall over. She leant there over the bowl, like she was waiting. Then she wailed. She lifted her hands and they looked wrong, like an old woman's hands, because they were covered in wet dough. She put her hands around my waist and called me darling.'

The boys wrap themselves around each other, weeping bright and bitter tears.

'I got the kerosene from out the corner and the cap came off easily enough and I upended it over her, wanting it to be done, for a line to be drawn. But I couldn't find the matches. She was moving about the room on all fours, her sari was getting in her way, it was caught under her knees, she could only move her arms, she was turning around and around like she had lost something, and I said to her, "Where are the matches?" I noticed that she was breathing in this strange way, like she was straining the air through her teeth. Anyway, I found the matches.'

All Abhik and Kaneer ever wanted was stories and hot milk. Cuddles now and then. A warm pallet. They've got stories now, all right.

'By this time she had got around the whole room on all fours, spreading the kerosene, so when I dropped the match on her the fire spilled off her on to the floor and the whole room went up, pushing me out of the room, and the worst of it is she is following me, she's standing in the doorway, burning, her hands, burning, pressed either side of the doorframe, and her head, burning, smoking like a chimney, the hair all gone, her eyes gone like cooked eggs but moving and her skin all white.'

Stories are their lifeblood now, their oxygen, their life support. Stories are their home. Their bricks. Their clay.

'She came into the room. Very gentle tread she had. Small feet. The room was filling with smoke, black, tarry, tasty, it rolled over her head. Wild it was, and when it went it was like it left this doll behind, and it was this doll came knelt down in front of me. Well, I forgot myself. And I did this thing. Look. I laid it on her head, you see, laid it there as though she were still my wife. Even though it was burning. Even though there was nothing there. Bone. Aah –' He gasps, hiding his face behind a crummy hand.

'What?'

'Nothing.' Ogan blinks, smearing his useless hand across a stubbled cheek. 'Got something in my eye.'

Saturday, 12 February, 2000: eight in the morning

Ogan Seth, wife-killer, flees to Mumbai's port area. Hiding his ruined hand under bandages and blarney, he talks his way aboard a dhow bound across the Indian Ocean for Muscat, in Oman. Fabrics, mainly. Spices. Machine parts. Break bulk. 'You'll have to sleep on deck.'

'Okay.'

'Under that Hilux there,'

'Okay.'

'I'll give you passage. Food. No pay.'

'Okay.'

'Sign here.'

Easy. Ogan's mark, his 'X', is much the same whichever hand he writes with.

'You've a bedroll?'

'No.'

'Well. See what you can find.'

At night Ogan lies, whimpering and sleepless, wrapped inside an 'antique' rug.

(Rug / US$22.4 SQF / 168 SQF)

The boat's dangerously overloaded, of course. The way it wallows whenever there's a chop puts Ogan in mind of horses struggling across a river, nostrils flaring, in the curry westerns he used to enjoy with his wife when –

Anyway.

Captain Egaz Nageen's a Thai who barely knows port from starboard. For sure, his paperwork's a forge or fudge. He spends all day studying seamanship manuals when he thinks no one is looking.

- Speak loudly and clearly when delivering your report.
- Even if you cannot properly identify the object seen smelled or heard say what you think at that moment.
- When searching for an object scan the sky the sea and the horizon from left to right and from top to bottom and from bottom to top and from right to left and back again.
- Remain at the helm until entirely relieved.

No one's fooled.

The voyage is peaceful enough, but the engine's underperforming and the crossing takes the best part of a week. Nageen says they'll put in at Ras al Hadd to resupply. It turns out he's always had this trip in mind, that he fancies himself as some sort of self-educated world traveller. A stolen library book, concealed among his clothes, says:

> Exhausted and demoralized by the sheer scale of the world they had hoped to conquer, the sheer numbing on-and-on-ness of everything, Alexander the Great and his expeditionary force returned at last, victorious yet self-defeated, and Niacus, Alexander's admiral, laid up the whole fleet in Ras al Hadd to slap on lime.

A dull time they must have had of it, too. Gravel hills. Green inlets. Sinking sands. The beaches are made of puffer-fish needles and oyster shells. After so many days, so many nights being slowly squeezed inside his brightly coloured, rasping rug (its colours strangely persistent in the night, as though the stuff were flecked with glass), Ogan decides to stretch his legs. He wobbles down the wooden jetty and follows the spoor of a wild fox to an abandoned seaplane-refuelling depot on the other side of the hill: '1933' above its door. Inside, under a large, rusted but still serviceable fuel tank, there is a buoy and a curl of fuel hose. Ogan, grateful for the shade, shuffles in. Under the buoy, Ogan finds a thing.

Some sort of thing. Red leather. Nasty. There's a tuck, a fold, he prises out a flap of leather, and inside there is a book, done in the same sickly red skin. Worth a bob or two, he's sure. He turns the pages. Pictures. Scales and fangs and eyes. Strange.

He leaves the fuel shed to examine the find more closely.

Alexander's hoplites leap to their feet, startled, and brandish their swords in his face. They are young: more boys than men. There's not a greybeard among them. They howl, peeling their lips back over blackened gums. Teeth, too, are in short supply. Ogan runs away screaming, pursued by catapulted stones and the spears of hula-skirted hypaspists. Overhead, other histories contend for domination of the skies. Avro 501s, held together with piano wire and prayer, wrestle in the turbulence kicked up by full-throated Rochester-built Short Cs. Oblivious to mankind's future conquest of the air, a party of unarmed Napoleonic expeditionaries are lovingly buggering each other in the shallows, hands copper-green with the soft coral to which they cling while, on a small table of flat rock just above them, plump Mesopotamian princesses sprawl on leopard-fur chaises longues, sipping sherbets under parasols of finely beaten human skin, and the air fills with a complex stench made of sweat, horse dung, aviation fuel, cooked oysters, rancid asses' milk and cordite.

The boys have ripped Ogan out of time. They have spread him thinly through history. They are doing this in part because they think he deserves it; mostly, they are doing it because they can. Ogan's not the only one who's been feeling restive after a long voyage.

A twofold and terrible djinn snaps at his heels as Ogan, alive at last to the majesty and tragedy of the human condition, scampers back to his ship, bursting with the need to atone for his paltry sins and misspent life. Returned seamlessly to present time, he runs the length of the jetty and flings himself upon his knees before Nageen, his master.

'Sir, do your duty: *I have seen the error of my ways*!'

He's sure as hell seen something's put the fear of God in him. Nageen sighs. He's just this second stepped on to dry land. His head's a-swim with nautical bullet points and handy ship-shape tricks, cheats and hints. Catechisms. Acronyms: ATON, LOB, POB, POD. He's clinging to his command by the skin of his teeth here. His only real nautical experience has been how to squat in the bows of a patched RIB, intimidating South Korean trawlers with a knock-off AK-56. He's done with all that, but the climb from there to here has been vast and scary. He's never crossed a whole ocean before today and there's no one to toast his achievement: just this lunatic sprung from the pages of a *Boy's Own* annual.

'Clap me in irons, begad!'

More likely (given the cost and weight of ferrous metals) the most this poor, deranged sod can expect is cable ties and a trip to the nearest hospital.

'I have killed! I have gone and besmirched my very soul!' Ordinary Seaman Ogan Seth has eyes that dance with rainbow light. A schizophrenic. All that Nageen needs.

Now that they've had their fun, Abhik and Kaneer withdraw. Playing up to everyone's idea of an angry and vengeful God is amusing, so far as it goes, but there's something much more urgent they have to deal with.

The red notebook.

They have seen this before – but where?

They arrive back at the fuel shed to find the book is gone. They go hunting about for it, dust-devilling their way into the past, but it is not there and soon even the buoy and the fuel hose are gone, deployed to fuel the seaplanes bobbing at anchor nearby. Further back and the fuel shed unbuilds itself, and there's still no sign of the red book.

They've come the wrong way. They've been looking for the book in the past. Rapidly they wind their way back to present time and into the future. Nine uneventful years scroll by before, all of a sudden, the book appears, beneath the buoy, dropped like an egg in a nest of decayed fuel hose.

They pause a moment, the book spread open between them, and gaze out of the door at the rocky platform, the empty sea, the jumbo jet-streaked sky. Nothing's changed much in nine years. Nothing's changed much in nine hundred years, come to that. The dry heat of the Middle

East swiftly disorders the past but it consumes nothing. There's no soil, no mulch, no mould to help things rot. There are oyster shells round here that Alexander's hypaspists cranked open, drank dry and threw aside.

The boys ruffle the pages of the strange red book that will one day be left here in the dark: a mystery why.

There are what look like games of snakes and ladders here. Ruler-straight arrows point up. Strange, sinusoidal lines sine down. There's writing, but it's hard to figure out. Passages have been scrawled crosswise over each other, offering more texture than sense. Stranger imagery, too: shamanic eyes and scales and fangs . . .

To Uncle Lothar
Wishing you a Merry Christmas
Vibeke

Now this almost never happens: that the boys are confronted with something stranger than they are. Cautiously they disentwine, letting go their sinusoidal form. The shed expands and blurs, its seams peel open, jetting blue light. In the dusty village, miles distant, that is Ras al Hadd's only habitation, cracked old men, flash-photographed against the mud walls of their houses, imagine that the old fuel dump has exploded –

But there is no sound and the light is gone almost as soon as it is noticed. A trick of the light, men say to each other, going on with their limited lives.

The fuel store, meanwhile, shrinks and comes back into focus. Its seams heal. Its mortar hardens. The blue light shrinks to a spark, a point, a full stop, locus *x* upon the graph. Pages turn and fan and blur . . .

The blow is so powerful, so fast, he does not see it coming. It all but decapitates him.

Gasping, lump-throated, Abhik and Kaneer reel away from Lothar Eling's Arctic agony, his death by polar bear, sweet fucking hell, *this* again!

Up until now the boys have not given much thought to the way other people's stories intersect with their own. Why would they? Stories weave their way around the earth, knotting themselves around each other as they go. Winds blow. Hearts desire. You may as profitably marvel at the way a point on one particular rice noodle edges up against a point on another rice noodle in a bowl of noodle soup. At a certain scale, coincidence is a given. A commonplace.

But to be brought back twice to Eling's lonely death: that's a hell of a lot of noodles. Or a very small bowl. For the first time in its existence, the twofold djinn feels restricted. Hemmed in. A plaything of coincidence rather than its master. What is it about this notebook? *What is it trying to say?*

The djinn coalesces and tries again. This time, it'll pick a different entrance point, a different owner. Entering a cold, dark, well-appointed house in Svolvaer, it hears

> *sides of cod chock-chocking as they dry on wooden racks, while inside, Eric Moyse rocks himself into uneasy dreams: the taste of krill, the flash of flensing knives.*

Dear heaven: *Moyse?* A name that's emblazoned on the world's every other shipping can!

> Eric Moyse, future founder of the shipping line, slumps in an old rocking chair before the stove. He wishes he did not have to go through it all again, but if the notebook belongs to anyone now it belongs to Eling's old professor, Jakob Dunfjeld.

Is that so? Well. The Djinn's not above taking sage advice. Once again it withdraws, regroups, needles in...

Monday, 8 April: four in the afternoon

Nearly four decades after he first demonstrated his mathematics to his peers at the University of Bonn, Professor Jakob Dunfjeld is in Copenhagen describing his academic odyssey to an audience of journalists and students. In his breast pocket, pressed hard against his chest, palpitating, a second heart: Eling's red notebook. It has become his constant companion.

In his youth, Jakob shared journal space with the greats: Hertz, Planck, Villard, Lorentz. Even now, with the old physics brushed away, he'll hold forth, quite unabashed, about 'the luminiferous aether'. In his lectures he lets the formalities drop and talks about Nothing. His little academical joke. 'Because "luminiferous aether", gentlemen, ladies, is Nothing clad in academical motley. All this talk of aether was only ever a sort of hand-waving, an act of prestidigitation, drawing attention away from the fact, gentlemen, ladies, that what we are actually talking about, make no mistake, is the structure of the Void . . .'

Nothing exists. Nothing – with a capital N. Between atom and atom. Between surface and surface. Nothing has to exist, or energy is trapped in matter, matter falls in upon itself, and the universe is reduced to a homogeneous dot. Nothing is the universal yeast, the cosmological baking soda, the air in God's balloons. 'There can be nothing, my friends, without Nothing!'

This is *greeted with polite laughter* and even *a smattering of applause.*

This Nothing, he goes on to say (the boys are riveted, to have their deep anatomy descried), this Nothing, being nothing, never gets in the way of Anything. Things move through Nothing and Nothing wraps itself around every Thing. 'In other words, Nothing is a fluid.'

At this point, among the more knowledgeable of his audience, there's a frisson of recognition. Because while Jakob was scrawling Nothing's drag and swirl on the blackboards of the Norwegian Physical Society – pictures reproduced in the pages of no less a publication than the *Zeitschrift* of the Königlich-Preußische Akademie der Wissenschaften – the edifice of that sort of physics was already crumbling beneath the predictive weight of special relativity.

Jakob came off better than most when the old guard was swept aside: 'It was as I was explaining the hydrodynamics of magnetic attraction and repulsion in mathematical terms to ever emptier lecture halls, that

I discovered vortices occurring at the boundary layer between the magnetic body and the surrounding fluid. Now, at first I found these vortices a great nuisance! Neither Hertz nor Kelvin ran into them. But then, neither man had ever admitted the possibility that the density of the fluid is dynamic, responding to several variables at once. Let that be the case, and circulation will arise in even a perfectly homogeneous fluid!' Not his words. Eling's. Eling saw it first. Eling realized how it all tied together. After years of study, and too late. The red notebook drags inside his jacket. Absently he lays his hand on his heart as though taking an oath. Perhaps he is. 'This is the point, gentlemen, ladies, this is the crux: *turbulence, even in an ideal fluid, is inevitable*.'

After his lecture, Jakob dines alone and catches the Malmö ferry to connect with the night train to Oslo. The sleeper cabin's curlicued brass light fittings and its paisley pillowcases only serve to remind the old and ailing professor how far he is from resting on solid earth. There is nothing to see out of the window. Were it not for the rhythm of wheel on rail, he might be dropping through the Void.

He closes his eyes and almost immediately – this is how it seems – the guard is hammering on his door. He opens his eyes. Light bleeds in behind the blind. It is morning. He sits up, pulls up the blind and leans his head against the window, using the vibration and the cold glass against his forehead to wake him up. He blinks blearily at Oslo's suburbs.

About two minutes outside the station, the train shudders to a halt. In the skies above the city centre, the Norwegian air force is putting on a show. About bloody time, is Jakob's bleak judgement. Given the hostile forces ranged against them across the Skagerrak.

He has pretty much given up hope of meeting the connecting train and is pulling out his pen and a letter to his daughter Vibeke –

> It still rankles that the editors of the *Zeitschrift* won't let me redub it the 'Dunfjeld–Eling theorem'. My study of his notes doesn't justify the change, apparently. 'Dunfjeld theorem' indeed. Indifference dressed as flattery.

– when the wheels beneath him give a lurch and the train putters forward into the station. Jakob steps down from his carriage and looks around for a porter. Which way is the baggage car?

Ahead of him, part of the station's ceiling explodes into fragments, showering the platform with glass. The crowd pulses and heaves as a single body. Jakob staggers. A woman screams. In the aftermath Jakob hears an aeroplane's engine, receding at speed, and it comes to him as a single thought, prepackaged and entire: not the Norwegian air force; the German one.

At the station's entrance commuters gather, looking out at the stalled and deserted intersections of Biskop Gunnerus gate, more as though assessing a rain shower than the air cover to an occupation. Jakob eases past them and heads west. Walking through the besieged city carries with it a perverse air of freedom amounting almost to vertigo. His shadow is a long figure laid out before him by the early morning sun, like an arrow for him to follow. Gunfire from the planes circling above his head is sporadic and, being directed at nothing in particular, it reminds him most of all of those scenes in the western serials he so much enjoys, when the villains ride into town firing their six-shooters into the air.

He walks calmly along empty roads. He is excited – but it is a species of excitement experienced in a dream, something disconnected from the will. (Already, he is dying.) He reaches the road that leads to Holmenkollen. The traffic here is heavier. Jakob holds out his hand, begging a lift. It will be his first act under the new dispensation. The thought of hitching a lift excites him even more than the fact of the invasion. He dreams up a stirring line for his diary tonight: We are all Adams in these first hours. We are all heroes, drunk on the possibility of action.

(In fourteen hours he will be dead.)

Home at last, he picks up the phone. The lines to Bergen and Narvik are down. He asks for the Oslo number of an acquaintance, another professor, of chemistry: 'Steitzl.'

'There are about a thousand German paratroopers parading through the centre of Oslo, I can see them from my window.'

'Paratroopers?'

'*Yes.*'

'What's it like?'

'Like? A thousand German paratroopers marching through Karl Johans gate? This requires metaphor?'

'What are we going to do?'

'Do? I'm going to tell you and the telephone operator what we should do? An operator who's by now been replaced by some well-scrubbed Berlin bierkeller tart? Good evening, Fräulein! And as for you, you old ass, get off the bloody blower before she takes your platitudes for some sort of code.'

At night, in his tiny cuboid bedroom, and as the time of his extinction approaches, Professor Jakob Dunfjeld dreams of a place with nothing in it. No matter. No heat. No energy. Nothing: not even light.

Waking, he clings to his dream. Picture it: unobserved and unobservable – perfect Void!

There is a heaviness in Jakob's chest. A pressing, breathless mass. He imagines it not as it actually is – a cancer, fluid welling in a stinking lung – but as primordial matter expanding at the moment of the world's beginning. It is a process that is almost purely mathematical: a rapid inflation of the nothingness that yawns between the components of matter. A stretching of distances.

It comforts Jakob, in the time of his dying, to think that things are clouds. Waking in the middle of the night, slathered in sweat, mouth and nostrils hot with the smell of it, he sits up, trying to control his breathing.

He sits on the edge of his bed, shivering, trying to get his breath. His dressing gown lies at his feet: a pool of deeper darkness in the unlit room. He cannot reach down to it. He will have to kneel.

So, he kneels.

Gently, the boys assist. They dull his pain. They sing to him, this good old man, this clever, disappointed man: how things are clouds.

Strange, that this should have become a prayer for him. To whom is he praying? The question is false. God is everywhere, interpenetrating matter and energy. So prayer is intransitive. I live. I pray. I die. Short sentences. Easy sentiments for the short of breath. All youthful lyric put away. Haiku his limit. He leans forward and coughs. Nothing comes. He waits for his breathing to begin again. He waits for his body to remember – and it does.

His arm jams in his dressing gown. He hasn't the strength to yank his hand past the twist in the sleeve. He stands, his arm twisted up and back, bird with broken wing. The boys are good at knots: the sleeve unravels, letting him in. It enfolds him. He does up his dressing gown with shaking hands. He is fifty-four years old and he is going to die, very soon now. Nothing two little boys can do about that.

He lights a lamp and carries it, hobbling, down endless stairs, into the ice-cave of his living room. The living space in this house is so big, the other rooms so impractically small, that he has been obliged to take a part of the living room for his study. His work space realizes a fantasy of accomplished old age. A big oak desk. On it, stained and dog-eared, Eling's ugly little notebook, still a source of fascination.

> The oceans will not cease to turn, nor the winds to blow—

A wing-back chair. The bear skin before the fire is so big and so white it is hard to credit, but it is real enough: one of Eric Moyse's youthful trophies. A gift. The effect of these things, cramped together for cosiness, and with no regard to the rest of the room, suggests a film set erected in the corner of a giant sound stage. Still, it is impressive.

The shelves are lined with books and journals. *Physikalische Zeitschrift*. *Die Naturwissenschaften*. Just look at him: the would-be geometer of the universe, become a human weathervane, a seer of herring! Still, it is a considerable accomplishment, worth more than a footnote in the history of science, to be the one to say why the winds blow and the oceans turn.

Shivering, Professor Jakob Dunfjeld unlaces his gown. He lets it drop on the floor. He nudges his nightshirt past his belly, his chest, gets it up under his arms and begins the painful process of getting the thing over his head. His chest feels sore and stretched: a container. Certain small, hard animals are groping blindly about in there.

He lies face-down across the bear skin, naked, and the fur's warmth reaches up for him. This good old man. The boys, touched by his tale, weave a little spell for him. Their genial gift. Fur grows up around him, soft, as sweet as grass, as he descends.

Now who is this, rifling the pages of the holy notebook? Why, it's his daughter, little Vibeke! Not so little now, of course. Aged and coarsened by her years of exploration. Toughened and at the same time made strangely merry by so many vagrant adventures. She's come back south to Oslo on a sad and necessary mission, and in the teeth of the spreading Nazi bureaucracy, to sort out her dead father's effects. This clever, kind old man: she sits and weeps a while. He was both mum and dad to her: a debt not meant to be repaid; meant to be borne. She'll bear it, heavy as it is, with pride. This lovely, funny, sad old man: her dad.

She boxes up his papers. She invites men she trusts, old colleagues of her father, to bear away his life's work and curate it as best they can. She writes letters to banks, solicitors, foreign institutions. Finally, and grudgingly, she fills out the necessary forms, telling the Quisling state the least it needs to know. All done, she pockets the red notebook: a keepsake for her on her journey – and vanishes into the north.

Two dead boys slither after her.

Saturday, 1 January 1944: six in the morning

In Norway's far north, morning is indistinguishable from deep midnight except that at this hour the air is colder, heavy with freezing dew. This is a place the old maps have down as Lapland. Inside the tent, safe behind walls of hide and lichen, Vibeke wakes to the nausea of her pregnancy.

In such utter darkness, to reorient yourself is an act of will: the recreation of the world. Vibeke imagines into being the dimensions of the shelter surrounding her. She listens, and out of the scrape and hiss of dormant branches she unpicks the distant lap and trickle of a stream of meltwater. She imagines the path to the stream. A fallen trunk. A patch of bog. A clearing. She imagines the stone circle and the fire on which the water is heated. The vessels in which it boils. Breakfast. Little by little, she builds a world to wake to, then sits up, tugs hides and blankets around her against the chill. She picks the moss out of her hair and concentrates on her breathing. The cold will ease the swimminess in her guts: she has only to breathe and wait.

The air in the tent is damp and thick. There are half a dozen sleepers in here with her. Sightless, night-blind, in her mind she contemplates her companions – sleepy and yet observant, one of them and yet apart, a refugee with Oslo eyes and brain, cast up by the war among these Arctic people.

The Lapps are a small, inquisitive lot, slow to smile. They treat outsiders with more curiosity than kindness. Nonetheless, they have taken to her.

Impossible to say why she never thought to come to an accommodation with the invader. She has no pressing love of nation. Her father was once the intellectual darling of Vienna, for heaven's sake. Not that her background need have come into it. All she ever had to do was pay a visit to Austvågøy's chief of police, Herr Birkeland. So what if he's a Quisling man? She imagines herself swapping notes with him on the nesting habits of shrike, the mating calls of fieldfares. Birkeland the tyrant, Herr Birkeland the jackbooted oppressor, is, when all is said and done, a local man. A bird-spotter! She's known him for years. She's shown him her drawings before now; he's as easily awed as a child. On Birkeland's say-so she could be living out the war in Eric Moyse's house. It is there for her use, after all. Clean sheets, and money in the drawer.

At the same time, she knows that none of this has ever been possible. There has never been any chance for her to remain in the Lofotens: not living as she chooses to live, the fairy of the ferns. Invading armies do not believe in fairies. Invading armies fear the footloose and the indigent. The casual labourer with his bag full of arcane tools. The wagon with its indeterminate load of men and food and fuel. For the same reason it has never occurred to her to fall in with Eric Moyse's escape plan either. What has England for her now? Only its own set of suspicions, regulations, restrictions, expectations. Easier for her to embrace the wild life she has been courting ever since she came to the Lofotens. Easier, by far, to travel north!

In Tromsø she found work as a teacher. It wasn't very satisfying. The little Lapp children didn't speak Norwegian and when she tried talking to them in their own language the school administrator told her that teaching in Samí was forbidden. She had to ask him: What's Samí?

'You've just got to keep speaking Norwegian,' he told her. 'They'll learn in the end.' Of course, they didn't learn.

She sits up in the dark, groping for the red notebook. Blindly, she scrawls with a burnt twig across its pages, in the style of a palimpsest:

> Downy birch forms the treeline, often 200m above the other species. Rowan, aspen, willow, grey alder, and bird cherry are common in lower elevations.
>
> Elk, red fox, hare, stoat and small rodents. Small bears in summer.

A nice irony this: the German invaders understood her. They were sympathetic. They were good boys, well-brought-up young boys: responsive to her civility. On her walks she was careful never to startle their lacklustre patrols, sure always to explain herself truthfully and fully to the miserable, half-frozen lads manning the checkpoints. They were, after all, her father's kind of people. Officers of the Twentieth Mountain Army, lonely and miserable in their chilly exile. Beguiled by her perfect German, her talk of Vienna and Bonn, they fed and clothed her more than the hatchet-faced fishwives of Tromsø ever did.

What she never expected, until it was too late, was the degree to which one or two of them might beguile her. Once or twice it happened that an officer induced her to slide off the stockings he'd given her: a hiss indistinguishable from a sigh. Such well-behaved young men!

The school fell apart. More and more men were billetted on the town against the threat of Russian counter-invasion. Soon the school was full of soldiers and there wasn't any room for the children. An order went out telling children to collect moss and leaves, medicinal plants, tea plants – that this outdoor work counted as schooling. Winter came and the school closed altogether: a 'fuel holiday', they said. Since by then the Lapp children she was teaching had neither clothes nor shoes, Vibeke knew it was over. So she followed the children. Together they collected moss and leaves, they collected medicines and tea plants, and, heading east, at last the children led her to the hidden places they called home. Look at our strange, pale friend! Ma! Pa! Look at our prize!

Come late spring, Vibeke, round-bellied, heavy with her firstborn, follows the clan east. They eke out a living in a lonely, colourless land of mosquito-ridden bogs and lakes. Human dwellings fall far behind them. They lay traps for wading birds and wild ducks. Not having game, they survive on bilberries boiled in salt water and occasionally on sorrel plants. Vibeke gives birth to a son, evacuating him into a nest of moss and lichen and feathers while the men sit a little way off and – for her sake, she likes to think, though chances are they're quite oblivious – sing slowly, bearing each syllable deep in the throat, and with a kind of boiling anger that never seems to go anywhere until it peters away at last, worn through by constant repetition.

She falls ill. For a long time she is silly with fever and cares only for the sight of her child. Her recovery is slow, so that this life of hers comes back to her in fragments, newly minted: no longer an experiment in living, but a life. Not a wilderness: a world.

In crabbed charcoal-ash shorthand, Vibeke sets down her adventures. The red notebook is virtually unreadable now to any but the most conscientious cryptographer. Her camp-mates watch her, dubious, as she hatches at that strange red fetish of hers and Vibeke records, as well and as economically as she can, her travels with these remote people: what she's seen and heard and done with them. Torrential mountain rivers strewn with great chunks of ice. Tracts of boulder-covered wilderness.

Closing the book, she bends to study her infant, stirring in his willow cot; at two years a beauty, trusting, eager to please: half-German child. Strange, that happiness should come upon her here, impoverished, unwed, and a mother – but is this not the happiness she has been moving towards all these years, since Eric Moyse, her patron, set her the task of recording the life of his Arctic home?

Faithful to her task, she's found a hidden treasure here: a way of observing that is, at the same time, a way of living. A freedom from society's absurdities that is, surely, a higher and more responsible way of being. A primitive life that, through its very directness, becomes a kind of science. She wishes she had the room and symbology to write all this down. Then again, by restricting herself to a brutally curtailed shorthand, does she not observe all the harder? Is her memory not keener, her understanding sharper? Neither has it escaped her notice that, the more observant and analytical she becomes, the more she resembles her companions – the bright-eyed, silent Sami with their furs and fires and elk.

Civilization has been dislocated by the war. It is possible that she will never see it again – at least, not in a form she would recognize.

There is a little light now. Grey motes finger their way between the overlapping hides of the shelter. Her companions, stirring out of sleep, turn and stretch under their blankets. Vibeke imagines herself surrounded by grey waves: a human sea.

As she stares into her son's eyes, bright with winter half-light, Vibeke feels a great excitement. Here, she thinks, or whispers, or thinks she whispers. Here, little Havard, here is the world, and it is no one else's, not any more. They have all gone away. Here is the world. Yes, it is cold. Yes, it is hard. And – yes – it is ours.

TEN

At the end of the war Reindeer-Sami, Sea-Sami, homeless families, gypsies, bankrupt fishermen, Russian deserters, all varieties of human rubbish, sweep down the Norwegian seaboard, mile after mile of them, all the way to Ålesund.

The police find Vibeke squatting in a ruined farmhouse twenty miles inland from Narvik with 'a party of labouring men': jargon at once petty and lubricious. Once labelled a delinquent, Vibeke is fair game for a justice system struggling to reassert its authority after years of wartime compromise.

So Havard, Vibeke Dunfjeld's bastard son, grows up an orphan: one of hundreds shivering in camps in Trondenes and Finnfjordbotn. His schooling begins in a series of dilapidated coal sheds. Later he is taken to a mountain lodge in Lahpoluoppal where there are no lamps and only one wood saw. When Lahpoluoppal closes, defeated by the winter, he is transferred to Narvik.

By the time rescue comes, in the spring of 1951, Havard Dunfjeld is eight years old and has spent more years in the orphanage than he ever spent with his mother.

It is a rescue as fantastical as any of Havard's orphanage-driven dreams. 'Dunfjeld, you're wanted in the office.' He's suspicious. The solid world is teasing him. It is aping his desires – desires he knows can find their true fulfilment only in his imagination. True emissaries are faceless, they are nameless, but this one has both a name and a face. An absurd, rosy nubbin of a face, congenitally happy and with a voice to match: 'Hello!

I'm Peder Halstad!'

Havard stands there. Not shy. Unconvinced.

Peder asks the boy many questions. Havard finds it strange, having to justify himself to a man he half-suspects must be a hallucination.

'Tell me about your mother.'

Havard remembers rucksacks, axes and saws. A few books and blankets. Odd tools sequestered in abandoned cottages. He remembers wire nooses and dead rabbits. Wild garlic in the gullies. Black water under dripping trees. A dog snaps at orchids and covers herself in marsh mud. Stunted thorns grow out of the stones. 'We went out before sunrise to lift lobster pots. We sat on rocks with fishing lines tied to our toes. We hunted the shoreline for branches and hatch covers. Sometimes the fishing crews threw us fish.'

Peder Halstad offers to take Havard for a drive. 'What do you think of that?' How could he know that Havard has only ever been in a car once before? That it bore him away from his mother? That she screamed after him. That he struggled free and turned to look out of the back window in time to see her being slapped in the mouth. Norwegian social services, *circa* 1946. Pounding a sundered nation together.

Havard and Peder walk slowly, side by side, out of the building and across the yard, its cracked surface marked out for games Havard and his dorm-mates have never learned to play.

Peder Halstad says, 'I've an idea you might like.'

Here it comes.

'I work for a man in business. A shipping man.'

Havard has visions of running away to sea. Of spending years before the mast. A whaling ship!

'This man knew your mother. He was her friend. After the war he looked for her, but without success. We have not found her. We have found you.'

The implication – that he has become the grail these men seek, powerful men in powerful black cars – counts for less with Havard than mention of his mum. How 'not found'? How 'lost'?

'He knows you're here. I mean, he knows, I've told him, how you live here. How you are.'

'Can I see him?'

'Of course you can see him. It might take a while. He lives in New York.'

'In America!'

'And London. And Oslo. He travels.'

'Does he travel on aeroplanes?'

Peder smiles. 'Now and again.'

'He's rich?'

'His name is Eric Moyse.' Peder looks at Havard: he expects a reaction. 'You've not heard of him?' He opens the door of the car and Havard climbs in.

Four years go by.

It is 1955, and Havard's just finished his first semester of high school. He flies to Chicago's Midway Airport with Peder and Peder's wife, Judith – a woman who qualifies these days as 'Mum'. (Peder, mindful of his employer's interests, has never stood for 'Dad'.) A car is waiting at the airport to take them to the New Bismarck, and while Peder and Judith share a meal in the hotel's dining room the child they are all but fostering flakes out in his bedroom, exploring TV channels over milk and a club sandwich. *Dragnet*. *Kraft Television Theater*.

Early the next morning a call comes: Eric Moyse is waiting in the lobby. Havard, Peder and Eric drive to a parking lot in Burnham Park with a view of the navy pier. The prototype container has been delivered.

Havard climbs out of the car. The cold hits him full in the face: it will snow today. He turns up the collar of his lumberjack shirt and pauses before the container: a corrugated-steel box, forty feet long by eight feet square. It carries no livery, no badges, no marks. It might have been deposited here by aliens: a blank on to which you might project any desire. Its raw, unpainted sides glisten in the low autumn light. Its doors are open: they swing back and forth in the breeze as though the box were trying to propel itself through water.

Peder manoeuvres the Dodge hard up against the container and clambers across the cab to get out of the vehicle. 'Havard? Come on!' Peder hauls himself on to the bed of the truck, and helps the boy up after him. From there they climb on to the cab roof, and from there on to the container. The steel box vibrates beneath their feet. It does not flex.

Havard surveys the city from a grand height of eight feet. Soldier Field. The Board of Trade Building.

'How is it?' Eric stands by the front of the Dodge, where the warmth of the engine takes the edge off the morning's chill. He is the very picture of anxiety, as though his adopted son and his friend were balanced on a mountain ledge or had climbed upon a berg which might at any moment roll over on top of them.

'Seems fine.'

'Havard?'

'Sure.'

'Well, jump about a bit.'

For ten full minutes Havard and Peder caper about on the roof of the container. They link arms. They dance round and round. The box does not sway, or ping, or flex, or buckle, or bounce. It rings like a bell. Peder sniffs. He calls down to Eric, 'Of course, we'll have to drop serious weights on this thing.'

'Of course.'

The container's bell-like reverberation sounds the death-knell for a small boy's dreams of running away to sea. From this point on there will be no more stevedoring, no more trimming, no more ordinary seamanship, no heave, no drag, no thrust, no groan, no weary back or throbbing arm or beer-parched throat, no barrel to roll, no crate to crack open, no cart to pull. The future's robots now, and cranes, and serial numbers, and coordinates. This is Eric's mission: to create and command a global trade in boxes and strip the meddlesome component entirely away.

∞

Sunday, 4 December 1960: midday

Fire engines and ambulances criss-cross the streets of Cardiff, braying: animals trapped in a barn. The river Taff is full to overflowing, but Eric Moyse has insisted on being dropped off at the edge of Gabalfa, seized, he now supposes (fed up, wet through, and more or less lost), by a desire to make this visit a pilgrimage of sorts: a penitential slump up to the derelict shrine of his undeclared and unrequited love.

Twenty years too late, Vibeke Dunfjeld has reappeared.

After a spell in prison, and free at last of the attentions of Norway's mental health system, she vanished from the Norwegian public record only to turn up in Cardiff, widow of a Lofoten merchant seaman who had served here during the war.

Peder Halstad has pieced this puzzle together: more and more he acts as Eric's eyes and ears, while his employer spends an ever greater part of his life on paper, shaping a commercial empire that grows more abstract by the day.

Vibeke Dunfjeld is a lecturer now. An *ecologist*. She is writing course materials for the Open University. No small accomplishment after years on the margins. Arrest and imprisonment. Self-harm. Hospital. Her father's surviving friends – one or two well-placed emeritus professors – have taken a discreet hand in her rehabilitation.

Gabalfa is a new estate: a crude mock-up of a future that has yet to emerge from the war's sticky ashes. Prefabricated houses and kerb stones on the skew. Houses rather less robust than the rorbu cabins – fishing boats, halved and overturned and fitted with a door – that his family once rented out to fishermen in Austvågøy.

Aberporth Road. Bacton Road. It is as though the war, not content with robbing Cardiff of many civic buildings, has gone on in the silence and relative calm of a phoney peace to destroy the city's very idea of itself. In place of the old buildings, however small they were, however mean, come these dull ideas of houses, Not houses but 'houses'. Not walls but 'walls', flat 'roofs' that cannot stand the touch of real rain. These are streets built by weary men. Men for whom contingent gestures are enough.

Eric's shirt collar feels as though it's shrunk a couple of sizes. His trousers are sodden and press, cold and clammy, against his thighs as he walks; they hobble him. His shoes are soaked through.

He is at the house now. No amount of abstraction, no amount of theory, can insulate him from this moment. He opens the gate. Crazy paving. A lawn more grey than green under the sky's woolly overcast. He knocks.

He has imagined this moment to death over the years, to the point of erasure: a needle blunting itself against the bleared grooves of a shellac record. The door opens and here is Vibeke Dunfjeld: a forty-five-year-old Welsh widow, part-time lecturer and ornithologist. The poignancy of this moment – the erosion of a remembered beauty, Vibeke's once sparkling eyes freighted now with experience and disappointment – barely registers against the crackle and white noise thrown up by Eric's years of lonely speculation and rehearsal. He has expected so much from this moment over the years, good and bad, that nothing the world actually throws at him can surprise him. This plain, square woman, these thin lips prematurely lined, the glassy, bulletproof quality of these eyes – these things neither surprise nor dismay him. He is aware, most of all, of a tremendous sense of relief. Clearly they are past the time when her sex might have had power over him. At last, after years of waiting, they are strangers!

Every outdoor garment Vibeke possesses is hung from wall hooks just inside the front door; as Eric enters he knocks a coat on to the floor. Rehanging it is a minor test of skill, like a child's puzzle. He picks his way over unopened envelopes, catalogues, notices for jumble sales, fêtes, public meetings. The hall is carpeted, its mealy colour made even more indeterminate by scuffs of mud and paint. An offcut, the carpet gives out a couple of feet short of the kitchen and a vaguely oriental blue linoleum takes over. There are clothes and undergarments over every chair back and radiator. Vibeke complains that she has nowhere to dry anything on a day like this. Sweaters. A child's stripy top. Tights. Vibeke has a child, then? Another child? Peder said nothing about this.

In the kitchen dolls slump in a delinquent row against a skirting board. Sheets of foolscap paper cover the kitchen table, spiralled and scribbled over, drawings half-done. Books: Hilda Boswell's *Treasury of Poetry*, Hilda Boswell's *Treasury of Nursery Rhymes*. Powder-pink forest sprites with schizophrenic eyes. Of the girl herself there is no sign. She must be at school.

Vibeke sits Eric down at the table, then turns to the sink where she engages in some indeterminate activity halfway between food preparation and washing-up. Eric studies her as she moves about the room: hunched, uneasy in her own skin. 'I suppose you'll want tea,' she says.

The mess filling this place seemed cheery after the bleak and empty street – but now that he is sitting down his impression of comfort is rapidly evaporating. These drawings, swept aside to make room for his tea – these aren't the child's. These are Vibeke's. An adult hand drew these. However disordered, this is an adult's way of drawing a bird. A face. A hand.

The dolls, slumped against the wall, return his stare.

'I suppose you have been wondering about Else.'

'Who?'

'My daughter.'

'Else. How lovely.'

Silence.

'How old is Else?'

'Eight.'

Eight: that was Havard's age, at his adoption.

'Do you take milk?'

He shakes his head. 'Lemon, if you've got it.'

She goes to the fridge and takes from inside the door one of those acid-yellow plastic lemons – a Jif lemon, for heaven's sake, mascot of the post-war shoddy. He says: 'I have pictures of Havard. If you would like to see them.' His sodden jacket is hung over the back of his chair: he reaches into it and pulls out his wallet. The snaps are crumpled and water-stained. He lays them on the table.

'Well,' she says.

He lays the pictures out on the table. Havard on a camel, with a view of the Sphinx. Havard on a hill overlooking the Golden Gate Bridge. Havard by the Niagara Falls. 'Anyway,' he says, 'I brought these for you.'

'You should have brought the boy.'

'The boy?' Eric thinks about this. 'Havard?'

'He must be seventeen.'

'Yes.'

'A young man by now.'

'I suppose.'

'Why didn't you bring him? Didn't he want to come?'

'I –' In a rising panic, Eric realizes he has no answer to this. 'I didn't think –'

Vibeke goes back to the sink, to whatever it is she is doing, or not doing, or pretending to do. 'It's all right,' she says.

He says to her, ready for anything: 'It must have been hard for you.'

Her smile is weathered. 'Hard. Yes.'

'What did they do? Where you were. Where they kept you. What were they trying to do?'

Vibeke appears genuinely puzzled: 'I think in the end they just wanted me to be somebody else.'

'Were you really so crazy?' A little levity. Nothing wrong with a little levity.

'They thought so. They had funny ideas about crazy. You wouldn't agree with them at all.'

'No?'

'Oh, no. Do you remember all those letters you used to write to me, about your climbing trips? Your Arctic walks? Weeks, months in the wilderness. Living in the teeth of it. Knowing it by living it. That is what you wanted me to understand.'

'Was it?'

'I loved your letters. They inspired me. I tell my students about them. About you.'

So, after all, there has been some way in which he has touched her! He remembers the white eagle. Her hand on his shoulder. Her gaze elsewhere, not on him, never on him. 'You were right, of course,' she says. 'Right about that kind of life. It was right for me. I'm glad I lived that life. In spite of everything, I'm glad.'

Dizzily, Eric tries to make sense of this. Her years of vagrancy are something he's assumed she would rather forget. Petty thievery. Courtrooms. Jail. On the contrary: she seems to have recast them as something heroic, something she chose – and Eric her mentor, the cause of it all!

Eric studies the inside of his cup. No leaves. No pattern. No future. Tea bags. 'You'll have to tell me what happened.'

Vibeke tells her story: how the stateless peoples of the far north were forced south by hunger. 'The Germans burned everything to the ground. Well, you know this.' She stole what she needed to survive. She raided bins and cellars and larders. 'Like a bear in winter!' Eventually she reached civilization. What was left of it. 'The government had passed a law against pulling a cart with horses. Can you believe that? They wanted us to be different people. They wanted us to be like them. They beat us into shape.'

'Yes.' He looks her in the eye. Out with it: 'And Havard, they took him away from you.'

'Yes.'

'They told me you were cutting yourself.'

'Oh,' she says. 'That. That's when I was inside.' She pushes up her sleeves to show him: a cobweb of thin white scars.

He stares at them. He wants to be sick. Her sexual power is gone but in its place comes something tougher. Something horrid. 'I looked for you.'

'And you found little Havard.'

'Eventually. They told me you had had a child.'

'Yes?'

'I looked for you. I wanted you. I –' He stops, dumbfounded. In the struggle to explain, he has finally declared himself, more than thirty years too late.

'You found my son instead.'

'Yes.'

'And you took him.'

'It was the least I could do. Given the way I feel about you. Given the way I've always felt about you. For heaven's sake, Vibeke, you must know how I felt, it can't possibly have passed you by.'

Her fractional shrug is all his disappointments rolled into one. 'Perhaps I have forgotten.'

He is too weary to argue now. Too weary even to mourn the death of this thing he has been carrying around all these years. This love, if that is what it is. 'Yes,' he says. 'Perhaps it's best forgotten. It was never . . . Being older than you, I suppose. I was afraid . . .'

'You could have got me out of there,' she says. 'If you had loved me, you could have set me free.'

He stares at the backs of his hands. He is as old as the century. He is sixty years old. Sixty! How did he get so old? 'I loved you. You were – I couldn't have cared for you. They told me that.'

'You took their word for it. The doctors. The police. Peder Halstad. You took their advice.'

Eric finds himself in a place where he can see no justice in anything he has done. 'Yes,' he says. 'I took their advice.'

'Poor Eric,' Vibeke croons. She picks up his cup and carries it to the sink and sets about making another pot of her ghastly tea. 'Never really in love is my guess.'

'You can think what you like.' The words are out before he can stop them. It's no small thing to say to a woman who has spent years of her life in mental hospitals: a delinquent labelled unfit to rear her own child. He closes his eyes, afraid to meet her gaze, aghast at his own stupidity. 'Excuse me,' he says. 'Forgive me. Look,' he says, as if this were an explanation, 'I need the toilet.'

Behind the locked door of her bathroom, safe at last, Eric's steadying breath comes cheaply perfumed: Yardley, Fabergé, Estée Lauder Youth Dew. He studies the shelf above the sink. No ambergris in this line-up. Perfumes that have never seen the inside of a whale's arse. He looks around him, ever more dizzy, ever more claustrophobic, hunting for something to latch on to. The room's as generic as a toothpaste advertisement.

He flushes the toilet and unbolts the door. Through the open doorway next to the bathroom comes a puttering: gas running dry in the bottle.

He discovers the sitting room. Here the welter of clutter and rubbish implies some intense, disordered industry. Vibeke has been cutting out pictures of birds and sticking them into scrapbooks. Ordnance Survey maps are spread out over the floor. A Calor gas heater stands in the centre of the room, spitting out a gluey heat. On a table in front of the window, piles of guidebooks and timetables frame a seated figure. A child.

'Hello.'

The girl turns round. Her face, so serious, reminds him so much of the child Vibeke that he forgets to breathe. 'Who are you?' There's no lightness in his voice at all. No friendliness. The girl climbs off her chair and edges around the room.

'I'm Eric. Hello.' It is too late for reassurances. All he can do is make way for her. She runs lightly out of the room.

He hears the kitchen door come open and Vibeke's voice, muffled by distance. Confronting mother and daughter together is more than he can handle. Let them discuss him for a minute, if they want to. Let Vibeke find him in here, what does it matter? Anything to get away from that kitchen, that yellow melamine, that bloody tea.

He explores the room. On the desk, between the piles of bird-watching pamphlets, he sees something. A cherry-red something. Hideous. He picks it up. He turns it over in his hands. Red leather.

It is Lothar Eling's notebook. He opens it.

> Perturbations will disrupt even an ideal, frictionless fluid, if it is effectively unbounded. So the weather will not die.

By some of Eling's sketches, the professor has added a line or two in the margins. There is other writing too. Cartoon snakes with dizzy eyes.

Vibeke's girl has been laying crayon over Eling's testament, his dying words. How could Vibeke let her daughter do that?

Beside the notebook is its case: a stiff, once waterproof wallet, stained now, scribbled over with felt-tip pens and flecked with shards of rub-on transfer. Head of cat. Leg of cartoon dog. Eric crams the notebook into its case and pockets it.

Vibeke and the girl, Else, are waiting for him in the kitchen. They are staring out of the kitchen window. He comes up beside them and he sees what they see, which is to say, nothing: a vast, still, grey pool. The Taff has burst its banks. Water, heavy with silt and coal dust from Taff Merthyr and Trelewis Drift, has overrun the convolutions of road, park and playground. Isolated by the rising flood waters, already the children's play apparatus has lost its landward familiarity and acquired the eerie mantle of abandoned dockyard machinery.

'It's going to come in the house!' Vibeke runs into the living room. Her daughter follows. Eric stares out of the window at the swelling gutters, the film of dirt winding fingers through the weedy lawn under the window. He is trying to get the sense of this, the scale, but he is a stranger here, he does not know the lay of the land, all he can see is the corner of the child's playground, the edge of a street, a few feet of lawn . . .

'Else, mind out the way!'

'But Mummy, I want to help!'

They are in the front room. Vibeke is plucking maps and books up off the floor. She's stuffing papers at random on top of books ranged along high shelves. She pauses, staring at the shelves. 'They'll never hold,' she says. 'When the wall gets wet the shelves will never hold. Christ.' It's only a prefab after all: panels of plaster held together by prayer.

Still, Eric can't muster anything like Vibeke's sense of urgency and a grotesque suspicion springs to mind: what if this sudden flurry and panic is just something she *does*? What if flood drill is part of her domestic routine? He knows nothing about Vibeke. She has, after all, for years been counted among the mad.

'Oh, God.'

What if this is just something she does? Every time a drain gets blocked, or leaves jam a gutter, or a main bursts . . .

At his feet he notices a spreading stain. He is seized with infantile horror – a visceral shame at the disobedient body. The stain spreads and spreads, between his legs and into the room, towards the frantic woman and her child. He turns, and the hall is wet, black with smuts. Something – a sort of fur – is growing up through the pile of the hall carpet. It is wet, but it is not water. It is more mineral than that. It has a colour and a sheen. It is the solid earth gone fluid around him. It prowls around his legs and tucks itself under a decrepit divan piled with toys, picture books and crumpled washing. 'Vibeke.'

A smell fills the room: loose stools and rancid food. The vomit of Gabalfa's sewers.

Her hand to her mouth, Vibeke gazes around the room, her eyes wide and helpless. Else, taking her cue from her mother, starts to cry. What can they do? It will all be destroyed. It is inevitable. The dolls in the kitchen are already drowning in the black slurry pouring in through the back door. The flood is over the soles of Eric's shoes, now. A fresh cold seeps between his toes.

Eric crosses to the desk. He lifts the lace curtain and looks out.

The streets are running with water. If it is water. Black water. Wavelets criss-cross each other, sheets drawn up over a bed. 'Dead water.' He remembers this. 'The propeller churns, but the boat doesn't move.' Children are running about. Splashing. Men and women wade through the street in wellington boots, carrying suitcases, carrier bags, nothing at all. He looks from house to house. He'd thought these structures follies, rosy-spectacled half-gestures. These houses are not childish. They are the product of an unspeakable and very adult realism. Their shabbiness is not an accident. It is integral. It is *meant*. Bodies, atom-flashed against these plywood walls will leave no prints, for the walls will fall away as fast as the bodies evaporate. These buildings have been made to serve present need, because the present is all there is –

'Eric!'

He looks at Vibeke, her elfin face thickened and coarsened by time. Her eyes, once mischievous, are merely schizophrenic now. 'There's nothing I can do.'

What would she have him do? Canute the waves?

'Nothing,' he says. 'Nothing!'

ELEVEN

Eric Moyse's merchant fleet served the Allies well during the war. His office preserves letters of thanks from the British Treasury, the US Maritime Commission. But Eric, while serviceable, has always had his sights set on the greater prize. Boxes and boxes and boxes in boxes. Whoever won that war won the world – but it was Eric's world they inherited. A world in a can.

Eric spent the larger part of the war behind a desk in Roosevelt Street, New York, with a view of the tumbledown East River pier. In those days the congested Brooklyn waterfront was lined with piers, transit sheds, multi-storey factories, all of them just a stone's throw from the water. Now the factories of Brooklyn are empty and all the clever money has moved south to deep water, new cranes, new railheads in New Jersey, Pennsylvania and Connecticut.

Eric is by now the undisputed king of discards, of Liberty ships and Victory ships. His fleet has cost him virtually nothing, and with it he has changed the face of the earth. Armed with an IBM 704 and a simulation punched into a stack of perforated cards, Eric has tripled the profitability of ships sailing between Hawaii and Oakland. Year on year his tracking systems grow bigger, more capable, and more expensive. In a single year he spends about $400,000 on computers to keep track of the 30,000 shipping containers plying his Pacific routes.

Eric Moyse's container shipping is the saving of American forces in Vietnam. In 1968 the US Army is taking more than two weeks to unload a boat at Saigon and its cargo tracking is so poor that the wharves at Cam

Ranh Bay are disappearing under the most bizarre surpluses. Hawaiian shorts. Crosses and candelabras. Eric Moyse's newfangled container-shipping operation ensures that US troops receive the right resources, on time, to prosecute the war. The line makes good money from the service, too. It used to be that ships supplying Vietnam returned home empty. Not any more: Eric Moyse has opened a trade route between Yokohama and the west coast of the USA and his ships return from Vietnam laden with Japanese textiles and televisions.

Though the doctors give him the all-clear, and it takes him no more than a night's observation in hospital before he's dried off and on a plane back to New York, friends and observers generally agree that 1960 marks a watershed in Eric Moyse's life. Gabalfa drowned and Cardiff Arms Park under four feet of slurry. He is never quite the same afterwards. People say the dark has taken him. Certainly, you can date the chunky sunglasses that are so much his visual signature from this date.

Blinkered, taciturn and monstrous, his eyes hidden from the glare of a whiteout that exists, by now, almost entirely in his own mind, Eric writes out endless lists. Antwerp, Felixstowe, Hamburg, Hong Kong, Kaohsiung, Kobe, Rotterdam, Tilbury, Yokohama. He sketches maps, charts, diagrams. He writes letter after letter to Power Electronics International, Inc., proposing investment in 'a gantry crane with one end of the bridge rigidly supported on one or more legs that run on a fixed rail'. He carves out territory after territory.

While his competitors are digging deep, investing in a new generation of high-performance cargo ships, Eric Moyse has his managers trawl breaker's yards for old oil tankers: big, slow ships, too wide for Suez, that steam around the world at walking pace. Every week, and on the hour, one of these rusting tubs disgorges your raw materials at the right quayside, on to the right trucks. What do you care how many months it's been at sea? Eric has seen what his competitors have not seen: that speed is not essential for a container line.

*

Friday, 23 July 1971

Eric has booked a table at the Dorchester in London's Park lane to wish Havard, his adopted son, a happy twenty-fifth. The Greek-American shipping tycoon Ari Onassis is staying at the same hotel. The men don't like each other much, but they can hardly ignore each other; not when they're sat at neighbouring tables in the same gold-papered dining-room.

Ari's finding it as hard as anyone to wrap his head around Eric Moyse's commercial reasoning. Jokes about Moyse's 'decrepit' and 'obsolete' fleet have become a staple of the better business sheets. How can such a slow, antique fleet be winning so much business? Now is not the time to pursue the finer points of commerce. Better to simply tease the little man.

Ari has not met Eric's son Havard before but, like everybody else, he feels he knows him already. Havard has broken out on his own with a boutique that's the rage of Soho. Richie Havens and Joan Baez were both seen wearing his threads at the Isle of Wight festival. Of course, Havard doesn't make the clothes. According to the papers he spends most of his time off his face in a corner of Manor Studios. Havard's playboy lifestyle distracts from a series of small, canny business decisions that have placed him, in his tender mid-twenties, at the heart of London's burgeoning music, art and fashion scene. In jumper and jeans he looks out of place here; he also, very obviously, has the sense of entitlement to run roughshod over the dress codes of establishments far more exclusive than this one.

Ari pushes his plate roughly towards the waiter. 'This isn't what I ordered.'

'Sir?'

'Bring me the beluga.'

'Sir, this is –'

'No, it isn't.'

Tight-lipped, the waiter takes up the untouched plate and carries it back to the kitchen.

Moyse stares at his foie gras, heart hammering with embarrassment.

Havard merely laughs. Ari impresses him. His cheek, his wit, his bigness. At the same time, Havard's bright eyes hold something more than humour. They carry something of his mother's schizophrenic shimmer – as though his visual field were no more than a parade of glossy surfaces.

The waiter brings Ari Onassis a fresh plate of caviar. The eggs are now appreciably bigger than before. Glossier, too. One can only hope the waiter spat on them.

'The trouble with you,' Ari says to Eric, 'is you have unimaginable wealth, yet you do not demand the best. It's indecent. It's unfair. Me, I always demand the very best. It's criminal, my friend, what little fun you get out of life.'

What is Eric supposed to say to that? 'I've had my moments'?

Eric has got Havard a gift done up in plain brown paper. (An affectation: why couldn't he just have bought gift-wrap like everyone else?) Ari reaches across the table and picks it up. 'What's this, then, a present?'

Havard's eyes glitter – when movement at a neighbouring table distracts him. Even Ari (turning the parcel over and over in his hands, barely resisting the impulse to open it) notices this: 'If it was a girl you were ogling, I could understand.'

Havard starts. 'Sorry.'

'Does the gentleman owe you money?'

'Nothing like that!'

'Well? Out with it.' Ari, who consumes everything, eats everything, tireless in his pursuit of everything.

Havard says: 'He's Said bin Taimur. The Sultan of Oman. Or was. He lives here now, in the hotel. I've heard he keeps a parrot.'

Ari puts the packet down again beside Moyse's plate.

'What is that, anyway?' Havard says to Eric, aping Ari's rudeness. He hasn't Ari's cheerfulness, or his scale. He sounds merely petulant. Spoiled.

Moyse sighs. 'For you.' He winces as the boy tears the paper roughly off. It is an ugly object. A square of – well, by its colour, what would you say? Old upholstery? Rotten meat? Inside the pocket is a book, bound in the same vile red leather.

'It belonged to Lothar Eling,' Moyse says. 'The man I found on Foyn. What was left of him.' How to explain what this book signifies? The spin of oceans. The incommensurability of desire. The circulation of the blood. Last, and critically: dead water. 'Your mother got him this notebook when she was a girl. A Christmas present. For his journey on board the *Italia*.'

Ari, exasperated, drops his fork – tiny as a toothpick in his fist – on to his plate. It tings. 'You got him a *book*?'

Havard says: 'Oh, Ari, for heaven's sake, this is *history* I'm holding. Lothar Eling invented weather modelling.'

Eric stares at his son. Where did he pick up this knowledge? With a sinking of the heart, he remembers Peder Halstad. Peder would have taught young Havard this. Peder has been more of a father to the boy than Eric has ever been.

'The weather?' Ari sniffs and goes back to his food. What's the weather to him? He and Eric and Erling Næss and all their generation have spent their lives ordering bigger and bigger vessels, to the point where storms cannot baulk their ships, cannot force a change in their courses, can hardly slow them down. They are beyond weather now.

'Is this my mother's handwriting?'

Moyse looks:

> To Uncle Lothar
> Wishing you a Merry Christmas
> Vibeke

'Yes,' he says, 'that's hers. That's your mother's hand.'

This is the story Eric tells his son: that he spent years looking for Vibeke, long after the war, and did not find her, and in his searching found Havard at last, her bastard child, abandoned in an orphanage outside Narvik. And in 1951, adopted him: all of this is true. After that the truth gets hard to bear. Cardiff, little Else, and the flood – these are private hurts. So Eric prevaricates. Elides. Finally, lies: 'Hard as I looked, I never found your mother.'

At the next table, Oman's old Sultan rises stiffly from his seat, drops his napkin on to the table, and makes for the door. An old man of royal blood, his every action is elegant, parsimonious, cold. As he limps away, Ari Onassis mimes a respectful applause.

After the meal Ari arranges to be driven to a club somewhere and Havard, grinning from ear to ear, follows in his wake. Eric traipses after them, the notebook tucked safely in his pocket. Havard, for all the interest he showed in it at first, has already forgotten it. 'My mother's hand' indeed. 'Thank you,' Havard calls, waving from the back of the Bentley. 'Thank you, Dad, for a great night!'

Well, thinks Eric, waving back: sod you. He rests his hand against the square bulk in his pocket. You would only have lost it. You would have written your phone number in it and given it to some girl – and then where would we all be?

Dead water. Ships that churn and churn and churn, for days, for years, forever. It's clear enough that Havard's not ready for this. Havard's not ever going to be ready for this. The burden is Eric's alone: he was a fool ever to imagine he could pass it on.

When people talk about shipping they talk about goods. They talk about televisions and motorbikes and cars and toys and clothing and perfumes and whisky. They omit to mention screws, pigments, paints, moulded plastics, rolls of leather, chopped-glass matting, bales of cotton, chemicals, dyes, yeasts, spores, seeds, acids, glues. And no one even thinks about waste. The single biggest worldwide cargo by volume is waste paper, closely followed by rags and shoes, soft drinks cans, worn tyres, rebars, copper wire. Almost everything can be recycled or repurposed. Nuclear and clinical wastes. Residues and contaminants. Industrial by-products. That these things move over the earth is a fact no one wants to confront, any more than they would want to handle the piss and puss their kidneys filter, minute by minute, from their blood.

Eric looks up, hunting stars, but the sky's blackness is as close and oppressive as the inside of one of his own shipping containers. The lights of the city obliterate the sky completely. He remembers the war, how blackouts let in the starlight, and on an impulse he crosses Park Lane and loses himself as best he can in the shadows of Hyde Park.

It feels strange to be stepping outside the city that has for so long surrounded him. When was the last time he climbed a hill? Tasted snow? Set foot aboard a ship? How has a life once steeped in the blood and ice of the hunt and dripping in the oil wrung from humpbacks and blues, from living giants, how can this vital life have fallen off so far? He is over seventy years old. He should be rooting himself again in the earth to which he will all too soon return.

He determines to recall his adventures and all the riches his parents' fleet brought home. Whale oil to light the lamps in every seaboard town from Narvik to Nagasaki to Maine. That he squeezed the breast of a dead blue once, to taste its milk. That the milk of blue whales is a thick, greyish jelly. That it tastes better than it looks. He remembers, he slit open its belly and used a tin jug to gather a couple of pints of barely digested krill. Boiled, krill has the taste and texture of North Sea shrimp. As he walks he clenches his hands, drawing back the bolts on disused memory. Sperm whales die slowly. Once, a sperm whale they had thought dead suddenly came back to life on the factory deck, thrashing out. They finished it off with knives. Did these things really happen? The whole business seems alien now, even preposterous.

The world is losing its colour, it is turning to paper, and it is his fault. He is convinced of this. With an IBM 704 and a stack of perforated cards he has cleared away the mess and confusion of the world's cargo ports – this is true. But this revolution has acquired a life of its own. It has turned his ships to paper. They sail across paper oceans now, carrying paper goods. They lead – he leads – a paper life. How has he come to this? To have swapped his homeland for a flag of convenience, his years before the mast for an unending schedule of India Club lunches with Lloyd's 'names'?

By the time he reaches the Serpentine, Eric knows he is going to be sick. Even here, in the midst of the park, he cannot see a single star. Where the path runs up against the water he kneels and reaches down and splashes bird-fouled water in his face. It feels gritty. He shivers and the shiver runs through him, back and forth, a furred and bright-eyed fever-creature. He thinks of Vibeke's letters: her pet Pippi, chattering in terror.

He vomits cleanly into the water. He waits for a second heave, for a third, but it does not come. He has evacuated himself with trademark efficiency.

Something unfurls in the corner of his vision.

A handkerchief.

He rocks back on his haunches and takes it, half-blind, eyes streaming. He wipes his eyes, his mouth. His guts are a foreign territory: there is not much pain, but there is sensation. His normally senseless innards have a form: lapping corrugations, crafty left-hand spirals, tucks, folds, involutions.

He looks up and around, dumbly proffering the ruined handkerchief.

Said bin Taimur, deposed Sultan of Oman, raises a hand in polite refusal. Serious, unsmiling, Said's face is at once severe and vulnerable.

Moyse wonders what to do with the disgusting thing in his hand. He blows his nose on it. He gets to his feet and crams the soiled handkerchief into his trouser pocket. 'Thank you.'

The Sultan bows.

Two old men by a lake. Shadows in a city-lit night. Two players who dominated a stage that is already being dismantled around them. They are both, in their way, significant figures, worth more than a footnote in the history of their time. They do not need to be introduced. Said offers Eric Moyse his arm. The gesture, the offer of human warmth, is almost too much for Eric. After so many years. Such cold. Eric brushes a hand over his face, hiding his tears, dashing them. He takes the old man's arm. He feels the Sultan's tremble, the spill in his walk: hard to say who is supporting whom. And how strange this is, this proximity, considering the kind of life the Sultan has led. Considering the divine right of kings.

'You must go slower,' the Sultan says.

'I am sorry.'

'Forgive me. I am lame.'

'Of course.'

'Would you like to know why I am lame?'

Moyse doesn't know what to say to this.

'I am lame because on the day I was deposed I contrived to shoot myself in the foot.'

'You did?'

'This is an expression, of course. Shooting yourself in the foot.'

'Yes.'

'Yes. Only with me it was not an expression. I actually shot myself in the foot. Bang.' The Sultan shrugs. 'It caused much hilarity at the time.'

Eric's own birthday comes just a couple of months later. He celebrates at the Frontier Hotel in Las Vegas, watching Diana Ross and the Supremes. After the concert he retires to the penthouse suite, orders all light bulbs removed from the apartment, and behind bespoke blackout curtains that utterly extinguish the desert sun he writes a string of clumsy, blind-handed memos giving his staff explicit instructions not to look at him or speak to him unless they're spoken to. For six months he subsists entirely on black tea, chocolate and pemmican: Arctic rations.

Dead Water. A surplus arsenal, big enough to shake the world, orbiting unseen across five oceans. Think about it. Think about the distribution of risk. Eric does. Eric has to. Eric has to keep it all in mind. How many containers? How many cargoes? He commits nothing to paper. How many numbers, keywords, check digits? Absolute deniability. Absolute personal control.

On 16 October 1975 hotel security men accompanied by local law enforcement officers and federal agents order Havard's staff aside and break into his apartment.

It is empty.

∞

Eric Moyse's disappearance inspires intermittent headlines, an article in the *New Yorker* by Bob Woodward, a conspiracy cult, several unsuccessful airport-book 'exposés' of the shipping industry, and an A-certificated Lew Grade thriller stirring Telly Savalas and Elliott Gould. Eventually the line abandons its staggeringly expensive global manhunt, Eric Moyse is presumed dead, and on 1 October 1976 his adopted son Havard is appointed president.

Many of the firm's old guard vanish at this point, pensioned off or internally exiled. (The line is a complex global entity, big enough to contain any number of elderly factions and lost causes.) Havard, succeeding to the board, appoints Peder Halstad as his personal adviser.

The arrangement is short-lived. Peder, an old man, finds Havard's Muscat headquarters unbearable. 'You spend six months of the year glued to the air conditioner, the skies are white, the air tastes of iron filings, and you expect me to enjoy the weather!'

'It's sunshine, Peder,' Havard insists. 'Many people like it. Please. Stick it out for six months.'

Peder does exactly that.

The last straw comes when Havard takes him out of Muscat on a day's snorkelling trip. On a rocky shelf beside a beach since swallowed by a Saudi hotel complex, Peder and Havard watch as turtles come to nibble the reef just below their feet. Peder's golf club is full of talk about the coming economic miracle: how a city is springing like a phoenix from the poisoned creek in Dubai. Half Peder's friends are planning to retire there, or at least to 'somewhere in the sun'.

'I tell them, they may as well stick their heads in the oven and turn the grill on. Honestly, rivers and greenery are not God's curse.'

'Spoken like a true Norseman.'

'Thank you.' Peder cracks another Mountain Dew and refills Havard's cup. 'The point is, I've well-wishers coming out of my ears. Judith looked after me so well over the years, people assume I need to be *taken care of*. In the *sun*.'

'You can look after yourself.'

'Damned right.'

'The Great White Explorer.'

'That's me.'

'The man who faced the Arctic alone.'

'Well, until I got back to Cape North. After that I thumbed a lift.'

'Man against the elements.'

'Man *naked* against the elements.'

'Well,' says Havard. 'That's an image I didn't need.'

On the road behind them a coach pulls up. The doors open and out pours a seemingly endless stream of fat. It is hard at first to distinguish individual bodies. They are all exactly the same colour: the sterile grey-white of fridge-hardened lard. They are wearing bathing suits but folds of fat hide their clothing from sight. Every one of them is screaming. Not cheering. Not shouting. Screaming, and running for the sea. Havard goes over to talk to the driver and it turns out that these are tourists from Kiev.

'Ukrainians on a package deal,' Havard tells Peder, his old protector, laughing.

Peder shakes his head. 'Let me go, son,' he says. He has helped consolidate Havard and the Moyse Line within Oman's power structure. He has secured the company exclusive export rights to its medium sour crude. But he cannot work a day longer with Havard's oil man and 'regional expert', David Brooks

'I wish this wasn't such an issue for you,' Havard frets.

'It's not an issue. The man's a cunt. Oh, look at that.' He points. The Ukrainians have got hold of a turtle. They have dragged it out of the surf. They are trying to ride it along the beach. Peder lays an old hand on Havard's shoulder. 'Please, son, if you love me. I am really too old for this shit.'

Loaded in Rafah, Egypt, transferred to Genoa, Italy, to a ship bound for Hamburg, then transferred to a ship bound for the Deep Water Facility at Belledune, Abhik and Kaneer carve their twofold djinn path around the earth, victorious and everywhere.

That grumpy old sod Eric Moyse has had his uses after all. Boxes and boxes and boxes within boxes: this story has swallowed the earth.

They have the world wrapped up now – all the world's bounty travels in shipping containers and every shipping container is a scale in their skin. Day after day, from port to rail yard to lorry park, Abhik and Kaneer trundle down a street near you.

They pay very little attention to the small but necessary part of their being that men call Dead Water. They are no longer very boyish, so they are not especially fascinated by their own excretions and emissions. Dead Water is their lymphatic system, their twofold body's drain: what's there to pay attention to?

Then it comes, grey and wrinkled like a brain: the pollution cloud presaging the catastrophic floods of 1976. Rain, bituminous and grainy, splashes a container being hauled on the back of an antique Tata truck along the GTR, west to east, to a scheduled sailing from Mumbai. The truck driver's not slept in fifty hours, not since Patna, and the medicine that's been fuelling him has grown fangs. It bites. Needles shoot through the driver's left shoulder as he drives and down his whole left side. He gasps, but he will not stop, he will not pull over, he cannot afford to, he has a schedule to keep and seventeen kids to support, in three cities, to three separate and unwitting wives, so he keeps rolling, ignoring the signs, ignoring the pain, through Firozabad and out, towards the badlands of Uttar Pradesh, along the Sher Shah Suri Marg.

It rains and rains. The road grows slick. The windscreen wipers falter. The driver yawns and does not see the bite in the road. The truck plummets down the embankment, hurling the hapless driver high into the branches of a margosa tree. Its load, improperly secured, goes bounding down the bank, over and over, booming and bellowing, MOYSE MOYSE MOYSE MOYSE MOYSE, and rocks to rest, upside down, just a few feet away from where a small boy stands, soaked through and frozen with horror, under a rain of knife-like leaves.

Abhik and Kaneer confer, their talk a susurration so faint it could be anything: a sound, a scent, a movement of lightless surfaces against a lightless ground. There's something about this kid, they're sure. Some great, ironic promise.

Cursing, the twofold djinn disentangles itself from disordered contents of the can. Outside, the boy, gripped by an obscure impulse, runs his hand back and forth over the wall of the can and the container doors swing open.

Boy and djinn behold each other, but the living child's eyes, inadequate to express the djinn's terrible twofold majesty, present it to him only as illimitable dark. Squinting, he approaches.

It is *Rishi Ansari*!

Rishi Ansari

This sound, this sussuration – savour it. This is the sound of dead boys laughing.

Midpoint reversal, on the button. Structure to make a struggling, sceptical playgoer weep with relief. Oh! the boys embrace. What luck! A path regained. A clew out of their maze. Their story's back on track at last. Can this be true? A journey half-done, a puzzle halfway solved? Oh, yes.

The kid steps inside, over the aluminium lintel. His footfalls make no sound on the plywood floor as he edges into the dark.

Rishi Ansari. Serviceable and anonymous. Komatsu boy. Oh yes, we're having *you*.

TWELVE

Rishi's father, Keshav Ansari, adores fairgrounds. Twice a year, before the flood robbed him of his two eldest sons, he would drag his family to the fair in Firozabad.

After flood and funerals, there's only Rishi wants to accompany him. So Keshav takes his sole surviving boy to visit the fair 'one last time'. Keshav's half-blind with glaucoma by now. He won't let Rishi have charge of the money, but he can't see well enough to count it. The stallholders and the fairground men have to do it for him. Money falls through his fingers like water, leaving him angry and bitter. The fairground is full of thieves, he says.

Rishi sets his father down on a plastic chair, grumbling over a paper plate piled with dried fish and brinjals, and goes off to explore the arcades. On the side of one booth, a spray-painted Clint Eastwood chews a cheap cigar. The booth sells silver dollars. You feed money into the machine and type a short message on its chunky keyboard.

Rishi types: AADI + RAM

His brothers.

Next he has to choose something for the middle of the coin. There are six designs to choose from. Rishi picks

Shanti.

Peace.

Something like the tone arm of a record player feeds a silver blank into the press. The hammer falls with a satisfying, floorboard-shaking thump. The coin drops into the hopper at his feet. Some hidden apparatus has contrived to wrap it in a plastic baggie. It's fiendishly difficult to open. He has to use his teeth.

He gets the coin out of the bag and studies it. It's only a cheap thing, but it's something he has made. He pockets the coin and promises himself that he will always carry it with him.

Rishi and Vinod's friendship begins innocuously enough. They are neighbours, after all. I dare you to madden that cow. I dare you to steal those keys. To drink this bottle. To climb that roof. To break his window. To shit on her laundry.

'Boys!'

Now here comes Vinod's cousin Yash, arriving unexpected on the scene, the summer after the floods. 1977.

Yash Yadav: a thing beached and abandoned. An animal capable enough in its own environment but poorly suited to its present surroundings. Vinod thrusts Rishi under Yash's nose, showing off his playmate as you'd show off a model boat or the steering wheel off a wrecked car; Yash peers at Rishi and sniffs. Yash sniffs at everything, as though compensating for faulty vision. The milk cans. The mango trees. Yash is fat, with a rolling gait he's copied from Amitabh Bachchan in *Sholay*, a cowboy movie he's already seen three times in Lucknow.

Rishi and Vinod are playing shoot-outs in the rain, Rishi with a tin toy, Vinod with his father's rusted old service Browning. Vinod needs both hands to lift it and the one time he managed to pull the trigger it snipped a lump out of the webbing between his thumb and forefinger. Now he just swings it around and yells 'Bang'.

They turn a corner of the house, arguing over the rules of their game ('Vinod, you have to at least point the thing, if you don't point the thing there's no point . . .'), and come upon Yash, by the parlour window, pressing Rishi's sister, little Safia, six years old, up against the wall.

She has hold of her doll; she's clinging to it fiercely and Yash is trying to tear it off her. Safia yelps like a wounded puppy. Already Yash has a taste for intimidation. He has his hand over her face.

'Yash.' Vinod sounds exactly like his father. 'Leave her alone.'

Yash is impressed. His sneer is uncertain of itself, ready, at an instant's notice, to transform itself into a smile. 'She a friend of yours?'

'Well, what do you think?' says Vinod, and he lifts the gun and pulls the trigger. The safety's on. He finds the catch and thumbs it forward, takes aim, fires again. Of course, the gun is empty. A toy. Yash doesn't know that. Vinod's attention to detail has him sweating.

He runs and tells, and that night Old Samey carries Vinod, his son and heir, into a barn, lays him down on a blanket of straw, and whips him until he bleeds. Yash is there. Watching.

Things are happening for Yash. Some family plan has him travelling into Firozabad with Old Samey once, twice a week. He comes home from these trips stuffed with his own importance and as conceited as an old cat. You can tell from the way he speaks (too loud, too much from the hard palate) that he is discovering the power of his own ego. Scowling in front of the mirror every morning. Straightening his sandals under the bed at night.

One afternoon, when Yash is away with Old Samey, Rishi goes to the usual bathing place to swim and finds Vinod and Safia coupled on the riverbank.

Safia flicks herself closed, drawing up her knees to hide her nakedness. Vinod, bucked and abandoned, looks for all the world like a baby tipped out of a pram. His fast-wilting erection swings between his legs, ridiculous and infantile as a rattle. It takes him a moment to spot Rishi's face among the bushes.

He isn't going to say anything. Around here, girls have been burnt for holding hands, for an unchaste look. Round here is the kitchen-accident capital of the world, and there are relations Rishi doesn't trust: grim-faced, disappointed men in hamlets west of here, always crapping on about honour as they pick their feet and suck their ulcered gums. It isn't Safia he's trying to protect, so much as his father. Poor Keshav, his eyes wide with glaucoma, trying to hold his own in some bitter family row. His mother screaming. 'Show us what you're made of!' No.

So Rishi becomes the couple's protector, and in 1982, after several youthful years' fumbling and mooning, Vinod finally gets to inseminate his sister.

There is, for a while, a great deal of wailing and slapping going on, Witchy old aunts come visiting with vile herbal preparations. Safia refuses to drink them. Rishi stands up for her. 'How dare you!' their mother cries. Rishi bears the blows, but it takes all his self-control not to grab his mum's wrist.

Keshav listens from his corner, his eyesight almost gone, and the pupils of his eyes wider than ever, perpetually surprised: 'What's happening? Is anybody going to tell me what is happening?'

'You go talk to them, Keshav!' their mother implores. 'It's not right!' – badgering him and badgering him until Keshav heaves himself from his chair and taps his way down the lane to Old Samey's house.

Why Samey agrees to his neighbour's mumbled and embarrassed marriage demand is a question that keeps Chhaphandi's gossips busy for weeks. The word is he wants to teach his eldest a lesson.

The night before the engagement, Rishi strings mango leaves over their door and ties banana plants to either side of the gate. Then, once Safia is awake and ready, he opens the gate and Vinod and about fifty relatives and friends parade in, dancing over ground strewn with rice and coloured powders. They sit Safia and Vinod down on wooden planks. A priest mumbles Sanskrit nothings at them; the couple stare straight ahead, rigid as statues, not once daring to look at each other. The engagement party lasts long into the night, and marriage follows, like clockwork, two months later.

Old Samey insists on a dowry, of course.

'A dowry!' Rishi's mother clasps her hands over her heart, her gestures broad and violent, as though miming a fatal knife attack.

'It's only a formality,' Keshav soothes.

'After what that boy did!'

'Really. It doesn't matter,' Keshav mumbles, eyes flickering, distracted, over the bare walls of their little house. Hard to say what matters to him by now. Wide-eyed as a child, he is taking his first, tentative steps into a private world.

A dowry, then: a means by which Old Samey might salvage a little family dignity from the couple's rushed courtship and Safia's all-too-obvious bridal bulge. Rishi can go to work for the Yadav family and pay regular instalments out of his wages. The exact amount isn't important. Everyone can see that Vinod and Safia are in love. That, the toothless old men of Chhaphandi agree, misty-eyed, ought to count for something. But time is what it is.

The river, which robbed the Ansaris of two boys and a home, doesn't stay put. It meanders, and settles into something like its old pattern, giving back the land it took.

Old Samey is delighted. In the aftermath of the floods, there's a boom in the construction trade, and land recovered from the river is perfect for the new brickworks. Old Samey buys new machinery, digs ditches, sets foundations, and advertises for extra labour: some out-of-work farm labourers, but itinerants too, beggars and *bhangis* from Lohardaga. Real scum.

Rishi stands with his father, blinking through the smoke of a dozen bonfires at the ruined land. Trees and undergrowth have been grubbed up, old field-lines scraped away by iron teeth. Old Samey's brand-new Komatsu (185hp, powershift transmission, enclosed cabin) crosses and criss-crosses Rishi's birthplace, marking out a series of trenches.

Rishi has grown up thinking that this land would one day be his. Fields for him to tend and grow a little rich by. Crops to harvest, money to spend. Land for him, in turn, to hand on to a son.

He says to his father. 'Old Samey wants me to work the digger. There. In the brickworks.'

Keshav nods.

'It will pay for Safia's dowry.'

'Yes.'

'Dad. There must be something we can do.'

Keshav's eyes are sucking absences.

'Please.'

Please show us what you're made of.

The vacuum he glimpses in his father's eyes goes deeper than anyone suspects. By 1993 Keshav is dead and his widow is spending her days decorating glass bangles, cutting them against a spinning wheel. Bangle-making: the occupation of her widowhood. Safia has two children by Vinod and seems happy enough living under Old Samey's roof. Old Samey gives Vinod charge over the family brickworks, and Rishi is still its Komatsu man.

Every day Rishi trundles a saffron-yellow earthmover back and forth over land that should by rights belong to him. He moves bricks from one corner of the yard to another. He shovels ash into holes. The money is good, but Old Samey keeps most of it to pay for Safia's dowry. Odd that the debt grows bigger as the months go by.

The change in Rishi's fortunes arrives in the guise of a catastrophic failure of the steering rack on Old Samey Yadav's Padmini Deluxe. Late one morning, driving home from a building site, Vinod's father swerves to avoid a truck and hurtles off the Sher Shah Suri Marg at around 60 mph. The slope of the embankment matches the arc of the falling car so closely the Padmini kisses the ground, hurtles into some fruit bushes, and rolls to a halt, undented.

Labourers in the fields run to the car to find Old Samey grinning, upright in his seat, clutching the wheel. They mill around the car, yelling, pointing at their flattened fruit bushes. They hammer on the door and the windscreen, yelling for compensation. Look what the old fool has done. Look at all our lovely fruit.

No one tries the doors. There are rules to this game. They are waiting for the old man to make a move. To wave his hands about in protest. To drive away, or try to. They are sportsmanlike, in their way. They need an excuse before they pull him out and kick him half to death, and he just sits there, smiling. (If they'd known him when he was alive, they'd have known straightaway that something was wrong. Old Samey never smiled in his life.)

Vinod takes his father's death hard. He wants to grieve, but he doesn't know how. Instead, he rages, explaining repeatedly to the police how his father had only just taken the Padmini in to have the steering tweaked. 'Those fucking grease-monkeys all but killed him!' Of course, the police aren't remotely interested. If the shock of the accident caused an old man's heart to stop beating, what business is it of theirs? A fragile heart, unable to cope with the knocks of life, is not their concern.

So Vinod reaches out and Yash agrees to drives over from Bombay. 'I'll see what I can do,' he says.

Vinod and Rishi are sitting in a roadhouse, arguing about money, when Yash rolls into town. The place isn't much: a square bunker of breeze blocks and wire-reinforced glass. The white emulsion smothering the interior is the establishment's sole stab at decoration. The walls are bare, the tables melamine, the floor concrete, the air heavy with old fat. A car pulls up outside and Yash stumbles over the step into the restaurant. 'Come see,' he calls to them, cutting to the chase, as though the years of his absence, his training, his years on the beat in Mumbai, were no more than a moment's absence. A trip to buy cigarettes.

Rishi and Vinod follow him out, mesmerized by his familiar bulk, his unprecedented drunkenness, and the weird Elvis roll of his hips. Yash Yadav is all grown-up. He is a policeman.

In the forecourt are half a dozen trucks, a shoe dangling from each tailgate: the trucker's talisman. Some mopeds. Yash's car: a clapped-out Standard Gazelle. Yash hunkers down by its right front wing. 'Doesn't look much, does it?' He reaches up inside the wheel arch and pulls something free. He stands up, peeling gaffer tape off the stock. He shows it to them: a smart new police-issue Glock 17. 'Polymer frame and five and a half pounds of pull. Some hot-head *gandhu* fucks with me, he fucks with death.'

Squirming as best they can out of the way of the weaving barrel, Rishi and Vinod try to steady Yash down and get him into the roadhouse. Yash insists on tucking the gun into the waistband of his trousers. He's CBI now: a plain-clothes constable with the Central Bureau of Investigation. He wants to celebrate.

'We can't go in there with that thing.'

Yash is adamant. He has passed a firearms course.

Rishi and Vinod help him round the back of the building, where string mattresses slung around short wooden posts make hammocks for drivers plying the Sher Shah Suri Marg. At least, they try to.

'A moment.' He stumbles off towards his car.

Vinod sucks his teeth. 'Can you believe they've given that oaf a gun?'

Yash has a personal supply in the car. He returns with the bottle. He's already opened it, releasing into the air a pungent chemical smell with an undertone of burnt sugar. Yash takes a swig and hands it round. The stuff is as strong as it is rotten. Rishi tries to read the label in the weak exterior light.

KASHMIR RUM

Yes: Rishi can read. Not that you need much skill to interpret the three big Xs printed, blood-red on black, beneath the brand name. Under them comes an admission, CONTAINS FLAVOURS, and in smaller letters, along the bottom, FOR SALE IN JAMMU AND KASHMIR ONLY. This rotgut is a long way from home. A gift from one of Yash's army friends, perhaps: souvenir of one of those drear winter camps that fill whole valleys of shit-brown Ladakh. Holding the Himalayan line. Keeping the Moslem hordes at bay. Rishi takes another slug and fights a gagging reflex. No wonder the they don't drink if this is all they have to hand.

Yash is in a mood to celebrate. He wants to show off, and he has plenty to show off about: 'I recently completed the Advance Commando Combat System of Professor Doctor Rao,' he announces, climbing on to the webbing of his crude string bed. He keenly communicates the professor's insights concerning Vital Organ Striking and Subclavian Artery Termination, 'One Enemy, One Chance, One Strike, One Kill!' The bed frame creaks as Yash bounces back and forth, cantilevered hips in constant hula motion, arms sweeping and chopping the air.

Rishi and Vinod gaze at him, captivated, waiting for him to fall through the netting or for the gun to go off in his pants.

Rishi and Vinod stretch out side by side on string mattresses, slugging cold beer in the dark, while Yash, a wakeful drunk, lectures them on the nature of the insurgent Mohammedan machine. Its networks, its *hawala* economy, its sleeper cells.

Three young men, bullshitting the dark.

Yash tells them: 'You can beat a man bloody, but a night in a refrigerated truck is cleaner and faster.'

Morning brings them back to the matter in hand. Over chilli-egg sandwiches, between bare walls, hunkered over a melamine table, Vinod explains the circumstances of his father's death. 'Those cunting retards fucked Dad's car. They as good as killed him.'

'Not in law,' says Yash.

'Their carelessness –'

'The lack of evidence –'

'Fuck's sake –'

'*Not in law*, I said.'

A pause.

'There are things the law cannot do.' Yash's statement hangs over them a second: a general sentiment regarding the human condition. 'Off the books, we still have one option.'

'What?'

'We can ruin them. We can take their garage off them and kick them into the street.'

'How?'

'There are papers Mohinder Gidh can draw up.' He turns to Rishi. 'But he will need your help.'

'My help?'

'Mohinder can show you the documents he needs. He can show you what to make.'

'Make?'

'Come on, Rishi,' Yash sighs. 'Vinod's told me what's in that tin of yours.'

Each week Rishi visits Devnagar and collects glass blanks for his mother to cut against her wheel. The journey from Chhaphandi to Devnagar and back is too much to do in a day, so Rishi spends the night with a cousin of his mother's. After they have eaten, his auntie goes to bed – she's forever dropping with tiredness – leaving Rishi free to pursue his hobby. On the roof, basking in the city's churn (spinning wheels and screaming babies, insults hurled from house to house, squeal of pulleys, snap of clothes pegs, slam of ten thousand doors), he pulls his biscuit tin out from under the plastic water tank and sorts through the dollars there.

The trouble with the dollar-stamping machine – a constant of his life, and still sporting its Clint Eastwood paint job – is that while he can compose pretty much whatever message he wants around the edge of the coin – 'Board of Intermediate Education', 'Bihar School Examination Board' – the centre of the coin must feature a novelty motif.

Happy Birthday

Love

Souvenir from Firozabad

So Rishi embosses his legal-looking documents very lightly, rubbing the paper over the circumference of his chosen dollar with steady strokes of a soft eraser. The impression this leaves is weak-wristed, but the stamp is fraudulent anyway so this isn't a huge problem. Growing adept, Rishi has even begun cutting his printing blocks by hand, using the chewed-up jewellers' tools that litter the city's bric-a-brac stalls. And with this reconditioned kit he counterfeits what so few round here can afford: a paper life.

'You don't have to make masterpieces,' Yash assures him. 'Just make documents good enough that if someone asks, Mohinder can hold them up and say he was honestly duped.'

Rishi thinks about it. An idea comes to him. Really, a very good idea.

'Write off the dowry.'

Rishi's demand surprises them both. Yash laughs.

'Years I've been driving your family's fucking earthmover around and what have I ever had to show for it? What wages have I ever seen? I've paid you Safia's dowry many times over and you know it.'

Confused, Vinod glances at Yash.

'After all,' Yash says to his cousin, 'you're getting a going concern out of the deal. You're getting an entire auto business. You can afford to be generous.'

Vinod takes a swallow of Pepsi and swills it around his mouth, scowling, judging the vintage. After a minute or two of this charade, he holds out his hand: 'So we're done,' he says, and Rishi shakes his hand.

Once Rishi has some money in his pocket, he goes in search of a companion. He finds a girl from Agra. Educated. A catch. A prize. Pali Ghoshdashtidar. They marry. In Firozabad he gets a foreman's job in one of the city's glass factories and his mother comes to live with them in Devnagar.

They don't rub along too badly. Once Rishi's off to work in Firozabad, away go the pots, the pans, the cushions, the few domestic knick-knacks that make their home. Out come the gas bottles, the lathes, the burners, spools of solder.

Men tend the kilns in the centre of town and it is their grievances and disputes which make the headlines, but in reality the city's industry is driven by the women and girls in places like Devnagar, squatting in poorly lit rooms like this one. Pali is a businesswoman and expects to be taken seriously. Rishi's mother hides her fear of her daughter-in-law behind a tremulous smile.

By the time Rishi gets home, Pali has packed away the children and his mother has prepared their dahl. They move around their room in silence, rearranging their few possessions. They eat, and for a while the smell of food erases the day's busy milling of glass blanks: hot electric leavings in the air.

Rishi's mother piles their dishes into a bowl of grey water and washes them herself: servile work performed without complaint. We spend all day with children, Pali and I, ordering them about, keeping them in check, seeing to their cuts and scrapes, what do we want with a house-girl cluttering up the room of an evening? (In truth, she is glad of a way to demonstrate her humility to her scary daughter-in-law.)

At night a curtain, drawn from wall to wall, divides the room, offering the couple a little privacy. Rishi's mother sleeps among the piled-up lathes and wheels, boxes of irons and solder spools.

It's a bad time for the brickmaking business. Word's gone round the camps that indentured labour is done for. This, anyway, is the pronouncement from Delhi. Politicians are on the TV saying that there's no longer any place in modern India for employment practices that border on slavery.

Which is all very fine, but urban sentiments fall on stony ground in Chhaphandi. Freeing the serfs into *what*, exactly? In roadhouses up and down the Sher Shah Suri Marg, Vinod explains the matter: 'The only other work these people get is shovelling shit. Literally, shovelling shit. Maybe one or two get to change the dressings in charity hospitals. What kind of life is that?'

Next, the Communist Party roll into town, stirring up trouble, inflaming the workers at the Yadav Brickworks. A couple of days later, a mother of two, Samjhoria Nankar, declares herself free, downs tools, and walks out of the Chhaphandi brickworks to attend a rally. She comes back, of course, to eat Vinod's food and burn his fuel, but she doesn't go back to work, oh no, she just sits there ('the fat pig'), all the while demanding her 'rights'. That's why Vinod has been taking a lathi to Samjhoria Nankar's back.

There have been fights at the brickworks before, of course. It is a place of hard knocks. Whenever upstart *bhangis* win at cricket, the rich boys of the village ride up on their Enfields and beat them down to size with bike chains. It is in the nature of things. In this region the wealthy make their own justice. Terror is a tool of control, cheaper and more effective than the law. Horror inspires fear, and fear inspires respect.

Vinod's escalating harassments of the Nankar family have been anything but calculated. More like the tantrums of an overgrown child. Rishi comes home one evening from his shift at the glass factory and finds Pali's milling operation still in full swing. 'Late delivery?'

Pali elbows past him with a tray of bangles. By the door sit beaded bags, loaded with samples wrapped in brightly coloured tissue. Pali is due aboard the Kalindi service tonight. She's going to New Delhi to play the aspiring businesswoman, displaying rural handicrafts to a discerning urban market. If she secures good orders, as she expects, almost everyone in the street will be able to afford a brand-new plastic water tank this year.

'I've been busy entertaining your friend,' Pali grumbles. 'Yash Yadav is on the roof with your mother.' She turns off the gas taps, one by one. The Bunsen burners gutter out even as the girls are working.

'What the hell is my mother doing on the roof?'

'Flirting.'

Rishi takes the dregs of liquor from behind the portable television and climbs the ladder.

Yash, the region's counter-terror tsar, is a man people turn to for advice regarding agitation, insurrection and incitement. He's the one who says to backbenchers, newscasters, clueless relatives and dotty old women where the national rot is to be found. The toothless old men of Devnagar adore him. He is their shining boy. He is, to hear them speak of him, the youthful embodiment of every ancient courtesy. He wears pressed shirts. He wears a watch. He shakes their hands in the morning. He buys them tea. He loses to them at backgammon and chess.

Yash can bowl over toothless old women too: Rishi's mum has given him the embroidered cushion to sit on and has even brought Pali's best china up on to the roof. The plates are piled with kids' food: halva, kulfi, sugared almonds. At Rishi's arrival she stands, yabbering like a schoolgirl. 'Rishi! Inspector Yadav and I have had such a fascinating afternoon! He has been telling me *everything* – so shocking! What would we do without him?'

Yash says: 'Let's talk in the car.'

Rishi rides to Chhaphandi in Yash's brand-new, saffron-yellow Maruti Zen. The front passenger seat is set so low he can barely see over the dashboard. The car's wallowing suspension makes him feel seasick – not that he's ever seen the sea.

While they drive, Yash tells Rishi the news. Vinod has come to blows again with Manjit Nankar. He claims that he caught Manjit interfering with the Lohardaga girls. The pair of them must have been drunk, for neither one managed to land a decisive punch. Bleeding and panting, they plunged into the shadows behind the Nankars' hovel. 'Someone left a hod-carrier lying around.' Yash draws his sigh from a deep well of weariness, as though human incompetence generally is his personal burden. 'This Manjit person tripped over it.'

The blade buried itself in his skull, killing him instantly. The news, the horror of it, has an almost physical mass: it sinks in. 'Who knows about this?'

'You. Me. I phoned Mohinder. Safia and the kids know by now. A bunch of *bhangis*, you know, kiln-workers. I have that in hand.'

It takes Rishi some while to map the enormity of Yash's plan. 'You can't expect me to do this!'

Yash won't even give him the satisfaction of a reply. Rishi has bought his way out of his dowry obligation by becoming Yash's little helper, and little helpers do what they are told.

Defining the southern edge of the kiln-workers' compound, broken pallets lean in teetering piles against the walls of a forty-foot-long shipping container. The container fell off the Sher Shah Suri Marg years before, rolling down the embankment, grey and relentless, like one of those elongated dice from the cricket game Aadi and Ram played with Rishi sometimes. Howzat! The Yadavs use it now to store tools and equipment. They keep the kerosene in there.

About fifty workers live beside the kilns. Most are teenage girls, itinerants from Lohardaga. Their huts are thrown up as and when they are needed. Each girl gets one room, which doubles for cooking and sleeping. The rooms aren't big and the older girls are taller than their rooms are long. This doesn't matter so much, and the girls can still stretch out at night as the rooms don't have any doors. Some of the girls have made doors of sticks and straw to keep the dogs out, and the more enterprising ones have made roofs of straw to protect them from the sun.

Vinod and Yash are waiting by the container. As Rishi shambles up, Vinod unfastens the padlock securing the container door and tugs the locking bar. The hinges squeal. The keys to the Komatsu are hung from a string just inside the door. Vinod throws them to Rishi and Rishi climbs into the Komatsu.

The Lohardaga girls, woken by the engine's growl, poke their heads out to see what's going on. The sardar dropped them off only a couple of months ago and they've yet to acquire much discretion. (Vinod's memorable assessment: 'In the fields they piss themselves where they stand and they don't even think to cover themselves.') That said, they can smell trouble brewing under their noses. They flee their hovels and scamper through the cornfields with their few possessions balanced on their heads. One takes her door with her, a square of battered corrugated iron.

Rishi, more nervous than anything, laughs.

Vinod and Yash pour kerosene into the house that, only hours before, served as the Nankars' home while, high up in his cab, Rishi listens to the clank of buckets, the splash of kerosene, a baby's cries stifled by a mother's hand. A dog's barking, a cockerel's crow.

Vinod Yadav lights a rag and throws it into the empty hut. The *whoomp* of ignition is felt more than heard. The oily, brazen flames of the fuel die back quickly and leave the hut smouldering steadily. There is little inside to catch light other than the fabric of the hut itself. The straw roof blackens and caves in quickly; corrugated-iron sheets tumble into the ruin. Streamers of white smoke spring from the mud walls as though the hut were a cracked kiln. In the cab, his view framed by the tubes of the safety cage, Rishi feels weightless, as though he were on board a fairground ride.

At Yash's signal he puts the Komatsu into gear and rumbles forward. He takes the front wall of the hut clean off, jamming to a halt in a cloud of dust and ash. He yanks the Komatsu into reverse and wobbles out of the wreckage pile. He stops, applies the handbrake, and lowers the front scoop. Vinod and Yash disappear into the container. They come out again lugging something in a sheet. Rishi watches, pressing his hands into his groin. Vinod and Yash manhandle the bundle into the scoop. The vehicle tips forward slightly on its suspension, then rights itself. Rishi pulls a lever, raising the scoop's hydraulic arms. Yash waves at him: Rishi stops the scoop. Yash and Vinod disappear into the container a second time. Rishi waits. They reappear, lugging a second roll.

'What?'

Neither Yash nor Vinod will look at him as they heave it into the scoop. The Komatsu rocks and creaks.

'For the love of God, what have you done? Yash?'

They turn their backs on him, surveying the burning house, then Yash wanders over to the shipping container a third time and comes out with a coal bucket. Rishi watches as Yash carries it back and sets it down beside Vinod. It is full of potatoes.

Vinod looks at the bucket. He picks up a potato. He weighs it in his hand. He chucks the potato into the wreckage of the Nankars' hovel. He picks up another. Yash joins in. Potatoes. Why are they throwing potatoes into the wreckage?

The Nankar woman demanded better wages for the family. She said they were starving. She even lodged a police complaint about it. So this is the idea: let the busybodies come. Let them have their enquiry. When they do, they'll find food here, right inside the remains of the Nankars' home.

Potatoes.

Rishi wrestles the Komatsu into reverse gear. He turns the vehicle roughly round, sending bars of lemon light through the safety cage and on to his lap. Heavy tyres churn the dry earth as he drives out of the compound. The sun is shining through the branches of the trees as he draws clear of the kilns.

There are a couple of hard nuts among the workforce, so the Yadavs can expect some do-gooders to come snooping around in the next few weeks. Some handwringing scribbler from the Janwadi Lekhak Sangh. Still, it will be hard for the workers here to drum up a public protest if there are no corpses to protest around.

The fire pit is not new. Rishi used to burn waste from the brickmaking operation here. Old rags, articles abandoned by absconding workers, broken pallets. He drops the bodies into the pit and uses the Komatsu to cover them with old tyres. Once the tyres are alight, their thick, liquid smoke fills the complex: a choking stink. The burning tyres will break the bodies down.

He strips off his shirt and jumps down from the cab of the Komatsu. The sun is hot on his back. He wades through weeds, through lumps of cow shit, teeters on discarded fence posts and broken kerb stones, slides on a scree of abandoned gravel. Behind him, a column of black smoke rises, thick and knobbled like a spine. It rises and then, at a certain height, it meets an invisible barrier. Something. He is no weatherman. Though it occurs to him, as smoke flattens off and spreads towards him, thick as ever and wrinkled like a cauliflower, or a brain, that when fluids of different densities and temperatures pour into each other, they make layers, and where these layers meet, internal waves will form.

He stares at the smoke and the smoke furrows its brow and stares back at him. He looks away, afraid, for the first time, for their children. Abhik and Kaneer. Twins. Not that he knows them, or remembers them, or could even tell you why their names come easily to him. No. Not their children.

Not little children. Not even Yash Yadav would, could –

Caught between strata of different densities, the smoke cloud curls into a rope and stretches out across the sky. In the low and dirty light, oil-droplet rainbows sheen its sides. A cow wanders past, driven from its grazing by the stench of Rishi's fire, and ambles down the cart track towards the railway line.

Pali will be boarding the Kalindi Express about now.

THIRTEEN

Important changes follow upon the Firozabad rail disaster. With Pali dead, torn apart in the crash, Rishi finds life in Devnagar unbearable. His mum can't operate the bangle factory on her own, and hasn't the eyesight left to work for herself any more, so it's arranged that she moves in with Safia, to help with the boys. Shubi and Ravi. Safia needs all the help she can get since Vinod came out of hospital, his arm a swollen and infected stump. Rishi and his mum arrive at Old Samey's around noon. Rishi still thinks of this as Old Samey's house, though Samey is dead and it's Vinod who's ostensibly head of the Yadav household, and Safia who rules the roost.

The place has changed little since childhood. A coat of paint here. A mended window frame there. This is the same drive Rishi and Safia staggered along the day they lost their brothers to the flood. This is the verandah rail Old Samey leant against, chewing tobacco, watching them, eyes cold and shimmering like puddles. Over there is the barn where the Ansari family lived like cattle, waiting out the rains.

Mum is out of the car and halfway up the steps before Rishi has even applied the handbrake. 'I've come to stay with you!' she cries, with obvious relish. A hundred thousand Bollywood movies have prepared her for this classic comedy entrance: the monstrous mother come with her luggage to darken youth's hand towels, to eat through its larders, overstarch its sheets, and overdiscipline its children.

Safia, trapped in a dialogue that is half tradition, half misremembered rom-com, shows her mother love. Makes her tea. Feeds her sweets, Shows her to a room that she can call her own, and leaves her there, at last, to nap a while.

'Why not stay with us?' she asks Rishi, when they are alone on the verandah.

It is a gesture as futile as it is touching. Home to what? There have been too many losses, too many tears in the fabric. Aadi and Ram, drowned in the floods of 1976. His father, swallowed by the emptiness inside him. His wife Pali.

Rishi visits now and again as the months go by, to give his sister a break. He sits with his mother. He tries, over and over again, to explain to her who Pali was, though why he feels the need to confuse her and upset himself, over and over, is beyond him. 'She made things out of glass. Don't you even remember the glass?'

From the window of his mum's room, Rishi can just about make out the little parcel of land that should have been his in the first place. He could buy it now, of course. He could buy it several times over, but why? For what? The few family that are left to him are all Yadav's little helpers now, one way or another.

Of them all, only Vinod has resisted his cousin's patronage, for reasons he will not rehearse and anyway no one wants to hear. Since the rail disaster – almost a year ago now – Vinod's disappearing acts have been growing in number and duration and no one has really tried to do anything about it, except maybe Safia. ('He's so depressed, Rishi. He seems so *defeated*. Can't you talk to him? Please?') Safia has tried to bring the two of them back together. 'My husband misses you,' she's said to Rishi on any number of occasions. But Vinod is failing. More than that: he is wilfully tearing up his own life. Rishi's not seen him since they covered over the killings at the brickworks. He's staying well clear. He'll not become the straw a drowning man might grab.

Safia stays loyal to her childhood sweetheart, of course. She was always a good girl. She says will not divorce Vinod, even now he has more or less abandoned her for the life of an itinerant. Mum, meanwhile, helps her manage her shame.

*

When he moved out of Devnagar, Rishi took a single room in the Motellissimo Motel, ten miles out of the centre of Firozabad. He's still there a year later. From the outside, the place might be decades old. Inside, it reveals its modernity. Folded like a piece of origami from a single wipe-clean surface, the Motellissimo offers superior hygiene for the better class of traveller on the Sher Shah Suri Marg. Foremen and junior managers. Men without wives or children.

Each morning he sets off towards the city and the print shop Yash Yadav has bought for him. (Say what you like about Yash Yadav, he knows how to bring on talent.) Businesses along the Sher Shah Suri Marg bring Rishi their day-to-day copying and collating. Once the day's business is done, he pulls down the shutters and tackles the Yadav family's confidential affairs: documents to smoothe the family's expansion from construction into long-haul along the GTR, from long-haul into the import-export game. His biscuit tin gathers dust. He's learning computers. He's mastering Photoshop. This double trade is how he's been able to afford a car, a saffron-yellow Maruti Zen – even if it has gone and got itself stuck in third gear.

The annual monsoon is on its way. There are no clouds but the sky is thick, trembling with a tension Rishi imagines he can hear. Below him, spread before him as he rides the embankments of the Sher Shah Suri Marg, the countryside stretches and bubbles. Layers of sky bend and twist and cavitate, generating hot, invisible bubbles in the sky. As Rishi drives home to the motel, his day's work done, he sees clouds of birds racing the poison cloud: banks of filthy, sand-laden moisture from the Arabian Sea. Worms wriggle across the road. Forgetting himself, Rishi reaches for a higher gear – but the car is broken, there is no higher gear.

Come to that, there's no gear stick.

His hand touches living skin, dry skin, warm and scaled, and a rippling of smooth muscle beneath. He squeals, the Zen swerves, catches a pothole with his nearside wheel, and lollops into a bank of weeds.

The car stutters and dies. Rishi scrambles out, winded and sore from his collision with the steering wheel. Where the hell is it? How's he going to find it? More to the point, how the hell is he going to kill it?

Rishi edges his way round the car, peering through the windows, half afraid that the snake, whatever kind of snake it is, not any snake he's seen before, will try and strike him through the glass. Then it comes to him that the snake must have somehow wormed its way into the car from underneath, which means –

Rishi skips away, badly spooked, afraid of what might be weaving towards him through the grass. He steps into a cowpat.

A car appears on the horizon. Rishi squishes his way to the roadside and tries to wave it down, but the vehicle, a green Honda, does not stop, and Rishi freezes there a moment, trying to make sense of what he's glimpsed: his old, broken, half-forgotten friend and brother-in-law Vinod Yadav, riding the chicken-strap next to a woman whose lips are pulled back, as though by acceleration, over grey shark's teeth.

Rishi shivers in the day's liquid, rapidly escalating heat. It will rain tonight for sure. He walks beneath the sky's grey and spreading wound, covering the half-mile to the nearest roadhouse as quickly as he can. It would not do to be caught in the poison shower.

Rishi finds it easy enough to find a truck driver prepared to pull him out of his ditch for a few rupees; much harder to answer the driver's torrent of friendly questions. Who is he, anyway, and what does he do?

Month by month, Rishi's answers to these questions are becoming increasingly vague. 'I drive a Komatsu.' An obvious lie. You only have to look at his clothes. His shoes. Rishi has done well from his work with Yash Yadav. In the last year he has lost his wife – torn limb from limb and scattered piecemeal, one of hundreds, over the wreckage of the Kalindi and Purushottam Expresses – and he has, into the bargain, felt the old certainties shift from under him – family honour, personal reputation – but he has a decent wardrobe, and a car, even if it is still stuck in third gear.

Gingerly, Rishi takes his seat at the controls of his weirded car. There's the gear stick, reassuringly dull and plastic and useless. The day's twisted weather must be throwing up hallucinations.

He can't wait to be home. First, he has an errand to do. Under a sky grown purple with threat, he kangaroos his way along the Sher Shah Suri Marg at speeds not exceeding 20 mph, ready at a moment's notice to hurl himself bodily into the road. It's night by the time he arrives, exhausted and nerve-fried, at the mouth of a dirt track overlooked by a sign for Apollo tyres.

His errand: to tell Yash what he saw when he was inspecting his car – that Vinod's back in town, with company.

This is the worry, a fear quite as pressing as any snake bite: that by covering up Vinod's killing of Manjit Nankar – and worse, compounding his death with the execution of his wife – Yash and Rishi have laid themselves at the mercy of Vinod's conscience. This didn't seem much of a risk at the time, but Vinod's been falling apart ever since the rail crash, very visibly falling apart, and getting Manjit Nankar's death off his conscience might be the single best thing Vinod can do for himself these days. Then where will they all be?

Rishi turns down the dirt track. The forecourt lights are out, but light bleeds through the shutter of an upstairs room. He sounds his horn and watches the window, waiting for Yash to appear. When no one comes he climbs out of the car. The house is quiet. There's no music, no TV. There's a car drawn up here, a cheap Japanese saloon, its dark paintwork indistinguishable from the shadows it casts across the forecourt.

A green Honda. Is he too late? He should run – but where?

Rishi heads for the corrugated-iron lean-to at the side of the house. Under the roof, grey against the darkness, a police car stands on blocks and, beside it, Yash's latest acquisition: an Opel Corsa.

The shutters of the upstairs room clatter open. A shadow moves in front of the window. Here it comes . . .

'Who's there?'

Rishi walks out again, and into a square of yellow light.

'Rishi?'

'Yash.'

The air snaps and Yash rises, silhouetted against the muzzle flash. He is naked. He passes through the open window and turns in the air, a cork screwing its way out of a bottle. He turns head over heels and lands, seated, a few feet away from the car, one leg outstretched, the other tucked unnaturally beneath him, with a queer elegance: *ta da!* – a gymnast completing a routine.

Rishi moves towards the wreck. He's not seen Yash without his clothes since they all went skinny-dipping as children. Time has not so much aged Yash Yadav as accreted to him, rounding and folding and filling.

Yash's torso slumps at a subtly unliving angle. The impact has broken his spine. 'Ah,' he says, just about alive. His lips are moving and perhaps he's saying something, but Rishi can't hear because in the room upstairs a woman is screaming. A second gunshot claps her shut. Rishi looks up at the open window. He tries to find his voice but there's no spit in his mouth, no air in his lungs.

In his mind he is running, running, but his body is calmer than he is. It walks him past the car – a metallic green Honda, glistening in light pouring from the open window – and leads him under the lean-to. From here it isn't more than twenty feet to the side entrance.

The door is unlocked. He steps into the hall. He closes the door behind him. The whole floor is in darkness. He finds the stairs and climbs. Light spills on to the landing from a door, barely ajar. He palms it open. He sees a small wardrobe, a chest of drawers and a sideboard, and on the wall above it a film poster. Soldiers and mountains. On the sideboard there's a set of car keys and a gun. He enters the room, his attention snared by the gun. He recognizes it. It is Samey's old service Browning. His Hi-Power. The one he and Vinod played cowboys and Indians with when they were children. He sees a woman's legs, sprawled spastically across the bed. The rest of her is hidden behind a crouching form. Vinod Yadav is bending over her, wobbling for balance, tugging at her with his remaining hand.

'Vinod.'

'Rishi.' Vinod reaches for his childhood friend, desperate, drowning. 'Help me.'

'What have you done? Vinod?'

'Help me to dress her.'

The woman is Safia. Rishi's sister. Vinod's wife. She is making small, urgent gestures with her hands. She is naked. A pool of blood spreads under her hips.

'She's going to be all right.' Vinod clambers off the bed. He gets behind her and tries to get her to sit up. Not so easy with only one arm. He slips his hand under her shoulder and pulls. Her eyes spring open. She says, 'I can't feel my legs.'

Rishi puts his hands to his head. His head pulses. An unfamiliar muscle is pumping away inside there: 'Vinod. Go downstairs. Get Yash into the back of the pickup. We can't leave him outside. Go on.'

'Only I can't feel my legs.'

'Is she going to be all right?'

'Vinod, I know what I'm doing. They taught us things in the factory. Punctures, burns. Go downstairs. I have this.' Rishi leans over his sister. The mess that's left of her. He's dimly aware of Vinod running out of the room. 'What happened?'

'I tried to snatch the gun.'

'It's going to be all right.' He looks for something to keep her warm. There are no blankets.

'He surprised us.'

'Vinod.'

'Yes.'

'Vinod burst in on you.'

'Rishi? Where are you?'

Rishi is standing by the window, looking into the yard. Vinod is framed in light cast from the open window, staring at the havoc he has made of Yash Yadav.

'Rishi?

He turns back to the bed. 'I'm here.'

'I can't feel my legs.'

Rishi looks at her, sprawled there. His temples thrum: an unfamiliar rhythm. His breathing comes fast; it's as though he were running.

'Help me.'

A muscle in his head is flexing, working, burning all his breath. It brings a picture to his mind. A picture of the future. Safia crippled. Her reputation done for. A figure of fun. Kids will throw stones at her in the street. He's a child of these villages. He knows what goes on. The petty cruelties of this place.

'I can help you,' he says. He picks up a pillow and brings it down over her face.

She claws at him, clutching and tugging at his shirt. In her shock and confusion it does not occur to her that her life is already over.

'Rishi!'

It is Vinod, outside in the forecourt.

'Rishi!'

Rishi lets go of the pillow and climbs off the bed and goes to the window.

Vinod is still standing beside the body of Yash Yadav. 'I can't find the keys to the pickup.'

'They're in the lid of the toolbox. In the flatbed behind the cab.'

From the bed there is a sound, like bathwater curling down a plughole. He turns back into the room. Safia is trying to crawl off the bed. She is trying to drag herself forward. Her fingers pluck uselessly at the sheet. He can see the entrance wound now: a little well of blood, shimmering and wobbling like a jelly in the small of her back. As he watches, fresh blood trickles across her hip, over the smears.

Rishi turns her on to her back and puts the pillow over her face a second time. Now, it seems she understands.

Afterwards Rishi goes downstairs.

Vinod has got the pickup started. He backs it towards the house. Rishi walks over, waving him into position, then raises his hand. Vinod stops the truck and climbs down from the cab. 'How is she?'

'She's all right.'

Yash is dead. At least, he is no longer moving. Rishi and Vinod stand together, looking down at his crumpled remains.

Whatever has influence over Vinod's mind at this moment – whatever pill or powder, whatever endogenous chemical response to events, or to the horror of events – it has removed from him all sense of anxiety. Impossible to imagine Vinod bursting into Yash's bedroom. Impossible to imagine him killing Yash. 'We shouldn't blame Safia,' Vinod says, recalling in tranquillity an atrocity barely a minute old.

'No,' says Rishi. He has barely had time to register what he knows: that Yash – after how many years of waiting? – was taking Safia into his bed.

'Because people will say.'

'Yes.'

'Because of this bastard.' Vinod hawks up his phlegm and lets fly. A gobbet of mucus lands on Yash's bent head.

Rishi gives an involuntary shudder – someone walking over his grave. Imagine it. Vinod, under interrogation by the Firozabad police! Vinod spills his story out to some yawning regional prosecutor. Vinod rots in prison and everything that Yash has built – the haulage company, the shipping business, Mohinder's legal career, Rishi's own print shop – the whole empire goes up in smoke.

'Come with me.'

'Where are we going?'

'I don't want Safia left alone. You can wait with her while I deal with Yash.' He leads Vinod to the side door, up the stairs and into the bedroom. Safia lies spreadeagled on the bed, her hands raised over her head, her fingers curled like claws around invisible prey. Around every manicured nail there is a thick semicircle of blood. Her tongue lolls out of her mouth. Her eyes are wide open. Rishi stands, poleaxed by the horror of it, while Vinod runs to the bed and hurls himself on to his wife.

Imagine this: a husband driven mad by jealousy. A casualty of passion. A husband who loved too much. Rishi takes the Browning from the top of the dresser. He checks the safety. 'Vinod.'

Vinod turns.

Rishi shoots him in the face, and the hammer snips a neat wedge from the webbing that stretches between his thumb and forefinger. Sucking at his bloody hand, Rishi bends down and retrieves the gun.

Vinod is squatting on the bed, weaving from side to side, in thrall to a private music. His left eye is sunken and bleeding. Rishi hefts the gun in his left hand and shoots his old friend a second time, through the nose. Vinod nods at Rishi as though he understands, as though he approves. He opens his mouth. No sound comes. He lies down on the bed, over his wife.

Rishi secures the safety catch and puts the gun back on the sideboard. It is done. Safia has died in the arms of her husband. Once people are safely dead, the toothless old men of Chhaphandi are a sentimental lot. Rishi can rely on them to make something Shakespearean from this mess.

He goes downstairs, out of the door, and round the cars parked under the lean-to. He climbs up on the flatbed of the pickup and releases the drum. He hauls down a few lengths of chain. He drags it under Yash's arms a couple of times and secures the hook as tight as he can to the chain. He operates the winch and Yash's body thumps and scrapes its way on to the flatbed of the truck.

He climbs up into the cab. The keys are in the ignition. He puts the pickup into gear. He rocks the heavy vehicle up the track and turns on to the highway, under the peeling sign for Apollo tyres.

The brickworks are only ten minutes' drive away. Rishi turns off at the patch of hard-standing and rocks the truck gently down the embankment and on to the lane, lined with margosa trees, that leads to the kilns. He turns off the headlights. He eases through the abandoned workers' camp, fingers numb around the steering wheel. He parks up and tries to catch his breath. The air enters him in fits and jags. If it is air. Most of it is water. A muscle in his head beats and beats against the backs of his eyes. He learns to breathe through the contractions. He is only weeping, after all. A man who weeps is not broken. This is what he tells himself.

The key to the shipping container is hidden in its old place. Rishi unlocks and removes the padlock and tugs at the doors.

Yash hangs from his chain like the winning fish at a weigh-in. Rishi pulls a lever, the pickup's engine changes tone, and the crane extends its stubby pneumatic arm. Yash glides gently over and on to the earth directly over the lip of the container door. Rishi unfastens the hook and uses the motor to haul the chain out from under the corpse. He straddles the body and heaves, gathering the body into the dark.

He empties drums of kerosene over the floor. The container is watertight and leans slightly, so that the liquid pools in one corner, by the door. Rishi stumbles around in the dark, grabbing and feeling for cans and canisters, unscrewing and tipping, until the atmosphere inside the container – all solvent and alcohol – threatens to overcome him. He stumbles out over the lip of the door, swings it shut, and uses the padlock to secure it again.

Kerosene has a high ignition point. You can't set light to kerosene with a naked flame. But you can set light to petrol. From the pickup's toolbox he pulls out a length of hose. He uses the hose to siphon petrol out of the fuel tank and lets it puddle under the pallets stacked against the container.

Rishi has no matches and there are no matches in the glove compartment. He remembers the cigarette lighter in the truck's dashboard. He turns the engine over, pushes the coil in to heat it, and when it is red hot he touches it to the wet earth. The petrol ignites with a sound like a crashing wave. Flames leap up around the pallets.

Rishi turns away and runs. He does not see the explosion. He does not see the container swell suddenly; how it loses its hard edges, and how, for just an instant, it turns soft and belly-like. He feels the concussion. He feels the rush of air against his skin as the container doors come open. There is a sigh on the in-rushing air as, behind him, the shipping container inhales.

He knows without looking that the innards of the container are aglow, white-hot, the contents charred beyond recognition. Not that anyone will sift through it all, because what would be the point? A few old buckets. Tools. Fuel oil. Kerosene. The leavings of a dead concern.

Yash, left where he was, naked and defenestrated, would have inspired nothing but contempt. Imagine it now, though. Picture it: Yash Yadav, who killed his lover and her husband, then fled into the night! This is a figure to conjure with . . .

Rishi walks east along the highway. There are no cars at this time of night, and no Tempos. Only the trucks ply back and forth across this vast country and this vaster night. When their lights approach he steps off the road. Sometimes the road has good ditches and he lies down in them to hide. Sometimes there are no ditches and he stumbles into a wilderness of tall grass, cow shit and shredded tyres. He conceals himself as best he can, shifting as the headlights approach and pick out for him the galloping inadequacies of his hiding place.

Rishi, the clodhopper, coming late to everything, serviceable and slow – Rishi has no part in this tale. He must not feature. He must not be pictured. He must not be imagined. He must be erased.

He comes to the peeling sign for Apollo tyres.

He thinks it is going to be hard, the thing he has to do; but the muscle in his head contracts, contracts, contracts, and deep knowledge overcomes him. He was born for this. All his life he has been building to this. He washes away the little bit of Yash's blood that he finds drying on the step by the front door. He climbs the stairs and enters the bedroom and smudges and polishes, shifts and drapes and angles bodies and objects the way he must if this is going to work. He works steadily and without emotion. He knows what he is doing. He has practised this many times. He has sat, hour after hour, surrounded by old engraving tools, scissors and scrapers, sanders and fillers, practising for this moment. Years he has spent, cutting and printing, rubbing and scraping. No way he could have known, until this moment, that it was all for this. That all his paper games were preparing him for these rooms, these limbs, these stains.

He leaves the house and, with the key from the sideboard, he unlocks Yash's Opel Corsa. He climbs in behind the wheel, leans over, and stows the Browning Hi-Power in the glove compartment.

He turns the key in the ignition.

He feathers the accelerator and puts the car into gear.

The Sher Shah Suri Marg stretches before him. Agra. Delhi. Mumbai. Rishi settles himself against the Opel's comfortable upholstery. The car feels sporty under his hands.

A mile down the road he comes to a bridge over the river. It is the river they played in as children, but the bridge is new. He leans over and opens the glove compartment. He pulls out the Browning and hurls it off the bridge.

It hits the water.

It hits the water.

It hits the water.

He weeps, remembering picnics on a green riverbank. He thinks about friendship. He thinks about family. He weeps away these timeless values. These constants of a man's life dissolve in his tears and when they are gone, they leave him whole. They leave him healed. This is what he tells himself. He restarts the engine. He moves up gear after gear after gear.

A mile on, with the road empty before and behind him, he experiments with the radio. A little later, when the road surface improves, he sees what the Opel's fifth gear can do. A mile further on, he gets the air conditioning to work. It begins to rain, a poison shower, and the windscreen wipers come on automatically to sweep the rain away. The pounding in his head has eased. His labour is done. He thinks about his sister, about friendship and green water, and games that did not end but only soured. Tearless now, emptied out, he knows that he must live with tonight's issue, and that this will be possible.

So he heads west, owing nothing. He was born Rishi Ansari, but that is all anyone knows, or remembers, and soon enough they will forget even that. He has never been very important. He reaches around his neck and pulls out the talisman he has worn since childhood. A silver dollar. Round the edge: AADI + RAM. His brothers. He must enter this new world the same way he entered the last one: with nothing at all. He understands this. He opens the window and throws the dollar on its leather thong into the rushing downpour.

There. At last. He wipes his eyes. He wipes his face. He is a perfect blank.

Part Four

FOURTEEN

David Brooks considers himself an explorer; and after so many adventures above the snowline or carrying his own water, it's a shock to him to learn that life under sail is anything other than a privileged species of caravanning. A couple of weeks' back and forth to Melville Island across the normally calm Arafura Sea uncovers how little he knows.

He says to her, as they struggle to reef sails in a hail of spray, 'This place is really shallow. Fifty metres tops.'

'Other line.'

'Because, look,' he laughs. 'These waves make no fucking sense.'

'Other line!'

The wind generator falls to the foredeck. It lands at her feet.

'Fuck's sake, Dad.'

David's daughter Ester grew up by the sea. She has photographs of herself as a toddler, netting for eels in the culverts behind the house in Carrum Downs, south of Melbourne. There was no EastLink then and she remembers pasture stretching all the way to the horizon either side of the Mornington Peninsula Freeway. She remembers crushing herbs underfoot and the smell of them rising. She remembers ducks, swans, rails, pelicans, rare migrants from northern Asia. She remembers wading through tall grass and losing sight of the road the way you lose sight of land in a small boat. She remembers levels, sluices, rats. She remembers low embankments and, behind them, the weight of the ocean. Where Ester spent her childhood the sea is higher than the land.

Stuck at home with her mother – a kind, humourless woman, given, since the separation, to prolonged, cheerless affairs with predatory junior academics – Ester has grown up hammering at the world as though it were a TV screen. It is her father's fault. Just often enough to inflame her frustration, David Brooks reappears and flies Ester out for weekends to the less travelled parts of the earth. Surabaya. Yangon. Kuching. For the sake of the child, as he would have it: the roundedness of her education.

David Brooks returned to Oman after the 1970 coup brought Sultan Said's son, Qaboos, to power. A former British Desert Intelligence Officer, he soon fell in with Anthony Ashworth and the rest of the new sultan's nascent intelligence community. Bankrolled by the British, Qaboos's regime was replying to the long-standing communist rebellion in the south of the country by building roads and hospitals and schools. Teams of Royal Engineers dug wells for Dhofari villagers. Japanese transistor radios were handed out in Salalah's markets. Former rebels were granted amnesty if they joined irregular units organized and trained by the SAS. Quitting the army, David continued to work as a civilian consultant. He met Ann, Ester's mother, while working for the public affairs office of Moyse Line.

In the summer of 1999 Ester passes her Higher School Certificate and David, by way of congratulation, sends her an air ticket to Darwin. He says he has a surprise for her.

They arrange for David to meet her at the airport, but of course he doesn't show. Instead, there's this Pakistani cab driver holding up a sign, but Ester walks straight past him without seeing. They run into each other once everyone else has departed. The cabbie says: 'This is going to cost extra.' Ester doesn't have any money and just gets in the cab. The cabbie drives her to the Novotel on the Esplanade, opposite Bicentennial Park. David's in the bar in a shirt and tie drinking Budweiser from a bottle and reading Ken Follett's *The Pillars of the Earth*. David won't take any shit from the cabbie. Ester leaves them arguing and goes up to the desk to check in. A minute later David comes up beside her, flashing an American Airlines credit card. 'Any incidentals, charge this.' He drops the card on the desk and the clerk, busy at his terminal, glances at the unfamiliar plastic, fudges his typing, has to start over. 'One moment, sir, I need to make an impression.'

'You do that.' David picks up the card and plays with it, tapping each corner in turn against the counter. The cab driver has vanished.

'Sir?'

'Yes?'

'Your card?'

'Sure.'

The desk clerk gives Ester a plastic key.

'Mind you take her bags up to her room.'

'I can manage –'

'You're coming with me, kiddo.' David heads for the revolving door. He isn't getting any younger. You can tell from his walk which is his bad leg.

Ester glances towards the bar. 'Don't forget your book.'

'Wasn't mine.'

David isn't much over forty, heavy across the shoulders, a regular at the Sydney Harbour swim, and since Ester last saw him his hair has turned to steel. It doesn't age him at all. If anything, it makes him look taller. This is as well: at five foot seven and with one calf-bone shorter than the other, he's a good six inches shorter than his daughter. He takes her round by Packard Street to where his friend's yacht is moored: a sloop with a fractional rig, he says, ten metres on the button. 'You'll see.' He sheds his tie in concession to the afternoon heat, rolls it around his fingers, and dumps it in his trouser pocket. Years pounding the wilderness, clinging to the chicken-strap of the company Toyota, have given him a taste for business clothes. They are his holiday gear: a chance to sharpen up.

'Where's your jacket?'

'Back at the hotel. I'm staying with you, kiddo.' In fact, he has a room at the Mantra, next door. 'Come round and use the pool in the morning and I'll show you the charts.'

'Is it okay? Can I use the pool?'

He pulls a face: '*Can you use the pool?*' He takes her arm and points into the marina. 'There.' Ester knows by now that David's surprise is more for him than for her.

You don't set sail from Darwin to Timor without amassing a boxful of official paper. David's business acquaintance, Rishi Ansari, who's lent them his boat, has found a way around the worst of the bureaucratic headaches by entering them in a five-month rally to Langkawi, the idea being they'll withdraw after the first leg.

Race day comes round. Departure times are staggered to let the more serious contenders get ahead of the flotilla. Ester and David set sail after lunch.

There is very little wind. The ocean surface is either butter-flat or with an oily swell so light it hardly rocks the boat. David spends dawn and dusk on the roof of the cockpit reading *The 7 Habits of Highly Effective People*, while Ester potters, rearranging their gear, fixing the fiddle rails back on the stove where they flew off during their stormy acclimatization in the Arafura. Woman's work. Ester suspects that the boat – well equipped but badly arranged – has never before been out of sight of land.

'I don't suppose Rishi even knows how to take it out of the harbour,' David says. 'It's a status thing with him. Self-made man and all that.'

'Expensive.'

'He's done well. Import–export. We did some work together in Singapore.'

She says: 'Dad, you should look at what I'm doing.' This, after all, is why she is here, isn't it? To teach him to sail. David, sun-dazzled and dizzy, peers earnestly into cupboards and drawers and chests.

Storms appear on the horizon: white anvils with skirts of dirty cloud. One passes overhead, and they cut through the rain-lashed water at about six knots. Otherwise the cloud towers travel around them with agonizing slowness, in no prevailing direction, as though they were alive: motile. Ester and David sit watching them for hours, trying to gauge how the waves are going to develop – but they never do.

Rounding the north-eastern corner of Timor they find the current running against them; it throws up an uncomfortable chop. By now, though,

David's confidence is up. The weather map shows a system approaching with strong southerlies and David wants to ride the front into Dili before heavy rain traps them in Baucau. Ester raises all the sail they have and the wind, running at about twenty knots, drives them along their route so smoothly, so precisely, they feel as though they are being towed.

Ester sees the easterly before it hits: a darkening of the sea racing towards them like the shock wave of an explosion. Suddenly the wind is coming at them from two directions at once. The whole boat shivers and rears, and the waves, no longer square-on, thunk the hull: a fleshy sound.

Ester yells at David to disconnect the wind vane. She steers by hand, trying to keep the waves square to the stern. David shouts at her to put the helm over. She knows it's the wrong thing to do. Still, some reflex twitches: she does as she is told. The genoa backwinds against the spreader tip. Contesting forces hold the canvas utterly rigid: a metal sheet hammered into shape. Then the sail rips from head to foot.

They heave to and settle down to wait out the squall. Ester lashes the tiller. They set storm sails. Now that the boat has its prow to the waves, they no longer seem to tower so steeply and the fleshy smack of wave against hull isn't nearly as sickening as it was. The rain comes sheeting down and David manhandles Ester off the deck. Inside the cockpit, Ester sees that he is laughing. 'Here.' He pulls a couple of tins of beer from the cooler and hands her one. She cracks it open and swings her way aft to stare at the rain.

'Dad.'

He is sitting at the chart table with his back to her, legs hooked around the bench. Head in his hands. Still laughing.

'Dad.' Ester looks back out of the window, not believing what she has seen. At first there is only sea. Then, as the swell rolls under them, tipping them forward, the horizon wheels into view. What's left of it. The thing bearing down on them already takes up half the sky.

Ester throws her tin at him: '*Dad.*'

David bumps against her as the bow of their little boat rises, pressing them against the companionway door. The boat trembles and flexes as the wave rolls under them. They tip forward.

It can only be a ship. It looks more like a building.

David pushes past Ester, tripping her over. She topples and cracks her head on the table. He yanks the door open and pulls himself into the cockpit. Rain blows into the cabin. The boat tilts. The rain changes direction. Ester's head throbs. She's going to be sick.

David shouts something. How the air is gone.

He clambers inside.

'What?'

'Flare gun!' It's already in his hand. He's learned his way around the new storage, after all. The boat tilts. He braces himself against the companionway door and fires. Against spray and grey water the flare is about as impressive as a kid's sparkler. It hits the side of the wall and explodes.

The waves crash and spit. There is no sky. The wall is perfectly vertical, as though cemented to the ocean floor. Everything goes dark.

A few years later – Christmas Day, 2004 – David laughs and lifts his can of Coke, toasting the memory. 'And if that's not enough, some cunt turns a hose on us.' Below the hotel verandah, Phuket's feral dogs are fighting among the restaurant's bins.

Ester remembers the white jet hitting her father full in the chest, knocking him across the afterdeck. He wrapped his arms around a winch housing as the hose played over him, forcing him back against the lifeline. The jet changed direction. It hit the moulding around the companionway door, spraying sea water into the cabin, plugging her mouth . . .

'They were using the hose to push us away.' David drains his Coke. 'Bastards probably saved our lives.' He leans back in his chair, arms behind his head. He wants to show off his swimmer's muscles to Peter, sitting opposite him: a South African yachtsman, a great red tower of a man.

Peter's skin cooks more than it tans. There is a swollen quality to him, like a roast tomato, ready to burst. He is fit enough: big enough to wield his weight. Ester feels sorry for his family, having to share their cabin with all that bulk. Peter draws heavily on a local cigarette, turns towards where the dogs are hiding, and throws the butt over the balustrade. He pauses, waiting for a reaction from the shadows. Nothing. 'They were trying to get rid of you.'

'They were trying to push us away.'

'They thought you were pirates.'

'On a ten-metre sloop?'

'Should they care what you are? They're a whale. You're fry.'

David's not finished his story. 'Soon after, we found the engine wouldn't start.'

The ignition-key housing was cracked. Whenever water got into it, it shorted the circuit and the diesel tried to turn over. Tried, but couldn't: they'd left the engine in gear to jam the propeller while they sailed. Now there wasn't enough life in the batteries to start the engine; and without the engine they had no way to charge the batteries. 'In a storm, in the middle of a shipping lane . . .'

Normally, David manages to make this a funny story: a joke told against himself. Tonight it's different. It's ugly. A brag. A bid for attention. Ester gets up from her chair. 'I'm going to say goodnight.'

John and Sarah, the elderly English couple sitting next to her, wish her sweet dreams.

Ester's departure has an immediate effect upon David. He leans back precariously, rights himself; his front chair legs click against the floor tiles. 'Bright and early in Rawai, yes?'

Ester smiles, says nothing. He watches her go. You can see how nervous he is, how much he fears his daughter's disapproval. They met at the airport this morning and she has yet really to meet his eye. Ester wants this holiday to work. She needs her father back in her life, but she can wind him up a little. She owes him that.

Sarah, sensing an awkwardness, applies the linctus of her conversation: 'Rawai! Such a lovely spot.'

'We're going scuba diving.'

'Lovely.'

There are only diehards left on the verandah now. David Brooks. Kevin from San Francisco. Peter the South African. John and Sarah, the quiet, elderly couple from England (their eyes too bright, their smiles too polite; they've heard all these stories before).

Kevin tells his tale: 'All these bloodcurdling things I kept hearing about the local pirates got me so scared, I did that thing, you know? You scatter a box of tacks over the deck before turning in for the night? About two in the morning a lump of driftwood knocks against the hull. I go running out, wrench in hand, barefoot . . .'

The story raises a chuckle. Nothing raucous. In their drunk, they have become philosophers.

Sarah says: 'Half the time they're just trying to sell you fish.'

'They boarded me.'

All eyes on David again.

'This kid and his old man. In harbour, of course. These things almost always happen in harbour. No one ever says that.'

Grumbles of assent.

'Kid had a gun. I don't know guns. Some sort of gun. Not a handgun.'

'Ay-Kay.' Peter wants them all to know he's on first-name terms with assault weapons.

'It wasn't so bad. They wanted money, cigarettes. My boat was just a hire. Very simple. Old. No fancy electronics. But it gets under your skin. The old man showing you photo-booth snaps of his kids while his eldest pokes you in the ribs with a gun muzzle. I don't suppose it was even loaded.'

'Probably bloody was.' Peter again. 'As well that you stayed calm.'

'Calm?' David frowns, staring at the table. 'I was scared.'

It's John's turn. The elderly Englishman. God forbid he and his wife ever attempt to return home: their England's long gone. He pulls a book out of the pocket of his navy-blue blazer and shows it to them: a battered paperback with a two-tone cover. He holds it up for them to see. He's presenting it to them. He's *making a presentation*. Behind the unparodiable precision of his costume – blazer, whites and deck shoes:

the ex-colonial yachtsman abroad – you get a glimpse, in this moment, of what lies beneath. The regional manager. The systems analyst. One of British manufacturing's trusty but surplus second lieutenants.

'Tarutao's a Thai prison island that got mislaid in the last war. One day the supply ships simply stopped coming.' John says that starving prisoners and warders joined forces and turned to piracy to survive, establishing a pirate dynasty that's even today the scourge of the Andaman Sea. 'Jolly good read,' he assures the company, hauling himself out of his chair. The book is by a local novelist. John found it in Phuket Used Books in Mueang.

Perhaps John's book report is a parting shot: a way of saying he doesn't believe a word of the stories he's heard this evening. David would like to think so. Better that than an old man chuntering on, out of his depth.

'Come along, John.' Hooking her arm in his, Sarah leads him away.

At about 2 a.m., Ester wakes to find there is just one soda water left in her fridge. It is one of those cans that practically vanish in your fist, good for diluting a single G&T. She knows she should drink more water and that she'll suffer for it in the morning if she doesn't, but she hasn't the energy to go downstairs to the Coke machine. She just cracks open the can, slugs it down, and crashes out again.

About 5 a.m. she stumbles off to the toilet and after that she manages to sleep – only to be woken, around 8 a.m., by the bed. It's shaking.

By the time she comes fully awake the tremors have stopped. Twenty minutes later they start up again. In the light threading through bamboo blinds she watches her little turquoise Schweppes can jangle its way to the edge of the bedside table, and off. She gets up, kicks the can under the bed with her heel, and heads to the bathroom a second time. The tremors are a novelty for her: unnerving, but not strong.

In flip-flops, bathing suit, bikini and sarong, and with a belly full of paracetamol, she heads over to the beach-side Starbucks. She carries her double-shot latte to a table with a view of the beach. The water is running out. Kids are jumping in and out of rock pools exposed by the tide. She doesn't pay this much attention until, halfway through her coffee, she finds tourists leaning across her table for the view. The sea has not merely withdrawn. It has vanished. There are fish flopping about on the rocks.

People are walking where the sea should be. Even the locals are gathering to look. She follows them, the cup still in her hand. Crusts of wet sand give under her heels as she heads for the rocks of the exposed seabed. She passes a local man and his son; they are gathering huge fish in a carrier bag. She comes to the rocks. They are too sharp for her feet. She stands there, chugging coffee, looking out to where the sea has gone. Now, if it went away so quickly –

Yes: it's coming back.

Children run back up the beach, squealing. Now everyone is running. There is a piece of driftwood rolling about in the surf. Something happens to Ester's eyes – there's a small snapping sensation as they adjust to the scale of the thing – and she sees that the piece of wood is a boat. There are people in it. She turns and runs back to Starbucks, out of the way of the water. She doesn't run fast, as though admitting the size of the oncoming wave will add to its strength. People are standing around the bar. She pushes in among them. Nobody pays any attention to her. They have eyes only for the water. She shoulders her way through and out of the building and across the street. There's a tremendous bang as the wave hits the sea wall. Safely on the other side, and in the shade of a concrete stairway, Ester dares to look around. Spray fills the sky: the wall has contained the waters. There are people on the road, leaning on each other, knocked breathless, shocked. Others are laughing.

Something rises behind them. Something black and absolutely flat: a metal sheet. Foam fizzes along the sheet's leading edge, and it falls. Vehicles topple over. The sky is white. A wall of dirty black foam punches its way across the road towards Ester, shaking chairs and palm fronds and people and a couple of dinky purple sofas in its fists: Starbucks' entire contents, fittings, staff and clientele.

David sleeps through the night-time tremors, only to be woken by a loud bang. He thinks of bombs. A terrorist atrocity. The Dhofari rebellion. He opens his eyes wide, his body stiff and straining under the sheet.

It is absolutely quiet. There is no birdsong. He gets to his feet and opens the blinds. His room lies at the back of the hotel, overlooking the pool. He snatches a robe from the foot of the bed and opens the verandah doors. There is something wrong with the pool. The water level is too high. The water slops over his feet, sending bottles of shampoo clattering over the decking and – what are those grey things?

Fish. He is surrounded by little flapping fish. The water is black. A sewer main must have burst. He hobbles back to his room and shuts the door.

There's shouting in the corridor. He goes to open the door. As he turns the handle something ice-cold slaps his ankles. Water is squirting into the room through the bottom of the doorframe.

The door bangs open. Black water engulfs him. He sprawls. He gasps for air and swallows something sharp. He flails, pulling at the furniture, toppling it into the water. It floats.

He sneezes. It feels like he's swallowed a razor. He spits out a mouthful of greenish foam and gets to his feet. He leans against the door jamb. The water is roiling around his knees, unable to choose a direction. Sneezing and coughing, he wades into the corridor. The lights are out. In the dimness, he can't see the water for debris: napkins, passports, bedsheets, nappies, shattered wood, Formica. He has a dim notion that he has to gather things. Penknife. Passport. Sunscreen. He turns back into the room. The first car rolls into the pool. Then the second. The wave does not compute. The wave cannot be coming towards him because his room is at the rear of the hotel. Mist fills the air, obscuring his view of the pool. Shadows loom in the mist. They take on form and dimension. A motor scooter smashes through his windows on a tide of broken glass and corrugated iron.

The swell carries Ester across the road. She glimpses her hotel, then the water folds over her. When she comes up again, she is being hurled towards a building she does not recognize. It is built over a sunken parking area. Water curves, dips, rushes under the building. The current drags her along a concrete awning towards the sink-hole. She grabs hold of an exposed rebar. She levers herself on to her elbows and leans over the concrete shelf with the water rushing around her legs. The water is trying to pull her off and carry her under the building.

When the surge eases, she pulls herself on to the shelf. She is bleeding everywhere. Where she grabbed the rebar, her palm is gashed open, There are two dribbling slashes across her breasts where the water dragged her along the awning. Her legs look as though someone has gone at them with a lawn strimmer. The water is full of glass.

By now the water is receding, taking with it the contents of the hotel lobby: computers, TVs, filing cabinets, children, tables, panelling. From up the road the water streams back, bearing off whole bungalows. Cars. People. Sheets of corrugated iron go past at twenty, thirty miles per hour, skimming and slicing the surface of the water.

A dark line appears on the horizon. Another wave.

David heaves himself into the corridor and there's an old man rooted there, frozen; they practically touch noses. 'Christ!' The man's all bloodied up, his face a streaked thing, bacon, barely human. 'Sarah.' Blood streams through his hair and down his face. He says: 'This isn't my hotel.' He's wearing a yachting blazer. It's John, the Englishman.

David says, through a throat that burns, 'You need to sit down.'

'I was on the beach with Sarah.'

David reaches out for him. Is there any part of him that's safe to touch? 'Where's Sarah?'

'What?'

'Come with me and sit down.'

'This isn't my hotel.' John turns away from David and stumbles down the hall. The back of his skull is off. There are wet things in his head. At the foot of the stairs he kneels down. David doesn't know how to help him. John heaves drily into the water and rolls around and sits on the stair and says, 'We've got to find the can.'

'It's gone, John. Where do you think it's ended up, after all this?'

'Well,' John grumbles. 'You would say that. Wouldn't you?' He makes like a cat, bringing up a fur ball, and his face just, well, *sticks*. It jams there, so that he can no longer speak. He only hoots.

'I'm coming back,' David tells him. 'I'll find somebody. I'm coming back for you.' He climbs the stairs to the roof. A couple of dozen people have gathered here, blocking his view of the sea. Taller than the rest, Peter the South African leans on the parapet, an SLR camera pressed to his face. Someone screams and people pull away from the edge and he sees past Peter to a towering wave that has no water in it at all: only gas heaters, air conditioners, people, motorcycles and cars.

The building shakes. The wave forces its way down an alley. People fall into him, screaming. Peter is still at the balustrade, the camera pressed to his face. David, light-headed, sways forward and joins him.

Peter is using the camera's telephoto lens to scour the beach. 'They went down there this morning,' he says. 'Suzie and the kids. She took them for a swim.'

Along the coast waves criss-cross each other, mounting and bursting. The beach bungalows are falling apart. Corrugated-iron sheets spill into the water. Beds, TVs, plastic ducting, washing machines. Wreckage grinds together, creaking and banging. Horns and alarms fill the air. A tuk-tuk has been hurled into the crown of a palm tree.

Peter says: 'Where's your daughter?'

'I don't know. I saw John.'

'Where is he?'

'He wanted us to go and find the can.'

'Fuck the can.'

'That's what I told him.'

'The can is gone.'

'I know.'

'I mean. Look.'

'Yes.'

Peter stands with his face pressed to the back of his camera. His family is lost as surely as the can is lost: there's no point in his standing here. 'Peter. Come on.'

'I'm fine. Go find your daughter. Go, take care.'

David stares at Peter. They have never liked each other. David leaves the roof and heads downstairs. John has vanished. In his place are two French girls. The waves have torn all their clothes off. There are deep punctures all over them, as though someone has attacked them with a fork. David helps the girls up the stairs. The stairs are thick with mud. The girls whisper their thanks. Everyone keeps calling him 'doctor'.

He goes back down, counting the number of landings, and stops where black water, thick with turds and tampons and shampoo bottles, slops over his feet. Ester's room is under water.

Ester climbs on to the apex of the roof. She gets her bearings. She is about half a block away from their hotel. Above her, on the balcony of a neighbouring apartment block, a woman wrapped in a sari encourages her boy to jump. Hand in hand, they make the leap. They fall straight through. Ester, sitting athwart the ridge tiles, feels the whole roof flex as they hit it, and disappear.

Ester works her way along the roof. At the edge of the building she looks for a way across the alley. The water has receded, leaving behind a tangle of refrigerators and mattresses. The waves have driven a Toyota Hilux tail-up into the wall below her. She lowers herself into the flatbed. The cab's rear glass is missing. She climbs through. The cab is full of blood. She crawls over the plastic fascia to the driver's side door and scrambles out through the window.

From here she's able to reach a balcony on the first floor, but the room beyond is jammed with shattered furniture. She climbs back over the balcony and gingerly works her way down the rubble, through a webwork of fallen power and telephone lines, and into the water. It is black, opaque, it comes up to her knees. Straining for sounds of a third wave, she wades round to the back of the hotel, stubbing and cutting her feet on rebar and lawn chairs.

An explosion has taken away the back wall of the kitchen. The inside is a maze of tangled metal, vents and dangling wires. The swing doors to the dining room are blocked, but something has punched a neat hole through the plasterboard wall. She crawls through. The dining room is under about a foot of slurry. The flood has stacked the entire contents of the room against the left-hand wall. Twenty tables, a hundred chairs. The tower leans, wobbles and falls. Spray scuds the ceiling. It falls as rain as Ester pulls her way towards the lobby.

People are fleeing the hotel. If you time it right, you can run out of the main lobby and get far enough up the road to be beyond the reach of the waves. The sea is still ugly. Surges just a couple of feet high are more than strong enough to wield sheets of corrugated iron like scythes. People are shouting instructions and warnings. Their voices keep getting lost in the din of the helicopter as it buzzes the beach, back and forth, filming the destruction.

Ester leaves the hotel. By now she feels as though she's hobbling on stumps. She's kept her dressing gown. Some people out here are naked. Others are fully clothed and sit surrounded by luggage, as though at any moment a plane might arrive and pluck them off the hillside. People squat by the roadside with their backs to the sea, staring sullenly at nothing. A truck passes, full of women and children. Word has gone round there's another big wave on the way. Someone jumps up and points out to sea, triggering Mexican waves and screams and pointless, circular running. Most people here have no fight left.

Ambulances pass her on their way up the hill. She picks up her pace. If they find David first and he is injured and they carry him away, it might be days before she finds him. She picks a dirt path and goes exploring. There's a chance David wasn't in the hotel when the waves struck. There's a chance he went for a walk, a chance that he didn't choose to explore the beach.

A local man passes her, carrying a heavy pan. It has scrapings of rice in it. He's been bringing food to the survivors. He glances back at her, looks her up and down, and says something in Thai.

'I don't –'

He shuffles his feet, nods at her, and walks away. She watches him go.

There, on the path: he has left her his shoes.

It finally dawns on Ester that perhaps David is in Rawai. It would be just like him to have gone there at the crack of dawn, bossing the scuba guides around, checking, double-checking, triple-checking their gear. She knows her hope is crazy. Still, she turns around and hobbles down the hill, back to town.

The sea is calm and glittering grey: a sheet of foil. The waves have swept cars and tuk-tuks off the streets and stripped the leaves from the trees. There is a surface cleanliness about everything, but each building is either a gaping concrete shell or a rubbish heap, and already there is a smell over everything: not rotten, but wrong. The smell of deep ocean.

There are vehicles running along the coastline now, all heading in the opposite direction. Beyond the town, the traffic dribbles away to nothing. Still, she presses ahead. Her legs aren't working properly. They are bleeding again, everywhere, all over.

Sand covers the road, and she is just about to sit down in it, she is putting her hand out to steady herself, when two things happen. She sees that the sand is gritted with tiny fragments of glass, like shattered Christmas baubles; and just ahead of her, she sees a Toyota. Bungee-roped to the back of it there's a mountain bike. A Marin. Ester laughs, and stamps a tattoo of thanks to the cargo gods. She wrestles the bike to the ground.

The coast is not as she remembers it. Here and there, in puddles, things flap and shiver. The skies are empty: these stranded fish will die long before the birds return to finish them off. Shoals of shrimps have left vivid streaks in the earth: great strings of pink. There is much bare earth where the vegetation has been torn away. There are no dogs.

She expects the ground to be a quagmire but the water has run clean off the land, stripping it so that the going is easy. The earth and the sand have formed a mottled map over the road, a two-tone, dun-coloured thing, ancient and weathered and smooth as velum. It is obvious, after only an hour of this, that she is lost. This is, literally, a new country. There are no trees.

She crosses a riverbed. There is no bridge, no sign of a bridge, and the riverbed is inexplicably dry. Ester climbs off her bike. This has to be Rawai. Only there are no buildings. Stiff and sore and thirsty, she drops her bike in the dirt and casts around for the line of the road. There is nothing at all.

A flat dribble of earth and sand spreads in a brown-paper fan before the sea. Where the earth and the sea meet, a shipping container sits beached half out of the water. One of its doors has come open. It swings to and fro in the wind, squealing.

She is very thirsty. Her forehead throbs. The skin there feels as tight as a steel plate. Raw from the sun, she shakes out her dressing gown and wraps it around herself. The wind whips the gown around her legs. For a while she hesitates. There is only one possible refuge David could have found here, and there it is, half in, half out of the surf, its doors swinging in the wind. Once she looks inside the container and does not find him, then that is the end. Her father will be irretrievably lost.

The container is old and rusted and lacks any obvious markings. It is so dilapidated she wonders if it might not have sunk long before and been lifted from the seabed by the great waves. She catches hold of the door as it swings in the wind. It's heavier than she expects. She staggers, taking its weight, and opens it wide.

She steps inside the can. Impossible to imagine there is a rear wall to this thing. Its darkness goes on forever. Her bare feet slap the plywood floor: a fragile sound. She moves forward. Seawater swills around her feet. The container groans. It yawns. She stares into the darkness and she sees, just a few feet away from her, a shadow. A man, or the form of a man.

It is not David. It is somebody else.

FIFTEEN

Missing men. Spilled containers. Ships run aground. The Indian Ocean tsunami has thrown Moyse Line into chaos. At Muscat airport Tanya Dix, PA to the company president Havard Moyse, waits for Ester by the gate. No easy, ex-cabin crew courtesy from her. Ester feels instantly put in her place as Tanya, clicking her way towards the VIP lounge, rattles off a series of questions Ester cannot possibly answer. What is she here for? Who does she need to see? What does she need? When by? She thinks Ester's a businesswoman. Ester follows her through the airport's semi-restricted spaces, past glass-walled rooms stuck over with lining paper. Through the gaps Ester glimpses grey-faced US soldiers, crates of Tanuf mineral water, rucksacks as big as body bags. 'Do you know where you're staying?'

Ester wants to cry.

In the VIP lounge, Ester's luggage is waiting for her. Tanya uses her phone. 'Where the hell is the chopper?' she says, pouring Ester an apple juice one-handed from a carton into a heavy crystal tumbler. 'Here.' She kicks the fridge door shut. 'No point waiting for service in this hole. *Hello*?'

Ester has never flown in a helicopter before, let alone over the Empty Quarter. The clouds scattered below them cast shadows on the sand: regular pools of blue in a desert that's as pink as a rose.

The airstrip is exactly that: a narrow corridor of dirt, surrounded by a camel fence. There are landing lights but no amenities. A four-by-four –

one of those new, low-slung Land Rovers – is waiting for her. The driver's door opens and out steps the most beautiful boy Ester has ever seen. 'Ester Brooks.' He's like a fawn.

'Hello.'

'How was the journey, Ester?'

Bambi's name is Tim. Tim has been working in the A'Sharqiya region of Oman for four years and, up close, you can see the damage his skin has taken from the sun. The desert is not kind to white beauty. 'Have you been to Oman before?'

Tim gives her his two-minute orientation. People call Oman a Gulf state, but most of the country faces east across the Indian Ocean. Its western border is drawn ruler-straight, gifting it a considerable chunk of Arabia's Empty Quarter. For practical purposes the country is little more than a fertile strip sandwiched between a mountain range and the sea. Tim's done this before, a lot. He might be an air steward describing the safety features of a plane.

Like Tanya, Tim thinks Ester's here on business. Ester doesn't want the embarrassment of having to explain what she's really doing – that she's here to receive condolences for her father's death – so she keeps him talking.

It takes time to develop an eye for the beauties of this place, but Tim's been here four years now and he has no plans to leave. He points out the sights as they drive. Patterns in the rocks strewn either side of the road suggest an ancient settlement. Heaps of stones gathered here and there are pre-Islamic grave mounds. This was a city, once.

There is a cliff, and a path, and at the bottom of the path there is a jetty, and a boat. After hours of airborne sedation, Ester finds the going slippy and difficult. Things here are as simple and crude and remote as she was warned they would be. There aren't many billionaires invite you to their hideaway with advice to bring sensible footwear.

Their boat to the island is a spruce, speedy runabout of a sort very familiar to this Melbourne child. For some minutes they drive parallel to the cliff-face. The swell, as waves collide and redouble, is nauseating.

It doesn't help that Tim wants to show Ester a recent wreck. A trawler came to grief last year against these rocks and it's still reasonably intact. It comes in and out of focus through the turquoise water as they rise and fall. An engine block. A funnel. Then they are away, round the bend and into open sea, following the waves south-east to the tiny island Havard – after much prickly negotiation with the Omani government – has made his own.

The island's high rocks suggest a Hearst-scale gothic hideaway, but the back of the island is broken and crinkled and there are bays filled with sand imported from the interior.

The buildings are stone: traditional structures that blend comfortably into the stark landscape. The palms are fed desalinated water. A plastic liner surrounds each grove, keeping out the salt of the sea. 'If you see a dying palm,' Tim tells Ester, as they coast towards the beach, 'it means seawater's penetrated the water table. You won't see that here but you will every place else.' Before 1971, Tim tells her, there were no metalled roads outside the capital, Muscat. No schools. No hospitals. Oman's coastal highway – the first – is hardly development gone mad, but it has wounded the landscape, and all along Oman's seaboard the date palms are dying as aquifers are diverted to supply the hotels and resorts the new road has made possible.

Tim thinks Ester's here to write about the island. Havard Moyse spends most of his year in Dubai and frequently lets out his island home to holidaymakers.

Tim uses a walkie-talkie to call ahead. Havard Moyse, sixty years old and looking forty, waits for them in a cove overlooking the ocean. The scene is photogenic to the point of parody. A lone, barefooted figure in cargo pants and a loose white shirt, Havard stares across the blue ocean as though posing for a book cover. Sunlight catches in hair bleached more by the desert sun than age. The effect, so kitsch, so religiose – so breathtaking – renders Ester speechless, and perhaps this is why Havard takes her for a newly arrived guest. 'Do you kitesurf? No? Tim can give you a lesson. We have an hour or two before sundown, don't we, Tim?

You must stretch out after your journey. Where've you come from?' His warmth is so unforced, his solicitude so flattering, Ester is tempted to play along.

Tim is there to lever them back on track.

Havard's face falls. 'Ester, I'm so sorry. It's the desert. It does things to the mind.'

Havard's patter sees them from the cove, along a sandy path and a few concrete steps, to a pavilion made of palm wattle. There are sofas and, on a carved sandalwood table, a plate of Turkish delight and a silver bucket full of crushed ice and cans of Mountain Dew. 'I hope you've got a sweet tooth,' says Havard, casting a critical eye over this minimal hospitality.

They sit. They talk about the tsunami. How can they not? Moyse Line lost dozens in facilities along the coast of Tamil Nadu, plus a handful at sea. It is strange to hear Havard talk about 'his people' in this way: as though a shipping line were like any other kind of business. The truth, the great open secret, is that global shipping concerns like Moyse Line boast barely any physical reality at all. Moyse Line occupies two floors above a private art gallery on East 72nd Street in Manhattan. Less than twenty people inhabit its shabby white rooms, and most of them are in public relations. Havard Moyse's ships, sailing under the convenient dayglo flags of one landlocked tuppenny nation or another, are chartered from companies registered in islands in the Caribbean. Their crews are hired by agents in Jakarta and São Paulo. The seamen who carry his containers around the earth are effectively stateless and spend their lives in steel cabinets. Shore leave is a thing of myth: since 9/11 most countries will not even let them off their boat. The truckers work for a thousand and one small-time companies.

Havard leans forward, hands clasped. 'Not to know what happened. Not to know where. To not have a body to mourn. I'm sorry, it's not my place to talk about these things.'

Of course it is. It is why she is here: Havard knew her father.

'It was after the coup.' Havard reminisces. 'In London. We were staying at the same hotel. The Dorchester, on Park Lane. He was minding the old Sultan there.'

The little David told Ester about his work with Moyse Line – Dhofar, the coup, bin Taimur, Tony Ashworth to dinner – has convinced Ester that the line is embroiled in Oman's shadowy, if benign, government apparatus. It's not the only company in this position. Sultan Qaboos famously mortgaged his country to British oil interests to pay for his roads and hospitals and schools. There are worse ways to pull a country out of poverty. 'I never got to know David that well,' Havard concedes. 'He ran interference for me in Singapore. Counter-piracy, I mean. Until MALSINDO cleaned the Strait.'

It's so much Dutch to her, but she can see that Havard means well.

'He helped look for Eric Moyse, my father, when he disappeared.'

Ester hides her surprise behind her drinks can. She swallows hard. 'Dad didn't tell me that.'

Havard smiles, trying to put her at ease. 'He wasn't supposed to. Anyway, we didn't find him. You did.'

Ester stares into her soda, remembering.

The container has cracked, letting in the heat and stink of the beach. But the corpse's eyes have sunk long since. Light pools uselessly in the empty, leather-lined sockets. Seated there, upright yet settled, a deathly misshape, his head erect, his tongue black fabric chewed half-off by dusty, tombstone teeth, Eric Moyse, missing these thirty years, confronts her: the robber of his tomb –

'You can imagine the speculation there's been in the press.'

Is this why she is here? To be briefed? To be cautioned to silence?

Havard says: 'Eric's container was adapted so that it could be opened from the inside. It wasn't his tomb. I wish the papers wouldn't call it that. He lived in it. Hid out in it. It does happen. Traffickers use cans all the time, and not everyone travels steerage.'

'What was he doing in there?'

'I think he was hiding.'

'Who from?'

Havard shrugs. If he's afraid of her speaking to the press, he shows no sign of it. 'Us. Me. Who else is there? The line.'

Havard's seen his dad. It was on the news. He's travelled to Phuket. Was driven through its splintered streets, to the Vachira Phuket Hospital. Saw his father mummified: rictal, drawn, but still his dad, his flesh turned to reddish leather, his hair to wool, his fingers into sticks. A doll, in other words. Time's plaything, unwrapped after thirty years of faceless, nameless circling. Eric Moyse, founder of Moyse Line. Impossible to imagine the character of his son's dreams now.

Come nightfall, Havard phones London. Lyndon Ferry, Moyse Line's director of public affairs, is still at his desk. Havard says: 'I don't think she knows.'

A silence as Lyndon thinks this through. 'Is this a good thing or a bad thing?'

'I don't know.'

'So we think her father really died in the tsunami?'

'Ester certainly thinks so. For God's sake, Lyndon, a quarter of a million people perished. What are the chances David walked away?'

'Don't talk to me about probabilities. We've got David's daughter stumbling upon Eric Moyse's container.'

This is ungainsayable. 'I still think we're looking at a simple coincidence. Think about it, Lyndon. I gave David the assignment to Phuket. So what if he made a holiday out of it? So what if he took his daughter with him? He wasn't the only one.'

Lyndon laughs, without humour. 'You're right there. It was quite a circus, from what I hear.'

'So Ester's finding the container – yes, that's a coincidence. A big one. But it's a coincidence that was waiting to happen. If it hadn't been her it could have been any one of a number of people. That South African wasn't far behind.'

'What about this daughter of his? What's her name? Ester?'

'What about her?'

'Do you think she took anything out of the can? Any keepsakes?'

'Lyndon, she's twenty years old. What she saw, it scared her half to death.'

'There must be something has been lifted from the can,' Lyndon says. 'Otherwise . . .' He trails off.

'Otherwise what?' Havard's never really bought into the idea that Eric Moyse would have spent the years of his hermitage writing out, in fair hand, all his lifetime's secrets. 'Eric kept Dead Water in his head for thirty years and when the pressure finally became too much he ran away to sea where nobody could find him. God knows how many years he lived hidden in that can. Why would he ever choose to write his secrets down?'

'Even Eric can't have thought that he would live forever. He knew he would have to hand Dead Water over to somebody at some stage.'

This is an old argument; the same argument they've been having since Peder Halstad retired and Lyndon Ferry stepped up as Havard's chief of staff. Without Eric Moyse, nobody knows how Dead Water operates. Self-sustaining, apparently secure, and under nobody's control: it's a liability to stagger the mind.

'I'm going to do what I can for David's daughter.'

'Will she talk to the cameras, do you think?'

'And say what? We've had journalists and camera crews crawling over the can for days.'

There's been no sense in trying to conceal the story. Better to let it burn bright and burn out quickly. Eric Moyse is not a household name, not a Randolph Hearst, not a Howard Hughes, not even a Donald Crowhurst. Still, his odyssey carries a hint of each of those great stories and there's nothing to be gained by pretending that it hasn't happened: Eric Moyse, missing since 1975, makes a grand, posthumous entrance on the back of a killer wave.

The puzzle – what was Eric doing in one of his own containers? – has been overshadowed by the tsunami itself. This much is public knowledge: that the box was rigged to sustain Eric Moyse through a lengthy incarceration. A portable air-conditioning system. Car batteries. Cooking facilities. A chemical toilet. Books. Russian literature. (A row of uncracked spines: sooner death than to have to trace, over seven hundred indifferently translated pages, the sorry events behind Anna Karenina's inconsiderate passenger action.) A chest of clothes. A table and a chair. No notebooks, no papers, no personal revelations. No dying obsession, no madness, no grand delusion. No hint of Dead Water.

'So what are you going to do for her?'

'What?'

'Ester. What are you going to do for her?'

'Oh.' Havard hesitates. He remembers his school in Narvik, and Peder Halstad's visit. It is vanity, of course – pure narcissism – to be trying to rescue Ester the way Peder rescued him. Rescue her from what? For all he knows, Ester's already leading a perfectly good life. Still, he has to do something, for her father's sake. 'I thought I might offer her a job.'

Muscat shows off its little wealth by wasting its water. Petunias stretch in an unbroken line for the fifty kilometres between the airport and the city. Behind the flowerbeds lush hedges rise to a man's height, topiaried to resemble waves. Guest workers are everywhere: yellow boiler suits, palm-frond brushes, hoses.

Navigation is difficult because Muscat is four old towns run together. All roads lead to a centre – but which centre? After a while you learn to steer by the topology: each district has its distinctive nook in the hills. Havard and Ester arrive at the Intercontinental as the sun, hidden behind the Jebel range, begins lighting the dust clouds from below: an eerie, neon-pink glow. Palm trees ring the swimming pool. Their fronds are dry and broken, jointed like fingers. As they weave they make a sound like knives being sharpened. A mechanical whining from behind the hotel heralds the arrival of the evening bug men, keeping the mosquitos at bay with petrol-driven DDT sprayers.

Inside the bar a Brazilian six-piece sets up. A parrot screeches.

'It's a robot.'

Ester draws a fine grey pashmina away from her hair and settles it around her shoulders. 'You're kidding.' This evening she is anything but little-girl-lost. Impossible to think of her as a dead colleague's child.

'Time it.'

'Really?'

'Every three minutes,' Havard tells her, 'like clockwork. Go on. And the lawn around the pool is AstroTurf.'

They find a table. The walls of the bar are hung with photographs taken from old travel books. A lot of boats disgorging hemp sacks and balsa crates on to a lot of ramshackle quays. Joseph Conrad shading into Graham Greene shading into Humphrey Bogart in *The African Queen*. 'All this –' Havard waves at the walls. Crates and sacks and stacks and barrels, little boats and little harbours. 'All this is gone. Everything ends up in a box these days.'

Heavy men like great black towers, sweating in the sun.

'Eric ended it all. All those dreams of running away to sea. He turned the whole world into – oh, I don't know. A branch of Wal-Mart.'

There's nothing Ester can do for the line in Oman, but Dubai is less than a day's drive away. In the megaports of Port Rashid and Jebel Ali, the two biggest deep-water facilities on earth, there is work for her. 'If you want it. In the offices of Dubai Trade.'

He brings up the website on his Palm: *Dubai's one-stop web portal for shipping agents, freight forwarders, air agents, clearing agents, hauliers, free-zone companies and import communities.* 'It would be something different,' he says.

He tells her stories about Dubai. How its amphibious architectural wonders – The Palm and The World and all the rest – are already silting up. How its high-rises have to be built slightly corkscrewed so that, as the desert sun moves around the wet concrete, the structure will set true. He delivers each anecdote in the same bland, amused way, as though doling out sweets to a child. Havard has had close colleagues since Peder Halstad, but no lieutenants. He has been photographed with beautiful women, but he has never married. He is telegenic and no stranger to celebrity photo shoots, gossip columns, and even movie premieres. For all that, he is still a shipping man: by definition a grey, elusive man in an even more grey and elusive industry. He is more like his father than he will ever admit.

Ester says: 'I'll think about it.'

The next day Havard takes her to the beach. Muscat's surfing beach feels more remote than it actually is. No one's ever built tall here and it doesn't take much to hide the city. A line of palms. A shallow dune. The mountains beyond are hidden by storms. The sky is pearled, heavy with dust from the interior. They sit in the sand, eating flatbread, drinking wine. Iranian apples. Baklavas.

Ester watches the waves. She watches the kitesurfers spin and fly; their wings are perfect Cs, sickling the blue air. Each component of the view makes a distinct and separate impression upon her. There's a secret here she's not getting. Some relationship between body strength and wind and wave. An invisible magic that every so often snatches gravity away and turns this wet and furious activity into something else: an aerial acrobatics. 'I'd like to try that.'

It is as though someone else spoke. Someone who knows her better than she knows herself. She stares and stares.

The kites give a true picture of the wind; the surfers a true picture of the waves. Connecting them are monofilament lines, invisible and strong, like propositions in logic. The argument hums through those lines. The secret vibrates through them. How wind and waves relate. She wants to be out there. She wants to understand. Not surf, not fly, not spin, not trick her way into anything. Just understand. 'I've got to try that,' she says.

That night Havard takes her back to his house in Ruwi. The floors are so highly polished it feels as though she is walking on glass. The doors are lacquered and as reflective as mirrors: as they talk their way into their first clinch she keeps glimpsing, in dark connecting rooms, suave couples whose quiet intimacies exclude her.

The living room is the size of an airport lounge. There are piles of travel books, histories, big picture books about local crafts. In place of ornaments, scattered around the living room, on the corners of shelves and propped in corners, there are whale bones. Ribs like cutlasses. A single vertebra the size and approximate shape of a kitchen stool. Havard is already dressed, waiting for her to surface. He tells her, 'The locals must have chopped it up to get rid of the stink. They must have buried most of it. Anyway, they dragged this bit of spinal cord into the lagoon and that's where I found it. It still had a nylon rope running through it. I searched and searched, but I never found its skull.'

As he talks, he undresses her. He wants them to do it in the middle of the room. He feels her spine. He feels its whole length, and round, and in, mouth suckered to her little tit.

Her eyes are wide open. She barely blinks. 'Oh,' she sighs, as he enters her, 'go on, then.' She imagines villagers waking one morning to find a whale beached on their shore. The flesh rots but the bones remain. They persist. In the dunes: they circulate. 'Fuck me.'

'You're crying.'

'Fuck me.' She imagines them, hauling at it. 'Fuck me, if you're going to.' Dragging it from place to place. Disturbed by it. Inspired.

Tuesday, 15 March 2005

The kite moves truly to the wind; the board moves truly to the wave. Between them, caught there, the body flexes, seeking an accommodation. The secret – how wind and wave are one – wracks the body, runs through the body, then vanishes, leaves the body trembling, the mind amnesiac.

Every weekend Ester tries to drown herself in the shallows of a Dubai surfing beach the ex-pats have christened Wollongong. She sines. She sputters. She splashes into the sea. You can tell she's a novice from her brand-new gear. A Concept Air SLE kite. An F One wakeboard, too narrow for a beginner.

The rich dilettantes who've taken ownership of Wollongong think nothing of buying a fresh quiver every six months. Overgrown kids who care about this season's colours. SLEs in a particular shade of lime. They're engineers, mainly, from South Africa. Management consultants.

IT bandits. They drive their balloon-tyred pickups right up to the water. 'What do you do?' they ask her, over coffee, over Pepsi, over Mountain Dew. They expect her to say that she's a PA or something. A junior oil executive. At very least, an English teacher.

Ester's a clerk. Each morning she gets in her rental car and joins the slow shunt past private surgeries and road-mending crews into Jebel Ali. 'I proofread the names of the ships.'

Some of them say, 'Is that all?' Others dig themselves even deeper: 'Is it interesting?' Everyone asks her, 'How long are you going to do that?' and she replies, 'I don't know. It's my job.'

She wears her more than sun-bleached hair in a fussy, feathery, Tank Girl topknot. Her narrow features show interested boys what she will look like when she's old. She is very thin and deliciously sun-damaged. Like everyone, she hides her eyes behind shades, but you can glimpse little laughter lines at their corners. She looks at you with a kind of glee, as though she was this huge bird, wondering which end to pick you up by.

Havard said he was going to find Ester an apartment, but she's still got her all-right room in the Golden Tulip Seeb Hotel, a couple of miles from the airport. When she's not at the beach she spends the time tapping away at her laptop, chatting online with friends back home. She assumes the knock at her door is the maid wanting to come in and make the bed. It isn't.

David smiles. 'Well,' he says, 'look at you.'

He opens his arms for a hug.

They eat at a restaurant in the Madinat Jumeirah. The Madinat's a resort complex: a Venetian fantasy dropped wholesale into the desert, there to convince the tourists that Dubai, fifty years ago, was something more than a small fort and a malarial creek. It takes the cabbie a good half-hour to work out which of its forty-four restaurants David's booked a table at.

Father and daughter look as if they're on their way to a wedding reception. David is wearing an ice-cream suit and no tie; Ester's in a sunflower-yellow dress, her hair done up in a bun secured with an artificial sunflower: an exceptionally lovely stewardess from an Asian airline.

'December 2004. A severely corroded Moyse Line shipping container turns up unscheduled at a tiny shallow-water quay in Rawai. You remember. Phuket.'

Ester finds her voice. 'We were going to go diving.'

'Inside the container the dock-workers find a mummified corpse. You weren't the first to find Eric Moyse, Ester. The Thai police were. The corpse has no ID but there's a notebook stuffed with addresses and Phuket's chief of police, who's no slouch, gets on the phone and contacts every address he can decipher. Ness Ziona. Farnborough. Groom Lake. 85 Albert Embankment. And the call comes back: leave the body alone. Leave the can alone. Leave everything the fuck alone. Why? Because 85 Albert Embankment is the headquarters of MI6, Langley is the home of the CIA, Ness Ziona is home to the Israel Institute for Biological Research, Qinetiq is based in Farnborough, and Groom Lake is slap-bang in the middle of Area 51. A couple of weeks later, a bunch of us descend on Phuket, all of us with our wives and our children in tow, our swimming trunks, our factor 20. All of us hungry for a peek inside the container.'

'You were working.'

David makes a face. 'When am I not working?'

Ester doesn't want to think about how lonely her father's life has been over the years. She doesn't want to feel sorry for him. 'Where've you been?'

David clasps his hands in front of him: a dumbshow of sincerity. 'Eric Moyse was a good man. This is something everyone agrees on. During the Second World War he handled sensitive cargoes for the Allies. Some of those cargoes were weaponized. Most weren't. For the most part Eric handled wastes and surpluses. Stuff that no one, at that time, knew how to dispose of. After the war Eric developed a system for hiding sensitive military-industrial wastes in the global shipping system. Things it's best people don't open, but valuable enough you can't throw them away. Chemical and biological weapons. Fissiles. You know those amnesty bins the police roll out for kids to throw their guns and knives away? Moyse Line is a bin for WMD.'

'Is this an answer? This is you telling me why you disappeared?'

'Yes.' He reaches for her hand.

'I *mourned* you!'

'It is an explanation. Listen. Dead Water was only ever a temporary arrangement. A hold-over from the war. Nobody wanted to use Dead Water longer than they had to. After the war, one by one, Eric's clients began withdrawing their cans from the programme. But it's like jumbling the lock on a suitcase. Jumbling's the easy part. The difficulty, if you don't have the combination, is getting the damned thing open again. If you wanted your can back, you had to ask Eric. And Eric wouldn't tell anyone the combination. You have to remember the times. Cuba. Angola. The paranoia back then. The way Eric saw it, he was saving the world from itself.' He reaches into his jacket and pulls out an ugly square of reddish stuff. A leather pouch. Inside there is a notebook, covered in the same leather, and inside that a handful of water-damaged photographs.

'The morning of the tsunami, very early, I was in Rawai. I was talking with the chief of police there. He gave me this.'

David lays his hands over the notebook. He does not open it. 'Dead Water.'

'Speak normal.'

'This book contains the combinations, the algorithms, to operate Dead Water. Eric had it with him in the can. You want to hide a leaf? Stick it in a tree. You want to hide a code? Hide it in a maths book.' He opens the notebook and shows her. The pages are written over multiple times in a dizzying palimpsest. There is more than one hand at work here; even a child's crayon drawings. David closes the book. He says: 'I can't bear my home any more.'

David has a bungalow in Mona Vale, less than twenty miles north of Sydney. 'I can't bear the sound of the sea. The waves.' The tsunami has given him nightmares. He's sleeping most nights on the floor of a friend's apartment in Eastlakes, where the early-morning roar of incoming Qantas red-eyes provides him with the alibi he needs for his worsening insomnia. 'They'll declare me dead in a few weeks. I want you to have the bungalow.

Everything the solicitors offer you, take it. You don't have to worry about me. I'm catered for.'

Ester is trying not to cry. 'Will I see you again?'

'Of course you'll see me again.' He holds out his hand. He wants her to take it. He wants her to touch him. 'That's why I'm here.'

Day after day, without cease, sensitive cargoes drift around the earth. *Merdif Chiba. Mitsubishi Spirit. Morning Emperor. Moyse Bluethroat. Moyse Skua.* 'All we're interested in,' David tells her, 'is Havard's well-being. Havard is the public face of the company, but you have to understand, Ester, the line is big. We, the people I work for, we're something else.'

'Spies.'

'Government liaison.'

'Where were you?'

'I'm sorry, Ester. I'm truly sorry. But I had to disappear. Dead Water has to be kept a secret. Especially from Havard. Look what happened to his dad. We can't let him put himself through what Eric went through. We don't dare.'

Ester looks into her father's eyes.

'You can help us,' he says. 'You can help us to help him.'

From this point on, pretty much everything in Ester's life becomes contingent upon everything else. If she wants to stay, if she wants to prove herself useful in this indeterminate adult world, then it is up to her to carve a place out for herself.

Havard returns to Muscat. They spend a few evenings together. After a couple of weeks, in this city or that, Dubai, Muscat, they find themselves sharing a bed.

Ester's father phones her every day, never from the same number. Ester confirms Havard's safety. His wellness. His fitness. It occurs to Ester that her father, or whatever shadowy interest he represents, has hired her as Havard's jailer; but she is by now so disoriented she doesn't even feel able to tell Havard about David's reappearance. David's told her not to, and why would she disobey him? She has been manoeuvred into a place from which ordinary, honest communication strikes her as both arduous and risky.

As the months go by, David's phoned debriefings of his daughter grow more detailed and more complex. His questions take longer to answer. They require research. Of course there's something wrong. Of course Ester is afraid; but if she tore all this up now, what would she have left? A thirty-five-hour flight to Melbourne. Another room, another house-share. Evenings drinking sour beer, avoiding old boyfriends. Bodyboarding. Friends' weddings.

Vessels sailed from Jebel Ali Terminal 1
as of Tue Mar 22 20:14:26 GMT+04:00 2005
201 items found, displaying 131 to 145

Vessel	**MOYSE BLUETHROAT**
Voyage	0
Rotn	216945
Arrived From	SADMM
Sail To	AEFAT
Berth Date	07-MAR-05 23:25
Berth	56A
ETD	08-MAR-05 23:00
Cut-off Date	
Start/Finish Work Date	
Sailed Date	08-MAR-05 23:15

So she sits, rattling and mousing her way through another windowless day in Jebel Ali, each day a little more the true believer, dreaming of the day when everything will come right and Havard will know, and understand, and thank her for this great and secret service she's performed, and together they will drive her very own sports car home through the world's Eighth Wonder, past tallest towers and undersea hotels, surreal ice palaces and pink technology parks.

SIXTEEN

It is 2002. Five years have passed since Vinod Yadav absconded with Roopa's car and ruined her plot to bring Yash Yadav to justice. Since then Roopa has been living in Mumbai: the plain, unsmiling single mother of a five-year-old son. Her policing days are over. These days she makes her living as a private investigator.

Roopa is one of only a handful of female PIs in Mumbai, and she is probably the best of them. On her fussy, Flash-ridden website, she explains that she is fluent in Hindi, English, Bengali and Punjabi. She handles her share of marital cases, but her primary focus is commercial. Her early career in the ACB has given her specialized knowledge and expertise in cases of industrial espionage, misappropriation of funds, breach of contract, inventory losses and employee-related theft.

Her reputation is good and her work has been growing lucrative. Come March 2002 she can afford a plane ticket and she returns to Firozabad in style.

Firozabad: city of chandeliers, of *satta* and cheap alcohol, city of debt. She dresses smartly and wears her best teeth. No one, glancing at her now, would know her for bright, smiling, eager Assistant Sub-Inspector Vish. In the central police station of the city of Firozabad she shuffles and barges with the mass, a civilian now, a supplicant. She's come to speak to Nidra's husband, Arun. She's come to track down leads in her never-ending hunt for Yash Yadav.

'Roopa? Roopa Vish?'

Arun does not recognize her at first. When he does, he does not smile.

He's cool to her, but Roopa's confident he won't turn her away. The morning after her assault it was Arun and Nidra who turned up at her house to give her a lift into work. It was Arun who broke into her house and found her bleeding and toothless in the ruin of her mother's furniture.

Arun's an inspector now, tasked with lifting the Yadav family's baleful influence over Firozabad's law enforcement, long after Yash Yadav himself fled into the toils of the Mumbai syndicate.

'You know this?' Arun leans forward, captivated. 'You know that Yash has gone to work for the Mumbai branch of the family?'

Roopa shrugs. She's a civilian: her knowledge is her own, to dispense or retain at her leisure. After years of chain of command, the novelty of being a private citizen still pleases her. 'When he fled Chhaphandi the family got him out to Singapore. I've seen paperwork there that connects him with the Wong crew in the months before MALSINDO started scouring the Strait. Since then Yash Yadav's been writing *hawala* notes to pirate crews from Trincomalee to Hong Kong.'

She could tell Arun any number of tall tales. She's spent years mapping the Yadav family's activities along the Strait and in that time she's had men come up to her claiming to be bulletproof. In Sumatra she tracked down one pirate gang, not one of them over sixteen, who said that with the right ritual they could make their RIB invisible. She's spent weeks at a time on derelict fishing platforms or hiding out in orchid farms. She's spent longer, truth be told, sitting in the waiting rooms of lawyers, officials, security experts and policemen. The stories they've told her are hardly less outlandish. How men disappear from jail. How bank accounts fill or empty on a whim.

The character of piracy has changed since her father's day. Modern piracy has less to do with the ships themselves than with the blizzard of paperwork through which they sail. You can steal a ship with the right notarized form. You can operate a ship under the noses of its owners eight months of the year and no one any the wiser. With the kinds of profits you can make, you can afford to hire and pay the crew you've 'captured'. It's a white-collar crime now, as abstracted in its way as the shipping industry it feeds upon. Most hijackings aren't reported. Most ships are returned without a ransom. Why steal a boat when you can borrow it? Nab a ship, use it to shift a drug cargo across the China Sea. Or don't handle anything illegal: just lease the ship out to some desperate import-export hack with a letter of credit about to expire. When you're done, hand the ship back to the owner with a nod and a wink. The less the company bemoans the seizure of its ship, the more affordable its insurance premiums, so nobody says anything.

'And Somalia?'

'Somalia's a sideshow,' Roopa sighs, enjoying this despite herself. 'There's only so much mileage to be had from a bunch of amateurs. They're getting into gun battles on board Russian ships. Everyone knows this is beyond stupid.' Russians and Israelis carry guns. You do not fuck with them. Not while the rest of the world and the International Chamber of Commerce are still telling themselves that you can defend a quarter of a million tons of container ship with axes and fire hoses. 'The pressure will come on Somalia soon enough and then the pirate syndicates will move elsewhere, probably back to Malacca, or Hormuz, or even Brazil. Squeezing piracy is like squeezing a balloon. The people orchestrating this stuff work out of mobile phones. Half of them live in bloody Canada.'

Professional, multinational piracy runs under the surface, right across the Indian Ocean, from Karachi to Dar es Salaam, from Sur to Bandung. It's a desk-bound business, reliant on newfangled skills: cryptanalysis and ADSL, network administration, even AI. Mumbai's pirates recruit from universities now, from SIES and the Tata Institute. Its quaysides are as quaint and lifeless as Brooklyn's piers.

As a port of origin Mumbai is an irrelevance, and even Mumbai's reputation as a destination for stolen goods is only what one would expect from a megacity of its size. Mumbai's an egg that's long since cracked, dispersing crews and gangmasters around the globe. Only a very few old-style players remain in the city: has-beens who play nostalgic gutter games with home-made ammunition. Roopa has lost count of the number of threats she has received. Not long ago, a mafia shooter blasted away at her with a cottage-industry pistol that police later found in a nearby drain, its barrel fashioned from a Land Rover steering column.

She gives Arun to understand that she is working for a commercial client: a big shipping company. The Yadav syndicate has stolen one too many of its ships. They've set her on Yash Yadav's trail once more: 'Funny how these things come round.' Every word of this is a lie. Not a day has passed that Roopa has not held Yash Yadav in her sights. Yash Yadav is her own business: something her other cases fund. She is her father's daughter. Single-minded. Obsessed.

Arun has the files she needs. 'The All India Bar Association say they have a file on Mohinder Gidh an inch thick,' he says, pushing a much thinner file across the desk towards her: police notes covering the last eight years. 'Mohinder Gidh is still practising in Firozabad and his paperwork's clean. Since the garage murders and Yash Yadav's disappearance in 1997, nothing's arisen to suggest he has connections with the Yadav clan.'

While Roopa reads Arun leans back in his chair: it's his turn to spin a tale. 'Gidh's from Mumbai. A middle-class kid who wanted to be a surgeon when he grew up. The nearest he ever got was a clerical job in his father's law firm, selling medical certificates for a thousand rupees a time to people claiming to have come from the area affected by the Bhopal poison cloud. When the police caught wind of the scam, Gidh fled and washed up here.'

'You think he still works for the Yadavs?'

Arun raises an eyebrow. 'Round here, who doesn't?'

Early the next evening, Gidh makes his approach. He won't come inside Roopa's motel. He doesn't want to be seen. He's phoning Roopa from his car – he sounds a million miles away – to tell her he's waiting for her to meet him outside.

Roopa finds him in the darkest corner of the motel car park, draped over the steering wheel as though guarding it from thieves. He gestures her into the seat beside him. Arun has got him to agree to tell her everything he knows about the garage murders and the night Yash Yadav vanished from Chhaphandi.

Mohinder starts the car and pulls away with a tentativeness that cannot disguise the mashed state of the gearbox. He tells Roopa what she already knows about the Chhaphandi killings. That while Yash Yadav was riding a desk as the region's counter-terror tsar, a country cousin by the name of Vinod Yadav caught him with his wife. How, in the row that followed, both Vinod and his wife Safia were killed.

Roopa doesn't interrupt him. Her gums are hurting her today. There are shards of dentine, spars of bone, still buried in the quick of her jaw. They stir sometimes. Blade-sharp. They circulate. Besides, she wants to hear the story from Gidh's mouth. She wants to know how much he genuinely wants to help her; how much he wants to take advantage of the moonlight to spin a ghost story. The account Gidh delivers is as unembroidered, puzzling and gap-riddled as the original police reports – and, for that reason, all the more chilling.

According to the police, this is the most likely sequence of events: Vinod, catching wind of Safia's unfaithfulness, drives round to Yadav's garage and surprises her in the arms of his cousin, Yash Yadav. In a jealous rage, Vinod shoots Safia. There is a struggle (the prints on the gun are hopelessly blurred) and Yash shoots Vinod. Yash panics and flees, leaving his lover and her husband bleeding to death on his bed.

They are halfway to Chhaphandi and the moon is newly risen above a black, unpeopled horizon. Mohinder Gidh is hunched forward over the wheel, peering into the dark. In the light coming through the windscreen only half his face is visible. It looks as though it was made of paper.

'And Yash Yadav?' She raises a hand to catch her spittle. 'Have you heard anything from him?'

A Tata truck, running without lights, looms out of the shadows, blasts its horn and thunders by. The slipstream buffets the rickety little car towards the edge of the embankment. With surprising presence of mind, Mohinder presses smoothly on the gas, allowing the wheels to spin freely through the gravel. He tweaks the wheel, and the car wiggles its way back on to the Sher Shah Suri Marg. 'Miss Vish.'

'Roopa.'

'As you like. Let's not waste our time fencing. Of course I am in regular contact with Yash Yadav. You know this. Why else would you have come all this way?' They crest a hill: off to the right is a stand of trees. Mohinder turns in at a dirt driveway, overlooked by a sign for Apollo tyres. They coast a couple of hundred feet along a narrow, sloping drive and into the forecourt of a two-storey house thrown together out of white-painted breeze blocks. There are no lights. The place is deserted. Mohinder leads Roopa to the door and reaches into his pocket for keys. As he fumbles through them he tells her: 'Yash Yadav writes to me. He sends me regular amounts of money to spend on the boys.'

'He has children now?'

'Not his children. His lover's. Safia and her husband Vinod had two sons.'

Roopa doesn't trust herself to speak. It is painful for her to recall how badly she overplayed her hand. She as good as sent Vinod here. She as good as propelled him to his death.

'I can't imagine either boy will want to live here,' Mohinder says, 'but I maintain the place. When Shubi and Ravi are of age, they can sell it.' Up these stairs is the room Yash Yadav left dripping with blood. 'Meanwhile Yash pays for the boys' education.' He holds Roopa's gaze a while. 'Looking after the boys: this is all the business I do for Yash Yadav now. You should tell your client that. Tell me.' Here it comes. 'Why is your client interested in Yash Yadav? Is your client a shipowner?'

Anything Roopa says will, she is sure, get back to Yash Yadav. This is the moment for her to reveal absolutely nothing. God only knows why she says what she actually says: 'It's a personal matter.'

Her job. Her marriage. Her child. Her *face*.

'I see. Do you want to see the room?'

They climb the stairs.

The door is open. There is a sideboard and above it, tacked to the wall, a faded portrait of Amitabh Bachchan. An old movie poster. *Sholay*. Seeing the poster, Roopa is transported back to that horrendous police report

Arun showed her: easily the most unsettling legal document ever to have passed through her hands.

The officer who first bumbled his way up to this room was a probationer, barely into his twenties. He'd been sent to pick up the keys to a recently repaired patrol car. He had only the vaguest notion what his report should include and so he included everything. Entering the room, he observes: 'It was virtually empty.' He notes the movie poster. A small wardrobe. A chest of drawers.

> There was a rug over the floor, and a pile of bedclothes. Opposite the sideboard was a bed. A woman lay there naked, her eyes open, and a man lay on top of her, fully clothed, without a face.

Imagine him, shambling up to the bed. Poor bastard. Imagine his legs, the numbness in his feet. Imagine his hands; the weight of them, in that moment.

Gidh takes Roopa back to his offices above a tile shop in a hilly, unfashionable part of Agra. To climb wide concrete stairs, past sinks and cisterns and boxes of bathroom fittings, and then to pass through smoked-glass doors into Gidh's dim, IBM-lit interiors, is to stumble upon a villain's secret headquarters.

He pours them both a Johnny Walker. He tells Roopa that Vinod's murdered wife had a brother: a Komatsu operator called Rishi Ansari. 'Rishi still works for Yash Yadav.'

Roopa swirls the liquor around her mouth, a fire, a medicine to cauterize a wound. Dizzily, pain-drunk: 'He does?'

'In Mumbai. All Yash's correspondence comes through him.'

Through lips made numb by whisky: 'Safia's brother works for the man who murdered her? Why?'

'People like that, poor people, they take what they can get, don't they? He's done all right from it, too. Runs a wrecking yard in Mumbai Port Scrapping Area.'

'Rishi Ansari.' It isn't much of a lead, but at least it's local. Getting her man is all very well, but Roopa can only afford so many air tickets.

SEVENTEEN

Late afternoon. Rishi Ansari is taking his ease on the terrace of his favourite Mumbai bar: the one with the slow but kindly service and the view over Juhu Beach. He's watching a crowd of Saudi speculators gathered around a table at the opposite end of the verandah. This lot have been coming here every Thursday night for weeks now. 'Another good week's work!' the Saudis scream at each other, gone deaf, the insides of their ears coddled to cream by mobile microwaves. Another bay, another beach acquired! Another village levelled! Another date orchard drained! Rishi watches them tugging at their cut-off dishdashas, their faces disfigured by lust, their eyes hot coals behind their Ray-Bans as they tap their feet to the Latin beat pulsing inside the bar. He watches as they sip up their Pepsis, their Pepsi and Johnny Walkers, then – oh, to hell with it – their Johnny Walkers, neat. A couple of hours of this and they will reveal their utter and conspicuous devotion to sin, and Rishi smiles, because watching them makes him feel honest.

As he watches, he works at his phone, transferring money from one account to another. He hits a button, piloting paper boats up paper creeks, under a canopy of paper trees. He hits a button, and leaps from registry to registry, continent to continent, laying down patterns of false-positive information. He hits a button, and skips from dry carrier to tanker to dry carrier. He hits a button, and circumnavigates the earth, from the Bahamas to Panama, from Malta to the Maldives. No two-bit forger from the sticks could ever hope to perform miracles like these. But Yash can. Yash Yadav, long dead, but resurrected; he speaks again through Rishi's paper ventriloquism.

Rishi hits a button, numbers burning up the screen: complex financial operations reduced to a thumbed stereotypy that only his broker can decode. So much money to his nephews, Ravi and Shubi. So much to poor, nerve-wracked Mohinder Gidh . . .

Mumbai's Port Scrapping Area in Darukhana is where ships that have been plying the Indian Ocean for over half a century come to die. It is male territory. By day: flames, risk, work, frequent injury, falls, fires, explosions, subtle debilitations wreaked by exposure to oils, lubricants, paints, cargo slop. By evening: thin dahl and ashy chapattis, songs, booze, violence and sleaze.

Roopa Vish passes sheds where oxygen is compressed and bottled for the ship-breakers' yard. An oxygen-cooking oil mix burns hot enough you can use it to cut a ship's hull into strips. The strips are loaded by hand on to lorries and Tempos and handcarts and carried inland to the rerolling factories where coke-blackened men with seared lungs drag the strips through pit furnaces cracked and crazed with age and overuse. They feed the glowing scrap through graduated rollers to make rebars: ribbed reinforcing rods for South Asia's building trade. Men coming off-shift stare at Roopa frankly, with no hostility. It's early evening, and carbon has filled every pore of their faces, making them impossible to read.

She passes yards devoted to reclaimed chandlery: linoleum, life jackets, piping, air-conditioning units, beds, canned goods, furniture. One square of fenced-off earth sells old injection-moulded bathroom cubicles.

She reaches the coast. It is on fire. She imagines some cataclysm. D-Company have deployed their first fuel-air weapon. Pakistan has dropped a puppet nuke. Eventually her eyes adjust. The fires engulfing the beach are flaming pools of engine sludge and the wrecks are only empty ships, waiting to be dismantled. Men cut up a ship's engine with cooking-oil torches. Roaring diesel winches haul the pieces through the gutted hull. Sometimes the hawsers break and recoil, whipping through the air before they plunge, like striking snakes, and bury their severed heads in the sand. The end of a hawser once speared the roof of a Tata truck rumbling innocently along the service road like a flatulent Hindu shrine.

It missed Rishi Ansari by inches.

He cracks open a can of Thums Up, the local cola. He's lying in his hammock on the verandah of his workshop: a smart concrete bunkhouse overlooking the final resting place of the Greek reefer ship *Frio Dolphin*, built in 1979. To its left lie the remains of the British general cargo ship *Kerie*, built in 1978. The empty space to its right is reserved for the German general cargo ship *Mercs Wadduwa*, built in 1967. A pilot will run it aground sometime tonight.

'What you environmentalists don't understand . . .' Rishi treats Roopa Vish to his orientation speech. Ship-breaking is a necessary industry, and from politicians to foremen to cutters, the people of Mumbai speak of it with pride, impervious to the West's nannying. Rishi's the same: he assumes anyone in Western clothing is an eco-fascist and setting outsiders right about the view – the flames, the smoke, the stench of bilge and solvent and hot oil – is a task he has performed many times.

'Mohinder Gidh sent me.'

Now Rishi understands, or he thinks he does. Mohinder has told him to expect a prospective client, a professional woman who requires a speedy, discreet service: documents and identifying materials.

Rishi Ansari is not in the scrapping business. Dominating his workshop is a government security press. Roopa can tell that's what it is because a stamped metal plate on the side reads: India Security Press – Brigadier Road. It's a measure of Rishi's confidence that he hasn't even prised off the badge. On a table covered with newspapers sits an Alps MD-5000 printer, a laminator, a box of 5 mil pouches, a bottle of Interference Gold paint, a can of Damar spray varnish, Mylar, latex paste . . .

Mostly, Rishi Ansari works for the shipping industry. Worldwide, one in ten seafarers admits to using counterfeit certificates. Many more – one in five – are happy to shop their friends. Fraudulent papers are most often wielded by the officer class. Many seafarers are keen to start earning money as soon as possible; others are desperate to obtain a quick promotion. Many wish to hide awkward facts about their health or age. In the course of a career at sea most hands have stumbled across at least one junior officer who's yet to learn the difference between port and starboard. Since 9/11 Rishi has been exceptionally busy. Watermarks, laminated cards, magnetic readers, holograms, computer databases. Between them, bin Laden and Bush have created the conditions for a minor economic miracle in Darukhana. Every month some bright bureaucrat in the International Chamber of Commerce dreams up another security measure, and within weeks it has become just another veil for the stowaway, pirate or terrorist to hide behind.

Roopa's parking permit is not yet ready. The yellow ribbon of Rishi's MD-5000 has fused to the print head. The cheapest replacement he can find on the Internet is $700 – a swingeing amount of money – and there is no guarantee he will receive the goods. 'eBay is full of tricky people,' he says, with not a trace of irony.

He's had more luck with her ATM card. The hologram is impressive. He basks in Roopa's attention: 'HG-107 diffractive film. Great under a desk lamp but be careful, the hologram vanishes under diffuse light.'

Roopa doesn't care one way or the other and hands him 2000 rupees for a piece of fake ID that won't work on a cloudy day. She knows what she's doing. She lays her hand on Rishi's arm. 'That's wonderful,' she says – and smiles. Twenty thousand rupees these cost her: the smallest, whitest and most even teeth in her extensive dental arsenal. 'Rishi, I remember you.'

Rishi's shoulders stiffen.

'I met you in Chhaphandi's brickworks.'

His fear is palpable.

'After the rail crash. When Vinod was in hospital, having his stump seen to. Do you remember? A policewoman came round to see him about a family of scheduled-caste labourers. You were there to fob me off.'

Rishi makes to move past her, towards the door, out of there. Roopa lays her hand on his chest. 'It's all right, Rishi,' she croons. 'It's okay.'

'What do you want?' A small, high voice.

She knows what makes him tick. 'I want what you want,' she says. Surreptitiously, she flicks her tongue round her upper gum, the left side, above her tiny porcelain canine. There's a fragment bursting through. She can taste the blood. She's tanked with codeine today, half off her face. 'I want the man who killed your sister and your brother-in-law.'

Rishi blinks at her.

'It's why you're here, isn't it? Yash's little helper.'

Rishi tries to swallow.

'Don't you see? You're just like me.'

'I am?' He stares around the room: this little wainscot empire he's built under the shadow of the Yash family syndicate: 'I don't know who you mean.'

'Together,' Roopa whispers in his ear. Touches it with her tongue. Explores it. Paints a little pinkish blood inside it. Laughs. 'Together we can kill him. Would you like that? Rishi? Would you?'

Nothing.

'It's why you're here. It's why you're working for him. Shielding him.' Something comes out on her tongue. A tiny bit of grit. 'Isn't it?'

He shakes his head. He can't believe his luck.

'You don't fool me,' she says.

EIGHTEEN

There are indigents tottering around Mumbai's port sector who have had their arms boiled off, their feet hoofed lengthways with roofing shears. You do not fuck with the Yadavs, and if they ever find out who Roopa Vish really is, and that she has a score to settle with Yash, the Yadav syndicate's new, elusive and all-powerful boss, they will take their time killing her. Rishi knows the fun they'll have with her, before their graceless *coup de grâce*. Poor Rishi: he wishes with all his heart he'd never got Roopa into this. There it is. She's in it now, has been for nearly a decade, and nothing to be done.

Convincing Roopa that he is Yash Yadav's creature, his gatekeeper and private secretary, has been the acme of Rishi's career, centrepiece of his forger's art. With one perfectly turned lie, he's turned Roopa from a liability into his most reliable helper! Poor Roopa, who thinks she's spent all these years working her way up through the organization to become Yash's most trusted courier. Poor Roopa, who imagines she has come ever closer, through Rishi, to a man fifteen years dead!

Strange, that Roopa's well-being should have come to matter so much to him. He is not without feeling. He is not without conscience, or regret. He is not, all in all, a bad man. He is just bad enough.

Poor Roopa. Rishi wonders: at what point, in all these years of deception, did Roopa cease to be a game for him? At what point did she become more than a counter for him to move around at will? Ruined as Roopa is, driven as she is, dangerous as she is, Rishi's spent the best years of his life asking himself: dare I let her see more? Dare I invite her back to my apartment? Dare I show her my boat? Dare I cook her a meal? It's taken him a long time to build up the courage. Absurd how long it's taken him. Years. Evenings round at her place in front of the television. Meals out. Visits to the fair. Treats for Nitesh, a teenager now. Poor Rishi, edging with a painful slowness into someone else's life, and no one's getting any younger here.

Every quarter Rishi relays a mythical order from his mythical boss, Yash Yadav, and sends Roopa on a mission to the UAE. Every quarter she bears *hawala* notes and documentation across the Indian Ocean. Coordinates. SIM chips. Account numbers. Maritime documents of all kinds. Even cash money.

She waits. (This is her plan.) She waits. She works. She waits. One day she will meet Yash Yadav again, in person. Then, she'll kill him.

Any streetwise crew of twenty years ago would have picked up Roopa's scent in days. They would have found her son, her mum, her family's home in Thane, her ACB profile, the registration number of her car. But the syndicate's old street-corner crews, its has-been razormen and shooters, are following barrow-boys and trimmers, firemen and stevedores, into the same quaint dockyard oubliette. Origins hardly matter these days and the Yadav family is a 'Mumbai syndicate' in name only. From its paymasters to its deckhands, there's not one in the firm who does not work out of a mobile phone, and all the smart money lives in Toronto. The distributed nature of modern piracy is keeping Roopa alive, but this cuts both ways, and Roopa, though safe enough, is no nearer to the truth about Yash Yadav than she was when she first visited Darukhana nearly nine years ago. She is wasting her life away on a vendetta that no longer makes any sense – and Rishi is helping her waste it.

He presses a slip of paper into her hand. 'The documents will be PDF'd inside Ester's BlackBerry. Email them to me on this number. Memorize it. When you've made the call, take the chip out of the phone and throw the phone and the chip into the creek.'

Roopa says nothing.

He puts his arm around her shoulders, drawing her in. 'Yes?' It is a role Rishi has got down pat and he is so very good at it and, oh, so very weary of it: Yash Yadav's little helper.

They are sitting together on the threadbare sofa in his workshop in Darukhana, under the pitiless overhead lights Rishi needs for the close work he does: weaving money out of paper, foils, thread, ink. Rain hammers against the workshop walls. Roopa spent the afternoon helping him lay canvas offcuts over the worktables, printers, screens and tablets, cutting mats and laminator. Together, they've waterproofed what they can against the coming storm. Now the wind is driving the rain under the wooden shingles of the roof. In one corner of the hut it's actually raining. Raindrops wind down plastic wires and drop, fizzing, on to the naked bulbs that light the room. Rishi's had to turn off the fan because the air it blew was so damp that it started to short and filled the hut with the smell of burning. Roopa can still taste it on the roof of her mouth.

'How much longer, Rishi?'

He kisses her.

'How many more?'

He runs his fingers through her hair 'Roopa. Darling. Something will turn up.'

Roopa leans into his hands. A strange ménage, this must seem to her: two broken people, both with reasons to see Yash Yadav expunged, both nudging each other nervously towards the point of action, both becalmed. She will not take much more of this, but what else can Rishi do? Yash cannot be killed twice.

By now, Roopa has pretty much reconciled herself to the idea that Rishi is and always will be Yash Yadav's creature. A coward. Roopa does not trust him. She thinks that if Yash Yadav ever left his Western eyrie and visited Mumbai, Rishi would shop her to him in seconds. Not because he does not love her, but because he fears Yash Yadav more.

After all these years of waiting it's got to the point where Roopa, unillusioned, is pretty much relying on Rishi betraying her. It's the only way she can see to draw Yash Yadav into the open.

Does Rishi see yet how this works? Does he see how elegant this is?

He unbuttons her. He bares her. He encircles her with his arms. He brings his mouth down to her breast. Poor Rishi: it's not going to make a blind bit of difference. We're going to strip him of every comfort. We're going to rob him of every happiness. Because he deserves it, yes. But most of all because this is our idea of fun.

∞

In the 1970s, when neighbours like Abu Dhabi were letting their harbours silt up, confident that all the wealth they'd ever need would well up out of the ground for ever, Dubai's Sheikh Rashid chose to play the long game. He kept his city's harbour dredged. He built up imports, offered tax breaks and brought the builders in. Now the clothes on every Middle Eastern back and every luxury good, not to mention every bite of food they eat, passes through Dubai.

Whole nation states have been suckered into Dubai's fantasy. Ukrainians. Iranians. India thinks it runs Dubai: who else builds its buildings? China thinks it owns Dubai: who else lays its roads? Nobody runs Dubai. No surprise, then, that it's the money-laundering capital of the world. Occasionally armed police raid an attic in Deira, Dubai's old quarter. A man is led away and sometimes shot. Now and again a headless corpse is found slumped in a pool of blood in one of the city's subterranean car parks, and children fishing in the creek watch as a heron rips beakfuls of hair from a human head. In Dubai everyone is anonymous and significant at the same time. Roopa feels it. Roopa loves it. Bent on killing Yash Yadav, who ruined her and all her hopes, still, Roopa allows him this: she enjoys working for him. Yes, she loves her job!

Now, here come the Jumeirah Janes. Ex-pat TEFL-ers, HR managers, trophy wives close to expiry date. They run things in Dubai. They're the Emirates' unacknowledged power, First Ladies all. Only they're not getting any younger.

From the shadows of the surf shop, half-concealed and unremarkable,

Roopa Vish watches them. Yash Yadav had her beaten long ago into such a shape no observer can ever hold her in mind for long. She could sneer at these white bitches if she wanted: they would pay her no attention. She could laugh and spit at all that vanity on depilated legs. She does not sneer. She does not envy them or think them spoiled. She understands. She knows they know that age will do to them, and soon, what Yash's pliers did to her years ago: their every smile will break. Unnoticed, disregarded, crouched there in her grim blue salwar and baggy kameez, Roopa feels for them, that they have to cross this sandy lot on their way to nips and tucks (it's wall-to-wall plastic surgeons round here), and run the gamut of all the twenty-something hardbodies strolling in and out of the surf store, bronzed muscles quivering, unbrassiered breasts gambolling like puppies under Rip Curl vests. When the surfer chicks pass by, Roopa imagines she hears the Janes clench their capped and whitened teeth in rage.

It's not their fault: Dubai has maddened them. In the car here, as Nitesh drove – at fourteen, an adept at the wheel, and Rishi has cooked him an international licence the fiercest traffic cop would pass – Roopa remarked the adverts on Dubai's towers: 'Live the Life', 'We've set our vision higher'. Even the white-goods retailers have names like Better Life and New Hope.

Their mark parked up in front of the surf shop and Nitesh parked three rows down and stayed in the car while his mother got out and crossed the lot and settled herself in the shadows of the shop; and now even Nitesh, even her own son, finds it hard to spot her in the rear-view mirror, or even to hold in memory that she's there.

Every once in a while Roopa turns and looks in through tinted plate glass.

Ester's toying with a wind-meter.

She's buying herself some heel straps.

She's leaving the shop.

She's wearing cut-off jeans and a running bra. Over her shoulder she's lugging along her kitesurfing bag: a black flying fish against bright red and white. She's young – young as Roopa was when her looks were torn out with pliers. She has her more than sun-bleached hair done up in a fussy topknot. From her features Roopa can see what she will look like when she's old. If she lives that long. She's far too young for this game. White, besides – an outlier in the pirate demographic. She'll be some nigger's moll, is Roopa's guess, playing above her age. Then again, what is the right age to be carrying stolen shipping information through Dubai? The thugs that form Yadav's front line – gambol-toed monkey-boys swinging *bolo* swords and box-cutters – they're barely in their teens. Give her another year and Ester will be capable of anything. 'Radicalized' is today's buzzword. A pirate queen, shackling Bangladeshis to an anchor chain.

Roopa follows Ester to her car and walks on past to where Nitesh is waiting. Traffic's heavy: they join the stream two vehicles behind their mark and trickle after her in second gear. Again, Roopa's eye is drawn to the messages on Dubai's innumerable hoardings, and here and there covering entire faces of a complete but empty high-rise. Every time she visits Dubai – three, four times a year – Roopa finds the ads have grown yet more extreme, evoking, with a welling hysteria, the dream-logic of this fabricated place. Aspiration as an endless Jacob's ladder. Perfect your car, your phone, your home, your face. Perfect your labia. Plastic surgeons line the way to erotically sterile encounters at the Burj Al Arab hotel. Then what? Then where? The elevators only go up. Take a helicopter ride into the future. Cheat death. Chrome the flesh. Every advert they ride past features a robot. A perfected man. A smoothly milled thigh or tit. A cyborg sits at the wheel of a latest-model four-wheel-drive, limbs webbed promiscuously around the controls. A phone blinks in a stainless-steel hand.

Dubai's a vital entrepôt but most of its goods are containerized and handled by machines outside the city. A different, small-time trade holds sway along the creek road, in the centre. Its pavements and central reservations teem with tourists and Russian prostitutes in roughly equal numbers. Ester is heading back to her hotel. Nitesh parks up at the kerb. Roopa gets out and waits. Nitesh drives off. Across the creek, dhows packed to the gunwales with second-hand Toyota Hiluxes prepare for their voyage to Somalia. Piles of tyres, plucked off wrecked and defunct cars, are being hauled by hand and dropped into the rusted holds of boats bound for retreading factories in Navlakhi and Karachi.

Ester reappears. She's changed her clothes. She's wearing a white shirt, open at the collar, under a beige, loose-fitting trouser suit: clothing to blend her into that part of Dubai life lived almost exclusively by ex-pat men. Roopa crosses the road after her.

Some dhows are made of fibreglass these days, but there are plenty of wooden hulls left, white with lime, and plenty being built. The deck-houses are almost always wooden, cut here and there with repeated decorations. Easy to imagine that these tiny break-bulk ships are the last survivors of a dying trade, but they're no such thing. Container shipping serves the great ports of the earth, but there are few enough of them, and none in northern Africa. For the behemoths of Maersk and Moyse, Hapag-Lloyd and Evergreen, that coast offers no haven. So, with no deep harbours, north Africa depends on little ships, and all of them, every few months or so, tie up along the creek in Dubai. From China, mattresses. Piles of flashlights. Chairs, tables, oxytetracycline injections. Chilean softwoods. Foam mattresses. Drums of sorbitol from Mumbai.

Ester boards a passenger ferry for Deira. Roopa follows her on board. They cross the creek. It is prayer time when they land and the alleys of the old quarter are swimming in shoes, shoals of them, abandoned while men pray barefoot in its many mosques. At the end of prayers the streets are suddenly full again. Crowds of men – Turks, Somalis, Emiratis, Pakistanis – hustle this way and that with mats rolled under their arms. The poor, who have made do with collapsed cardboard boxes to kneel and bow on, are tucking them under gates and behind municipal bins, saving them for another time, another worshipper. The crowds clear.

Roopa has lost sight of her mark, but she is practised at this and does not panic. She moves, fast and purposeful, and relocates her a minute later, two streets over, in a cafeteria that keeps its stock on shelves above the customers' heads as though against the threat of shortage. Through plate-glass windows, the mark's bright trouser suit stands out against a ground of impeccable navy white. A couple of dozen Pakistani sailors are eating egg sandwiches, nursing cans of Mountain Dew. Most have wild red beards from making hajj. Their once in a lifetime visit to Mecca hasn't cheered them up at all. Roopa makes a call. 'She's clean. No minders. Here we go.'

'One minute, Mum.' Nitesh, grown up to this, is idling by the kerb barely two blocks away.

The call to noon prayer empties Deira as Ester enters the arcades of the souk. Her surf bag swinging from her shoulder, she weaves a path through shoals of shoes towards the junction of 38th and Al Jazira. She takes a seat in the cafeteria. Her contact's late. She orders a tea.

The cafeteria is filling up. Dapper Pakistani sailors with bright red beards exchange looks of conspicuous spiritual profundity over mint teas and egg sandwiches. A plain-faced Indian woman with loose dentures sits surrounded by bags from half a dozen boutiques, watching as her son breaks into his latest toy. Impossible to tell what it is. A hand-held game console. A toy, a phone, an MP3 player. Some indeterminate consumer good. He tugs at the packaging, lumpen and frustrated, a boy for whom bubble wrap and adhesive tape are the only barriers he has ever encountered between a wish and its fulfilment. There are bits of egg-box packaging all over the table. Occasionally his mother snaps at him: 'Careful, Nitesh!' She is one of those sour-faced women who are secretly frightened by their own children – and the boy, who looks about fourteen, overdressed in expensive, conservative jumper and slacks, shoots back looks of pleasure and gratitude: he has her measure.

He gets the thing into his hands eventually, whatever it is, and peels adhesive plastic strips from its screen and sleek black shell. The strips stick to his fingers and dangle, faintly amniotic, from his fingertips. Prissily he balls them up, rolling them until they drop, exhausted, on to the table.

It is a phone. It's no bigger than a credit card and yet the box is full of odds and ends that somehow plug into it – piece after piece, how do they fit into such a small space? Still, he can't get a signal. He leaves the table and wanders around the cafe, studying the screen, staring at it, or not even at it: through it, into the streamlined, solid-state future.

Ester looks at her watch. Where is her contact? What if something has gone wrong? She is afraid of being spotted. If she is being paid to watch Havard, then who is being paid to watch her? Sensitive cargoes move over the earth. Nuclear cargoes. Biological cargoes. Living cargoes. Rerouted and delivered, on time, and with plausible deniability, thanks to her: her necessary work. This is what her father tells her. Who could have predicted her current importance? Who, seeing her move animated containers back and forth on a Dell flat-screen in Port Rashid, would ever imagine –?

She forces herself to breathe, to calm down. She'll wait another ten minutes. No more. She reaches into her pocket for her phone. She finds nothing. The blood in her fingers fizzes. The sweat she worked up walking here chills her armpits and the backs of her knees. On the floor, under her chair, she finds a mobile phone. Not hers. She turns it on. Stored in the memory are the numbers she needs. The exchange has gone ahead without her. It is accomplished. How –?

She looks round. It is a busy time. Most of the people who were here when she arrived have left already, replaced by strangers. The sailors have left, replaced by grumpy Turks in threadbare jerseys.

The shopper and her boy are gone.

Now it is evening.

Russian girls line the central reservation of the creek highway: a bed of human flowers. Saudis in tinted four-by-fours roll up and pluck them, one by one. Along the embankment the dhows are moored eight-deep. Behind stacks of Titanic mineral water, behind tables and mattresses and rolls of carpet, Roopa Vish leans against the rail reading Ester's BlackBerry.

Roopa Vish: a forgettable face travelling under an alias on a false passport. A deep-cover freelance who works for no one but herself. Who answers to no one, and who has never, in all the years she's known him, from '95 till now, spent more than three nights in a row with her boyfriend, Rishi Ansari. She is a perfect blank. An unstamped silver dollar. This, she supposes, is what people mean when they talk about freedom. Freedom is one of Roopa's more questionable attainments. If she was being perfectly honest with herself, right now, she would sooner be cuddling on the sofa with Rishi – but that's all done with. She is doing away with it. There is no going back.

Information on the Yadav syndicate's next target is stored as PDFs in the phone's message memory. She taps in the number of Moyse Line's anti-piracy hotline, hits a button, and waits.

The phone purrs in her hand. She hits the green button.

'Who is this?'

Roopa smiles a shark-grey smile. 'I thought that would get your attention.'

'Who is this?'

'A friend. I suppose you want to know which ship it is you're about to lose.'

A pause. 'If you have information relating to the seizure . . .'

'Oh,' says Roopa, airily, enjoying herself, 'I can do better than that.' She takes the phone away from her ear, scrolls the wheel, and presses a button.

Expected vessels in Jebel Ali Terminal 1
as of Tue Dec 11 16:24:50 GMT+04:00
118 items found, displaying 1 to 15

Vessel	KA-BHAM
Voyage	KB1103
Rotn	406945
Arrived From	SITTW
Sail To	AEBRM
Berth Date	07-DEC 23:00
Berth	
ETD	

Another, longer pause.

'What do you want?'

What does she want? She wants a job. Working counter-piracy for Moyse Line would set her up for life, she reckons. Assuming she can stay alive long enough to cash her first pay cheque. She's given Moyse Line notice of an imminent pirate attack, but she can do so much more. She can blow the gaff on the Yash syndicate's whole deep-water operation: blow it in a way that will demonstrate to Yash Yadav that he can't trust anyone – not even his creature, Rishi Ansari. Then – this is the idea – Yash will decide to deal with this mess himself.

Once Yash comes calling, Rishi will give her up, of course. So be it. Hatred's hotter than love every time, and she is her father's daughter. Kabir Vish, who pissed his home and family away to tread the reeking slums of Bombay. Who favoured legal kills over a warm bed and a loving wife. Who chose to die in a hail of bullets sooner than come home to kiss his infant daughter goodnight. Roopa's hatreds outshine even her dad's. Dad slaughtered half a dozen in police 'encounters'. She'll kill one – but such a one! Yash Yadav, the pirate-king himself. She wipes her eyes and grits her cheap ceramic teeth. It's time to summon the wobble-hipped, pliers-wielding monster from its lair.

She unfastens the brooch from her salwar and uses the pin to prise the SIM card from the phone. She throws the phone and the card into the water. She turns away and crosses the creek road to where Nitesh is waiting with the car. 'The airport,' she tells him, dry-eyed, her mouth set in a wrinkled line. Nitesh does not yet know that he will be returning to Mumbai alone. She won't tell him until the very last moment. Everyone is a coward in their own way and Nitesh brings out the coward in her. 'Let's have your phone, then.'

As he drives, Nitesh digs out the phone she bought him when they arrived in Dubai. She digs around in its menu for the gallery. Roopa has taught Nitesh well. Rattling off shots in the cafe, he didn't try to hide what he was doing. He wasn't discreet. He acted the way you'd expect a boy to act given an expensive toy to play with. He took photographs of everything. There are close-ups of the cafe tables, of catering drums of cooking oil, shelves of fish sauce and piri piri. There are blurred portraits of Pakistani sailors, beards bright red, naval whites immaculate. There are close-ups of cans of Mountain Dew. There are only four pictures containing the mark, Ester, and every portrait is clear and perfectly framed.

'I need this phone.'

'Okay.'

'I'll buy you another in Mumbai.'

Nitesh shrugs. 'Okay.' It's all one to him. For Nitesh and his generation these things are just one more common good, like light, like running water.

She hits a button and Nitesh's snaps of Ester – the syndicate's insider in Moyse Line – wing their way over to the line's counter-piracy office in Ramonville-Saint-Agne, France.

The phone rings.

'*Are you the same –?*'

'Yes. If you value the *Ka-Bham* at all, I think it's time we met.'

The next day Roopa hires one of those new, impractically low-slung Land Rovers, its dashboard full of dinky all-terrain controls, and heads east, out of the city, towards a rendezvous in Musandam with officials of the Moyse shipping line. This cloak-and-dagger approach seems silly to her, but they are badly spooked: '*If our Dubai operations are compromised so far, we cannot guarantee your safety. We have to get you out of there.*' In vain she's protested her skill as a detective, her ability to look after herself. '*If this is the Yadav syndicate we're dealing with, then we're not taking any chances.*'

Even with customs stops she expected to cross into the Musandam peninsula before sundown, but in the desert she's hit convoy after convoy of trucks – unreal, outsize vehicles returning to the crusher plants of Ras al-Khaimah – and it's already 3 p.m. by the time she reaches the outskirts of Wadi Almar.

The town, bleeding unimpeded along the Al Rams road, has become a sort of mall, laying out, as though on a conveyor, the aspirations of a developing world. Tasselled curtains, plaster lamps and flushing toilets. Carpets with dolphins woven in. Camel caravans moulded into the plastic headboards of super-kingsize beds. Brass-look bedsteads. Sofas soft and brown as turds.

Where the parade of tat begins to dribble off, Roopa stops for a hitch-hiker. He's a Bihar man. A construction engineer. A crane nerd ('. . . and they say the 960 will lift thirty tons more!'). He's on the usual eight-month contract: a seven-day week followed by four months' paid leave – so long as he stays the course. 'Men go crazy, you know?' Roopa knows. Construction in the Gulf stops altogether in summer, when the skies are white and people (if they're outside at all, which is seldom) huddle in pitiful scraps of shade. Even the more temperate months prove too much for some. The furnace-light, the dust, the scale of things.

A fence, not much higher than a man and topped with razor wire, runs rifle-straight beside the road all the way to a granular horizon. Behind the fence stretch mile after mile of prefabricated houses. The narrow lanes between them are slung with clothes lines. Construction workers sit in circles of shade, knocking pallets together. Here and there mounds of graded gravel rise in parody of the great, dying ranges to the south. The road begins to disintegrate, its surface crazed and sunken under the weight of so many trucks bound for Dubai with loads of boulders and gravel. The World and The Palm began life here, as the insides of mountains. Roopa pulls up under the shadow of a great artificial cliff, its face networked with scars and cuttings. Vehicles move against the rock. In the flat light of afternoon they look as though they're clinging to a sheer surface. Factories at the mountain's foot lift jointed fingers to stroke the cliff-face: conveyors so distant Roopa cannot see the belts moving. The distance from ground level to cliff-top is at least a kilometre. Slice by vertical slice, they are tearing the mountain down and crunching it up. Roopa opens her window. The sound of conveyors, graders and crushers is too distant to be deafening, but the scale of it insinuates itself inside her mind: a mountain being ground, day by day, to nothing.

Her new friend wants to swap addresses: the world's a village to him, one long Grand Trunk Road. She's happy enough to scribble her address on the back of one of his business cards. The legend on it reads: Oriental Crusher. She drives away, hazard lights blinking in farewell. Not long afterwards she loses her way.

She comes to a roundabout. There is a fountain at its centre: a dry cement tower clad in blue swimming-pool tile, sterile as a bathroom fitting. There isn't a hint of what places the roundabout might one day serve. No buildings. No traffic. No signs. It's just a tarmac sunburst in the sand, its exits blurred and feathered by encroaching dust. On the horizon there are whole city blocks that aren't even on a map yet. New developments, bankrolled by the Saudis. University cities thrown up at miraculous speed by Bangladeshi guestworkers. Fawn crenellations hover inches off the horizon on a carpet of illusory blue.

It's late afternoon by the time she finds her way again. The foothills of Musandam come into view.

She's booked a room in a guest house in Khasab, Musandam's only sizeable town. From here it's less than sixty miles over the water to the Iranian mainland. The Iranian island of Qeshm is only forty miles away. The border is so porous the police permit the smuggling of just about anything they can't see the harm in. The smugglers are Iranian and far wealthier than Khasab's local youth, who gather by the quayside to stare enviously at the speedboats: shallow spoons of fibreglass each powered by two 200hp engines.

'These days it's all goats for cigarettes.'

Roopa turns. Her contact is a white man, not any taller than she is, in a dark suit and a shirt without a tie. 'There was a time these boys bartered hashish for white goods. Dishwashers. Washing machines.' He holds out his hand. 'David Brooks.'

'Roopa Vish,' she says, returning the shake.

They stand together on the quay, watching the work.

'You gave us a hell of a scare,' he says.

'Where's the *Ka-Bham*?'

'In Sittwe, taking on a fresh crew.'

'There you are, then. It's as good as lost.'

'It's a tub. A tramp. Not remotely valuable.'

'You're happy to lose it?'

David shrugs. 'We're happy to wait and see what happens.'

'And the crew?'

'What about the crew?'

They watch the smugglers prepare. Their boats are more like planes; they can make the crossing to Bandar-Abbas in less than an hour.

David says, 'We brought you here to ship you out. If what you say is going to happen happens, then we think you can be valuable to us.'

Roopa shakes her head. 'There's something I have to do first.'

'Oh?'

'I have to be getting back to Mumbai.'

'Into the jaws of the tiger, then.'

Roopa says nothing.

'Come on,' he says. 'We have time to talk this through, at least. You coming all this way. Let's eat.'

There are expensive restaurants in town, but David leads her past them all and to a bare cream shell without a sign. Plastic chairs, stacks of mineral water in boxes, two industrial-strength ceiling fans and bulbous steel ceiling lights. Torn grey linoleum. David orders for them both and whole kingfish are brought to them on outsize plates. On the next table a party of eco-tourists are bragging at each other. Bulging waists over khaki combat pants. Camouflage camelbacks slung over the backs of their chairs. Big yellow scarfs to protect them from the sand. They're looking for leopard, they say. They insist on being friendly. They insist on leaning over and talking.

When Roopa and David leave the eco-tourists are lined up in the car park, eyes turned towards Iran. They're comparing GPS readings, getting wet over the number of satellites that hover above the Strait. David wishes them goodnight. 'Are they yours?' Roopa asks him, once they're out of earshot.

David smiles. 'Now that would be telling.' He leads her back across the apron of reclaimed land towards the harbour and her Land Rover. He's tucked her arm in his, old-school. He has a crabwise gait. If it's an injury, it's an old one; something he is used to.

The boys and the boats have vanished. 'Their boats are so shallow you can't see them on radar. Iran's Revolutionary Guard have fishing boats out there armed with rocket launchers. They never hit anything.' David is full of these factoids and little anecdotes. He has it in him to be a bore: a fact that Roopa finds strangely reassuring.

Now they are back where they started, looking over the water. David tells her: 'If we take the correct channels, if we pass your information to the International Maritime Bureau, our insurers will hike up our premiums across the entire fleet.'

Roopa shakes her head. 'An open and honest game is the only game I'm prepared to play.'

David's exasperated. 'Who made you World Policeman?'

Roopa shrugs. 'If that's your attitude, I'm sorry to have troubled you. To hell with it. I'll send everything I have to IMB's anti-piracy centre in Kuala Lumpur, let them sort it out.'

David reaches into the pocket of his suit for cigarettes. 'Jesus.' He doesn't offer her one. 'You really are pulling the tiger's tail, aren't you?'

'I want the Yadav syndicate to know I'm here.'

'Oh, they'll know, all right. Do you know what they do to informants?'

'I can look after myself.'

David draws deeply on his cigarette. 'Seizures of this sort, normally the line pays the buggers off.'

'Not this time. I want them to come after me.'

'Yes?'

'I have to flush him out somehow.'

'Him?'

Roopa says nothing more.

David takes the cigarette out his mouth. He pulls a face, as though it tasted bad. He grinds out the coal. He has an orthopaedic shoe, a built-up heel. 'Well,' he says, 'let's get this over with. Can you give me a lift to my hotel?'

Roopa unlocks the Land Rover, David joins her in the cab, and they pull away, across the gravel apron, and turn inland on a road that winds up into the mountains. They top a saddle and a deep scoop of still water extends before them. In the middle of the inlet there is an island.

'Telegraph Island. There's nothing there but rock. People there used to go crazy. Terrible messages got pinged to India. Obscene stuff. Lights in the sky. You know "round the bend"?'

Roopa has noticed that David likes these constructions. They are a way of getting people to express an interest in him.

'This is the bend they meant.'

'Where are we headed?'

'Wait,' he says.

They come out on a level plain. There is no habitation here, just a bowl of land under thin vegetation, divided by ruined dry-stone walls. David leans forward, feels under his jacket, and pulls out something so crude, so home-made, Roopa takes it for a car jack. She stares at it: functional, squared off, familiar. David swivels round in his seat and presses it to her leg, just above the knee. The road is a cinder track, well maintained, but there are ridges, ripples really, where heavy plant has rucked up the surface of the road, the way you'd wrinkle up a bedsheet. The mouth of the thing judders against her leg. David pushes the barrel firmly against the flesh of her leg and pulls the trigger.

Roopa's lower leg waves and writhes stupidly, expressively. Blood wells from the wound. Roopa feels a great weight on her, a fantastic yet invisible pressure, numbing and comforting her. Before she can even be grateful for it, the pressure lifts, and pain comes from deep inside her. She feels her leg stretch and explode. She falls into David's lap. He leans forward, turning the wheel of the Land Rover so that they coast off the road and over the gravel plane. He drops the gun into the glove compartment. It is still smoking. He closes the lid.

The engine stalls and the vehicle rolls to a stop. David pushes Roopa off his lap and into the footwell. He undoes his seatbelt, opens the passenger-side door and climbs out. He pulls Roopa from the car, into the night heat. Roopa's leg flaps and drags after her, a burning thing, a stinging thing, a giant stinging grub fixed to the stump of her leg by its sting, a hornet, a horsefly, a red thing, a maggot. David drops her on the ground, reaches in again, opens the glove compartment, pulls out the gun, turns and aims it at her face. He says, 'It's going to be all right.'

Roopa sits up. The gun jumps, and Roopa's brains spill out of the back of her skull and plop on to the ground.

NINETEEN

Captain Egaz Nageen shoulders his way out of the New Myoma City Development Supermarket (a lacquer-ware box for Suniti; a Mandalay Spiderman marionette for Sabir) and descends fractured concrete steps into a heaving high-street crowd, red with monks.

This place gives him the creeps. Once a bright and cheerful state capital (Suniti's guidebook says: 'Distinctive regional twists include the enjoyment of much spicy food'), Sittwe's showing the strain these days. Ten trillion cubic feet of natural gas have been discovered under the city and the presence and promise of all that untapped wealth has been steadily rising like damp into people's brains. Each time Nageen visits, there's some new species of predator cruising the town. In the early 2000s the Chinese and the Indians were the two main contestants slugging it out for Burmese government concessions. Then a plague of American 'observers' descended on the town – all of them posing as the same video cameraman for National Geographic. And it goes on. The whole circus has degenerated into farce this year, as the city's drunken and despised riot police play host to a party of pallid Kalmykians. Where the fuck is Kalmykia? Name a famous Kalmykian. Hands up who can spell Kalmykia?

Then – once he's run the gamut of Sittwe's human stew, Buddhist nut-jobs spitting at him as he goes – there are the hawkers gathered outside the gates of the Deep Water Facility. 'Look sir, look sir, MP3!' This snatch-and-grab mob annoys the hell out of him. Most of their gear has been stolen from ships berthed in shallow water a mile down the coast: they have stolen some barefoot fisherman's prized possession and now they're peddling it to him, who could buy this tat a thousand times over in any store in Dubai.

'Get out of my way! Hey!'

And he is in. No denying the relief he feels to find himself at once among the suited and the salaried. The blank-faced, unlovely office towers of the Sittwe Deep Water Facility are too few for all the bureaucrats flooding in to operate Burma's latest gas concessions. Daewoo have nabbed most of the purpose-built space, while bamboo scaffolding and aluminium ladders make toy tower-blocks out of shipping containers stacked three or four high: temporary offices for Focus, Westburne, Sinopec, Essar. The oil companies' logos are riveted, brightly optimistic, against their streaked and corroded walls.

Nageen enters a pine-panelled waiting room. He wants to put his bags down, he wants to sit, but the room's toffee-coloured vinyl armchairs are occupied. He joins a line of fellow latecomers circling the room, passing and repassing the same pencil-amended timetables and printed regulations.

USE OF WHISTLES

A whistle shall not be used within the limits of the Facility except:

(a) As a signal of distress; or

(b) To prevent collisions; or

(c) In fog, mist, heavy rainstorms or any other condition similarly affecting visibility; or

(d) In accordance with the Rules contained in this Order and for the control of tugs; or

(e) To test the whistle.

A few minutes of this and Nageen feels himself caught up in a subtle, predatory game of musical chairs. Outside, through plexiglass so fogged and scratched it must have been reclaimed from a dead ship, he can see over calm waters to the Layshinedaung lighthouse. At this angle, at this time of the afternoon, the sea is exactly the same colour as the sky. Truly, you can't tell them apart. Approaching the jetty, the launches might be spaceships, hanging in the air.

Around 4 p.m. a port service boat ferries Egaz Nageen to his new command, the MV *Ka-Bham*, a 120-metre Japanese-built general cargo vessel. Fully laden, a ship like this will reach a top speed of just under fifteen knots. Nageen knows from experience that her hull will prove a dog in bad weather, no autopilot will be able to handle her in a storm, and the rudder will cease to steer under five knots. These considerations are academic. The five-day map shows no weather that needs steering around. The ship has a dark blue hull and beige exhausts. Its deck is hidden under 40-foot steel shipping containers, stacked three high. The iron house is white: a five-storey superstructure spanning the ship, seventy feet from side to side. There are three red-painted derricks, two forward, one aft. This gear is a sure indication of the ship's age since these days even shallow-water ports boast their own gantry systems. The *Ka-Bham*, at twenty-five, is well on its way to retirement.

Climbing aboard, Nageen surveys the ship's superstructure with mounting dismay. The port-side door is held shut with a bicycle lock and the frame is knobbled under a fresh coat of paint: by the week's end the whole panel will be orange with rust.

He enters the iron house by a ladder to the first floor.

MUSTERPOINT IN NO.1 DECK ALLEYWAY
NO SMOKING
NO OPEN LIGHTS

The interior is cramped and ill-lit. The East European crews he prefers have a devil of a time on these Japanese tubs. Too small, too narrow, too low, like bedding down in a doll's house.

Most of the crew are asleep, catching what rest they can before they sail. Long ago – before Nageen's time – it took days to unload a ship and a ship's crew could spend most of this time resting and drinking and whoring themselves silly on shore. Such capers are relegated to the storybooks now. These days, time in port is measured in hours; junior officers pull twelve-, even eighteen-hour shifts, and regular seamen are rarely allowed off the ship. These days, a crew works itself to exhaustion in harbour and spends the voyage recuperating.

Successive crews have done their best to cheer up the mess room. Red paper lanterns from Chinese New Year dangle from the ceiling alongside gold, red and silver decorations proclaiming Selamat Hari Raya, the feast that ends Ramadan. There's a skeleton watch of three waiting for Nageen. First Officer Kamal, Chief Engineer Sen and Third Officer Waddedar greet their new captain warily. Nageen's reputation precedes him. He will keep them up all hours on pirate watch. He will have them chiselling away at all manner of minor repairs. His master's certificate may be a typical Marshall Islands knock-off but he has made the most of his years at sea. Many of his contemporaries still barely know port from starboard. Nageen, on the other hand, has worked to become the thing he once aped: a competent commander of ships and men.

The iron house is coming to life. The last boatload of chandlers and peddlers has arrived to wake his crew with offers of cigarettes, beer and toothpaste. The first officer excuses himself and Nageen hears him steering the peddlers firmly away from the officers' quarters.

Waddedar offers Nageen a cup of chai, but he declines. His wife and son turn up in a couple of hours. It will be Sabir's first sea journey with his father. Suniti will be struggling with too much luggage as usual. Till they arrive, he wants to be alone with his ship.

Two days out of Sittwe, at around half past six in the morning, the MV *Ka-Bham* is swallowed by the docks at Gangavaram. Not even swallowed. Imagine a piece of krill fetching up against the strainer-teeth of a whale. On the bridge Nageen's twelve-year-old son Sabir presses his nose against the glass, trying to wrap his mind around India's biggest deep-water port. The *Ka-Bham* is the largest ship he's ever sailed on and its maximum weight, including cargo, crew, fuel, passengers, and stores, is 12,000 tonnes. Port Gangavaram has been built to service super-Capesize vessels with a deadweight of 200,000 tonnes.

Gangavaram is so massive it keeps coming apart in the eye, falling away into the apparently unspoiled green of distant hills. There is nothing human in this landscape to give it scale: no high-rise, no temple, not even a town. It is spectacular and disappointing at once.

The pilot brings them bumping up against a mobile harbour, well to the side of the main channels: a maître d' seating underdressed diners behind a pillar. Two flesh-coloured cranes tower over the ship and pick through her cargo in a fraction of the time it would have taken using the ship's own gear, and by late afternoon they are ready to sail again.

Back at sea Sabir loses interest in the bridge and goes back to the captain's cabin. Truth be told, there is nothing on the bridge for Nageen either. Time at last to explore the ship. Noisy grille staircases lead into the vessel's body and bowels. The *Ka-Bham* is a fussy tub. There are five cargo holds, four forward and one aft of the engine room. The forward holds, A to D, are separated by twin transverse bulkheads, fitted out with narrow stairs. Hatches provide access to the holds at four levels. For a multipurpose vehicle, plying every halfway-deep port between Singapore and Saihat, this difficult internal design is a nuisance. Much of the cargo this trip is break bulk. Holds B, C and D have their tween-decks engaged, bearing all manner of bales, bags and drums. Below the tween-deck, in the main body of the hold, B and C are stacked high with palleted aluminium ingots, greasy and grey as fish under polypropylene wrap. Hold A, at the prow, is smaller than the others, and is designed for seawater ballasting. The containers here, like those on deck, carry every imaginable non-hazardous, non-perishable cargo, from mobile phones to sterile plasters.

The *Ka-Bham*'s fuel tanks run below the *Ka-Bham*'s cargo holds, on the centre line below holds A to D. Hold E, behind the engine room, has buckled guide rails and is being used exclusively for break bulk. Most of this is low value: solvents and chipboard furniture.

Nageen takes the stairs back up into the iron house and climbs, weary, to his cabin on the fifth floor. The officers' accommodations on the *Ka-Bham* are surprisingly comfortable after the lacklustre impression afforded by the rest of the ship. He has two rooms of equal size, overlooking the stern. The first room has his desk. It also has the biggest wardrobe, but Suniti says she's happy enough next door. There's a TV and a VCR in there to keep Sabir amused. Nageen glances in: the room is empty. Most likely they're in the mess room, playing pool.

Nageen has another half-hour in which to brood before visiting the bridge again. He sits at his desk and flicks through the lever-arch file containing the ship's paperwork. The crew are a worry. The same Spanish manning agents who've been providing him with strong motormen and oilers for over a year – and Croatian officers, conscientious and accustomed to low pay – have this time saddled him with a bunch of untested Bangladeshis. Their paperwork suggests experience but Nageen has a nose for these things. It could be worse: the *Ka-Bham* is heading north and west this month, towards well-policed Indian waters, and this gives him time to bring the crew up to snuff in time for Malacca in November. Still, it annoys him that in a few weeks he'll be expected to nursemaid this bunch of itinerants through the world's busiest narrows.

Suniti comes in brandishing a carrier bag: 'I got us a fish.'

'Good God, where did you find that?'

'You should get out more. There's an entire village living under the pilings not three hundred yards from where we were berthed.'

Nageen is appalled. 'In Gangavaram? You left the ship? We might have sailed without you!'

Suniti kisses the top of his head. 'Well, I wouldn't have gone hungry.' She opens the bag. This fish is big enough to feed most of the bridge crew. An old hand, she knows how to charm her way into the mess room. Nageen pulls beers out of their refrigerator, making room, and puts the fish inside.

Sabir comes in, wanting to know all about the ship. 'I'll show you round,' Nageen promises him, but the boy's curiosity isn't so easily sated. 'What's it done? Where's it been?'

What's Nageen to say to this? That the MV *Ka-Bham* is flagged in Tonga and mortgaged – through a Maltese holding company that exists only on paper as a mailing address in the capital, Valletta – to a Shanghai branch of Germany's Bayerische Landesbank? That it's operated by a company registered in Albania and Delaware, and maintained through layers of corporations in Austria and Liechtenstein? This much is evidenced by the papers in the lever-arch file on his desk.

'We're carrying ingots to Chennai!'

Admittedly, ingots of aluminium reclaimed from old drinks cans – but let the boy dream a little longer.

Covering 28 million square miles, the Indian Ocean is big: nearly thirty times the size of India. Run into trouble here and even the satellites may not be able to find you. Anyway, satellites provide only the most illusory reassurance. Providing real aid to a distressed ship involves more than mere intelligence. It takes ships and men. It takes guns.

Suppose you run into trouble at a point somewhere between the Maldives and the Strait of Hormuz. Who are you going to call? There are plenty of navies to choose from. Indian. Chinese. NATO. America has its Fifth and Seventh Fleets stationed here. It doesn't make any difference. Look at the map. The big blue void. Your nearest warship is, on average, half an India away.

Time was, the Strait of Malacca, several days to the south-east, presented the greatest threat to the world's shipping. Look at a map and you'll see why: a full third of the world's commerce passes between Indonesia and Malaya through a channel that's only a mile and a half wide. Since 9/11, while resisting the US's urging to militarize the zone, the region's governments have banded together to provide effective piracy suppression around the Strait. The most you get round there these days is a little thieving from the anchorages; the syndicates have moved their operations elsewhere.

That, of course, is the problem. Since the syndicates started operating phantom ships they have no need of a land base and can appear out of nowhere, anywhere on the Indian Ocean. The ocean is big and empty and boring. The chance of one particular boat falling victim to a pirate attack in the middle of such a vast, featureless expanse is remote. Staring into all that emptiness, it's easy to forget that on board a ship like the *Ka-Bham* the horizon is only about ten miles away. It's easy to forget how quickly you can be taken by surprise.

It is a captain's thankless task to remember these things and to infect his men with a certain amount of painfully manufactured paranoia. Ever since they manoeuvred clear of the Sittwe Deep Water Facility, Egaz Nageen has been playing the tartar, readying his inexperienced crew for the realities of the Indian Ocean. He has had the crew of the *Ka-Bham* on alternating six-hour watches since they left Sittwe, six days ago. They were exhausted when he arrived on board and he figures to get them into their new routine while sleeplessness and weariness are an ordinary condition of life. The ABs have responded better than he expected. His stern lectures and new routines have reminded them – after sixteen-hour shifts spent stacking crates and weeks at sea slumped in front of Bollywood videos – that the ocean should be an adventurous place.

Nageen's chief concern now is that they should sleep when they have the chance. Since they went full ahead, every fixture, fitting and door in the iron house has been softly, insistently rattling. Ghatak, the second engineer, reckons there's a problem with the cooling system.

Twin coastlines, Sri Lanka to port and Tamil Nadu to starboard, are thin veins on a mist-blue horizon.

'Port thirty.'

'Port thirty, sir.'

They are steering south, around Sri Lanka. No big boats can sail between Sri Lanka and India. The waters of Palk Strait are shallow enough that there was once a bridge joining the two lands. (A bridge built by monkeys and palm squirrels, if you believe the *Ramayana*.)

Nageen has time for a shower before he's needed again.

Sabir's in his room, wrestling with his Xbox.

'Problems?'

'I think I have to tune it in.'

'What?'

'The TV. Only there's nothing on the remote.'

'Let me shower and I'll take a look.'

He's in his dressing gown, forty minutes later, still trying to persuade the cabin TV that it's got a games console hung off the back of it, when the telephone rings.

'Captain, bridge.'

'Yes, I'm here.'

It is Kamal's voice, high with tension: 'Sir, we have a companion.'

A pale blue lozenge slips quickly and obliquely across the radar screen. Incredible as it seems, this close to the Sri Lankan mainland, they are being stalked.

'How long have you been watching this?'

'About an hour, sir.' Second Officer Bose is hesitant: he thinks he's done something wrong.

'Very good, Mr Bose,' Nageen reassures him. This is a busy, heavily policed coastline. No point in sounding the general alarm every time a fishing boat happens to shadow their course.

Egaz Nageen raises his head, his eyes filling with purple light as the sun sets over Trincomalee and sea the colour of wine. It will be night in less than twenty minutes: the pitifully short evening of the tropics.

If they are wolves, they will wait till dark before they close in.

Nageen throws on a windcheater and steps on to the balcony overlooking the starboard side. He lights a clove cigarette. He sees buoys and channel markers and nubbins of coastline, blued by distance. He sees sampans and fishing boats, sand barges and ferries. He cannot pick out his pursuers and he won't waste his time trying. Their boat – an RIB most likely, with a couple of 100 hp motors hung off the back – is picking its moment, just out of radar range, low in the water. Invisible. There's a fair chop this evening: waves high enough to obscure a low-riding boat. The wave action means that, even at this height, the horizon's only about five miles away: you could row there and back. The *Ka-Bham* is high-sided for a cargo vessel but the transom rides pitifully low – a height any reasonably athletic man might leap for. (The pirates of Malacca used bamboo poles; they would shimmy barefoot up their poles on to the decks of ships that rode ten, even twenty metres out of the water. Strange, Nageen thinks, that he should feel almost nostalgic for this and for so many sleepless nights.)

It occurs to Nageen to make this a drill. Old hands might sneer, but there are no old hands on this ship. He fancies some fun. He goes inside and picks up the phone. The alarm system is old and scratchy and makes a boring nee-naw sound. With painful slowness, still half-asleep, Nageen's men gather themselves into something approaching a watch.

Nageen patrols the platform. On the deck below two tiny men in white overalls and red hard hats are wrestling with a fire hose, a simple job made hard by exhaustion. For years the owners have insisted on operating with skeleton crews. Nageen has a dozen on board a ship built for twenty-nine.

The purple light of evening turns grey, then gutters out. Second Officer Bose wheels the ship's Aldis lamp, lighting up the ocean with long, majestic sweeps as though watering a garden. Nageen barks at him to slow down: 'Look what you're doing!'

It is coming. It is really coming. Riding the waves. No running lights: a rigid-hulled inflatable crowded with men. The deck officer's arc light sweeps, loses them, wobbles, finds them again. Impossible, at this distance, to make out how they are armed. Light artillery is common. Strafed by a Bofors gun for hours, an unprepared crew is quickly demoralized. A modified anti-aircraft rocket fired across the bows or into the side of its iron house has brought more than one ship to a full stop. The pickings are so rich these days, and the vessels so poorly protected, most ambushes are carried off with nothing more than *bolo* swords and box-cutters.

They know they've been spotted. They fall back. Nageen walks back to the bridge and orders evasive manoeuvres. The *Ka-Bham* cannot outrun the pirates but heeling over sharply enough, often enough, creates a hell of a wake.

Back outside, twin navigation lights spark in the darkness and now they return, more confident than before. They are waving, making an open approach. What possible difference do they think this will make?

The deck officer yells into his phone. Over the tremble of the ship, Nageen feels the shudder of auxiliary motors springing to life. Fire hoses spray the ocean wildly as the men fight to control them. It's not an easy job and they've had no training in it. The men in the boat are professionals. They rev forward, over the *Ka-Bham*'s first mighty swell, and topple in under the light, and vanish.

Nageen yells a warning. Miraculously the hoses begin to converge.

It's too late. There are men on deck. Too many men. *There is more than one boat.*

Nageen runs back to the bridge, slaps the big red panic button and sounds the call to muster.

He bursts into his cabin and Suniti shrieks, tightening her grip around their son Sabir. The alarm has woken them. They are still in their nightclothes. 'Get back to your room. Now.' He pulls the wardrobe open and yanks the clothes to the floor. The ship's safe is built into the back wall of the wardrobe. It is vital that he makes it easy for frightened men to find. The sooner his attackers get a little of what they came for – papers and passports, a little money, US and Japanese bills, a wristwatch or two – the sooner they can be persuaded to leave. Even better, he should open the safe before the attackers get here. The keys are . . .

The keys are in his coat, in the wheelhouse. He feels the pit of his stomach fall away. He turns, sees his wife still standing there, their boy cowering against her. 'For God's sake, get in the other room! Don't lock the door.' Locked doors make frantic men more crazed.

There's shouting in the corridor. Someone forgot to secure a door. More likely, the pirates have broken in through the windows. He cannot make out words. Please God no one's stupid enough to fight them.

The bridge gleams blue in radar-screen light. Gauges and switches twinkle: the grotto of an expensive Mumbai department store. The helm's at full stop. *Why?* Where is Kamal? Where's the bloody navigator? Where is Third Officer Waddedar? The bridge is abandoned. Nageen retrieves his coat, grabs his keys, and runs back to his cabin. Not much further. There are footsteps, the slap of bare feet on texturized rubber, and there they are, in the corridor, before him. They have ski masks. They have guns: knock-off AKs. One wields a cheater pipe. Another carries a sword.

Are they locals? They look like locals. Ragged. Feet that have never seen shoes. Please God they're locals. Nageen and this crew can afford to lose their watches, their wages, their passports, a trinket or two. ('Look! MP3!')

If only the pirates' AKs weren't so shiny . . .

Nageen forces himself to breathe, to rid his muscles of every heroic impulse. What this situation requires, above all, is man-management. He holds up the keys. 'In here.' He walks calmly to his cabin. The room is empty. His wife and child have hidden themselves in the other room. The wardrobe is open. The safe is clearly visible. Good. Nageen crosses the cabin in three strides and stands in front of the door leading to the bedroom, and his family.

Half a dozen nervous men edge after him into the cabin.

'The keys.' Nageen makes to toss the bunch at their feet – and freezes. There's a deafening commotion in the corridor. The pirates turn and turn about, trying not to point their weapons at one another. The youngest of them, a boy hardly into his teens, runs forward and digs the muzzle of his weapon into Nageen's midriff. Nageen falls back against the connecting door, staring at the barrel.

There's fighting in the corridor outside. There's a gunshot, the first, and the kid jumps half out of his skin and leans the barrel into Nageen's belly, and it occurs to Nageen, blinking with pain, that the kid wants him to get out of the way. He's trying to get through the connecting door to the other room. He's trying to hide.

It's too late. The battle has reached the door of the cabin. Nageen glimpses a fire axe, rising. It buries itself in the false ceiling and sticks there, hopelessly tangled. The lights flicker but stay on. The intruders move as a body away from the door, yelling, brandishing their guns. It is a stand-off.

Nageen can hardly draw breath. The kid has winded him and it comes out as a scream: 'The key –'

The kid, seeing the key in Nageen's hand, pulls the gun from his belly. The axe, tangled in the roof, falls to the ground. Nageen glimpses Bose, his navigator. There are others with him. The idiots have armed themselves. Knives from the galley. Twist-locks from the deck. Bright steel glitters in the poor fluorescent light. Children! Amateurs! Bunglers! He is, in spite of their foolishness, extraordinarily proud of them.

The kid throws the key to one of his fellows, who stoops to pick it up. His gun goes off. The bullet punctures the false ceiling, bounces off a steel joist, and enters Bose's skull through his left eye. Second Officer Bose falls, stiff as a tree, his knife cleaving a complex path through the intruders.

The boy threatening Nageen drops his gun and grapples him, pulling him away from the door. Nageen lets himself be hauled aside. The kid is too strong for his own good. He tugs the handle and it comes away in his hand. He kicks the door and it slams wide open, and, as he steps through, Nageen grabs the gun, raises it and fires, point-blank, into the boy's back.

TWENTY

On the same day, Havard Moyse, sixty-year-old adopted son of Eric Moyse, founder of the Moyse Line, flies into London's City Airport. It's rush hour, not worth the bother of booking a driver, and by 09:30 he's riding the dinky elevated Docklands Light Railway into town like any ageing salaryman. As usual, the interchange at Bank is a screaming nightmare and he has to stand on the Tube all the way to Bond Street, where he ascends to street level. He walks east towards Oxford Circus and fetches up in what used to be a dowdy Italian sandwich shop. Now the breakfast menu declares: 'Respect for the Sussex landscape and wildlife is a central part of the ethos of our Breakfast, featuring Milk from local small dairies, free-range Plymouth Rock eggs, Gloucestershire Old Spot sausages and dry cured bacon, Cox's apple juice, seasonal fruit, and tasty Local jams, mustards and *Marmalades!*'

Marmalades! With a '!' for God's sake.

Over breakfast he phones Lyndon Ferry: 'I'm downstairs.'

'I'm on a call. Come up.'

As usual, Lyndon has forgotten that Havard doesn't have the code for the door. As usual, he won't give it out. 'Buzz me, I'll let you in.'

The office is a large, featureless white room above a milliner's shop. Ferry has filled it with large fibreboard tables, the latest Apple computers, and a couple of cheap bouncy armchairs from Ikea. Outwardly it cannot be distinguished from any of the hundreds of other PR firms, Internet start-ups and would-be production companies that look, from their third- and fourth-floor eyries, over the relentless commodification of Soho.

Lyndon Ferry's own appearance and behaviour maintain the illusion: Ted Baker suit, candy-stripe shirt, no tie. Shoes that want to be anything but shoes. For Ferry and his generation industrial intelligence is simply another digital commodity: stuff to be mined, filleted, mashed up, repackaged. Everyone is in the intelligence business now.

Lyndon's crew – he calls them his 'crew' – are attending an OSINT conference in Cambridge. 'Open Source Intelligence.' Today, anyone with a broadband connection and half an ounce of sense can drill down to information once considered the prerogative of CIA analysts. Games designers, TV producers and TED junkies are the new intelligence elite. Most of Lyndon's operation consists of mashing up public data: everything from port plans to airborne imagery to LIDAR.

'It's a 120-metre unbadged Japanese cargo vessel called the *Ka-Bham*. Tongan registry, Valletta on the stern.'

Havard studies the paper cup he brought up from the cafe: '1066', cyan print on magenta. A cup that wants to be noticed. The coffee's a sight more drinkable than anything the Italians ever slopped out.

'Mitsubishi rolled it out of the Nagasaki shipyard in 1987.' Lyndon is still proffering the factsheet, insisting that Havard engage. It is, after all, his ship. Havard, president of Moyse Line, the world's third-largest container company, drains his cup and reads.

The *Ka-Bham*'s dead weight is 12,000 tonnes. A single screw powered by a 1,740 kW Wärtsilä, swallowing 480 litres of engine fuel per hour. It has its own gear: three wire-luffing MacGregor Navires. These cranes, if well maintained, are worth a good fraction of the boat.

'Well, we can write off the ship.'

'Yes.'

'What's the cargo?'

'In terms of value, aluminium. Running at US$1970 a tonne, we're talking just under the eight.'

Eight million dollars. Havard works this through. 'Which leaves a lot of cargo space.'

Lyndon nods, bouncing slightly in his Ikea chair. These chairs are,

Havard decides, with distaste, a sort of adult baby bouncer. 'Five holds. B to D are tween-decked and over the containers we've got consignments of razor wire, paint pigment, hardwood bundles and mixed recyclables: nothing over a thousand dollars a tonne. There's copper. We've fifty bundles of ingots, each bundle weighs a metric tonne. At today's price that's about US$360,000. The rest is –' He turns and reads from his screen. 'Well, shit, basically.'

'Let me see.'

The printer next to Havard's chair whines into motion.

Baby Cycle Toy	US$40.8544/unit	8 PCS
Toy Friction Car	US$47.9953	288 PCS
Toy Clock Mk0043263	US$126.853	24 DOZ
Tin Bowl [3 Pcs Sets] enamel Storage Bowl	US$19.33/DOZ	79 CTN
Ceramic Mug 11Oz	US$331.603/DOZ	2736 PCS
Coloured Lamb Skin Leather For Garment (Finished Leather)	US$692.5 SQF	324 SQF
Filteration Ceramic Media Ring Ball (72pcs/Ctn) (Fish Farming Accessories)	US$7.46247	2 CTN
Seaweed Extract Powder (Bio-fertilizer)	US$1828.24	500 KGS
Ceramic Tiles China	US$5039.05	1 LOT

'Have we had a demand?'

'It came through while you were in the air. I haven't had time to assess it.'

'Tell me anyway.'

'Fifty for the safe return of ship and crew.' Lyndon pauses to let this sink in. 'The ship, I'd say, is worth two.'

'What's the complement?'

'Twelve.'

'Feed them to the sharks.'

No reaction from Lyndon.

'I'm kidding.'

'There's a complication. The captain has his wife and son on board.'

Havard picks up his coffee cup, discovers it's empty, puts it down. 'Shit.'

'Do you want –?'

'Let's finish this.' Havard mulls over the ransom demand. 'Fifty million. Is it a typo?'

'Say what you're thinking.'

'*Five* million for boat and crew.'

'Yes.'

'But –' Havard hunkers forward in his chair. '*What's wrong with the boat?*'

A ship like the *Ka-Bham* is an ideal mothership. So why don't they just take it? Lyndon smiles. 'My first thought is: these are local lads on a spree. They want the cargo for resale but they've neither the money nor the organization to operate a mothership. They're not professionals. They're fishermen. Only then I saw this.' He scrolls back through his browser's history and beckons Havard over to the screen. 'I've been staring at this since you left Schiphol and I still can't make sense of it. Look where the *Ka-Bham* was taken.' He taps the screen.

'Bloody Sri Lanka?'

'I rang up a friend in Kuala Lumpur: the Piracy Reporting Centre has a list of harbour thefts in Sri Lanka as long as your arm, but in the last five years only a couple of half-hearted attempts at boarding a vessel in territorial waters. The country's on a war footing, for heaven's sake. Its navy cut its teeth on the Tamil Eelam. They have their coastline buttoned up. Or they thought they did.'

'Are we off the IMB radar?'

'The demand came through other channels.'

'So it is a professional job, after all.'

'Overpowering a ship a couple of miles outside Sri Lankan waters? I don't know, is that professional or just incredibly stupid?'

Absently, Havard casts around for his cup again. Cyan on magenta . . . 'They want to be noticed.'

Lyndon cycles further through his browser's history. 'They want *you* to notice. Who else would be interested? They're not going to earn themselves any headlines seizing the *Ka-Bham*. The Indian Ocean equivalent of a Tesco home delivery van. If it had been a VLCC or a Suezmax I could understand it . . . There.'

A crude sales graphic fills the screen.

'This is the only image we have of her.'

'Jesus Christ.'

'I'll get one of the interns to trawl for a tourist snap.'

'How long will that take?'

'Reverse searching an image of the *Ka-Bham*? If there's a photograph anywhere google-able, a couple of minutes. Then half a day chucking out the false-positives. *Ka-Bham* in public sources we can forget because I tried that over breakfast.' He gestures at the cup: 'Did you try their Old Spot bacon when you were down there?'

'Yes.'

'Flickr has a *Ka-Bhum* flagged Mongolia treading virtually the same waters, which is borderline annoying. For the deep net a mod_oai will take about twenty minutes. At worst we can have a 3D schematic by the end of the day and deploy Navy Seals by midnight GMT.'

'Don't bother.'

'We won't.'

This meeting's working assumption is that the line will pay up. If declared, a 12,000-tonne cargo vessel from the 1980s will cost more than its resale value in increased insurance premiums, so seizures of this kind are kept off the books. This is why the ransom demand makes no sense: if it's in the shipping line's interest simply to write off the ship, then why are the pirates trying to sell it back to them?

Most times the syndicate that seizes the ship rebadges it and operates it for as long as it takes to run a handful of drug shipments across the China Sea, returning it to the line at the end of a stipulated operating period. The shipping line gives the ship back its old identity and the pirates disappear. The original crews are almost never harmed; some have even remained on board for pay and lodging equivalent to anything they'd get from their usual manning agent. A pirate's standard defence is that he believed he was serving on a legitimate ship.

Sometimes the ship simply disappears. Repainted – a day's work – and under a different name and flag, it never sees land again. Phantom ships are the new menace: motherships from which syndicates controlled from as far away as London or São Paulo or Toronto can deploy RIBs to seize, loot and otherwise terrorize legitimate shipping. Phantoms are an idea as old as piracy itself and went out of fashion only for as long as the Strait of Malacca offered easier, land-based pickings. Securing Malacca with ReCAAP has smashed the tumour and reinfected the whole ocean.

'Are we missing something here? What about the crew?'

Lyndon shakes his head. 'A bunch of Bangladeshis under the command of a mediocre captain. His wife is a Bollywood star travelling incognito and his son is a computer whizz who's hacked the launch codes to the Fifth Fleet's tactical nukes.'

'Be serious.'

'The wife's a PA, the son's twelve years old.'

Havard retires to his chair by the door. A little rocking and comforting would be good right now. *Fifty million?*

Lyndon rattles away at his keyboard. He's enjoying himself. Like all his profession, he's attracted to the worst-case scenario: al-Qaeda scuttles a Very Large Crude Carrier in Phillip Channel, or blows up an LPG tanker in harbour, razing half of Singapore. Since events like this rarely happen more than once in a lifetime, Lyndon, priest-like, scans for auguries. Every atrocity is presaged by deep, difficult-to-interpret movements in the public and commercial commonweal: it's his job to spot them. No wonder he took to the merchant marine sector so early: an industry so bound in paper regulation, and at the same time so radically free of constraint, it has turned ships into quick-change artists, concealing, transforming and recreating them all within the space of half a dozen well-crafted emails. It is a paranoiac's paradise.

The printer by Havard's elbow spools up again. 'Just printing the shit.'

The shit. Certificate of insurance in respect to civil liability for pollution damage. Survey Certificate. Certificate of Registry. International Tonnage Certificate. International Load Line Certificate. Minimum Safe Manning Document. ISM Code Safety Management Certificate. Cargo Ship Safety Construction Certificate. Cargo Ship Safety Equipment Certificate. Cargo Ship Safety Radio Certificate. Cargo Ship Safety Certificate. Continuous Synopsis Record. International Ship Security Certificate. Crew list. Stowage plans. Seamen books. Crew contract papers. Maritime declarations of health. Derating certificates. Vaccination certificates. Oil record books.

In theory a ship's identity is never entirely falsifiable and in this rapidly rising pile are clues that might one day reveal the whereabouts of the *Ka-Bham*, however often it is reflagged and repainted. By this time tomorrow Lyndon's cheery, minimalist interiors will be so stuffed with teetering piles of unread, mostly unreadable, printout that the office will resemble something out of *Bleak House*.

The effort – a requirement set by certain obscure global certification authorities – is purely formal: insurance in case this matter finds its way, God forbid, into a courtroom.

Havard snatches the first stack free of the printer.

COMMUNICATIONS
INSTALLATION UHF RT MF/HF WIRE
TYPE: STR-580E SRG-1150DM
OPERATION TYPE: F3E/F2B/G3E/G2B J3E,H3E,J2B/F1B
SERIAL NO: 3573-0470 3553-0854
OUTPUT RATING: 25W 150W
FREQUENCY RANGE: 156-166.065MHz
0.5-29.999MHz

'Lyn.'

Lyndon Ferry reads the sheet. 'Nice.'

'On a twenty-five-year-old MV.'

'Overkill.'

'Yes.'

'Which reminds me.' Lyndon goes back to his screen and runs a history search. 'There. Aren't you glad we proprietized the software?'

Havard doesn't need to leave his seat to recognize the on-screen branding of SOSid, the world's most comprehensive satellite distress system.

'The Ka Bham has SOSid?'

'Had. The box was disabled within twenty minutes of the first distress signal.'

A SOSid signal is supposed to bounce off the nearest satellite straight to the International Maritime Bureau's Piracy Reporting Centre in Kuala Lumpur. Mindful of escalating insurance premiums, Moyse Line has added a level of discretion to its SOSid firmware so it can keep its lesser troubles to itself. This is not 'proprietization' so much as old-fashioned hacking and there's a legal team quietly preparing the line's defences against the day SOSid's makers find out what they've been up to.

'The captain hit the panic button at 14:45 UTC yesterday. There's a five-minute window within which we can doctor the timecode before we bounce the signal over to Kuala Lumpur. Given the low value of the ship and the cargo, I killed the bounce. The IMB know nothing of this.'

'Good.'

Lyndon crosses to the printer to rescue the next stack of printout. 'You know, I think somebody's after your attention. They want you to know they can take any vessel anywhere on the ocean, at any time. That's what I think. And a crew like that, a crew that can run the gamut of the Sri Lankan coastguard and disable a SOSid in twenty minutes – they don't make typos in their ransom demands.' He crosses to the desk and slaps the papers down. 'Now, you might want to be telling me what's so precious about a few crushed Coke cans and a container full of Chinese pedal cars that it's worth you installing SOSid on a tub like the *Ka-Bham*. Because if these pricks are who I think they are, taking the *Ka-Bham* out of Sri Lankan waters wasn't a bit of fun. It was a threat. Like snatching your car keys and dangling them over a drain.'

'Meaning . . .'

'They want you to know how close you came to having a well-equipped coastguard crawling all over a Dead Water boat.'

Havard studies his hands.

'Because when it comes down to it, really, what the hell else can this be about?'

Havard is shown to his room at the top of London's Dorchester Hotel. His bags are already waiting by his bed. What his office has found so essential to put in these three huge suitcases is a mystery: he doesn't expect to be here for more than a night.

Havard unpacks his laptop on to the table beneath the window. The porter unfastens his garment bag and arranges his suit on a hanger. Havard sees him out with a tip and the porter closes the door as he goes.

Lyndon Ferry has already uploaded the *Ka-Bham*'s manifest to Havard's laptop. Havard can ignore the break bulk, which leaves him sorting through 280 TEU – 'twenty-foot equivalent units' – of containerized goods.

Havard remembers the day he assumed the presidency of the line. He remembers the phone calls. Ness Ziona. Farnborough. Groom Lake. 'Where are our cans?'

With two million containers in motion over the earth at any one time, and no way to unpick Eric's code, Moyse Line relies on intelligent software agents to catch glimpses of the system Eric Moyse set in motion. The line's IT department has thrown any amount of code at Dead Water – everything from Glimpse to GAIS. Finally, under government pressure to deliver, Havard threw in the towel and phoned Google.

Havard types into his browser a secure, unindexed URL known only to him, Lyndon, and a couple of the line's more stable board members. What lights up the screen is, to all appearances, a public search engine. One by one, Havard pastes container cargoes into the search box.

It would only take a line or two of Java to automate this – but what would be the point? Peder Halstad, inducting Havard into Dead Water, said that only one container had ever fallen out of Dead Water, vanishing in transit along the Sher Shah Suri Marg in the Indian state of Uttar Pradesh. Years ago, and long before Havard's time. Everything Havard's ever had to deal with has turned out to be a false alarm. So Havard's content to keep the whole business a kitchen-table operation. Even Lyndon doesn't get to see which combination of cargoes lights up the board.

It's mid-afternoon by the time he hits upon the correct container.

There are currently six containers on line or line-chartered ships with the same contents, in the same quantities and configuration, as a container on board the *Ka-Bham*.

This, among all the brilliant things about Eric Moyse's system, is perhaps the most brilliant: it is platform-independent. It will function for as long as cargo ships carry containers about the seas. The contents are the code.

Havard pastes the serial shipping container codes into a text editor. Each code is twenty digits long.

The first two zeroes are an application identifier.

The next number is an extension digit set by the line.

The next three digits code for one of the member states of GS and are not manipulable. Every Moyse Line shipping container carries 788 in its serial number – the code for Liechtenstein.

The next five digits represent one or other arm of Moyse Line.

The serial number ends with a modulo-ten check digit.

Sweeping aside all this shrapnel leaves an eight-digit serial reference with which to identify an individual Moyse Line container.

Havard pastes the container numbers into a spreadsheet: they add up to 278,999,924.

He takes the figure back to eight digits by deleting the leftmost 2, then appends 6 to the right-hand side. Six is the number of matching containers. Now comes the magical part: the bit he has never quite wrapped his head around, no matter how many times he's had the Luhn algorithm explained to him. Six will function as a check digit for the number he has just created. He types the number into a Python applet and, yes, the check digit confirms it: the new number is valid.

The chances are very small that anywhere in the world there are six containers in transit each containing an identical cargo. The odds that these containers have numbers that add up to a new, valid, yet completely fictitious serial number, are infinitesimal.

This is not a false alarm. This is not a drill. There's a Dead Water cargo on board the *Ka-Bham*.

Havard Moyse hauls his way out of Victoria Underground station, dry-mouthed and afraid. After three days of booking his own taxis, ordering his own dinners, and making sure he turns up on time to confidential meetings, he's a nervous wreck. Good God, he can barely bring himself to ride the subway on his own! He leans against the stair-rail, a sixty-year-old man in a nice suit, clutching a fabric laptop bag to his chest. He shrinks from the crowds surging up and down. It's preposterous: Havard the milk-bathed pasha, come to a rough landing on the mean streets of Putney. He's going to have to do better than this.

It is Havard's third day off the radar, busy with activities it's best his office does not know about. His job, as president of the line, is ninety-nine per cent negotiation. The other one per cent is – well, call it plausible deniability.

For most of his life the line has felt like his family. The powers sitting around his boardroom table were all of an age, after all. They shared a vision and a history. The bitter truth, however, is that while Peder, on his pedestal, has only ever had the line, the others all went and got themselves other, better, richer lives: wives and children and homes and friends.

Havard is well looked after by his office but he is weary of pretending that his staff are family. They are more like nurses. 'When would you like the car, Mister Moyse?' 'Shall I arrange that telephone call for you?'

The Thames's meander has fooled him: he expects to come out at the river around Vauxhall Bridge, opposite the SIS Building, MI6 as was – even the secret services have succumbed to rebranding – but he ends up in Chelsea instead, staring with mounting panic at the shell of Battersea Power Station. There are no free cabs. There is nothing for it but to walk.

Grosvenor Road runs parallel to the river. It's a stretch of embankment Havard remembers from his youth, his tiny, soon-aborted stab at independence when he was borrowing small sums from Eric to support fairly ruinous retail experiments on Carnaby Street. He remembers early mornings, staggering, faintly stoned, out of boat parties at expensive moorings along here. The boats are still here, still pinned between pilings, square and unseaworthy; boats with mailboxes and electricity on tap. Behind them, a single police RIB cuts and slews about the river, having fun: CO19 firearms officers cling to its pontoons.

The road moves away from the river now, making room for an unfrequented Greek restaurant, a derelict drinking club, and weedy tennis courts. It's a strange stretch of river, as though the capital has suddenly forgotten itself. On the other side of the road from the river stands Dolphin Square: Gordon Jeeves's art deco 'city within a city'. Serviced apartments for men and women even more infantilized than he is. It was a hit in the 1930s. De Gaulle's Free French operated out of here. By the 1960s it was a joke and it's surely an even bigger joke now. Why in hell did the Home Office pick this for a rendezvous? The SIS is only across the river, so the choice isn't even discreet.

'Yoo-hoo!'

An elderly couple in fleecy tracksuits are braving the near-freezing river air to hit a tennis ball back and forth across a court with no net.

'Would you mind terribly fetching our ball?'

She must be about ninety, going by the way her face has fallen off the bone.

'There.'

Havard fetches the ball from the verge.

'Thanks awfully.'

He throws it over the chain-link.

'You're Havard Moyse.'

'I am?'

'The silly buggers phoned us only this morning when we already had the court booked.' Her tennis partner has joined her at the fence. He's a bit younger than she is, though his absurd jet-black hairpiece does him no favours. 'I'm John. This is Sarah. Can't waste a booking. Bad form.'

'Would you mind waiting while we get changed?'

'I – No, I don't mind.'

'There's a bar and grill in the Square. Very modern.'

'No, John,' says Sarah. 'You booked the Contented Vine.' She squints at him. 'You did book the Contented Vine, John, didn't you?'

'Yes, yes,' he says, quickly. 'I did.'

'Well, thank goodness for that.' She says to Havard. 'Do you know Sussex Street?'

The elderly couple go off to change and Havard, who has long since grown out of waiting for other people, searches Sussex Street out for himself. Sarah's directions are clear enough and though it's too early for lunch the brasserie is, as promised, already open. Havard is their first customer. A waiter shows him to a table at the back, where patio doors lead to a small paved garden shaded by a Taittinger-branded parasol. It has started to rain.

Havard is directed to a padded booth directly underneath a lurid four-foot-high acrylic painting of a lobster. Every so often he turns and cranes his neck to stare at the thing. He can't shake off the feeling that it's moving, ever so slightly, whenever his back is turned.

'Mr Moyse.'

Sarah's dressed in senior-citizen nondescript. John looks like he fell out of a *Carry On* film: a blue yachting blazer with a fried-egg crest, whites and – are those deck shoes? His feet must be frozen through. John hands him a Daunt's bag. 'Got you a present.'

Havard opens it. The red paperback inside is called *Sodomy and the Pirate Tradition*.

'English buccaneers can't all be William Dampier, you know. Anyway, I hope you like it.'

'Don't encourage him,' says Sarah. 'All week he's been emptying his cannons into the poop deck.'

Havard stares at them, helpless.

'So, what have you got for us?'

He feels around his wallet for the serial number. He's written it down on a slip of paper. He hands it to John.

John snatches it from Havard's hand, reads it, shows it to Sarah, and tears it to pieces. 'I do wish people would learn to memorize things,' he mutters.

'Come along now, John. Mr Moyse isn't a professional.'

'Bloody laziness is what it is.'

'John!'

'I'm not blaming him. I blame the schools.'

'Here we go,' Sarah sighs.

The barman comes over with drinks. John shoves the confetti he has made into the pocket of his blazer.

'Frankly,' Havard says, his helplessness turning to anger, 'I expected this would be dealt with by someone younger.'

They stare at him. 'Well, what would be the point of that?'

'Mr Moyse,' Sarah says, 'you surely don't expect young people to go crawling all over Dead Water boxes?'

'Hardly matters to us,' says John. 'A nasty leukaemia twenty years down the road is hardly our problem, is it?'

Sarah, meanwhile, is staring up at the lobster hanging above Havard's head. 'Oh!' she exclaims. Havard flinches. 'John! Don't you remember? Five oh three one two two two eight seven oh oh two? It's the yellow rain!'

'Yellow rain?' Havard's voice is hardly more than a breath.

'Ness Ziona. You remember.'

John stares at Sarah as though she's just torn all her clothes off. 'Sarah, for God's sake, and in a bloody restaurant –'

'"Yellow rain"?'

'Mmm?' For all his horror at Sarah's lack of discretion, when push comes to shove, John can't resist the chance to tell a tale. 'Oh. Yes. 1975. Yellow rain. This weird sticky yellow stuff started falling out of the skies over Laos and Kampuchea. Alexander Haig – he was Secretary of State – accused the Soviets of dropping mycotoxins. Only it turned out to be honeybee shit.'

'The Soviets dropped bee shit . . .?'

'T-2,' says Sarah, helpfully. 'A trichothecene mycotoxin. It infected the Soviets' wheat supply in the 1930s and they were the first to weaponize it.'

'Mould,' says John. 'Bread mould.'

'Abdominal pain, diarrhoea, vomiting, prostration.' Sarah counts the symptoms on her fingers. She's proud of this: a lifetime's recall still at her fingertips. 'Give it a few days and you've got fever, chills, myalgias – bone marrow depression?'

'Don't ask me,' says John.

'Pharyngeal ulceration. Laryngeal ulceration. Melaena, bloody diarrhoea, epistaxis, vaginal bleeding –'

'*Sarah.*'

'The Israelis suspended their weaponization programme in 1972 but they couldn't be persuaded to sign the UN convention. Indefinite secure storage was the obvious face-saver.'

John shakes his head. The rain has loosened his hairpiece: it is moving independently of him. 'They're a rum lot, the Jews.'

'John!'

'Well, it's time they signed.'

'I do hope you'll write to them, John, and tell them.'

'Sarah –'

'I do hope you will make the effort to share your important political insights with Benjamin Netanyahu.'

'If you're going to be like that –'

Havard thumps the table. It comes out of nowhere. He doesn't know he's done it until he's done it. He's as surprised as they are. 'Would you mind telling me what *the fuck* is on my ship?'

John flashes a mischievous grin. '*Was* on your ship.'

'Don't get upset,' says Sarah, rather put out. 'It's not alive. Not after all this time.'

'And what do I do?'

John folds his arms. 'What do you do? Absolutely nothing.'

Sarah says: 'Write it off. It's not a big ship, is it? Not a valuable cargo?'

'No,' he says, defeated. 'Not a valuable cargo.'

'We'll sort it out,' John drawls. 'We'll put a call in to Ness Ziona. It's their stockpile, after all.'

Sarah says, 'I'm afraid the crew will have to look out for themselves.'

TWENTY-ONE

There's a hand over his eyes, pressing his eyelids shut, he can't see, and in the few seconds it takes for him to return to consciousness, Egaz Nageen is made a child again. Let me see the surprise. Let me see what you got me. But the hand is not a parent's hand, Nageen is not a boy, and the hand over his face will not let go, it will not stop pressing against his eyes, and he wonders what this is, and then he remembers.

Egaz Nageen is cold all over. Every breath is a shudder. With every breath, gills spring open along his sides and ice-water gushes between his ribs. Only his eyes are hot, only his face, where the hand presses his eyelids shut, fiercely, as against a spring.

Time passes. A minute. Two minutes. Ice-water slops through every groove of him, every cranny round his grape-bunched lungs. How many breaths? Count your breaths. How many breaths to a minute? (He needs some grip, some control. He needs rhythm.)

He is aware, now, of other breaths, of other patterns of breathing, lapping and syncopating. They are together, then: the survivors. How many have been spared? How many killed? He's still in one piece, just about. There's been no payback, yet, for the boy he killed. Of course, he's valuable: the captain. He'll command a ransom. These other poor slobs are shark bait. Voiceless. Underskilled. Surplus to the industry's requirements.

What of Suniti? What about Sabir?

This room is not cold at all. The cold is coiled inside him. He pictures it. A bristle worm. The cold will shake him apart if he lets it. He needs something to put between himself and the cold. He needs an idea. Or not even an idea. An image.

He pictures the hand across his eyes, or tries to: fingers curled against his face. If this is a hand, there must be fingers. Are there fingers? If there are no fingers, then this cannot be a hand. If this is not a hand, then –

He bucks, blindfolded, his body smarting against its bonds. His hands are secured behind his back with a cable tie; his eyes are bound shut with a rag. His feet have been chopped off and discarded, and chains loop round and round the stumps of his legs –

His blood pounds and his heart hammers, robbing him of control. Panic is cold in his throat and the backs of his knees. He bites down on his lip, hard, and blood seeps out, salt against his tongue. He takes a breath. A breath. A breath. He cannot feel the binding around his ankles. He cannot feel his feet. He cannot feel a thing. He has to assume his ankles are bound with the same stuff that's pinning his hands behind his back. He has to assume his feet have gone numb, deprived of blood. He must conjure up things that are sane and real. He must assemble a world he can handle and predict. He cannot move; he cannot see, so he has to find some other way to hold on to the world. He experiments, twisting his wrists against each other. Plastic teeth chow down and the pain, catching him unawares, forces a sob from between clenched teeth.

'Shut up.'

Not his voice.

'Fucking shut up.'

Is it a voice?

'Shut up or we will kill you all.'

It is a voice all right.

Footfalls. Heavy boots. The men who boarded his ship had bare feet: big, splayed toes. Who's this in boots? He's chewing something sweet and faintly rotten. Arabian tea. Khat.

Nageen fights the urge to curse. He fights the desperate need to do something.

He lies there, absolutely still. But something spills out. A sigh. A snarl.

He feels the air moving around him as the man in boots draws back. 'Shut up.'

Nageen's head explodes.

Later – no telling how much later – Nageen wakes.

Footfalls. Heavy boots, receding. 'We will kill you all.'

Same voice. Same footfalls. No time has passed. This is what Nageen tells himself. This is what he decides. I have not lost time. He holds on to the thought, as to a buoyancy device. One by one he begins to reel the parts of himself together: burning hands, needle-legged feet, a face as puffy as a mushroom, the flesh inside his mouth senseless and shreddable as tissue. He chews his lip. He needs the taste of blood. Why will his lip not bleed?

He must not stir. He must not sob. What is that noise? Please God, he prays: don't let it be me.

It is a cadence he knows as well as his own, strained now, risen in the back of the throat. It is his son. Sabir is sobbing.

Footfalls. Heavy boots.

Nageen struggles to sit up.

'Head down.'

Nageen hesitates.

The boots approach.

He waits for the kick. He needs to draw attention away from his son.

A hand presses his head firmly to the floor.

'On the floor.' The man's breath stinks of khat: all green and rotten. 'Don't fucking look. None of you look. We'll spray acid in your eyes. Keep your heads on the floor. Keep your faces on the floor.' He rubs Nageen's face against the rubberized floor and the rag binding his eyes scrunches a little; it pulls at his lids.

Footfalls. Heavy boots. Sabir is sobbing as the man lands his first kick. He cries out. A second kick to his stomach turns the boy's cry into a gush of air, an unliving sound: a punctured inflatable folding up on itself. 'Shut up.'

Another blow: Nageen groans.

Footsteps.

'Don't. Fucking. Move.'

Egaz Nageen doesn't fucking move, and the man in boots moves away. As he goes he spits something out. It lands beside Nageen's face. A gob of paste. Spent khat.

Nageen's blindfold is dislodged a little. His eyes are fixed open against the cloth. His eyes are hot and wet and scratched. He cannot see a thing, but he is afraid to close his eyes, because if he closes his eyes, who's to say he will be able to reopen them against the restraining rag? Eventually, inevitably, the irritation becomes unbearable and Nageen squeezes his eyelids shut.

And opens them. Not all the way, but a little. Snake-eyed, he strains for the light.

Nothing. He cannot see.

He shuts his eyes. Opens them a little. Shuts. Opens.

Nothing.

Perhaps it is night.

Perhaps, if he waits long enough, it will be morning and he will be able to see.

It is a start.

Hours pass.

Around him men are struggling with their bonds. (Is Sabir all right? Is Suniti here? Where are they?) Every half-hour the man in boots returns to threaten them and kick heads. He is becoming useful: a clock.

The smell of him – the smell of khat – is overpowering and vile. He's chewing the stuff constantly, using it to steady his nerves. Nageen's chewed enough khat in his time to know that this man's only going to get more and more out of his head.

They've given him the job of guarding the hostages because he's the weakest, the most anxious, the one they'd rather not have under their feet while they secure the ship. They don't trust him so they've left him guarding the luggage.

Egaz Nageen forces a smile through broken lips, a chipped tooth. He wants to feel this. He wants to taste this.

They have made their first mistake.

Egaz Nageen wakes. His head feels as shapeless as a bag. It aches so much, the ache is a sound: a tinnitus that makes it hard for him to hear the rhythm of the ship.

There is nothing to see. No light. Still, Egaz Nageen squeezes his eyes tight shut, his lids scraping against the restraining rag, the better to listen. There is something wrong with the rhythm of the ship. There is something wrong with the engines.

Through the rubberized flooring, the rhythmic tremble of the engines has grown weaker and faster: the heart of a dying man.

Nageen's own heart begins to race: *they have switched to the diesels.*

At sea, a cargo ship runs on fuel oil, but fuel oil has to be hot or it clogs the injectors. For manoeuvres, slow and dead-slow propulsion, a big ship runs on cooler-burning diesel. They are manoeuvring. Are they coming into port?

Nageen flexes against his bonds. He waits for the shout, footfalls, the impact of a heavy boot. If they are being watched, then whoever is watching them is a good deal calmer than their first jailer. Nageen squirms against the rubberized floor, seeking purchase. There is nothing to lean against. He clenches his stomach muscles and somehow manages to get himself into a sitting position.

Upright he can feel, much more clearly, the motion of the boat.

They're still at sea.

Something strikes the ship. Not hard: Nageen imagines them coming alongside another vessel. Another blow reverberates through the hull. The sea is calm and they are in the middle of it. They are going to transfer the *Ka-Bham*'s cargo, and when they have transferred the cargo – what?

It's happened before and it will happen again. In the scrapping yards corpses are discovered in a ship's cold store, stripped of clothes, jewellery, teeth. Impossible to say whether they were crew or pirates, or whether they knew what they were, or cared, and besides the ship is dead and its paperwork leads nowhere, as usual . . .

Nageen bites his lip: the pain, trivial enough, is sufficient to bring him back to the present. He cannot afford nightmares. The whining and scraping is not Baba Yaga's house, scrabbling about the deck on chicken legs. The ship's gear is lifting containers off the deck of the *Ka-Bham*.

It's brave of them to be transferring cargoes in mid-ocean. There is a definite swell. They are under a deadline. The syndicates are run these days by men who have no special knowledge of the sea. They are as likely as any city shipowner to tell a captain to 'punch through' a storm.

He bites his lip. He bites it, bites it hard. The moment. Stay in the moment. It is all you have. The clangs and scrapes come at him from different locations, different distances, and all of them just slightly below him. The sounds are clues: it is up to him to decipher them. He listens, he concentrates, he pictures the layout of the ship. He turns his head slowly from side to side, guessing directions and distances.

He knows port from starboard now. He knows they are high up in the iron house. He knows where they are. This is the mess room. It smells right: under the fug of khat and urine and unwashed bodies. *He knows where they are.*

'Don't move.'

His breath catches in his throat.

'Don't you fucking move. We'll kill you all.'

Footfalls. Heavy boots.

'You think the owners care about you? The owners don't care about you. You think they're going to pay a ransom? They're not paying a ransom. You think we asked for a ransom?'

A click.

'We didn't.'

Nageen remembers being offered a cup of chai by Third Officer Waddedar. There is a kettle here.

'You think we want you to live? We don't. You think we want to share our food with you?'

The kettle boils.

Nageen hunches, tense as wire.

The kettle rattles, plastic, lifted free of its base.

Footfalls.

Water dribbles. Sabir screams. The screaming goes on and on. It doesn't stop. Steadily it loses whatever there was that was human in it. Whatever there was that was Sabir becomes pure pain, pure tone, and the scalding water pours and pours and pours, flooding Sabir, bloating him, washing his face away, his face just one big blister now, a white mask pricked with eyes: no more Sabir.

'We have acid. We will kill you all.'

Ships lie gutted on the black, poisoned sands of Darukhana. Cut open, they yawn like mouths. Rishi likes to imagine them breathing. He likes to imagine them smelling what he can smell: gasoline, tar, solvent, bilge water. He tears open a can of Thums Up and drinks to take away, if only for a moment, the taste of this place. His home. His kingdom. The seat of his power.

This is recycling in the raw. Greenpeace may hold their noses and bleat about carcinogens but virtually everything is salvaged from these ships. Industrial fluids. Sump oil. Materials of every description. Men clamber from deck to deck, tearing through panelling and asbestos to get at the plumbing.

It's low tide and the beach running between his workshop and the sea – *his* beach, his domain, fenced, signed, Private Property, Keep Out – his tongue of black and sterile sand stretches further than those pathetic kattas the river and Old Samey stole from him all those years ago.

The call comes through on the wrong phone. He answers it anyway: 'What's wrong?'

'Thank you for taking the call.' It's David Brooks.

'I can give you one minute.'

'Roopa Vish tried to sell Moyse Line documentation relating to the taking of the *Ka-Bham*.'

'What documentation?'

'All of it. Everything my girl fetched us out of Dubai.'

Rishi hunkers down against a dawning horror. 'We'll have to scuttle the ship.'

'Yes, we'll have to scuttle it.'

He closes his eyes. 'Go on.'

'Roopa contacted the line's Toulouse office and by a miracle their people patched it through to me. I had to make a decision. I'm sorry.'

Rishi doesn't have to ask what this is. He knows how this goes.

'It was quick,' David says. 'As quick as I could make it.'

Rishi begins to speak but it comes out all wrong. There are no words in it at all.

David says: 'Get the ship off the ocean as fast as you can.'

Rishi pulls himself together just long enough to say that he expects never to hear from David again.

'I'm gone,' David says, and cuts the line.

When Rishi's hands are steady enough, he taps out a text message. Nothing comprehensible: just a string of numbers. He dials and the message flies far, far out to sea, to a man whose name he does not even know. He takes the chip out of the phone and throws both chip and phone into the harbour. He is being so careful, but still he has no idea – none – what he is up against.

Egaz Nageen is learning to see.

Bit by bit he has turned himself around to where he knows the mess-room windows must be. Definitely, there is light. Nothing more than light, no form – but light itself is something. He tells himself this: a painstaking workman and fiercely sane. He is learning to see through the rag binding his eyes. He is learning to wring every mote of information from his tiny world.

The captives are fed. Porridge and fish bait. He eats, he gags, he eats more than he gags. He will keep this down. He gags again. Good God, are these men amateurs, after all? Are they only fishermen, driven by desperation? What's an amateur now? The Somalis are fishermen. For years they were reduced to eating fish bait. Now they take tankers at will.

These are not Somalis. Nageen knows what Somali sounds like. He has heard practically everything but Somali on board since the cargo was unloaded. Indonesian, Chinese, Malay, Thai. No, these are an old Malacca crew. He imagines them, bound to their mothership, stranded at sea since MALSINDO drove them out of the Strait. How many years since they set foot on land? Four years? Five?

They take him to the toilet. He stumbles as they pull him from the stall, deliberately slumps, and his head cracks the side of the stall.

The rag around his eyes is giving way.

Sabir's sobbing has shrunk to nothing now. The pirates have amended their mistake. No more heavy boots: just the slap-slap-slap of feet that have never known shoes.

'We will cut you up. Heads on the floor.'

No more games. No smell of khat. No more chai.

Have they taken the kettle away?

Night falls. (There is day and night now. There is time. It is something.)

Egaz slumps on to his side and tries to sleep. He wakes up and feels something against his cheek. A hard wad of something. A dried bolus of khat. He waits. He listens. He cranes his head and takes the dry lump into his mouth. He breathes deep, trying not to choke. His mouth is dry. His spit turns to foam. He waits, he breathes, he tries not to choke. Eventually the lump softens. He chews on dead stalks, dead leaves. He will use whatever he can get hold of to rebuild his world. The khat is chewed to nothing; there is no goodness left in it, none at all.

He chews and chews and chews.

There is light. Egaz sits up, stomach muscles straining. Much more of this and he will not have the strength to sit up any more. He listens, turning his head this way and that, trying to get his bearings. There is something wrong with the engine. There is something wrong with the ship. It is listing. Perhaps it is the wind, the direction of the waves –

No. The ship is listing. They have not trimmed the ship correctly. If the weather deteriorates, it will handle badly.

A can is lifted to his mouth. Dirty water. He drinks, tries not to gag, gags anyway, hunts for more but there is no more, the can is gone.

Slap – slap – slap. He glimpses movement through the rag binding his eyes. A mote of red as the can is pulled away from his mouth.

Esso.

It is an Esso can.

Night falls.

He tries to sleep.

'Egaz –'

'Shut up!'

Feet slap across the room, from door to window. (He knows where the door is. The window. He knows who called out for him. Suniti. His wife.)

Suniti cries out as something – a foot, a hand – clips her, hard, knocking her over. He hears her fall. She sobs.

'On the floor now. Heads down.'

Obediently, Nageen rolls on to his side.

'Kiss the floor, all of you.'

A different voice, from a different part of the room. A Thai. There are two of them. A Thai and – a Malay? Two of them. Now he knows, and knowing this, his world expands. Two men and an Esso can – and Suniti. Suniti is here.

He sleeps, sure now of his world. His wife. His son.

In the morning the ship is listing still further. There is something wrong.

He tenses against his bonds. His feet are dead. His hands tingle. He tries to sit upright, falls back, tries again, falls back.

There is something wrong. Have they turned him around in the night? Has he moved as he slept? The list is wrong. The list is to starboard now. Yesterday they were listing very slightly to port. It is light. He can very dimly make out the shape of the windows. He has not been turned around.

There is something wrong with the ship. He closes his eyes, squeezes them tight shut. He cannot hear a thing. Only breathing. There is no vibration. They are drifting. The breathing is very loud. Too loud. It is not only breathing; and the other sound, the not-breathing – it is not a sound he knows. What the hell is that sound?

It is coming from below.

He jackknifes, comes to a sitting position, feels a muscle tear. 'Hey.'

Nothing.

'Hey!'

No footfall. No acid. No threat.

'Hey!'

A constant hiss, far away, below them, below the engine room, where the cooling pipes run.

The sea valves are open.

Egaz Nageen drags his head back and forth across the floor of the mess. He gags, drooling vegetal spit. His broken lips burn. He shouts, barks: guttural noises, more animal than human. Shallow pimples in the rubber floor tiles scrape and snag at the rag bound round his eyes. Now there is no one to kick him or threaten him or burn him, getting rid of the blindfold is easy – just a matter of patience and time.

Slowly, slowly, he rolls the rag from his eyes. His vision flares. Ink blots spill across his eyes and resolve into images, pure black on pure white. The edge of a pool table. Lines and squares: windows. Slumped forms. His crew. His child. His wife.

Long white bars. The room's fluorescent strips are lit up. The generators are still running and even were they to die, even were they to be shut down, there are emergency generators hard-wired to the ship's grid. These days, when ships go down, they carry their light into the dark.

He strains, sits up, feels muscles in his stomach tear. He cries. Tears roll down his face as he bends long-crippled legs. His feet are useless knuckles. He thumps and scrapes, begins to move across the room. Around him men flex, blind grubs against the rubber floor. He recognizes them. Chief Engineer Sen, First Officer Kamal. His son.

Sabir's face is scalded white, blistered, smeared with blood where he has scraped the pustules open, fighting against the rag still around his eyes. Nageen is level with him now. Nageen wants to say how proud he is. He wants the first words from his lips to be words of love. He want his son to hear, his wife, and all of them, how much he loves his boy. 'Shut up,' he says, and kicks Sabir with senseless feet. 'Shut the fuck up.'

The boy keens, sobs, is overcome.

'I'll break your teeth, you don't shut up.'

Love, right now, would kill this kid as sure as a knife against his throat. Love will soften, will make a space for fear. Sabir will get no love from him. Not yet. If they go down, they'll go down spewing hate and rage. His promise to himself and all of them. They'll bloody fight. 'Keep still, you bloody fool.'

Sabir buttons up, his scalded lips pressed white, his body slackening against its bonds. Egaz thinks his heart will burst. This much he allows: 'I'm coming back for you.'

He thumps. He scrapes.

Why not an urn? Why not a samovar? Why not something bolted down? Whoever heard of a mess-room kettle? Stupid. Non-regulation. There's the cord. It's plugged in at midriff height, above the table, held by staples to the wall.

He leans against the table, takes hold of the leg with bound hands, and works himself backwards up the table leg, pushing and scraping. If he tips his head back he can feel the edge of the table. He uses his head, an extra pressure, kicks and heaves. He gets one shoulder on to the table edge. Don't turn. You turn, you fall. His stomach burns and rumbles, torn to shit. If he falls now he'll never have the strength to get up again.

He shimmies, gets a shoulder blade against the table edge. Some more. Don't turn. Not yet. Now –

He turns.

He sprawls against the table, weak-kneed, held there by his weight against the table edge. It digs painfully into the bottom of his ribcage. He's not quite on, no, not quite stable, if he slips . . .

He moves his feet. He hops. The table edge knifes its way under his ribcage and his forehead bumps against the kettle.

His weight is mostly on the table. He squirms, nudging the kettle sideways. It stops. It sticks. The wire feeding the kettle base is stapled to the table.

The kettle is plastic. The switch is under the handle. He heaves, sticks out his tongue, and licks the switch. The kettle wobbles on its base. He kicks, slips, recovers. He moves after the switch, tongue extended, hopeless, bestial, gets the switch under his tongue and lunges. The kettle rolls off the base and rocks away out of reach, against the wall.

Desperate, he lunges against the table. The kettle rocks. The table top is melamine. Nice, slippy melamine. He gets his feet under him and rocks against the table. The kettle skips and wobbles.

Six inches of this. Six inches to the side of the table. He breathes, he rocks, he hunts for rhythm. How long till it falls?

Behind him, blind grubs quest for light. 'Mr Nageen!'

'Shut up,' he gasps, 'shut up.'

'Mr Nageen, the sea valves!'

'Shut your face!'

The kettle falls.

Nageen tries rolling off the table, his feet slip out from under him and he falls, cracking his head on the rubber floor. His nose blooms, a dull flower of pain and tears spill from his eyes. Pain vices his forehead. He lies there, straining, clinging to consciousness. A minute goes by before he can think about anything but pain.

The kettle rolls by his head in a puddle of old water. Off its base. Powerless. Useless.

He's only half-done.

He shimmies back against the wall and jackknifes, inch by fractional inch, back to his feet. He edges round so his back is against the table, fingers weaving, feeling for the plug. He finds it, inches it out of the socket with his fingertips. It hangs off a staple. He gets hold of the plug and pulls, leaning against the flex. The first staple pops, his weight comes on to the flex and the cable stutters free as he falls to the floor. The kettle's plastic base flies off the table, lands, and snaps in two. Nageen stares from piece to shattered piece. The nearest is the biggest; the plastic nipple that powers the kettle is still intact. The wire is still attached.

There are power points under plastic housings all over the ship. He just has to find them.

'Dad.'

Sabir has worked his blindfold off. One half of his face is ballooned, unrecognizable. The other half is trying to smile. He nods spastically.

There is a ribbon of metal by his hip. A wire handle. Nageen rolls towards his son. Sabir sits up, shimmies round, gets his thumb under the wire and pulls. The housing lifts free. There are four plugs.

Sitting with his back to the panel, Nageen fumbles the plug into a socket. Is there any power? There's no way to know yet. How long before the power dies? Emergency generators feed lights and pumps and automatic doors. The ring main's an unknown. He plugs the wire in. Sabir's already wiggling over to the kettle.

'Mr Nageen?' The voice is controlled. Quiet. Manageable. It is Sen.

'Hold on, Mr Sen.'

Sabir nudges the kettle across the room with his forehead. This is going to take a while. Nageen allows himself a moment's rest. The crew are sobbing. Everyone but his wife.

Softly: 'Suniti.'

'I'm here.'

'Suniti.'

'Shut up.' It is Sen. 'Shut up.'

There are footsteps. Voices. They do not come closer. They do not retreat. There are men still aboard. There are men inside the iron house.

They wait.

Sabir whispers: 'Father –?'

Nageen shakes his head: shut up.

Minutes go by.

The ship lists to starboard. A swell runs under the ship. The kettle rolls over and comes to rest against its handle.

Footfalls, at a run.

They are gone.

Nageen lies back, raises his feet and drops his heels hard against the kettle housing. The plastic body pops from its base. This thing really is a piece of shit. Together, back to back, Sabir and his father manoeuvre the kettle base into the plastic nipple hanging from the power cord. Sabir has hold of the heating element. He drops it.

'It's hot.'

Nageen twists round as far as he can. 'Get it off the wire!'

Sabir tugs the wire out from under the coil. As it heats, it turns from bluish grey to grey.

'Okay.'

'Dad.'

'Okay.'

He can do this. His son's taken worse than this. He studies the coil, its position and angle, then shimmies round. The flooring is already responding to the heat. He can smell it. He can hear it. A faint hiss.

'To the left, dad.' Sabir's voice is iron-clad. 'Again. You're there.' Nageen brings his wrists down on the coiled metal and running, running round the coil, back and forth, back and forth, adepts of AC, the divine twins, Abhik and Kaneer, eager actors now in the drama they have set in motion, hiss self-laudatory prayers. They flare and flame, releasing him.

TWENTY-TWO

Havard's flight from Doha to Muscat leaves on schedule at 3.15 p.m. Everyone else on the flight is watching a film; Havard has his very own horror-movie on his iPhone.

Almost everyone in Ester's Facebook album is wearing surfing gear and grinning like an idiot. Every photograph is tagged, date-stamped and geo-tagged. Almost everyone tagged in her photographs has their own Facebook page. There's one exception. He's older than the rest and appears in just one shot, alone, standing with his back to the camera. Ester took this photograph when he wasn't looking. It's in Dubai. There's the sail-like Burj Al Arab hotel on the skyline and he's looking towards it, hand raised to shield his eyes, in a suit, for Christ's sake. Havard knows only one man dandyish enough to wear his suit to the beach. It's so obvious a clue it's almost an insult.

Lyndon's over the moon, of course. 'I always said David Brooks was a cunt.'

Havard, waiting at the gate for his flight to board, winced and lowered the volume of his phone. 'You weren't the first, Lyndon. Tell me something.'

'Sure.'

'Your investigating Ester. It was pure spite, wasn't it?'

'You send David to Rawai to examine the can and a few weeks later *his daughter* shows up in your bed? Well done with that, by the way.'

Havard said nothing.

'Come on, Havard, I have a job to do. No one here was particularly gunning for her. All this stuff is just a key-press away. We put about a hundred employees through the same checks.'

'I can't afford to know about that.'

'I'm just telling you.'

The trouble with Lyndon Ferry is he is an enthusiast. He wants to share with people the pleasures of his work.

The plane lands on time. A Land Cruiser is waiting to drive Havard through Muscat's hilly tangle to his house in Ruwi. Tall hills and crenellated houses. Corner supermarkets. Car dealerships. He unlocks the door and finds Ester slumped on his sofa, surrounded by bags and cases. She has been waiting a long time for someone to knock on this door.

'Ester.'

Her face is swollen. She's a mess. She will not look at him. What the hell is she doing here? 'I'm sorry,' she says.

'Ester.'

'I'm sorry!'

He sits down beside her on the sofa, among his whale bones and his fashion books, his pottery shards, industry awards and photographs. One way or another, he is going to have to explain to her that 'sorry' is not going to cut it. He gets out his mobile and calls up the picture Lyndon sent him while he was in the air. 'We have satellite imagery of the *Ka-Bham*.' He taps her shoulder with the phone. She averts her head. 'As you can see, the ship is lying on its side. Chances are it's already at the bottom of the Indian Ocean by now.' She will not look. On top of everything else, she is a coward. 'The *Ka-Bham* had a crew of twelve. The captain's family was aboard. His wife. His twelve-year-old son.'

Ester puts her hands over her face.

'Ester. We don't know yet if there are survivors. Even if there are survivors, we don't know if there's a boat can reach them in time. It's a big ocean.'

Ester slides off the sofa, away from him. Her silly, feathery topknot is quivering. He resists the impulse to touch it. To stroke it. Such a stupid girl. He goes to the kitchen and puts the kettle on. There's instant coffee in the cupboard. He makes two cupfuls and carries them back into the living room. 'Here.' He sets a cup down beside her.

On his mobile he calls up her Facebook page. The photograph is as blurry as hell. He shows it to her. Ester wraps her arms around herself. She is shivering. 'Ester, if you can tell me where your dad is, I can do something for you. I can help you. We all can. Christ.' He tries to laugh but it comes out very badly. 'I mean, we don't want you in any trouble.' Havard wants to tell her how much she matters to him now. He wants to tell her how lonely his life has been. It is all too late.

He has his office. He has his colleagues, and many of them are friends. They will have to be enough for him. He will manage. Old fool. 'We want to keep you out of the papers,' he says, as brutally as he knows how. She will believe this of him. It is the sort of thing a shipping magnate, a man in business, a moneyed man, would say.

Nothing.

'Where is David Brooks?'

'I can't.'

'He called you. Warned you. What? He told you to run?'

She nods.

'What did he tell you?'

'Oh.' She tries to smile. 'He spun me a line. The way he does.'

'He said you were in danger.'

'Yes.'

'So why didn't you run?'

'From you?' She hunts for the words. 'You're kind.'

'Thanks.'

'You've been kind to me.'

'Christ.'

'What?'

'What did he tell you about the boat?'

'That his people were trying to bring it into safe harbour. For the UN. He said when you found out what they were doing, you ordered it sunk.'

Havard runs his hands over his face. 'Oh, for crying out loud. *Sunk?* With what? My secret fleet of submarines?'

'There's no point going over it,' she says. 'You know how he hazes people.'

Now, there's the truth. David's talents – counter-piracy, counter-espionage, government liaison – have never been easy to corral. 'Where is he?'

She is looking at him, measuring him. She is feeling a little better. 'How did you get this, anyway?' she asks, peering at his phone. She is utterly mystified. 'Only Friends and Family can see this.' Poor child. She has no idea what privacy is, never mind secrecy. None of her generation have a clue. Theirs is the open-source intelligence upon which men like Lyndon Ferry feed.

'Ester?'

'I can't do this.'

'But you can let fourteen people drown.'

'I didn't know.'

'You didn't know pirates kill people?'

'I didn't know that was what – *I didn't know.*'

'You thought your father worked for the United Nations?'

'Don't.'

'That every VDU op in Dubai carries confidential papers around in her cellphone.'

She looks at him.

'You think that's what espionage looks like? A man in a vanilla suit and a stick, secretly bettering the world? Ester, espionage is an office in central London that does nothing all day but break into the Facebook pages of people as stupid as you are. How long do you think it took my friend Lyndon to crack your Dropbox account? Your Evernote account? Posterous, iTunes, all the rest of your shit? He's pulled enough sensitive information out of your cloud to put you in an Emirates prison for life. Tell me about David Brooks. Now.'

'He said –'

'What?'

'He said we were taking contaminated ships off the seas.' She puts her head in her hands. 'He made everything so – so plausible. So complicated.'

'I bet he did. Tell me where he is.'

'I don't know. Musandam. He said he was there a day ago. Said he was on a snorkelling trip. He could be anywhere by now.'

'Where are you meeting him?'

'I'm not.' She takes her hands away from her face finally. 'You're safe. He's shutting it down. Whatever it was we were doing. He's shutting it down.' She studies her hands. They are shaking.

Can he touch her? Comfort her? Havard lays his hand on her shoulder. She stands up quickly, away from him. He watches her to the door. 'What about your bags?'

'Bin them.'

'You know,' he says, 'I'm going to have to call people.'

'Call them.'

'The police. My office in London.'

'All right.'

'They will find you.'

'No,' she says, sadly. 'They won't.'

They have taken Nageen's sight, his dignity, most of his hope, his freedom, his mobility, his shoes, his socks, the keys from his pocket – even his small change. What they failed to take is the plastic voucher card he picked up at the New Myoma City Development Supermarket in Sittwe.

With burned and bleeding fingers Nageen eases the card out from the back pocket of his trousers. He wraps his fingers up in the rag that bound his eyes and takes hold of the card between the index and third fingers of his least painful hand. Gingerly, he brings the plastic into contact with the hot coil. Smoke rises. He breathes it in. Toxins swirl the pain in his hands into colours and he pulls his head away, afraid he'll faint. The colours die behind his eyes and he lifts the card to see. He blinks away his tears. He's burned a bite out of the card. Too smooth. Too rounded. He tries again. He's steady now. The smoke rises, smarting his eyes. He studies the card again. It's smouldering. He tries to summon up his spit but his mouth is full of foam. He drops the card and stamps on it with his bare foot, putting it out. He doesn't even feel the heat, the burns around his ankles are too fierce, too raw, to allow for more sensation.

He picks up the card. The bite is deeper now, and angled. It will do. He clambers to his feet and hobbles across the slanting floor of the mess towards the door.

The door is locked but it's only a mess-room door, a stupid internal door. He hunkers down, forces the card into the jamb above the lock and wiggles it down over the bolt. A stupid internal door with a stupid hotel-room lock: it disables the handle but the bolt moves freely. He leans and pulls. The bolt slips and pings back into place. He tries again, only this time he pulls at the handle with his free hand. The bolt pings and the door comes open.

The corridor is empty. He leaves the mess, pulling the door closed behind him. The main generator has died and the auxiliaries are whining. He heads downhill. There is a fire point. The axe is gone from its bracket. The first-aid kit is missing. He reaches the galley, puts his ear to the door and listens. Nothing. He tries the handle. It's unlocked. He opens the door a crack and peers, then swings the door wide. No one. He leans against the door jamb, breathing hard. He smells meat. The smell is rising from his hands. His stomach turns over and he spits.

Inside the galley, mounted on the wall, there is a first-aid cupboard. He pulls it open and runs his seared hand across the shelf, knocking the contents to the floor. He half-squats, half-falls to the floor, his ankles shooting fire, and fights the zipper round the lip of the sealed green pack. There are scissors in the lid. He palms them and uses the wall to help him back on to his feet. He hobbles into the corridor.

He's halfway to the mess room when he hears them. Footfalls. Heavy boots. A voice. Behind him.

Back the way he came, at the end of the corridor, there is a stairway. Iron-grille stairs ring out. Nageen hesitates, caught between the mess room and the galley. The scissors fall from his hand.

The voice stops, then picks up again: one half of a conversation. The iron stairs ring and ring and ring. A shadow scuds the wall behind the stairs. Nageen leans forward and starts to run. If you can call it running. Nageen stumbles downhill to the stairs.

Third Officer Waddedar is turning up the final flight, dragging his feet, his heavy boots, up the steps.

Waddedar. The pirates' plant.

'Mr Waddedar.'

The young man glances up, eyes dark with sleeplessness, and Nageen bares his teeth, and falls.

The men collapse in a pile at the foot of the stairs. Waddedar's head rings against the grille-work like the clapper of a bell. Nageen, barking, spitting blood, fights free of Waddedar's arms. He stares about him, wild-eyed. He thinks of water. Boiling water, streaming down on his son.

Waddedar groans. He blinks, cross-eyed and infantile, up at Nageen. Nageen casts around for a weapon. Waddedar has nothing on him. His mobile phone lies in pieces behind his head. Nageen picks up the half-shell of the phone and hammers at Waddedar's face. Waddedar opens his mouth to scream and Nageen hammers the casing into Waddedar's mouth. Waddedar gags. Pink spittle rises around the edges of the phone and Nageen's fingers slip about as he hunts for purchase on the casing. Waddedar bucks against him, boots loud against the grille-work of the stairs. Nageen gets on top of him, puts his hands together and brings his weight to bear. The casing cracks and edges in and blood wells from Waddedar's mouth. He's blinking as Nageen climbs off him, and flecks of foam spurt from his nose. Nageen brings his foot down on Waddedar's nose and feels it crunch under his bare heel.

He takes the stairs. The scissors are where he left them. If he bends for them now he will never get up again. He uses his feet, scraping and dribbling the scissors along the rubber floor to the mess room. He opens the door, clings to the handle and lowers himself down. He picks up the scissors, grips them with his teeth and paddles across the floor to where Sabir is lying. He's unplugged the coil. The room stinks of charred rubber.

Nageen works the scissors between his son's wrists and chews the blades down on the cable tie. His hands have no strength. He works and works. The boy's wrists are bleeding as he strains against the weakening band. It gives suddenly and Sabir cries out. Nageen falls on to his back as Sabir feels for the scissors. He takes them up and works at the tie securing his ankles.

Nageen closes his eyes.

Sabir tries to stand. He gets as far as his knees and shuffles to the nearest man. Chief Engineer Sen rubs his wrists, takes the scissors from the boy and cuts his ankles free. He stumbles to his feet, gripping the scissors.

'Sen –'

'Fuck you,' says Sen to all of them, and hobbles from the mess room, gripping the scissors like a knife.

Sabir is on his feet now. 'Wait,' he says, and follows Sen out into the corridor. Nageen groans and curls into a ball. A swell runs under the ship and outside there is a great and terrible groaning: huge animals are drowning out there . . .

'Mr Nageen, sir!'

It's Kamal, the first officer. 'Mr Nageen, I can see you, sir!' He's sat up against the wall below the window, scraping and banging his head against the wall, trying to be rid of his blindfold.

The ship is listing more now, thrown out of balance by its containers as they topple and strain against their wire lashings.

'Here.'

It is Sabir, back from the galley with a knife. Nageen watches as he frees Suniti. Suniti makes to embrace him but there's no time: Sabir pushes her to the floor, cuts the band around her ankles and crosses to the window. Kamal shuffles back against the wall, afraid.

Nageen says, 'Hold on, Mr Kamal.'

Suniti is on her feet. 'I'm all right.'

'Suniti.' He absolutely must not weep.

Sabir saws through the cable tie securing Kamal's legs. 'Good boy,' Kamal mutters, rubbing his ankles. 'Right.' He stands up, silhouetted against the window. The window explodes and his head goes with it.

Suniti screams and drops to the ground. Armour-piercing bullets strafe the mess-room wall. Sabir crawls towards Nageen. Suniti reaches out a hand. Nageen rolls towards her, grips her hand and pulls. Under a rain of flaming ornaments, calendars and shattered safety notices, Nageen, Suniti and Sabir shimmy towards the door. The gunfire cannot drown the cries of the men they are abandoning.

As they reach deck level, the strafing stops. Nageen waits, slumped against the wall, fast running out of strength, while his wife and son struggle to undog the iron-house door. Containers are toppling into one another out there: creatures from nightmare, bellowing in pain. The ship tips sickeningly to starboard and Nageen slides to the rubberized floor of the gangway. Even five floors down, they can still hear screams spilling from the mess room. Now there's a new sound: the motors of another ship. Not a workboat: something fast and manoeuvrable. It revs and slews around the stricken *Ka-Bham*.

Sabir opens the door a crack and looks out. 'No one.' The weight of the door is against them as Sabir and Suniti help Nageen jam his way through the gap and on to the deck.

Nageen cowers in the glare. He cannot see. He cannot breathe: the air's too rich for him. His sight pulses black and he staggers, trying to hold on, trying to keep his feet. At the stern of the boat, hidden by the superstructure, the pirates' boat is circling.

Suniti takes Nageen's arm and drags him after Sabir: they're heading for the containers. These are lashed lengthways to the deck, four abreast, but here and there the twistlocks have snapped and containers have toppled into their neighbours: it's only a matter of minutes before the whole lot gives way and slides into the sea.

Behind them the engine of the pirates' boat ratchets up a gear: they're coming round. Nageen finds his feet and topples forward into Suniti, propelling her into an alleyway between the stacks. Sabir is already there, crouching, craning up in fear as the topmost containers groan and tip with the motion of the boat.

They hunker here a moment. It's cool here between the bottom-most cans – cool, at least, in comparison to the sun-flamed deck – but they cannot stay. They are as fragile as insects here. The stacks have only to shift a couple of feet and they will all be crushed.

The pirates' ship comes starboard of the *Ka-Bham*, its motor rolling down. Its wash nudges the *Ka-Bham*'s lumbering hull: it tips, returns, tips, returns, swinging, port to starboard and back, a deadly see-saw. The ship is foundering, drifting out of true: it is side-on to the waves now and the end, when it comes, will come fast.

Above their heads the containers groan.

On hands and knees Nageen edges between the cans. They're stacked against each other, nose to tail, on top of the hatch covers. Between the hatches there's open space. Nageen bobs into the gap and back again, not daring to show himself for more than a second. He glimpses the pirates' boat: a real rusted piece of shit. In the bow men are wrestling with the innards of a Bofors gun.

He waits five seconds, then peers out again. The boat is past the gap, chugging gently forward and round the bow. Sabir and Suniti come up behind him. If the pirates spot them they will kill them: no doubt of that. They can't stay here either: the cans will crush them, if not in the next minute then in the minute after that, or the one after that. The ship is going to roll.

To starboard the sea, drunken, uptilted, rolls towards them and now, edging into view – yes – a dinky orange self-inflating life raft. A man kneels in the raft, paddling frantically. It's Sen. He's going backwards. The sea is against him. The breeze is against him. The breaths of two dead boys are against him. See them flexing in the sky! And here comes the pirates' boat. Slowly, inexorably, it rounds the bow of the *Ka-Bham*. The pirates open up with everything they've got. Handguns. AKs. The life raft shivers and shimmies, the roof shreds away, and Sen falls into the water.

Suniti pulls Nageen back into the dark of the alley. The pirates' boat revs and swings around the starboard side of the *Ka-Bham*. Its wash, coinciding with a swell, catches the ship broadside. The deck pendulums. Each moment longer, wilder than the last. A lashing wire snaps, whip-cracking the containers stacked above their heads. Nageen feels strong arms around him. He paddles ruined feet against the deck as the containers start to slide. He feels the passageway contract, the kiss of steel on his arms, and he closes his eyes.

Sabir falls back, dropping Nageen. Nageen's head strikes the deck. He opens his eyes. He's sprawled in the open space between hatches. The *Ka-Bham* is rocking, he reaches out to save himself from rolling, it's happening, it's happening now.

Far away, under the screams issuing from the shattered mess-room windows, Nageen hears the pirates' boat tearing at the water. Downhill, the sea rolls and slaps the inclined hull. Through intermittent walls of spray, he sees the pirates' boat, low in the water, half-hidden already by the ocean's soft swells: it is speeding away.

Seawater spills over the starboard rail. He turns uphill, sees only steel and sky. The ship is going to roll. Ahead of him, Suniti scrambles up the deck against the incline. She grabs the port-side rail and reaches down for Sabir. Sabir catches hold of her hand and reaches for Nageen. On bleeding hands and broken knees, Nageen climbs towards them. Sabir catches him under the arm. Nageen paddles his feet.

The *Ka-Bham* rolls.

Lashing bursts and containers thunder into the foaming water. Nageen flails and cracks his wrist against the combing of a hatch. *A handhold*: he clings. He pulls. Sabir lets go. The sea thunders up in a wave to lick Nageen's burnt feet. He paddles, grabs, misses, and falls backwards into the sea. He enters the water and cracks his back on something solid. Air bursts from his lungs in a great rush, turning him in the water. He sees something sliding beneath him: something white and corrugated: he imagines sandy shallows.

Letters slide before his drowning eyes:

The ribbed floor, so close he might touch it, resolves into the steel wall of a container. Egaz Nageen hangs face down in the water, breathless, weightless, without pain, submerged and staring as the can rolls under him, gathers speed, turns blue, turns pale, turns small, and disappears.

∞

Rishi has shut up the workshop in Darukhana. He's arranged passage to Toronto. All he has to do now is clear out the apartment.

He turns the key, letting himself in for the last time. What a shame that he has to leave all this behind! Rental on the place approaches the annual domestic product of Chhaphandi, and ever since Roopa started getting under his skin he's been filling it with furnishings that wouldn't look out of place in one of those glossy magazines of hers.

What the place really needed, he knows – more than money, more than things – was for them to stay here together more than a couple of nights at a stretch. Rishi himself has spent so little time here he's been sliding off things. He's been stubbing his toes on things, an inept guest in a too-expensive hotel room. The oven still had the plastic on – he found that out only last night, trying to warm up a take-away halloumi pizza. There are gadgets in his bathroom he's never found the uses for, shit-kicker that he is. Chhaphandi boy. Komatsu driver.

He's sorry to be leaving, and who can blame him? He loves the life he's led here. After Firozabad, after Devnagar, after Chhaphandi, who wouldn't love this life? Most everyone in the world would kill to have this life, even a week of this life, if only so they could just sit and think for once, not worrying about where the next meal was coming from.

Each comfort he has acquired has made him a little bit more the person he set out to be that night on the Sher Shah Suri Marg. Someone who appreciates a comfortable cushion, a well-cooked meal, a decent shirt. This is the person he wants to see in the mirror of a morning. Not some bloody beast of burden.

Passport, and cards, and keys, and phone. Don't look back. Don't give in. Relocate and regroup. Toronto. The uninspired choice of hungry men. He knows what he's doing.

The hire car's where he left it. He thumbs the phone on, tosses it on to the front passenger seat, and sets the car humming around him. Radio, air conditioning, motive force. Put it in gear. Drive.

Traffic's as bad as he expected: it takes him nearly an hour to arrive at the Port Trust gate. He's sorry to be leaving Mumbai. The city has been good to him. It has given him a place to work undisturbed. It has even brought him some happiness. Days out. Evenings in. A woman he cared for. A boy who might one day have called him 'Dad'.

A son! A home! Oh, run away, Rishi. Get out while the going's still good!

The dongle suckered to his windshield was weeks in the making and cost him a small fortune, but it does the job handsomely: the Port Trust barrier swings up automatically and he sails through at 20 mph. The road takes a long curve around warehouses and lorry parks. He pulls up under a concrete awning, opens his window and hands to the duty guard a paper that's all his own work (he's always taken pride in his work). The guard hands him a yellow hard hat and gives him directions to Riverside Upper.

He pulls up in a small, cramped square of tarmac under huge metal daisies. Floodlights and cameras hang off them like petals. He opens the window, smells diesel and the sea. A wall of containers stacked five or six high hides the water. There are regular four-foot gaps between each column of containers. Through the gap directly ahead of him he spots a red hull.

A straddle-carrier trundles past, lines itself up, and rolls over the stack in front of him, wheels filling the crawlways either side. Behind it blue mobile gantries trundle back and forth along the quay, whining like monstrous children. The crawler stops and a man in a yellow hard hat climbs out of his tinted glass cabin and down a ladder, and disappears.

The phone on the passenger seat jangles at full volume. Heart thumping, he fumbles for the green button.

'Sir, are you ready?'

He's ready. He's ripe. Get out of the car.

'We can see you. I think. Raise your hand.'

Do it.

'Thank you, sir. Now, you'll have to move fast. You see the alleyway straight ahead of you?'

'Yes.'

'Go three cans left.'

He's done this before, across the Indian Ocean, many times. When he started he hid out in the bilges of dhows. He's come up in the world since, but the principle is the same. Most people in his line of work travel this way, especially since the airports got so uncomfortable.

'Good. Now when you're in the alley we won't be able to see you and I don't suppose the mobile will work well either in all that tin. Just go all the way down to the quay and we'll pick you up at the other end.'

He reads as he goes: it's impossible not to. Hamburg Süd. Moyse. Maersk. CSAV. There is something magical in this: the world's bounty boxed up like so many heavy-duty Christmas presents. How the world goes round, packed, palletized, boxed, numbered, turned to paper, turned to figures, turned to logic gates and light, to symbols he will never grasp. Concepts that evaporate as soon as they are spoken. The world transfigured so we might have our dolphin lamps. Our mattresses. Our peacock-pattern drapes. We fight tooth and nail to keep this life of ours. You couldn't stop this if you tried.

'Yes, we see you.'

A huge blue gantry towers over him. No cabin. From this point on, everything's machine.

Looped umbilicals gather and stretch as its arms reach out over the cargo ship's forward hold. For the next three weeks, this will be Rishi's home. Genoa. Hamburg. Then the long Atlantic crossing. The batteries in the can his people have prepared for him have juice enough to sustain him for a voyage three times as long as the one he's contemplating now. He'll have lights. A bed. A TV and a laptop. A toilet. A satellite phone.

Security passes for ports in Egypt, Canada and Thailand. Three passports.

There is no one about. The noise of the gantry makes it hard for him to hear the phone. 'What was that?'

'Three stacks to your right. Left. To your left. Sorry.'

Start walking.

'Other way. Other way!'

The blue gantry rolls past him on wheels higher than he is. He's afraid. We can smell his fear, and the smell is good. Rishi's powerless here.

'To your right.'

So stop.

A forty-foot white Moyse Line container sits on its own in a space marked out by yellow paint.

'Go up to the door. Now. Open it.'

Rishi slips the phone into his pocket while he fights with the bolts. They come free. He digs the phone out of his pocket again.

'Listen. When you enter the container you're going to lose the signal. There's a cord just inside the door for the light.'

Oh no there isn't.

He steps over the lintel, into a fug of damp and solvent and epoxy resin. Behind him, the heavy steel door swings in the wind, dimming and brightening the interior walls, the plywood floor, the ribbed ceiling. He cannot make out the back wall at all, it is so dark. But he can smell it. He can smell it all right. What he did to Mummy. What he did to Daddy. The stinking shreds of burning tyres.

The doors swing open again and he catches his breath to see us, we are so beautiful. We snake towards him: rivers of glass dust. Shreds of yellow light! Clouds caught by the setting sun! Fields of colour, soft and wet as the insides of a peach! We are so beautiful, so uncanny, we might be a dream that's slipped into the waking world somehow. A dream that's spilled from heads other than his own.

He feels for the cord. There is no cord. He squeals like a girl to feel Us. The ripple of Our cold dry skin. He sees Us curling above him: Our colours and Our fangs. He smells Us: a breath of burning electrical insulation and dripping upholstery foam, fats and charred nylon, burning hair and paint fumes. We are so close now, Our twofold nature finds itself reflected in each of Rishi's eyes. To Kaneer, he excuses Daddy's death: 'It was an accident!' To Abhik, he sighs: 'Samjhoria – it wasn't my idea!'

Not good enough. We have a story to tell. A tale to comfort us in our long and limitless death. And this was always on the cards. This was always going to happen. What other kind of story would we ever choose?

He steps away from Us again, again, again. His footfalls make hardly a sound as he retreats further and further into Our Dark . . .

Now change the number on the can. One byte will be enough to keep him orbiting in here forever. It doesn't matter how much he screams. It doesn't matter how much he flails. No purchase here. No friction. No leverage. The propeller spins but the hull's not going anywhere.

Dead Water.

TWENTY-THREE

Nothing exists. Nothing has to exist, or everything becomes coincident with everything else, and the universe is reduced to a homogeneous dot. Picture a propeller, caught between layers of different densities: how it churns and churns, whipping up the foam on which the real world, the world we see and smell, depends.

In darkness and paralysis, Egaz Nageen dreams of a place with nothing in it. No matter. No heat. No energy. Not even light. Nothing except, just possibly, the potential for form. Waking, he clings to his dream, and from out of the big and deepening blue he gathers up the things he needs to sustain him.

He builds: Suniti's tears against his cheek.

He builds: Sen's raft has stayed afloat.

Sabir's small hands thump rhythmically against his chest. The whole raft lollops like a hotel bed as Sabir lands his weight, again and again, on his father's chest. Salt water fountains from his broken mouth. He gasps and gags in one seamless, wringing heave.

Through the open door of the life raft, he can see the *Ka-Bham* lying on its side, half-submerged. Its deck cargo is mostly gone, tipped into the sea. Only a few containers remain, tangled in wire lashing, near the surface of the water. With every swell they knock against the upturned deck. Swells break and cream along the iron house.

Nageen flits in and out of consciousness and still he builds. Workmanlike. Determined. Now Suniti is sitting on the slope of the *Ka-Bham*'s bow, cradling the life raft's nylon line. She's studying the waves that lap the hull a few metres below her. The *Ka-Bham* will take time to sink. When it does, she imagines it falling away in a broiling whirlpool of spume and spray. As if. 'Sit,' says Nageen, through a throat that can no longer sound: 'Calm down. Just hold on to the fucking rope.'

If the engine-room bulkhead has held this long, it's not going to burst now, so they have half an hour, maybe longer, before the ship goes gently down. Their best hope is to stay by the *Ka-Bham* for as long as possible. A cargo ship – even a small, half-sunken cargo ship – is easier to spot from the air than a life raft.

Item, some nylon line. Item, a supply of fresh water. Item, a sponge. A safety knife with a buoyant handle. Two bailers. A fishing kit and a mirror. No EPIRB. No radio. Not far away – behind him, thank God, where he doesn't have to look at him – Chief Engineer Sen lies face-down in a spreading pool of red.

Their captors' final mistake: they meant to leave no one alive. They ran out of time. If they'd had time, they could have made sure of it. Brought the *Ka-Bham*'s crew on deck. Pulled pillowcases over their heads. Beaten their heads in with twistlocks and cheater pipes. Or not even that: just zipped them to the anchor chain and let it go. God, imagine the shame of that: shackled to an anchor chain with *cable ties*.

Suniti pulls off her kameez and drapes it over her head to protect herself from the sun. Sabir totters the length of the *Ka-Bham*'s hull, his shirt held tented to hide his melted face. His lovely boy. His child. I love you. Oh, my treasure, how I love you!

The air is clear, but as the minutes pass, strange clouds come to spot the sky. Balls. Plates. Cigars. Nageen stares at them. High cloud. Ice cloud. There is a storm coming. Not for hours, but soon. The wind will blow the clouds apart. Then it will come for them.

Sabir, listen. When I was a young man, a fisherman, we would go out, me and my friends, in the dying of the day, with carbines hardened in old wars. Tarutao boys. We hunted trawlers: thieving South Koreans. We shook Australasian pensioners to the core with our threats, sacked yachts and pleasure craft, and came away with watches, passports, handfuls of paper money. To be perfectly frank with you, son, it made pleasant a change from catching fish.

Listen, Sabir. Starving men do not have a choice. But we did. We were not starving, my friends and I. And you know, Sabir? In the end, we did choose. Every one of us. One way or another, every one of us grew up.

Listen, Sabir. Sometimes, it takes a whole life to right yourself. So become the thing you ape, Sabir. Ape wisely and well. Become good.

A black dot burns the sky away: a tiny hole that shivers and expands. An eye. A mouth with fangs. A ring of bright blue light. A spinning snake. A machine with moving parts, wet and golden as the insides of a peach. Sabir raises his hands to the sky. He waves his shirt. His hard feet slap the burning hull. 'Americans!'

In an ocean bigger than thirty Indias: Americans.

Well then, thinks Nageen, not quite believing: bless America.

Fangs curl upon themselves, ploughshared to landing gear. Lemon-yellow feathers spring from under metal scales and churn the sky. The air shivers in the creature's down-draught and the life raft swirls and spins, takes on water, bobs and drowns and bobs again.

Nageen snorts, tastes salt and spittle. *True*. He bites his lip, tastes blood. *All true*.

A US Navy helicopter sweeps in close, turns the sea to foam, and drops a line.

Centuries ago, when sailors from Europe first encountered North African dhows, they marvelled that, for all their curving elegance, these exotic machines couldn't tack. Trade winds have driven dhows back and forth across the Indian Ocean for centuries and the pulse of their to-and-fro is so regular, so reliable, no one ever bothered to learn how to steer against the wind.

Powered by twelve-cylinder Suzukis a dhow these days can push twenty-five knots in an hour, but if the crossing from India takes longer than about five days, it will still put into Ras al Hadd to resupply.

Concealed inlets. Goat paths. Mudflats deep enough to drown a four-by-four. David Brooks steers his RIB to shore and bumps against the jetty. He climbs out and makes the boat fast against a pole so smooth it feels as though it is coated in glass. The planks of the jetty wobble and spring under his feet. Whatever fastened them has long since rusted away. The whole structure is held together by nothing more than habit.

A thin gravel path edges over steep, stony inclines, out of sight, round hills, to the island's hidden heart. Round the bend is a bend and around that bend is another bend. Madness and despair. Lights in the sky. He follows the path round the island. Waves have undercut the rock all around and in the overhang a greenish coral grows. It is not a living green at all. David pauses a moment and nudges a spur of the stuff with his toe. It is as soft as cream.

He comes to a level platform, inches thick in fish bones, oyster shells and pieces of calcified coral, and stands gazing over the shell of an old accommodation block. Its low brick walls are all that remain. He walks in among them. The wood from the roofs, long since collapsed, lies in a grey, spongy carpet at his feet. Around the next bend he comes upon a brick shed, far sturdier than the homes of the people who once served here. It is intact: a tall, windowless stone building, its corrugated-iron roof slathered with cement. Above the only door, chiselled into the lintel: 1933. The year of its construction. Seaplanes once stopped here to refuel on their way to India.

The iron door of the refuelling station is open. David goes inside. The whole of the interior is taken up by a gigantic fuel tank mounted on trestles. The floor is thick with the shed skins of gigantic snakes. There is a faint multicoloured sheen to them: dead rainbows. But with a mortal's talent for self-deception, David convinces himself that they are, in fact, the feathery remains of a fuel hose. In the midst of the skins, like an egg in a dragon's nest, sits an old orange buoy, the size of a man's head.

David scuffs ankle-deep through the rotten rubber, stirring it with his stick as though he were chivvying the ash of a dead fire. He jabs his stick into the mess, getting purchase on the concrete floor, then bends down and lifts the buoy.

He pulls a red leather notebook from his jacket and drops it into the nest. It will be safe here, until the next time.

'Towards a Unified Theory of Ocean Circulation.' Diagrams and spirals. Dead water.

He sits the buoy on top of it.

After years of this shit you get cynical. You figure, you may as well go work for yourself. 'The can I took off the *Ka-Bham* is stocked with canisters of a trichothecene mycotoxin produced by the Israel Institute for Biological Research in Ness Ziona and consigned to Dead Water around the time the Knesset was refusing to sign the Biological Weapons Convention. 10 April 1972, to save you looking it up. Years ago. The stuff will be safely dead by now. Don't tell my buyers.'

Ester's answerphone says: 'To re-record your message, press One.'

He presses One, and then the red button, killing the call.

The Pajero is waiting for him behind the next hill.

He drives for half a day through a landscape that looks recklessly young. Up-tilted rocks, like giant launching ramps, erupt from a sea of gravel.

Around lunchtime, to complete his disorientation, he finds himself abruptly fed on to freshly set Tarmac. The new coastal highway is radically unexpressive: a flat, monomaniacal idea, and when it ends, narrowing at last to a single lane, warning signs appear and the hillside is smothered in pink plastic sacks. David drives slowly over the hill, unsure of what he's seeing. Workmen crouch in the shadows behind big boulders, stripping the red plastic sleeving off rolls of copper wire. At the top of the hill two policemen in a patrol car ignore him as he passes. So that's it: they are getting ready to blow up the hill.

The road descends and weaves slightly inland to where Chinese derricks are pumping the water out from between the roots of dying date palms. He turns off the road at a coastal village and drives the Pajero at speed along firm tracks in the dunes to a view of the sea. The moon comes up over the Gulf of Oman. At this latitude the horns of a half-moon point up, parallel to the horizon, so that it looks like a cup. Inversion effects ripple and ridge its silhouette and lend it a fluted stem. The whole sea pulses green. Out to sea he catches isolated flashes: the movements of fish. Where wave overlaps wave, green lightning explores the join. Each incoming wave, curling on itself, wrings out some light. Phosphorescence lights up the foam scurrying over the sand towards his feet.

He dips his hand into the surf. It comes out flecked with stars. A wave comes and crashes and recedes. He watches as it runs back to the sea, leaving green lights in the sand, some brilliant, some dim, but thousands of them, strewn, curled, massed, riven by dark little rivers no wider than a fingernail. He thinks of the satellite photographs you see sometimes in airline magazines: the seaboards of great cities at night. A wave washes the city away. A few seconds later another appears. For a minute or more he stares at his feet as though the sand around were a gazetteer. Hong Kong . . . Singapore . . . Rotterdam . . . Yokohama . . . He thinks about great waves. About the births and deaths of civilizations. He is very tired. Bone-tired. He aches.

The next day he arrives in Sur and, glad to be free of the cabin for a while, wanders the streets, from the offices of National Biscuit Industries past tailors and launderers to the Turkish Sheep Restaurant on the far side of town. He sits on the promenade watching the fleet coming in: open boats draw up along the beach. There are about fifty of them, loaded to the gunwales with tuna. The surf is pink with blood and yet the men and boys wrestling the fish off the boats are in dishdashas so white, so pressed, so neat, it's as though the world has let its continuity lapse.

The fish are auctioned off by a Sur native wielding a silver-handled cane. The affair, apparently ill-tempered, keeps collapsing into laughter, only to resume at the same cut-throat pitch. Toyota Hiluxes line the promenade, their windscreens covered in blankets. Drivers stir inside the darkened cabs, snatching sleep before the all-night run to Dubai.

In the evening he forks up a plateful of sweet fish makboos on a terrace overlooking the offices of the Golden Cage Wedding Company. He says:

'If it's pirates you're after you should be here with me. Every other creek and lagoon they say Osama hid out there in the bilge of a dhow when he fled Afghanistan. Osama is the Bonny Prince Charlie of our age. Where are you?'

He does not delete the message this time. He leaves it on her phone. He wants her to know where he is. Absurd as this is. Absurd as he knows it to be: he wants her to come after him.

The next day, heading east, the hills grow sharper, darker, more pyramidal, and the sand of the desert disappears under a wine-coloured gravel, dotted here and there with prosopis trees, their canopies pruned by passing camels into natural umbrellas. A small range of crumbly red hills marks the point at which the earth surrenders to its own gravity. Beyond, the landscape acquires an absolute and mathematical flatness, before dribbling away into dunes and gravel beds, shallow lagoons and salt marshes. On the northern side of this spit is the Gulf of Oman. Southwards – a five-minute drive over weedy rubble and ferny succulents – lies the Indian Ocean. So he comes to it at last: Al Suwiah. The end.

The currents here sort the ocean's trash and hurl it on to the beach to make strange, apocalyptic waymarkers: here a line of shattered televisions; there a pink pool of dead shrimps, over there a shoal of plastic sandals. He picks his way through the sea's leavings – fragments of coral, plastic bottles, leathery rays. When the wind dies the air fills with flies and the stench of dead fish.

He walks for hours, courting a tiredness that will not come, past deserted fishing huts made of date-frond wattle and old fishing net. With the onrush of night, structures hidden in the day by dust and haze become visible. At the end of an old landing strip there's a navigation tower with a revolving blue-white light. Inland, jazzy red fairy lights blink in complex, shifting syncopations: air hazard lights for the transmitters of the BBC World Service.

In boxer shorts and barefoot he zig-zags east along the beach in the last of the light, following the tracks of turtles as they scoop their way up to the dunes to lay their eggs. The ground is covered in circular depressions where the young have dug up through the sand and away.

Back at the waterline the sea crushes its colours into the sand.

David thinks of Eric Moyse in his container, crossing from ocean to ocean and in and out of deep-water facilities from Rotterdam to Kaohsiung. Unrooted from everything, sensitive cargoes move, silent and unseen, over the earth. Or they do not move: a mystery that tantalized the crews of the *Dobbs* and the *Fram*. Dead water. It has not escaped his notice that, after all these years, and having committed so many trivial and not so trivial betrayals, and having sacrificed so very much of both himself and others, he has ended up, today, barely twelve hours' drive from where his journey started more than forty years ago. Bitumen and metal dust. *Italia*.

He goes back to the car and checks his phone. There are no messages.

He gathers driftwood for a fire. He comes upon a smooth grey piece from an old dhow. A decoration, a repeated spiral pattern, has been chiselled into the wood. He traces the figures with his finger. This way. That. This way. That. His finger races round the wood, chopping waves into froth: no headway here.

He lays the fragment down in the light of the fire, takes a picture of it with his phone, then tosses it into the flames.

Whatever else her father has done, he has been a good teacher. The first thing Ester does, she throws away her mobile phone. Next, she has to ditch the Land Rover.

She makes it out of Muscat easily enough and passes over the hills of Sohar in the last of evening, the copper-green of the earth turned mossy by the dying light. To either side of her rise hedgerows of plastic bunting. The road is up. The road is closed. She joins a tailback of Shinas-bound traffic composed almost exclusively of Toyota Hiluxes. Where the plastic hedges meet in a tangle of rusted cementation rods and gray drainage pipes a dented tin sign sends them trailing cluelessly, nose to tail, into the desert.

For twenty minutes Ester follows the cars in front into the wilderness. But a glance at the cabin compass finally convinces her that they are doubling back on themselves. They are curving back towards Sinbad's emerald mountains. They are lost. For a while, mesmerized by their collective folly, she follows the car in front and the traffic snakes out ahead of her, and it weaves obediently behind, and the whole convoy wriggles across the desert like a line of ants.

The spell breaks. Ester wrestles the wheel around and heads off on her own, southwards, into the dark. The cars behind follow her, obedient as chicks. She accelerates. The vehicle behind her catches her up, flashing its headlights, entreating her to slow down. It is not good to be followed like this.

She turns the wheel an eighth-turn to the right and holds it there. A minute passes. Another. She's driving one-handed, peering into the dark, ready at a moment's notice to grab the wheel and wrench it round to avoid an acacia tree, a big stone, a fault in the rock. The ground refuses to surprise and another minute passes. Now, to her right, she makes out a string of headlamps sweeping by her side window into the dark. She holds her hand steady on the wheel, exerting the gentlest pressure, and in another minute she has the traffic stream dead ahead of her.

Another minute and the traffic flow is on her left and she is merging gently in. The car that has been tailgating her nuzzles in three cars behind and the traffic behind it merges where it can – and then she loses sight of where the flows are blending.

For a while she orbits, an obedient mote, in the circus she has made. Then she cuts her lights, drops into manual, and floors the accelerator. This time she is too quick, too impetuous for anyone to follow. In the rear-view mirror she sees that the gap she left in the circle is already healed.

She does not want to reveal her position, so rather than flash her brake lights she lets the Land Rover coast to a stop. She climbs out. The ground is flat and rippled and hot through her trainers. The Land Rover's bodywork tings and crackles as it cools.

In the distance the great wheel she has made in the desert endures, vehicles following each other bumper to bumper. She wonders how long it will last. This eddy. This gyre. How turbulence maintains itself. Why the oceans do not cease to turn.

She waits for it to disappear – a bright snake, all glass and glitter, eating its own tail. She waits for morning. She waits to be alone. Once she is alone, she'll torch the car. Once she's torched the car, she'll walk away.

ACKNOWLEDGEMENTS

Many thanks go to men and families I cannot name (they know who they are), and to two I can: Anna Davis and Nic Cheetham towed this story into clear water.

S. I.

London, 2011